Praise for *Echo*

"SF hard enough to break a tooth on.

"An intricately inventive and coolly deterministic lesson in the futility of trying to outthink evolution, less a critique of human transcendence than an indictment of its basic assumptions."
—*Publishers Weekly*

"Watts's literary science fiction is engaging and stunningly bleak, but he asks all the right questions about our evolution."
—*The Washington Post*

"Watts provides some of the most provocative speculation on consciousness and perception in current science fiction."
—*Chicago Tribune*

"Every word has been tuned and polished: there's a perfectionism at work here, a refusal to write a novel that's merely as good as the last one if something better can be wrung from cutting-edge science and the English language. There is some real tour de force writing in this book."
—*Tor.com*

ECHOPRAXIA

PETER WATTS

A TOM DOHERTY ASSOCIATES BOOK TOR NEW YORK

ECHOPRAXIA

Copyright © 2014 by Peter Watts

A Tor Book
Published by Tom Doherty Associates, LLC
175 Fifth Avenue
New York, NY 10010

www.tor-forge.com

Tor® is a registered trademark of Tom Doherty Associates, LLC.

The Library of Congress has cataloged the hardcover edition as follows:

Watts, Peter, 1958–
     Echopraxia / Peter Watts.
          p. cm.
     "A Tom Doherty Associates book."
     ISBN 978-0-7653-2802-1 (hardcover)
     ISBN 978-1-4299-4806-7 (e-book)
     1. Biologists—Fiction. 2. Interstellar travel—Fiction. 3. Imaginary wars and battles—Fiction. I. Title.
PR9199.3.W386E24 2014
813'.54—dc23

2014015442

ISBN 978-0-7653-2803-8 (trade paperback)

Tor books may be purchased for educational, business, or promotional use. For information on bulk purchases, please contact the Macmillan Corporate and Premium Sales Department at 1-800-221-7945, extension 5442, or write to specialmarkets@macmillan.com.

First Edition: August 2014
First Trade Paperback Edition: June 2015

Printed in the United States of America

D   17

For the BUG.
Who saved my life.

CONTENTS

WE DO NOT DESTROY RELIGION BY DESTROYING SUPER-
STITION.

—CICERO

TO CONCENTRATE ON HEAVEN IS TO CREATE HELL.

—TOM ROBBINS

We climbed this hill. Each step up we could see farther, so of course we kept going. Now we're at the top. Science has been at the top for a few centuries now. And we look out across the plain and we see this other tribe dancing around above the clouds, even higher than we are. Maybe it's a mirage, maybe it's a trick. Or maybe they just climbed a higher peak we can't see because the clouds are blocking the view. So we head off to find out—but every step takes us downhill. No matter what direction we head, we can't move off our peak without losing our vantage point. So we climb back up again. We're trapped on a local maximum.

But what if there *is* a higher peak out there, way across the plain? The only way to get there is to bite the bullet, come down off our foothill and trudge along the riverbed until we finally start going uphill again. And it's only then you realize: Hey, this mountain reaches *way* higher than that foothill we were on before, and we can see so much better from up here.

But you can't get there unless you leave behind all the tools that made you so successful in the first place. You have to take that first step downhill.

—Dr. Lianna Lutterodt, "Faith and the Fitness Landscape," *In Conversation,* 2091

The *Crown of Thorns*
External Layout

Note: for clarity, only two of the six spoke-hab assemblies are shown.

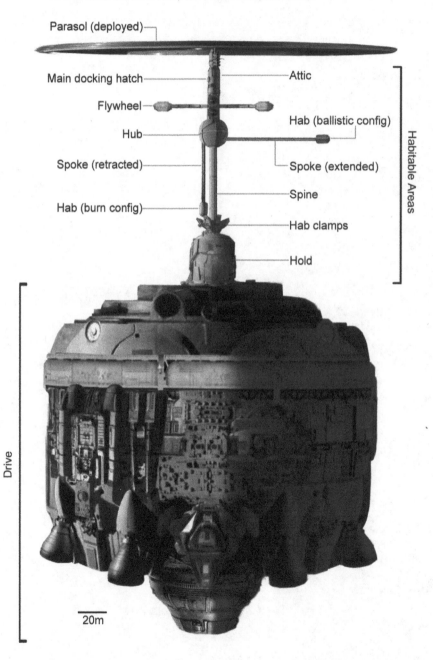

Parasol (deployed)

Main docking hatch

Attic

Flywheel

Hab (ballistic config)

Hub

Spoke (retracted)

Spoke (extended)

Spine

Hab (burn config)

Hab clamps

Hold

Habitable Areas

Drive

20m

PRELUDE

IT IS ALMOST IMPOSSIBLE SYSTEMATICALLY TO CONSTI-
TUTE A NATURAL MORAL LAW. NATURE HAS NO PRINCI-
PLES. SHE FURNISHES US WITH NO REASON TO BELIEVE
THAT HUMAN LIFE IS TO BE RESPECTED. NATURE, IN
HER INDIFFERENCE, MAKES NO DISTINCTION BETWEEN
GOOD AND EVIL.

—ANATOLE FRANCE

A WHITE ROOM, innocent of shadow or topography. No angles: that's crucial. No corners or intrusions of furniture, no directional lighting, no geometries of light and shadow whose intersection, from any viewpoint, might call forth the Sign of the Cross. The walls—wall, rather—was a single curved surface, softly bioluminescent, a spheroid enclosure flattened at the bottom in grudging deference to biped convention. It was a giant womb three meters across, right down to the whimpering thing curled up on the floor.

A womb, with all the blood on the outside.

Her name was Sachita Bhar and all that blood was in her head, too. By now they'd killed the cameras just like everything else but there was no way to take back the images from those first moments: the lounge, the Histo lab, even the *broom closet* for chrissakes, a grungy little cubby on the third floor where Gregor had hidden. Sachie hadn't been watching when Gregor had been found. She'd been flipping through the channels, frantically scanning for life and finding only the dead, their insides all out now. By the time she'd cycled through to the closet feed the monsters had already been and gone.

Gregor, who was in love with that stupid pet ferret of his. She'd shared an elevator with him this morning. She remembered the stripes on his shirt. Otherwise she'd have had no idea what to call the mess in the closet.

She'd seen some fraction of the carnage before the cameras went down: friends and colleagues and rivals cut down without remorse or favoritism, their gutted remains sprawled across lab benches and workstations and toilet stalls. And with all those feeds running through the implants in her head—with all her access to all that ubiquitous surveillance—Sachita Bhar had not caught so much as a glimpse of the creatures who'd done this. Shadows, at most. A flicker of darkness cast by some solitary stalker from a blind spot in the camera's eye. They'd done it all without ever being seen, without ever seeing each *other*.

They'd always been kept isolated. For their own good, of course: stick two vampires in the same room and their own hardwired territoriality would put them at each other's throats in an instant. And yet they were working together, somehow. At least half a dozen, confined, incommunicado, acting in sudden precise concert. They'd done it all without ever meeting face-to-face—and even at the height of the slaughter, in those last moments before the cameras died, they had remained invisible. The whole massacre had happened from the corner of Sachie's eye.

How did they do it? How did they survive the angles?

Someone else might have enjoyed the irony; she hid in a refuge for monsters, one of the few places in the whole damn building where they could open their eyes without risking a death sentence. Right angles were *verboten* here. This was where Achilles' heels were put to the test, a cross-free zone where geometry was precisely controlled and neurological leashes optimized. Elsewhere, civilized geometry threatened on all sides: tabletops, windowpanes, a million intersections of appliance and architecture just waiting for the right viewpoint to send vampires into convulsions. Those monsters wouldn't—

—*shouldn't*—

—last an hour out there without the antiEuclideans that suppressed the Crucifix Glitch. Only here, in the white womb—where poor, stupid Sachita Bhar had run when the lights went out—could they dare to open unprotected eyes.

And now one of them was in here with her.

She couldn't see it. Her own eyes were shut, squeezed tight against the butchery flash-burned into her head. She heard no sound but the endless animal keening in her own throat. But something drank a little of the light falling on her face. The swirling red darkness inside her eyelids dimmed some infinitesimal, telltale fraction, and she *knew*.

"Hello," it said.

She opened her eyes. It was one of the females: Valerie, they'd named her, after some departmental chairman who'd retired the year before. Valerie the Vampire.

Valerie's eyes red-shifted the light and threw it back at her, blood-orange stars in a face flushed with aftermath. She towered over Sachie like an insectile statue, motionless, even her breathing imperceptible. Moments from death and with nothing better to do, some subroutine in Sachie's head ticked off the morphometrics: such inhumanly long limbs, the attenuate heat-dissipating allometry of a metabolic engine running *hot*. Subtly jutting mandible, lupine as a hominid's could be, to hold all those teeth. Stupid turquoise smock, smart-paper/telemetry composite weave: Valerie must have been scheduled for physio work today. Ruddy complexion, the bloody flash-flood vasodilation of the predator in hunting mode. And the *eyes,* those terrifying luminous pinpoints—

Finally it registered: *Contracted pupils.*

She's not on Auntie U . . .

Suddenly Sachie's cross was out, last-ditch kill switch, the talisman everyone got on day one along with their ID: empirically tested, proven in the crunch, redeemed by science after uncounted centuries spent slumming as a religious fetish. Sachie held it up with sudden desperate bravado, thumbed the stud. Spring-loaded extensions shot from each tip and her little pocket totem was suddenly a meter on a side.

Thirty degrees of visual arc, Sachie. Maybe forty for the tough ones. Make sure it's perpendicular to line of sight, the angles only work when they're close to ninety degrees, but once this little baby covers enough arc the visual cortex fries like a circuit in a shitstorm . . .

Greg's words.

Valerie cocked her head and studied the artifact. Any second now, Sachie knew, this nightmare creature would collapse in a twitching mass of tetany and shorting synapses. That wasn't faith; it was *neurology*.

The monster leaned close, and didn't even shiver. Sachita Bhar pissed herself.

"*Please,*" she sobbed. The vampire said nothing.

Words flooded out: "I'm *sorry*, I was never really part of it, you know, I'm just a research associate, I'm just doing it for my degree, that's all, I know it's wrong, I know it's like, like *slavery* almost, I know that and it's a shitty system, it's a *shitty* thing we did to you but it wasn't really *me*, do you understand? I didn't make *any* of those decisions, I just came in afterward, I'm barely involved, it was just for my *degree*. And I—I can understand how you must feel, I can understand why you'd hate us, I would too probably but please, oh *please*, I'm just . . . I'm just a *student* . . ."

After a while, still alive, she dared to look up again. Valerie was staring at some point just to the left and a thousand light-years away. She seemed distracted. But then they always seemed distracted, their minds running a dozen parallel threads simultaneously, a dozen perceptual realities, each every bit as *real* as the one mere humans occupied.

Valerie cocked her head as if listening to faint music. She almost smiled.

"Please . . . ," Sachie whispered.

"Not angry," Valerie said. "Don't want revenge. You don't matter."

"You don't—but . . ." Bodies. Blood. A building full of corpses and the monsters who'd made them. "What *do* you want, then? Anything, please, I'll—"

"Want you to imagine something: Christ on the Cross."

And of course, once the image had been incanted it was impossible *not* to imagine. Sachita Bhar had a few moments to wonder at the sudden spasms seizing her limbs, at the way her jaw locked into startling dislocation, at the feel of a thousand blood-hot strokes exploding like pinpricks across the back of her skull. She tried to close her eyes but it doesn't matter what kind of light falls on the retina, that's not *vision*. The mind generates its own images, much farther upstream, and there's no way to shut those out.

"Yes." Valerie clicked thoughtfully to herself. "I learn."

Sachie managed to speak. It was the hardest thing she'd ever done, but she knew that was fitting; it was also the *last* thing she would ever do. So she summoned all her willpower, every shred of every reserve, every synapse that hadn't already been commandeered for self-destruction, and she spoke. Because nothing else mattered anymore, and she really wanted to know:

"Learn . . . wha . . ."

She couldn't quite get it out. But the short-circuiting brain of Sachita Bhar managed to serve up one last insight anyway, amid the rising static: *This is what the Crucifix Glitch feels like. This is what we do to them. This is . . .*

"Judo," Valerie whispered.

PRIMITIVE

Ultimately, all science is correlation. No matter how effectively it may use one variable to describe another, its equations will always ultimately rest upon the surface of a black box. (Saint Herbert might have put it most succinctly when he observed that all proofs inevitably reduce to propositions that have no proof.) The difference between Science and Faith, therefore, is no more and no less than *predictive power*. Scientific insights have proven to be better predictors than Spiritual ones, at least in worldly matters; they prevail not because they are true, but simply because they *work*.

The Bicameral Order represents a stark anomaly in this otherwise consistent landscape. Their explicitly faith-based methodologies venture unapologetically into metaphysical realms that defy empirical analysis—yet they yield results with consistently more predictive power than conventional science. (How they do this is not known; our best evidence suggests some kind of rewiring of the temporal lobe in a way that amplifies their connection to the Divine.)

It would be dangerously naïve to regard this as a victory for traditional religion. It is not. It is a victory for a radical sect barely half a century old, and the cost of that victory has been to demolish the wall between Science and Faith. The Church's concession of the physical realm informed the historic armistice that has allowed faith and reason to coexist to this day. One may find it heartening to see faith ascendant once again across the Human spectrum; but it is not *our* faith. Its hand still guides lost sheep away from the soulless empiricism of secular science, but the days in which it guided them into the loving arms of Our Savior are waning.

—*An Enemy Within: The Bicameral Threat to Institutional Religion in the Twenty-First Century*
(An Internal Report to the Holy See by the Pontifical Academy of Sciences, 2093)

ALL ANIMALS ARE UNDER STRINGENT SELECTION
PRESSURE TO BE AS STUPID AS THEY CAN GET AWAY
WITH.

—PETE RICHERSON AND ROBERT BOYD

DEEP IN THE Oregon desert, crazy as a prophet, Daniel Brüks opened his eyes to the usual litany of death warrants.

It had been a slow night. A half-dozen traps on the east side were offline—damn booster station must have gone down again—and most of the others were empty. But number eighteen had caught a garter snake. A sage grouse pecked nervously at the lens in number thirteen. The video feed from number four wasn't working, but judging by mass and thermal there was probably a juvenile *Scleroperus* scrambling around in there. Twenty-three had caught a hare.

Brüks hated doing the hares. They smelled awful when you cut them open—and these days, you almost always had to cut them open.

He sighed and described a semicircle with his index finger; the feeds vanished from the skin of his tent. Headlines resolved in their wake, defaulting to past interests: Pakistan's ongoing zombie problem; first anniversary of the Redeemer blowout; a sad brief obituary for the last wild coral reef.

Nothing from Rho.

Another gesture and the fabric lit with soft tactical overlays, skewed to thermal: public-domain real-time satellite imagery of the Prineville Reserve. His tent squatted in the center of the display, a diffuse yellow smudge: cold crunchy outer shell, warm chewy center. No comparable hot spots anywhere else in range.

Brüks nodded to himself, satisfied. The world continued to leave him alone.

Outside, invisible in the colorless predawn, some small creature skittered away across loose rattling rock as he emerged. His breath condensed in front of him; frost crunched beneath his boots, bestowed a faint transient sparkle to the dusty desert floor. His ATB leaned against one of the scraggly larches guarding the camp, marshmallow tires soft and flaccid.

He grabbed mug and filter from their makeshift hook and stepped into the open, down a loose jumble of scree. The vestiges of some half-assed desert stream quenched his thirst at the foot of the slope, slimy and sluggish and doomed to extinction within the month. Enough to keep one large mammal watered in the meantime. Out across the valley the Bicamerals' pet tornado squirmed feebly against a gray eastern sky but stars were still visible overhead, icy, unwinking, and utterly meaningless. Nothing up there tonight but entropy, and the same imaginary shapes that people had been imposing on nature since they'd first thought to wonder at the heavens.

It had been a different desert fourteen years ago. A different night. But it had *felt* the same, until the moment he'd glanced up—and for a few shattering moments it had even been a different *sky*, robbed of all randomness. A sky where every star blazed in brilliant precise formation, where every constellation was a perfect square no matter how desperately human imaginations might strain. February 13, 2082. The night of First Contact: sixty-two thousand objects of unknown origin, clenching around the world in a great grid, screaming across the radio spectrum as they burned. Brüks remembered the feeling: as though he were witnessing some heavenly coup, a capricious god deposed and order restored.

The revolution had lasted only a few seconds. The upstaged constellations had reasserted themselves as soon as those precise friction trails had faded from the upper atmosphere. But the damage had been done, Brüks knew. The sky would never look the same again.

That's what he'd thought at the time, anyway. That's what everyone had thought. The whole damn species had come together in the wake of that common threat, even if they didn't know what it was exactly, even if it hadn't actually *threatened* anything but Humanity's own self-importance. The world had put its petty differences aside, spared no expense, thrown together the best damn ship the twenty-first century could muster. They'd crewed it with expendable bleeding-edgers and sent them off along some best-guess bearing, carrying a phrase book that spelled *take me to your leader* in a thousand languages.

The world had been holding its breath for over a decade now, waiting for the Second Coming. There'd been no encore, no second act. Fourteen years is a long time for a species raised on instant gratification. Brüks had never considered himself a great believer in the nobility of the Human spirit but even he had been surprised at how little time it took for the sky to start looking the same as it always had, at the speed with which the world's petty differences returned to the front page. People, he reflected, were like frogs: take something out of their visual field, and they'd just—forget it.

The *Theseus* mission would be well past Pluto by now. If it had found anything, Brüks hadn't heard about it. For his part, he was sick of waiting. He was sick of life on hold, waiting for monsters or saviors to make an appearance. He was sick of killing things, sick of dying inside.

Fourteen years.

He wished the world would just hurry up and end.

He spent the morning as he'd spent every other for the past two months: running his traplines and poking the things inside, in the faint hope of finding some piece of nature left untwisted.

The clouds were already closing in by sunrise, before his bike had soaked up a decent charge; he left it behind and ran the transects on foot. It was almost noon by the time he got to the hare, only to find that something had beaten him to the punch. The trap had been torn open and its contents emptied by some other predator who'd lacked even the good grace to leave a blood spatter behind for analysis.

The garter snake was still slithering around in number eighteen, though: a male, one of those brown-on-brown morphs that vanished against the dirt. It writhed in Brüks's grasp, clenched around his forearm like a scaly tentacle; its scent glands smeared stink across his skin. Brüks drew a few microliters of blood without much hope, plugged them into the barcoder on his belt. He swigged from his canteen while the device worked its magic.

Far across the desert the monastery's tornado had swollen to three times its predawn size, pumped by the midday heat. Distance reduced it to a brown thread, an insignificant smoky smudge; but get too close to that funnel and you'd end up scattered over half the valley. Just the year before, some Ugandan vendetta theocracy had hacked a transAt shuttle out of Dartmouth, sent it through a vortex engine on the outskirts of Johannesburg. Not much but rivets and teeth had come out the other side.

The barcoder meeped in plaintive surrender: too many genetic artifacts for a clean read. Brüks sighed, unsurprised. The little machine could tag any gut parasite from the merest speck of shit, ID any host species from the smallest shred of pure tissue—but pure tissue was so hard to come by, these days. There was always something that didn't belong. Viral DNA, engineered for the greater good but too indiscriminate to stay on target. Special marker genes, designed to make animals glow in the dark when exposed to some toxin the EPA had lost interest in fifty years before. Even DNA computers, custom-built for a specific task and then tramped carelessly into wild genotypes like muddy footprints on a pristine floor. Nowadays it seemed like half the technical data on the planet were being stored genetically. Try sequencing a lung fluke and it was even money whether the base pairs you read would code for protein or the technical specs on the Denver sewer system.

It was okay, though. Brüks was an old man, a field man from a day when people could tell what they were looking at by—well, by *looking* at it. Check the chin shields. Count the fin rays, the hooks on the scolex. Use your *eyes,* dammit. At least if you screw up you've only got yourself to blame, not some dumb-ass machine that can't tell the difference between cytochrome oxidase and a Shakespearean sonnet. And if the things you're trying to ID happen to live inside *other* things, you kill the host. You cut it open.

Brüks was good at that, too. He'd never got around to liking it much, though.

Now he whispered to his latest victim—"*Shhh . . . sorry . . . it won't hurt, I promise . . .*"—and dropped it into the kill sack. He'd found himself doing that a lot lately, murmuring meaningless comforting lies to victims who couldn't possibly understand what he was saying. He kept telling himself to grow up. In all the billions of years that life had been iterating on this planet, had any predator ever tried to comfort its prey? Had "natural" death ever been so quick and painless as the killings Dan Brüks inflicted for the greater good? And yet it still bothered him to see those small diffuse shadows flopping and squirming behind the translucent white plastic, to hear the soft thumps and hisses as simple minds tried to drive bodies, suddenly and terrifyingly unresponsive, toward some kind of imaginary escape.

At least these deaths served a purpose, some constructive end transcending the disease or predation that nature would have inflicted. Life was a struggle to exist at the expense of other life. Biology was a struggle to understand life. And this particular bit of biology, this study of which he was author, principal, and sole investigator—this was a struggle to use biology to help the very populations he was sampling. These deaths were the closest that Darwin's universe would ever come to altruism.

And that, said the little voice that always seemed to boot up at times like this, *is so much shit. The only thing you're struggling to do is wring a few more publications out of your grant before the funding dries up. Even if you nailed down every change inflicted on every clade over the past hundred years, even if you quantified species loss down to the molecules, it wouldn't matter.*

Nobody cares. The only thing you're struggling against is reality.

That voice had become his constant companion over the years. He let it rant. *Either way,* he told it after it had run down, *we're a shitty biologist.* And while his own guilty plea came easily enough, he could not bring himself to feel shame on that account.

It had stopped being a snake by the time he got back to camp. He stretched the limp and lifeless remains along the dissecting tray. Four seconds with the scasers and it was gutted, throat to cloaca; twenty more and the GI and respiratory tracts floated in separate watch glasses. The intestine would have the heaviest parasite load; Brüks loaded the GI tract into the 'scope and got to work.

Twenty minutes later, a retinue of flukes and cestodes only half-cataloged, something exploded in the distance.

That's what it sounded like, anyway: the soft muffled *whoompf* of far-off ordinance. Brüks rose from his work, panned the desert between spindly gnarled trunks.

Nothing. Nothing. Noth—

Oh, wait . . .

The monastery.

He grabbed his goggles off the ATB and zoomed in. The tornado was the first thing to draw his eye—

—That thing's going pretty strong for so late in the day—

—but off to the right, directly over the monastery itself, a puff of dark brown smoke roiled and drifted and dissipated in the lowering light.

The building didn't seem to be damaged, though. At least, none of the façades he could see.

What are they doing over there?

Physics, officially. Cosmology. High-energy stuff. But it was all supposed to be theoretical; as far as Brüks knew the Bicameral Order didn't perform actual experiments. Of course, hardly anyone did, these days. It was machines that scanned the heavens, machines that probed the space between atoms, machines that asked the questions and designed the experiments to answer them. All that was left for mere meat, apparently, was navelgazing: to sit in the desert and contemplate whatever answers those machines served up. Although most still preferred to call it *analysis*.

A hive mind that spoke in tongues: that was how the Bicamerals did it, supposedly. Some kind of bioradio in their heads, a communal corpus callosum: electrons jiggling around in microtubules, some kind of quantum-entanglement thing. Completely organic to get around the ban on B2B interfaces. A spigot that poured many minds into one on command. They flowed together and called down the Rapture, rolled around the floor and drooled and ululated while their acolytes took notes, and somehow they ended up rewriting the Amplituhedron.

There was supposed to be some rational explanation to justify the mumbo jumbo. Left-hemisphere pattern-matching subroutines amped beyond recognition; the buggy wetware that made you see faces in clouds or God's wrath in thunderstorms, tweaked to walk some fine line between insight and pareidolia. Apparently there were fundamental insights to be harvested along that razor's edge, patterns that only the Bicamerals could distinguish from hallucination. That was the story, anyway. It sounded like utter bullshit to Brüks.

Still, you couldn't argue with the Nobels.

Maybe they had some kind of particle accelerator over there after all. They had to be doing *something* that sucked a lot of energy; nobody used an industrial vortex engine to run kitchen appliances.

From behind, the metallic tinkle of displaced instruments. Brüks turned.

His scasers lay in the dirt. On the bench above them the gutted snake watched him upside down from its dissecting tray, forked tongue flickering.

Nerves, Brüks told himself.

The discarded carcass shivered on its back, as if the gash down its belly had let in the cold. Flaps of tissue rippled along either edge of that wound, a slow peristaltic wave undulating along the length of the body.

Galvanic skin response. That's all it is.

The snake's head lurched up over the edge of the tray. Glassy, unblinking eyes looked this way and that. The tongue, red-black, black-red, tasted the air.

The animal crawled from the pan.

It wasn't having an easy time of it. It kept trying to roll and crawl on its belly but it didn't *have* a belly, not anymore. The ventral scales that would have pushed it along, the muscles beneath had been sliced apart, every one. And so the creature would manage a half twist every now and then, and fail, and resort to crawling on its back: eyes wide, tongue flicking, insides emptied.

The snake reached the edge of the bench, feebly wavered a moment, dropped into the dust. Brüks's boot came down on its head. He ground it deep against the rocky soil until there was nothing left but a moist sticky clot in the dirt. The rest of the creature writhed, its muscles jumping to the beat of nerves jammed with noise and no signal. But at least there was nothing left that could possibly please-God *feel*.

Reptiles were not especially fragile creatures. More than once Brüks had found rattlesnakes on the road hours from the nearest vehicle, spines crushed, fangs shattered, heads reduced to bloody paste—still moving, still crawling for the ditch. The kill sack was supposed to prevent that kind of protracted agony. You turned the animal's own metabolism against it, let lungs and capillaries carry the poison to every cell of every tissue, bringing a quick and painless and—most of all—a *complete* death, so that it would not wake up and fucking *look* at you, and try to *escape,* an hour after you'd scraped its insides away.

Of course, there were zombies in the world now. Vampires, too, for that matter. But the twenty-first century's undead were strictly Human. There was no reason anyone would want to build a zombie snake. This had to be another contamination artifact; some accidental genetic hack that shut down the MS receptor sites, maybe triggered a rogue suite of motor commands. Had to be.

Still.

He'd really hoped the ghosts would be easier to handle out here.

There weren't nearly as many ghosts in the desert, for one thing. For another, none of them were human. Sometimes he wished he could feel half as much for the thousands of *people* he'd killed.

Of course, basic biology explained that particular double standard as well. He hadn't had to face any of his human victims, hadn't looked into their eyes, hadn't been there when they'd died. The gut was not a long-range organ. Its grasp of culpability degraded exponentially with distance; there'd been so many arcane degrees separating the actions of Daniel Brüks from their consequences that conscience itself entered the realm of pure theory. Besides, he'd hardly acted alone; the guilt diffused across the whole team. And their intentions, at least, had been beyond reproach.

Nobody had blamed them, not out loud, not really. Not at first. You don't pass judgment on the unwitting hammer used to bash in someone's skull. Brüks's work had been perverted by others intent on bloodshed; the guilt was theirs, not his. But those perpetrators remained uncaught and unpunished, and so many had needed closure in the meantime. And the distance between *How could they* and *How could you let them* was so much smaller than Brüks had ever imagined.

No charges had been pressed. It wasn't even enough to revoke his tenure. As it turned out, it was only enough to wear out his welcome on campus.

Nature, though. Nature always welcomed him. She passed no judgments, didn't care about right or wrong, guilt or innocence. She only cared about what worked and what didn't. She welcomed everyone with the same egalitarian indifference. You just had to play by her rules, and expect no mercy if things didn't go your way.

And so Dan Brüks had put in for sabbatical and filed his agenda, and headed into the field. He'd left behind his sampling drones and artificial insects, packed no autonomous tech to rub his nose in the obsolescence of human labor. A few had watched him go, with relief; others kept their eyes on the sky. He left them, too. His colleagues would forgive him, or they wouldn't. The aliens would return, or they wouldn't. But Nature would never turn him away. And even in a world where every last sliver of natural habitat was under siege, there was no shortage of deserts. They'd been growing like slow cancer for a hundred years or more.

Daniel Brüks would go into the welcoming desert, and kill whatever he found there.

He opened his eyes to the soft red glow of panicking machinery. A third of the network had just died in his sleep. Five more traps went down as he watched: a booster station, suddenly offlined. Twenty-two beeped plaintively a moment later—proximate heat trace, big, man-size even—and dropped off the map.

Instantly awake, Brüks played the logs. The network was going down from west to east, each dead node another footfall in a growing trail of dark ragged footprints stomping across the valley.

Heading directly for him.

He pulled up the satcam thermals. The remains of the old 380 ran like a thin vein along the northern perimeter, yesterday's stale sunshine seeping from cracked asphalt. Diaphanous thermals and microclimatic hot spots, dying since nightfall, flickered at the threshold of visibility. Nothing else but the yellow nimbus of his own tent at center stage.

Twenty-one reported sudden warmth, and disappeared.

Cameras lurked here and there along the traplines. Brüks had never found much use for them but they'd come bundled as part of the package. One sat on a booster that happened to be line of sight to number nineteen. He brought it up: StarlAmp painted the nighttime desert in blues and whites, a surrealistic moonscape full of contrast. Brüks panned the view—

—and almost missed it: a slither of motion from stage right, an amplified blur. Something that moved faster than anything Human had any right to. The camera was dead before Nineteen even felt the heat.

The booster went down. Another dozen feeds died in an instant. Brüks barely noticed. He was staring at that last frozen frame, feeling his gut clench and his bowels turn to ice.

Faster than a man, and so much less. And just a little bit *colder* inside.

The field sensors weren't sensitive enough to register that difference, of course. To see the truth from heat signatures alone you'd need to look inside the very head of your target, to squint until you could see deltas of maybe a tenth of a degree. You'd look at the hippocampus, and see that it was dark. You'd listen to the prefrontal cortex, and hear that it was silent. And then maybe you'd notice all that extra wiring, the force-grown neural lattices connecting midbrain to motor strip, the high-speed expressways bypassing the anterior cingulate gyrus—and those extra ganglia clinging like tumors to the visual pathways, fishing endlessly for the telltale neural signatures of *seek* and *destroy*.

It would be a lot easier to spot those differences in visible light: Just look into the eyes, and see nothing at all looking back. Of course, if it ever got that close you'd be dead already. It wouldn't leave you time to beg. It wouldn't even understand your pleas. It would simply kill you, if that's what it had been told to do, more efficiently than any conscious being because there was nothing left to get in the way: no second thoughts, no pulled punches, not even the basic glucose-sucking awareness of its own existence. It was stripped down to pure reptile, and it was *dedicated*.

Less than a kilometer away now.

Something inside Daniel Brüks split down the middle. One half clamped its hands over its ears and denied everything—*what the fuck why would anyone must be some kind of mistake*—but the other remembered the universal human fondness for scapegoats, the thousands who'd died thanks to dumb ol' Backdoor Brüks, the odds that at least one of those victims might have been survived by next of kin with the resources to set a military-grade zombie on his trail.

How could they.

How could you let *them . . .*

The ATB hissed beneath him as its tires inhaled. The charge cord pulled him briefly off balance before tearing free. He plunged through a gap in the trees and down the scree, skidding sideways: hit the base of the slope and the desert spun around him, slimy and frictionless. The stream nearly took him out right there. Brüks fought for control as the bike one-eightied, but those marvelous marshmallow tires kept him miraculously upright. Then he was racing east across the fractured valley floor.

Sagebrush tore at him as he passed. He cursed his own blindness; these days, no self-respecting grad student would be caught dead in the field without rattlesnake receptors in their eyes. But Brüks was an old man, baseline, night-blind. He didn't even dare use the headlamp. So he hurtled through the night, smashing through petrified shrubs, bucking over unseen outcroppings of bedrock. He fumbled one-handed through the bike's saddlebags, came up with the gogs, slapped them over his eyes. The desert sprang into view, green and grainy.

0247, the goggles told him from the corner of his eye. Three hours to sunrise. He tried pinging his network but if any part of it remained alive, it was out of range. He wondered if the zombie had made it to camp yet. He wondered how close it had come to catching him.

Doesn't matter. Can't catch me now, motherfucker. Not on foot. Not even undead. You can kiss my ass good-bye.

Then he checked the charge gauge and his stomach dropped away all over again.

Cloudy skies. An old battery, a year past its best-before. A charging blanket that hadn't been cleaned in a month.

The ATB had ten kilometers in it. Fifteen, tops.

He braked and brought it around in a spray of dirt. His own trail extended behind him, an unmistakable line of intermittent carnage wrought upon the desert floor: broken plants, sun-cracked tiles of ancient lakebed crushed in passing. He was running but he wasn't hiding. As long as he stayed on the valley floor, they'd be able to track him.

Who, exactly?

He switched from StarlAmp to infrared, zoomed the view.

That.

A hot tiny spark leapt against a distant slope, right about where his camp would be.

Closer, though. And closing fast. That thing could *run*.

Brüks swung the bike around and kicked it back into gear. He almost didn't notice the second spark sweeping across his field of vision, it was so faint.

He saw the third clearly enough, though. And the fourth. Too distant to make out shapes on thermal, but all hot as humans. All closing.

Five, six, seven . . .

Shit.

They were fanned out along the valley as far as he could see.

What did I do, what did I do, don't they know it was an accident? *It wasn't even* me, *for chrissakes, I didn't* kill *anyone, I just— left the door open . . .*

Ten kilometers. Then they'd be on him like ravenous wolves.

The ATB leapt forward. Brüks pinged 911: nothing. ConSensus was live enough but deaf to his pleas; somehow he could surf but not send. And his pursuers *still* weren't showing up on satellite thermal; as far as the skeyes could see he was alone down here with the microweather and the monastery.

The monastery.

They'd be online. They'd be able to help. At the very least the Bicamerals lived behind *walls*. Anything was better than fleeing naked through the desert.

He aimed for the tornado. It writhed in his enhanced sight, a distant green monster nailed to the earth. Its roar carried across the desert as it always did, faint but omnipresent. For a moment, Brüks heard something strange in that sound. The monastery resolved in the gogs, huddling in the shadow of the great engine. A myriad of pinpoint stars burned there against a low jumble of stepped terraces, almost painfully bright.

Three in the morning, and every window was ablaze.

Not so faint anymore: the vortex roared like an ocean now, its volume rising imperceptibly with each turn of the wheels. It was no longer stuck to the horizon. StarlAmp turned it into a pillar of fire, big enough to hold up the sky or to tear it down. Brüks craned his neck: over a kilometer away and still the funnel seemed to lean over him. Any second now it would break free. Any second it would leap from the ground and slam back down, *there* or *there* or *right fucking here* like the finger of some angry god, and it would rip the world apart wherever it touched.

He stayed on course even though the monster ahead couldn't possibly be made of air and moisture, couldn't possibly be anything so—so *soft*. It was something else entirely, some insane Old Testament event horizon that chewed up the very laws of physics. It caught the glow from the monastery, trapped that light and shredded it and spun it together with everything else that fell within reach. A small gibbering thing inside Daniel Brüks begged him to turn back, *knew* that the creatures stalking him couldn't be worse than this, because whatever they were, they were only the size of men but this, *this* was the very wrath of God.

But that hesitant little voice spoke again, and this time the question lingered: *Why is this thing running so hard?*

It shouldn't have been. Vortex engines never really *stopped,* but at night they weakened in the cooling air, diffused and idled until the rising sun brought them back to full strength. To keep a funnel this size running so hot, so late at night—that would almost draw more energy than it yielded. The vapor from the cooling cells would have to be verging on live steam—and now Brüks was close enough to hear something *else* against the jet-engine roar, a faint creaking counterpoint of great metal blades, twisting past their normative specs . . .

The monastery lights went out.

It took a moment for his goggles to amp back up; but in that moment of pure, illuminating darkness Daniel Brüks finally saw himself for the fool he was. For the first time he saw the pin-point heatprints *ahead* of him, closing from the east as well as from behind. He saw forces powerful enough to hack surveillance satellites in geostationary orbit, but somehow unable to blind his antique Telonics network to the same heatprints. He saw a military automaton, ruthless as a shark, fast as a superconductor, betraying its own approach from kilometers away when it could have avoided his traplines entirely and killed him in his sleep.

He saw himself from high overhead, stumbling across someone else's game board: caught in a net that closed around but not *on* him.

They didn't even know I was here. They're after the Bicamerals.

He pulled to a stop. The monastery loomed fifty meters ahead, low and black against the stars. All windows abruptly shuttered, all approaches suddenly dark, it rose from the landscape as though born of it: a pile of deep rock strata breaching the surface of the world. The tornado loomed beyond like a whirling gash in space-time, barely a hundred meters on the other side. The sound of its rage filled the world.

On all sides, candles closed in the darkness.

0313, his goggles reminded him. Less than an hour ago he'd been asleep. It wasn't nearly long enough to come to terms with your own imminent death.

YOU ARE IN DANGER, the gogs told him helpfully.

Brüks blinked. The little red letters persisted, hovering off at the corner of his eye where the chrono readout should be.

COME ON, THEN. DOOR'S OPEN.

He looked past the command line, panned across the darkened façades of the monastery. There, ground level: just to the left of a broad staircase that underscored the main entrance. An opening, barely big enough for a man. Something burned there at body temperature. It had arms and legs. It waved.

MOVE YOUR ASS, BRÜKS, YOU SELF-ABSORBED IDIOT.

SEALING ENTRANCE IN   15s

14s

13s . . .

Brüks moved his self-absorbed idiot ass.

FOR THEY HAVE SOWN THE WIND, AND THEY SHALL
REAP THE WHIRLWIND.
—HOSEA 8:7

INSIDE, THE DARKNESS was bright chaos.

Human heat signatures flickered across Brüks's goggles at point-blank range, coruscations of false color in frantic motion. The heat of their passing painted the surroundings with fainter washes of red and yellow: rough-hewn walls, a flat dead light panel for a ceiling, a floor that yielded unexpectedly beneath his feet like some ungodly hybrid of rubber and flesh. Off in an indeterminate distance, something stuttered and wailed; here in the hallway the human rainbows moved with silent urgency. The woman who'd invited him in—a petite writhing heatprint no more than 160 centimeters tall—grabbed his hand and pulled him forward: "I'm Lianna. Stay close."

He followed, switching the gogs to StarlAmp. The heatprints vanished; bright greenish stars moved in the void left behind, always in pairs, binary constellations jostling and blinking in the dark. A word popped into his head: *luciferin*. Photophores in the retinas.

These people had eyes that doubled as flashlights. Brüks had once known a grad student with similar augments. Sex had been—disquieting, in the dark.

His guide threaded him through the starfield. That distant wailing rose and fell, rose and fell; not words exactly, but syllables, at least. Clicks and cries and diphthongs in the dark. Bright eyes rose before him, seething with cold blue light. Amplified photons limned a gray face full of lines and angles. Brüks tried to steer his way around but that face blocked his way, eyes glowing with such furious intensity that his goggles had to dial back the amplification to almost nothing.

"*Gelan,*" the face croaked. "*Thofe tessrodia.*"

Brüks tried to take a step back; bumped into traffic, rebounded.

"*Eptroph!*" cried the face, as the body beneath gave way.

Lianna pushed him sideways into the wall—"Stay *right there*"—and dropped to the floor. Brüks switched back to thermal. The rainbows returned. Brüks's assailant was on his back, heat sig bright as a solar flare, muttering nonsense. His fingers fluttered as if stabbing an invisible keyboard; his left foot tapped an agitated tattoo against the elastic flooring. Lianna cradled his head in her lap and spoke to him in the same incomprehensible tongue.

The chronic background roar of the vortex engine rose subtly in pitch. Stone trembled at Brüks's back.

A hot bright figure appeared down the corridor, swimming

against the stream. Within moments it had reached them; Brüks's guide passed her charge to the newcomer and was on her feet in an instant. "Let's go."

"What was—"

"Not here."

A side door. A flight of stairs, sheathed in the same rubbery skin that turned their footsteps into soft squeaks. It corkscrewed down through cooling bedrock that dimmed with each step in the goggles' sights, but that compact body glowed like a beacon ahead of him. Suddenly the world was silent again but for their own footsteps and the distant, almost subsonic thrumming of the vortex engine.

"What's going on?" Brüks asked.

"Oh. Mahmood." Lianna glanced back, her eyes bright garish blobs, her mouth a crimson slash of heat. "Can't always control when the rapture hits, much less which node. Not the most convenient thing in the world but you don't want to miss the insights, you know? Could be time travel, for all we know. Could be a cure for golem."

"You understood what he was saying."

"Kinda. It's what I do, when I'm not bringing lost sheep in from the desert."

"You're a synthesist?" *Jargonaut* was the street name. Glorified translators, charged with bringing esoteric transhuman tablets down from the mountain, carved in runes simple enough for pitiful baseline Humans to half understand.

Rhona had called them *Moses mammals,* back when she'd been in the world.

But Lianna was shaking her head. "Not exactly. More of a— you're a biologist, right? Synthesists would be rats. I'm more of a koala bear."

"Specialist." Brüks nodded. "Narrower niche."

"Exactly."

A faint orange stain appeared on the thermoptics: warmth from below.

"And you know who I am because . . ."

"We're on the bleeding edge of theistic virology here. You think we don't know how to access a public database?"

"I just thought you'd have better things to look up when you were being attacked by zombies."

"We keep an eye on the neighborhood, Dr. Brüks."

"Yeah, but what—"

She stopped. Brüks nearly ran into her, then realized they'd reached the bottom of the stairs. Bright heat spilled around a corner dead ahead; Lianna turned and tapped his goggles. "You won't be needing those."

He pushed them onto his forehead. The world reverted to a dim wash of blues and grays. The rough stone to his left broke the feeble ambient light into jagged fragments; to his right the wall was smooth gray metal.

Lianna was already past him, heading back up the stairs. "I gotta go. You can watch from down here."

"But—"

"Don't touch anything!" she called back, and was gone.

He stepped around the corner. The ceiling panels here were as dead and dark as every other he'd seen in this place. The room— really, more of a cul-de-sac—was lit solely by a band of smart paint covering the far wall from waist-height to ceiling. It glowed with a haphazard collage of tactical displays ranging from hand-size to two meters across. Some of the feeds were coarse green mosaics; others rendered images high rez and razor-sharp.

A man in a loose tan coverall paced back and forth before the displays, at least two meters from his fuzzy slippers (*slippers?*) to the cropped salt-and-pepper thicket on his head. He spared a glance as Brüks approached, muttered "Glas-*not*," and turned back to the welter of intel.

Great.

Lianna the koala had told him he could watch, though. He stepped forward and tried to make sense of the chaos.

Upper left: a satellite view so crisp it nearly hurt his eyes. The monastery sat dead center, a bull's-eye on the board, aglow with telltale thermal emissions. But it was the only hot spot in the whole window; whatever orbital eye he was looking through had been precisely blinded to all those other heatprints closing in the darkness. Brüks reached for the display, his fingers set to zoom the mag; a grunt and a glare from the slippered monk and he desisted.

So much for orbital surveillance. The monastery had its own cameras, though, judging by the mix of StarlAmp and thermal windows looking out across the desert. They painted the night-scape in palettes from every band of the visible spectrum, cool blues and rubies intense as lasers, color schemes so chaotic Brüks wondered whether they were really functional or just a reflection of some deviant Bicameral aesthetic. Candles glowed in each of *those* windows, and they all looked the same.

Four klicks out, and closing fast.

Something sparkled on one of the displays, a tiny bright sun-dog in the dead of night. The image flared a moment; bright electronic snow fuzzed the display. A brief, bright nova. Then a dark dead hole in the wall, NO SIGNAL flashing from its center.

The monk's fingers flew across the paint, calling up keyboards, zooming displays. Windows sprouted, panned brief landscapes, evaporated in turn. Three of those views sparked and died before the Bicameral had the chance to retire them gracefully.

They're taking out our cameras, Brüks realized, and wondered distantly when he had started to think of these rapture-stricken deviants as part of *we*.

Less than three and a half kilometers now.

A new set of windows bloomed across the wall. The pictures flickering in these frames were grainier than the others, desatu-rated, almost monochrome. And while they, too, panned the des-ert, there was something about those views, something different yet familiar—

There. Third window over: a tiny monastery hunkered on the

horizon, a tiny vortex engine. *This* camera was looking back from way the hell across the desert.

That's my network, Brüks realized. *My cameras. I guess the zombies left some alive after all* . . .

Brother Slippers had tapped into a half dozen of them, zoomed and cycled through each in turn. Brüks wasn't sure how useful they'd be: cheap off-the-shelf things, party favors to lure impoverished researchers into springing for a package deal. They had the usual enhancements but the range was nothing special.

They seemed to be sufficient for Slippers's purposes, though. Second window from the left, a heat source moved left to right about a hundred meters out. The camera panned automatically, tracking the target while he amped the zoom. The image resolved in slow degrees.

Another one of the monastery's eyes flared and died, its overlaid range finder fading a moment later: 3.2 kilometers.

That's almost nine meters per second. On foot . . .

"What happens when they get here?" he asked.

Slippers seemed more interested in a distant heatprint caught on number three: a small vehicle, an ATB, same basic design as—

Wait a minute—

"That's my bike," Brüks murmured, frowning. "That's—*me* . . ."

Slippers spared him a glance and a head shake. "Assub."

"No, *listen*—" It was far from a perfect mug shot, and Telonics's steadicam tracking algorithms were the envy of no one in the field. But whoever sat astride that bike had Brüks's mustache, the square lines of his face, the same multipocketed field vest that had been years out of style even when he'd inherited the damn thing two decades before. "You're being hacked," Brüks insisted. "That's some kind of recording, someone must've—" *Someone was* recording *me?* "I mean, *look* at it!"

Two more cameras down. Seven so far. Slippers wasn't even bothering to clear the real estate by closing the channels. Something else had caught his eye. He tapped the edge of a window that looked onto a naked-eye view of the desert sky. The stars strewn across that display glittered like sugar on velvet. Brüks wanted to fall into that sky, get lost in the stark peaceful beauty of a night without tactical overlays or polarized enhancements.

But even here, the monk had found something to ruin the view: a brief flicker, a dim red nimbus framing an oval patch of starscape for the blink of an eye. The display clicked softly, an infinitesimal sharpening of focus—and in the next instant the stars returned, unsullied and pristine.

Except for a great *hole* in the night hanging over the western ridge, a vast dark oval where no stars shone.

Something was crawling toward them across the sky, eating the stars as it went. It was as cold as the stratosphere—at least, it didn't show up on any of the adjacent thermal views. And it was *huge*; it covered a good twenty degrees of arc even though it was still—

No range finder. No heatprint. If not for whatever microlensing magic Slippers had just performed, not even this eclipse of ancient starlight would have given it away.

I, Brüks realized, *have definitely picked the wrong side.*

Twenty-three hundred meters. In five minutes the zombies would be knocking at the door.

"Carousel," Slippers murmured, and something in his voice made Brüks look twice.

The monk was *smiling.* But he wasn't looking at the cloaked behemoth marching across Orion's Belt. His eyes were on a ground's-eye view of the vortex engine. There was no audio feed; the tornado whirled silently in the StarlAmped window, a shackled green monster tearing up airspace. Brüks could hear it anyway— roaring in his memory, bending the ducts and the blades of the substructure that birthed it, vibrating through the very bedrock. He could *feel* it in the soles of his feet. And now Brother Slippers brought up a whole new window, a panel not of camera views or tactical overlays but of engineering readouts, laminar feed and humidity injection rates, measures of torque and velocity and compressible flow arrayed along five hundred meters of altitude.

Offset to one side a luminous wire-frame disk labeled VEC/PRIME sprouted a thousand icons around its perimeter; a hundred more described spokes and spirals toward its heart. Heating elements. Countercurrent exchangers. The devil's own mixing board. Slippers nodded, as if to himself: "Watch."

Icons and outputs began to move. There was nothing dramatic in the readouts, no sudden acceleration into red zones, no alarms. Just the slightest tweak of injection rates on one side of the circle; the gentlest nuzzle of convection and condensation on the other.

Over in its window, the green monster raised one toe.

Holy shit. They're going to set it free . . .

A wash of readouts turned yellow; in the heart of that sudden sunny bloom, a dozen others turned orange. A couple turned red.

With ponderous, implacable majesty, the tornado lifted from the earth and stepped out across the desert.

It came down on two of the zombies. Brüks saw it all through a window that tracked the funnel's movements across the landscape: saw the targets break and weave far faster than merely human legs could carry a body. They zigzagged, a drunkard's sprint by undead Olympians.

They might as well have been rooted to the ground. The tornado sucked those insignificant smudges of body heat into the sky so fast they didn't even leave an afterimage. It hesitated for a few seconds, rooted through the earth like some great elephant's trunk. It devoured dirt and gravel and boulders the size of automobiles. Then it was off, carving its name into the desert.

Back in its garage, swirls of moisture condensed anew where the monster had broken free.

The vortex was past the undead perimeter now, veering northwest. It hopped once more, lifting its great earth-shattering foot into the air; pieces of pulverized desert rained down in its wake. A distant, disconnected subroutine in Brüks's mind—some ganglion of logic immune to awe or fear or intimidation—wondered at the questionable efficiency of throwing an entire weather system at two lousy foot soldiers, at the infinitesimal odds of even *hitting* a target on such a wild trajectory. But it fell silent in the next second, and didn't speak again.

The whirlwind was not staggering randomly into that good night. It was bearing down on a distant figure riding an ATB.

It was coming for *him*.

This isn't possible, Brüks thought. *You can't steer a tornado, nobody can. The most you can do is let it loose and get out of the way. This isn't happening. This isn't happening.*

I am not out there . . .

But something was, and it knew it was being hunted. Brüks's own hacked cameras told the tale: the ATB had abandoned its straight-line trajectory in favor of breakneck evasive maneuvers that would have instantly pitched any human rider over the handlebars. It slewed and skidded, kicked up plumes that sparkled sapphire in the amped starlight. The vortex weaved closer. They swept across the desert like partners in some wild and calamitous dance full of twirls and arabesques and impossible hairpin turns. They were never in step. Neither followed the other's lead. And yet some invisible, unbreakable thread seemed to join the two, pulled them implacably into each other's arms. Brüks watched, hypnotized at the sight of his own imminent ascension; the ATB was caught in orbit now around its monstrous nemesis. For a moment Brüks thought it might even break free—was it his imagination, or was the funnel *thinner* than it had been?—but in the next his doppelgänger lost its footing and skidded toward dissolution.

In that instant it *changed*.

Brüks wasn't certain how, exactly. It would have happened too fast even if whirling debris and the grain of boosted photons hadn't obscured the view. But it was as though the image of Daniel Brüks and his faithful steed *split* somehow, as if something inside was trying to shed its skin and break free, leaving a lizard-tail husk behind for the sky-beast to chew on. The maelstrom moved in, a blizzard of rock and dust obscuring any detail. The funnel was visibly weakening now but it still had enough suction to take its quarry whole.

Still had teeth enough to smash it to fragments.

The undead broke ranks.

It wasn't a retreat. It didn't even seem to be a coordinated exercise. The candles just stopped advancing and *flickered* back and forth in their windows, nine hundred meters out, directionless and Brownian. Far behind them the sated whirlwind weaved away to the north, a dissipating ropy thing, nearly exhausted.

"Dymic." Slippers nodded knowingly. "Assub."

Back on the pad a newborn vortex chafed at its restraints, smaller than its predecessor but *angrier,* somehow. Yellow icons blossomed across vec/prime like rampant brush fires. Overhead, something was eating Gemini feetfirst.

Another window opened on the wall, a hodgepodge of emerald alphanumerics. Slippers blinked and frowned, as though the apparition was somehow unexpected. Greek equations, Cyrillic footnotes, even a smattering of English flowed across the new display.

Not telemetry. Not incoming. According to the status bar, this was an outgoing transmission; the Bicamerals were signaling someone. It all flickered by too fast for Brüks to have made much sense of it even if he *had* spoken Russian, but occasional fragments of English stuck in his eye. *Theseus* was one. *Icarus* another. Something about *angels* and *asteroids* flashed center stage for a moment and evaporated.

More glyphs, more numbers: three parallel columns this time, rendered in red. Someone talking back.

Out in the desert, the zombies stopped flickering.

"Huh," Slippers said, and raised a finger to his right temple. For the first time Brüks noticed an old-fashioned earbud there, an audio antique from the days before cortical inlays and bone conduction. Slippers inclined his head, listening; up on the wall a flurry of red and green turned the ongoing exchange into a Christmas celebration.

Over on VEC/PRIME, orange and red icons downshifted to yellow. The chained vortex stopped thrashing on its pad and whirled smoothly at attention. Halfway to the horizon, the last vestiges of its older sibling dissipated in a luminous mist of settling dust.

The desert rested quietly beneath an invisible thing in the sky.

Just a few minutes ago, Dan Brüks had watched himself die out there. Or maybe escape in the nick of time. Something like him, anyway. Right up until that last moment when the maelstrom had chewed it up and spat it out. And right at that moment, the zombies had come—unglued . . .

Assub, Slippers had said then. At least, that's what Brüks had heard. *Assub.*

Ass—hub?

"A.S.?" he said aloud. Brother Slippers turned, raised an eyebrow.

"A.S.," Brüks repeated. "What's it stand for?"

"Artificial Stupidity. Grabs local surveillance archives to blend in. Chameleon response."

"But why me? Why"—in the sky, invisible airships—"why *anything*? Why not just cloak, like that thing up there?"

"Can't cloak thermal emissions without overheating," Slippers told him. "Not for long at least, not if you're an endotherm. Best you can do is make yourself look like something else. Dynamic mimicry."

Dymic.

Brüks snorted, shook his head. "You're not even Bicameral, are you?"

Slippers smiled faintly. "You thought I was?"

"It's a monastery. You spoke like . . ."

Slippers shook his head. "Just visiting."

Acronyms. "You're military," Brüks guessed.

"Something like that."

"Dan Brüks," he said, extending a hand.

The other man looked at it for a moment. Reached out his own. "Jim Moore. Welcome to the armistice."

"What just happened?"

"They came to terms. For the moment."

"They?"

"The monks and the vampire."

"I thought those were zombies."

"*Those* are." Moore tapped the wall; a heat source appeared in the distance, a lone bright pinprick well behind the line. "*That* isn't. Zombies don't do anything without someone pulling their strings. She's coming in now."

"Vampires," Brüks said.

"Vam*pire*. Solitary op." And then, almost as an afterthought, "Those things aren't good in groups."

"I didn't even know we let them out. I actually thought we were pretty scrupulous about keeping them, you know. Contained."

"So did I." Pale flickering light washed the color from Moore's face. "Not quite sure what her story is."

"What's she have against the Bicamerals?"

"I don't know."

"Why did she stop?"

"Enemy of my enemy."

Brüks let that sink in. "You're saying there's a *bigger* enemy out there. A, a common threat."

"Potentially."

Out in the desert, that dimensionless point of heat had grown large enough to move on visible legs. It did not appear to be running, yet somehow crossed the desert far faster than any baseline was likely to walk.

"So I guess I can go now," Brüks said.

The old soldier turned to face him. Regret mingled with the tactical reflections in his eyes.

"Not a chance," he said.

EITHER WAR IS OBSOLETE, OR MEN ARE.

— R. BUCKMINSTER FULLER

TWO GUARDS STOOD at the door halfway down the hall, one to each side, like a couple of dark golems in matching pajamas. Brüks had not been invited to the party inside but he followed Moore at a distance, hanging back along the edge of the corridor for want of any other destination. Bicamerals brushed past in both directions, going about whatever business involved the domestication of weaponized whirlwinds. They seemed unremarkable in the morning light slanting through the windows. No arcane ululations. No vestments or hooded robes, no uniforms of any kind that Brüks could make out. A couple wore denim. One, preoccupied with a tacpad as he passed, was stark naked except for the tattoo squirming along his chest: some kind of winged animal Brüks was pretty sure didn't exist anywhere in the taxonomic database.

They still had stars in their eyes, though.

Ahead, Moore stepped between the guards and into the room. Brüks sidled up in his wake. The sentries stood still as stone, barefoot, faces forward, their beige coveralls identically featureless. Empty holsters hung from their belts.

Their lightless eyes wouldn't stop moving. They jiggled and jerked in panicked little arcs, back and forth, up and down, as though terrified souls had been buried alive in wet cement. Someone coughed softly down the hall. All four eyes locked on that sound for the merest instant, froze in synchronized quadrascopic far focus: then broke, and resumed struggling in their sockets.

There was a market niche for zombies, Brüks had read, among those who still took their sex in the first person. He tried to imagine fucking any creature possessed of such eyes, and shuddered.

He passed by on the far side of the hall. Parallax served up a moving slice of the room behind the door: Jim Moore, a tabletop holo display in standby mode, a handful of Bicamerals nodding among themselves. A woman: lean as a greyhound beneath a mimetic body stocking, a bone-pale face under a spiky shock of short black hair, jawline just a bit more prognathous than any card-carrying prey might feel comfortable with. She turned her head as Brüks crept by. Her eyes flashed like a cat's. She bared her teeth. On anyone else it would have been a smile.

The door swung shut.

"Hey. Hungry?"

He jumped at the hand on his arm but it was only a woman, dreadlocked and gracile and with a smile that warmed his skin instead of freezing it. Her skin was uniform chocolate, not the rainbow swirl of false color it had been the night before; but he recognized the voice.

"Lianna." He grunted, taking her in. "You're the first person I've seen here who's actually dressed like a monk."

"It's a bathrobe. We're not really into gang colors around here." She jerked her chin down the hall. "C'mon. Breakfast."

They selected their meals from a commons that looked reassuringly like a conventional cafeteria bar (cloned bacon, Brüks was relieved to see; he'd been afraid the Bicamerals would be vegan traditionalists), but they ate sitting on the sprawling steps of the main entrance, watching the morning shadows shorten by degrees across the desert. The quiet hiss of an idling tornado drifted over the ramparts behind them.

"That was quite the night," Brüks said around a mouthful of egg.

"Quite the morning, too."

He raised his eyes. Far overhead, the contrail of some passing airbus etched a line across the sky.

"Oh, it's still up there," Lianna remarked. "Kinda flickers in and out of the higher wavelengths if you stare hard enough."

"I can't see it."

"What kind of augments you got?"

"For my eyes? Nothing." Brüks dropped his gaze back to the horizon. "Got wired with cryptochrome back when it was the Next Big Thing, thought it would help me find my way around down in Costa Rica. You know the ads, *never be lost again*. Except suddenly I wasn't just seeing Earth's magnetic field, I was seeing a halo around every bloody tacpad and charge mat. It was distracting as hell."

Lianna nodded. "Well, it takes some getting used to. Give sight to the blind, takes time to learn how to see."

"More than I had the patience for. Pigment's still sitting back there in my retina but I got it blocked after about a week."

"Wow. You're old school."

He fought back a twitch of irritation: *Half my age, and she's probably already forgotten the difference between the meat she was born with and the chrome that came after*. "I've got the usual brain boosts. Can't very well get tenure otherwise." *Which reminds me*—"I don't suppose there's any Cognital on the premises? I left mine back at camp."

Lianna's eyes widened. "You take *pills?*"

"It's the same—"

"It'd take about ten minutes to fit you with a pump and you take *pills*." Her face split into a big goofy grin. "That's not old school, that's downright *Paleolithic*."

"Glad you find it so fucking amusing, Lianna. You have the pills or not?"

"Not." She pursed her lips. "I guess we could synthesize some. I'll ask. Or you might ask Jim. He's, well . . ."

"Old school," Brüks finished.

"Actually, you'd be surprised how much wiring he's got in his head."

"I'm surprised to even find him here. Military man in a monastery?"

"Yeah, well, you were expecting us all to wear bathrobes."

"He's here to help you in your war against the vamps?" Brüks set his empty plate beside him on the step.

She shook her head. "He's here to—he just needed a place to work through some stuff. Also I think he's kinda spying on us." She cocked her head at him: "What about you?"

"I got herded," he reminded her.

"No, I mean, what were you even doing out in the field? There any species even left out there that haven't been RAMrodded and digitized?"

"The extinct ones," Brüks said shortly. Then, relenting: "Sure, you can virtualize anything in the lab. Still doesn't tell you what it's doing out in the wide wet world with a million unpredictable variables working on it."

She looked out across the flats. Brüks followed her gaze. There, just off to the northwest: the ridge upon which his own home had crouched lo these past two months. He could not see it from here.

"You gonna tell me what's going on?" he said at last.

"You got caught in the crossfire."

"*What* crossfire? Why were the zombies—"

"The vampire," Lianna said. "Valerie, actually."

"You're kidding."

She shrugged.

"So Valerie the Vampire summons her zombie forces against the Bicamerals. And now they're all sitting together just down the hall, munching chips and cocktail wienies because—Moore said something about a common enemy."

"It's complicated."

"Try me."

"You wouldn't understand." She tried for a smile—"You're behind on your Cognital"—but it fell flat.

"Look, I'm sorry I crashed your party but—"

"Dan, the truth is *I* don't really know a whole lot more than you do at this point." She spread her hands. "All I can tell you for sure is, well, you gotta trust them. They know what they're doing."

She stopped just short of patting him on the head.

He stood. "Glad to hear it. Then I guess I'll leave you to your games, and thanks for the meal."

She looked up at him. "You know that can't happen. Jim already told you that much."

"Are you going to tell me where my bike is, or do I have to walk?"

"You can't leave, Dan."

"You can't keep me prisoner."

"It's not us you have to worry about."

"Who's *us*, this time? Bicamerals, vampires? Koalas?"

She pointed north across the desert, squinting. "Look out there. On that ridge."

He did. He saw nothing at first. Then, briefly, something glinted in the morning sun: a spark on the escarpment.

"Now look up," she said. A distant shard of brightness stabbed his eye from high to the east, a reflection of sunlight off empty sky.

"Not us," Lianna repeated. "You."

"Me—?"

"People like you. Baselines."

He let it sink in.

"Valerie must have hacked a fair number of sats just getting her pieces into position. As far as anything in orbit could tell, this whole chunk of desert just dropped out of existence for a good four hours last night. That got people's attention. Someone probably slipped a drone or two under the ceiling in time to see our engine going through its paces—and those dance steps are, shall we say, a bit beyond what passes for state-of-the-art out there." Lianna sighed. "The Bicamerals have been spooking the wrong people for years now. Too many breakthroughs, too fast, the usual. They've been watching, all this time they've been watching. And now, as far as they can tell, we're in some kind of gang war with a bunch of zombies.

"They are not going to let this pass, Dan. Now that they've caught a glimpse behind the curtain they'll have thrown a net over the whole reserve."

And I, Brüks reflected, *don't blame them one goddamned bit.* "I'm not part of this. You said it yourself."

"You're a witness. They'll debrief you."

"So they'll debrief me." Brüks shrugged. "You haven't told me anything. I haven't seen anything they haven't, if they deployed drones."

"You've seen more than you realize. Everyone does. And they will know that, so your debriefing with be *aggressive*."

"So that makes you, what? My personal guard? Here to feed me, and walk me, and make sure I don't wander off into any of the rooms where the grown-ups are talking. And yank on my leash if I try to leave. That about sum it up?"

"Dan—"

"Look, you're giving me a choice between a vampire with her zombie army and *you baselines,* as you so delicately put it."

She got to her feet. "I'm not giving you a choice."

"I have to leave sometime. I can't spend the rest of my life here."

"If you try to leave now," she said, "that's exactly what you'll have done."

He looked down at her: thin as a pussy willow, she only came up to his chest.

"You going to stop me?"

She looked back without blinking. "I'm gonna try. If I have to. But I really hope it doesn't come to that."

He stood there for the longest time. Then he picked up his plate.

"Fuck you," he said, and went back inside.

Within his prison, she gave him all the space in the world. She backed right off as he stalked down the hall, past the murmuring of the devout and the hyperkinetic gaze of the frozen zombies, past the closed-door deliberations of enemies-of-enemies and the open doors of dorms and studies and bathrooms. He moved without direction at first, following any corridor that presented itself, backtracking from every cul-de-sac, his feet exploring autonomously while his gut churned. After a while, some dull sullen pain behind his eyes brought him back to the here-and-now; he took more conscious note of his surroundings and decided to revisit Moore's basement watchtower, as much for its relative familiarity as for any tactical insights he might glean.

He couldn't find it. He remembered Lianna leading him through a hole in the wall; he remembered emerging from it after the armistice. It had to be off the main corridor, had to lie behind one of these identical oaken doors that lined the hall, but no perspective along that length seemed familiar. It was as though he was in some off-kilter mock-up of the place he'd been just an hour before, as though the layout of the monastery had changed subtly when he wasn't looking. He started trying doors at random.

The third was ajar. Low voices murmured behind it. It swung inward easily; flat panels of vat-cloned hardwood lined the space beyond, a kind of library or map room that looked out onto a grassy compound (half sunlit, half in shadow). Past sliding glass doorways, arcane objects rose haphazardly from that immaculate lawn. Brüks couldn't tell whether they were machines or sculptures or some half-assed hybrid of the two. The only thing that looked at all familiar out there was a shallow washbasin set atop a boxy waist-high pedestal.

There was one of those inside, too, just past a conference table that dominated the center of the room itself. Two mismatched Bicamerals stood at the table's edge, gazing at a collection of dice-size objects scattered across some kind of hard-copy map or antique game board. The Japanese monk was gaunt as a scarecrow; the Caucasian could have passed for Santa Claus at the departmental Christmas party, given the right threads and a pillow stuffed down his front.

"From Queensland, maybe," Santa remarked. "That place always bred the best neurotoxins."

The scarecrow scooped up a handful of objects (not dice, Brüks saw now; a collection of multifaceted lumps that made him think of mahogany macramé) and arranged them in a rough crescent across the board.

Santa considered. "Still not enough. Even if we *could* sift the Van Allens dry on short notice." He absently scratched the side of his neck, seemed to notice Brüks at last. "You're the refugee."

"Biologist."

"Welcome anyway." Santa smacked his lips. "I'm Luckett."

"Dan Brüks." He took the other man's nod for an invitation and stepped closer to the table. The pattern decorating the game board—a multicolored spiral of interlocking Penrose tiles—was far more complex than any he remembered from his grandfather's attic. It seemed to move at the corner of his eye, to crawl just so when he wasn't quite looking.

The scarecrow clicked his tongue, eyes never leaving the table.

"Don't mind Masashi," Luckett remarked. "He's not much for what you'd call normal conversation."

"Does *everyone* around here speak in tongues?"

"Speak—oh, I see what you mean." Luckett laughed softly. "No, with Masashi here it's more like a kind of aphasia. When he's not linked in, anyway."

The scarecrow spilled a few more mahogany knuckles with chaotic precision. Luckett laughed again, shook his head.

"He talks through board games," Brüks surmised.

"Close enough. Who knows? I might be doing the same thing by the time I graduate."

"You're not—?" Of course he wasn't. His eyes didn't sparkle.

"Not yet. Acolyte."

It was enough that he spoke English. "I'm trying to find the room I was in last night. Basement, spiral stairs, kind of a war room bunker feel to it?"

"Ah. The Colonel's lair. North hall, first right, second door on the left."

"Okay. Thanks."

"Not at all." Luckett turned away as Masashi clicked and rolled the bones. "More than enough antimatter to break orbit, anyway. Least it saves on chemical mass."

Brüks stopped, hand on the doorknob. "What was that?"

Luckett glanced back at him. "Just drawing up plans. Nothing to worry about."

"You guys have *antimatter*?"

"Before long." Luckett grinned and dipped his hands into the washbasin. "God willing."

Most of the tactical collage was dark, or writhing with analog static. A half-dozen windows flickered fitfully through random points of view: desert, desert, desert. No satcam imagery. Either Moore had shut down those feeds or whoever was behind the blockade had walled off the sky as well as the horizon.

Brüks tapped experimentally on an unlit patch of paint. His touch provoked a brief flicker of red, but nothing else.

The active windows kept changing, though. Some kind of motion sensor built into the feed, maybe: views would pan and pounce, flash-zooming on this flickering shadow or that distant escarpment. Sometimes Brüks couldn't see anything noteworthy at the center of attention: a falcon grooming itself on a skeletal branch, or the burrow of a desert rodent halfway to the horizon. Once or twice a little fall of rock skittering down a distant slope, scree dislodged by some unseen disturbance.

Once, partially eclipsed by leaves and scrub, a pair of glassy reflections looking back.

"Help you?"

Jim Moore reached past Brüks's shoulder and tapped the display. A new window sprang to life at his fingertip. Brüks stepped aside while the soldier stretched the window across the paint, called up a feed, zoomed on a crevice splitting a hillock to the south.

"I was trying to get online," Brüks admitted. "See if anyone out there's picked up on this whole—*quarantine* thing."

"Net's strictly local. I don't think the Bicamerals actually have Quinternet access."

"What, they're afraid of getting hacked?" It was an ongoing trend, Brüks had heard: defensive self-partitioning in the face of Present Shock, and damn the legal consequences. People were starting to weigh costs against benefits, opt for a day or two outside the panopticon even in the face of the inevitable fines and detentions.

But Moore was shaking his head. "I don't think they need it. Do *you* feel especially lost without access to the telegraph network?"

"What's a telegraph?"

"Exactly." Something caught the Colonel's eye. "Huh. That's not good."

Brüks followed the other man's gaze to the window he'd opened, to the crevice centered there. "I don't see anything."

Moore played a little arpeggio on the wall. The image blossomed into false color. Something glowed Euclidean yellow in all that fractal blue.

He grunted. "Aerosol delivery, looks like."

"Your guys?"

The corner of Moore's mouth curled the slightest bit. "Can't really say."

"What's to say? You're a soldier, right? They're soldiers, unless the government's started subcontracting to—"

"Biothermals, too. They're not trusting their bots to run things." There was a hint of amusement in the old soldier's voice. "Probably baselines, then."

"Why's that?"

"Fragile egos. Low self-esteem." His fingers skipped across the darkened wall. Bright windows flared everywhere they touched.

"At least you're all on the same side, then, right?"

"Doesn't really work like that."

"What's that supposed to mean?"

"The chain of command isn't what it used to be." Moore smiled faintly. "It's more—organic, these days. Anyway." Another finger dance; the window dwindled and slid to an empty spot along the edge of the wall. "They're still setting up. We've got time."

"How was the meeting?" Brüks asked.

"Still going on. Not much point hanging around after the opening ceremonies, though. I'd just slow them down."

"And let me guess: you can't tell me what's going on, and it's none of my business anyway."

"Why would you say that?"

"Lianna said—"

"Dr. Lutterodt wasn't at the meeting," Moore reminded him.

"Okay. So is there anything *you* can—"

"The Fireflies," Moore said.

Brüks blinked. "What about—oh. Your common enemy."

Moore nodded.

Memories of intercepted negotiations, scrolling past in Christmas colors: "*Theseus*. They found something out there?"

"Maybe. Nothing's certain yet, just—hints and inferences. No solid intel."

"Still." An alien agency capable of simultaneously dropping sixty thousand surveillance probes into the atmosphere without warning. An agency that came and went in seconds, that caught the planet with its pants down and took God knew how many compromising pictures along God knew how many wavelengths before letting the atmosphere burn its own paparazzi down to a sprinkle of untraceable iron floating through the stratosphere. An agency never seen before and never since, for all the effort put into finding it. "I guess that qualifies as a common threat," Brüks admitted.

"I guess it does." Moore turned back to his war wall.

"Why were they fighting in the first place? What does a vampire have against a bunch of monks?"

Moore didn't answer for a moment. Then: "It's not personal, if that's what you're thinking."

"What, then?"

Moore took a breath. "It's—more of the same, really. Entropy, increasing. The Realists and their war on Heaven. The Nanohistomites over in Hokkaido. Islamabad on fire."

Brüks blinked. "Islamabad's—"

"Oops. Getting ahead of myself. Give it time." The Colonel shrugged. "I'm not trying to be coy, Dr. Brüks. You're already in the soup, so I'll tell you what I can so long as it doesn't endanger you further. But you're going to have to take a lot on—well, on faith."

Brüks stifled a laugh. Moore looked at him.

"Sorry," Brüks said. "It's just, you hear so much about the Bicamerals and their scientific breakthroughs and their quest for Truth. And I finally get inside this grand edifice and all I hear is *Trust* and *God willing* and *Take it on faith.* I mean, the whole order's supposed to be founded on the search for knowledge, and Rule Number One is *Don't ask questions?*"

"It's not that they don't have answers," Moore said after a moment. "It's just that we can't understand them for the most part. You could resort to analogies, I suppose. Force transhuman insights into human cookie-cutter shapes. But most of the time that would just get you a bleeding metaphor with all its bones broken." He held up a hand, warding off Brüks's rejoinder. "I know, I know: it can be frustrating as hell. But people have an unfortunate habit of assuming they understand the reality just because they understood the analogy. You dumb down brain surgery enough for a preschooler to think he understands it, the little tyke's liable to grab a microwave scalpel and start cutting when no one's looking."

"And yet." Brüks glanced at the wall, where AEROSOL DELIVERY glowed in shades of yellow and orange. Where a murderous tornado had rampaged the night before. "They seem to solve their conflicts pretty much the same way as us retarded ol' baselines."

Moore smiled faintly. "That they do."

. . .

He found Lianna back on the front steps, supper balanced on her knees, watching the sun go down. She looked back over her shoulder as he pushed through the door.

"I asked about your brain-boosters," she said. "No luck. The assembly line's booked or something."

"Thanks for trying," he said.

"Jim might still be holding. If you haven't asked him already."

He shifted his tray to one hand, used the other to rub away the vague pain behind his eyes. "Mind if I join you?"

She spared one hand to take in the staircase, as broad and excessive as a cathedral's.

He sat beside her, picked at his own plate. "About this morning, I, uh . . ."

She stared at the horizon. The sun stared back, highlighting her cheekbones.

". . . sorry," he finished.

"Forget it. Nobody likes being in a cage."

"Still. I shouldn't have shot the messenger." A sudden chilly breeze crawled across his shoulders.

Lianna shrugged. "You ask me, nobody should shoot anybody."

He raised his eyes. Venus twinkled back at them. He wondered briefly if those photons had followed a straight line to his eyes, or if they'd been shunted around some invisible spillway of curves and angles at the last nanosecond. He looked around at the cracked desert floor, lifted his gaze to the more jagged topography in the distance. Wondered how many unseen agents were looking back.

"You always eat out here?"

"When I can." The lowering sun stretched her shadow along the ramparts behind them, a giantess silhouetted in orange. "It's—stark, you know?"

Ribbed clouds, a million shades of salmon, scudding against an orange and purple sky.

"How long does this go on?" he wondered.

"This?"

"They lurk out there, we wait in here. When does somebody actually make a move?"

"Oldschool, you gotta *relax*." She shook her head, smiled a twilit smile. "You could obsess and second-guess for a solid month and I guarantee you wouldn't be able to think of anything our hosts haven't already factored five ways to Sunday. They've been making moves all day."

"Such as?"

"Don't ask me." She shrugged. "I probably wouldn't understand even if they told me. They're wired up way differently."

Hive mind, he reminded himself. Synesthetes, too, if he wasn't mistaken.

"You *do* understand them, though," he said. "That's your job."

"Not the way you think. And not without a fair bit of modding on my own."

"How, then?"

"I'm not sure," she admitted.

"Come on."

"No, really. It's a kind of Zen thing. Like playing the piano, or being a centipede in Heaven. The moment you start to think about what you're doing, you screw up. You just have to get into the zone."

"They must have trained you at some point," Brüks insisted. "There must have been some kind of conscious learning curve."

"You'd think so, wouldn't you?" She squinted up at some invisible behemoth he still couldn't see. "But they kind of—bypassed that. Zapped my fornix with just the right burst of ultrasound and next thing I know it's four days later and I have all these reflexes. Not so much that I understand them as my *fingers* do, you know? Phonemes, rhythms, gestures—eye movements, sometimes—". She frowned. "I take in all these cues, and equations just—come to me, piece by piece. I copy them down and I send 'em off. And the next day they show up in the latest issue of *Science*."

"You never examined these *reflexes* afterward? Played the piano really slowly, taken the time to watch what your fingers were doing?"

"Dan, they *won't fit*. Consciousness is a scratchpad. You can store a grocery list, jot down a couple of phone numbers—but were you even aware of finishing your supper?"

Brüks looked down at his plate. It was empty.

"And that's just a couple of swallows half a minute in the past. You ever try holding, say, even a single chapter of a novel in your head? Consciously? All at once?" Her dreads swept back and forth in the gloom. "Whatever I'm doing, it's got too many variables. Won't fit in the global workspace." She flashed him a small, apologetic smile.

They program us like clockwork dolls, he thought. Way off to the west, the sun touched gently down on a distant ridge.

He looked at her. "Why are we still in charge?"

She grinned. "Who's *we,* white boy?"

He didn't. "These people you—work for. They're supposed to be *helpless,* that's what everyone says. You can optimize a brain for *down there* or *up here,* not both. Anyone comfortable thinking at Planck scales, they can barely cross the street unassisted up in the real world. That's why they set up in the desert. That's why they have people like you. That's what they tell us."

"All true, more or less," Lianna said.

He shook his head. "They *micromanage tornadoes,* Lee. They turn people into puppets with a wink and a wave, they own half the patent office. They're about as helpless as a T. rex in a daycare center. So why haven't they been running things for years?"

"That's like a chimp asking why those hairless apes aren't slinging bigger feces than everyone else, if they're so damned clever."

He tried not to smile, and failed. "That's not really an answer."

"Sure it is. Everybody goes on about *hive mind this* and *synesthesia that* like they were some kind of superpowers."

"After last night, you're going to tell me they're *not?*"

"It goes so much deeper than that. It's *perceptual*. We're so—

impoverished, you know? We don't look out at reality at all, we look *in* at this model, this caricature our brains cobble together out of wavelengths and pressure points. We squint down over hand-written notes that say *two blocks east, turn left at the bridge* and we think that reading those stupid scribbles is the same as seeing the universe passing by on the other side of the windshield." She glanced over her shoulder, to the edifice at their backs.

Brüks frowned. "You think Bicamerals can see outside the windshield."

"Dunno. Maybe."

"Then I've got some bad news for you. Reality went out the window the moment we started mediating sensory input through a nervous system. You want to actually perceive the universe directly, without any stupid scribbles or model-building? Become a protozoan."

A smile lit her face, startlingly bright in the deepening gloom. "Wouldn't that be *just* like them. Build a group mind complex enough to put any hundred baseline geniuses to shame, and use it to think like a paramecium."

"That wasn't exactly my point," he said.

The sun winked good-bye and slid below the horizon.

"I don't know how they do it," she admitted. "But if what they see is even *closer* to reality—well, that's what you call transcendence. Not the ability to *micromanage tornados,* just—seeing a little more of what's out *there.*" She tapped her temple. "Instead of what's in *here.*"

She stood, stretched like a cat. Brüks rose beside her and brushed the desert from his clothes. "Then transcendence is out of reach. For our brains, anyway."

Lianna shrugged. "Change your brain."

"Then it's not your brain anymore. It's something else. *You're* something else."

"That's kinda the point. Transcendence is transformation."

He shook his head, unconvinced. "Sounds more like suicide to me."

· · ·

He felt his eyes start up under closed lids, stepped out onto that razor-thin line between dreamtime and the waking edge: just enough awareness to see the curtain, not enough to notice the man behind.

Lucid dreaming was a delicate exercise.

He sat up on the pallet, phantom legs still wearing corporeal ones like the abdomen of some half-molted insect. He looked around at furnishings that would have been spartan to anyone who hadn't just spent two months sleeping on the desert floor: a raised sleeping pallet a couple of meters long, dipped in some softer, thicker variant of the fleshy synthetic lining the floors. An alcove in the wall, a medicine cabinet fronted with frosted glass. Another one of those washbasin pedestals, this one with a towel bar bolted to the side facing the bed: a hand towel draped over it. The cubby Luckett had tucked him into for the night, all pretty much the way it looked when he was awake.

He'd learned to launch his dreams from a platform anchored in reality. It made the return trip easier.

Brüks flexed his temporoparietal and ascended through a ceiling of polished granite (that was surmise—he'd forgotten to take note of its composition in the waking world). The monastery spread out around, then below him: dwindled from a life-size fortress to a tabletop model on a cracked gray moonscape. A fingernail moon shone bone-white overhead; everywhere else, a million stars glinted hard as ice crystals against the darkness.

He flew north.

It was minimalist magic: no rainbow bridges or talking clouds, no squadrons of aircraft piloted by tyrannosaurs. He'd long since learned not to strain the credulity of whatever mental processes indulged his presence here, critics that had lived in his head since before his dreams had even been lucid. Some inner skeptic frowned at the thought of a space-faring bicycle and dreaming eight-year-old Danny Brüks found himself stranded between the stars. Some forebrain killjoy snorted at the giddy delight of flying and suddenly he was entangled in high-tension wires, or simply ejected back into consciousness at three in the morning, spat out of sleep by his own incredulity. Even in dreams, his brain had been selling him out since before he'd had hair on his crotch. As an adult he'd had no use for them until his limited baseline learning curve had run out of waking hours, forced him to learn new techniques in his sleep lest academia's new-and-improving generation devoured him from behind.

He could fly now at least, without thought or self-subversion. He'd learned that much through years of practice, through the induction hardware that had once guided his visions when REM started up, through the exercises that eventually let him ditch those training wheels and do it all in his own head. He could fly, into orbit and beyond and back if he wanted to. He could fly all the way to Heaven. That was where he was going now: the northern lights swirled in the sky directly ahead, a blue-green curtain shimmering above his destination like a star of Bethlehem for the Holographic Age.

But no talking clouds. He'd also learned not to push it.

Now, ghostlike, he passed through Heaven's fortifications and descended into its deepest levels. Rho languished there as she always did, alone in her cell, still wearing the paper smock and slippers she'd worn in Departures when they'd told each other it wasn't good-bye. A cuff around her left ankle and a dozen links of corroded chain shackled her to the wall. Hair hung across her downcast face like a dark curtain.

Her face lit up, though, as he descended through the ceiling.

He settled beside her on the stone floor. "I'm sorry. I would've come sooner, I just—"

He stopped. No point in wasting precious REM with dreamed apologies. He tweaked the script, started again.

"You wouldn't believe what's happening," he said.

"Tell me."

"I've got caught up in some kind of war, I'm trapped behind enemy lines with a bunch of—really. You wouldn't believe me."

"Monks and zombies," she said. "And a vampire."

Of course she knew.

"I don't even know how I can *be* here. You'd think with all this stuff happening I'd be too wired to even sit down, but—"

"You've been going straight for twenty-four hours." She laid her hand on his. "Of *course* you're going to crash."

"These people don't," he grumbled. "I don't think they even *sleep,* not all at once, anyway. Different parts of their brains take—shifts, or something. Like a bunch of dolphins."

"You're not a dolphin, and you're not some augmented wannabe, either. You're *natural.* Just the way I like it. And you know what?"

"What?"

"You're going to keep up with them. You always do."

Not always, he thought.

"You should come back," he said suddenly. Somewhere far away, his fingers and toes tingled faintly.

She shook her head. "We've been over this."

"Nobody's saying you have to go back to the job. There are a million other options."

"In here," she told him, "there are a billion."

He looked at her chain. He had never consciously forged those links. He'd simply found her like this. He could have changed her circumstance with a thought, of course, as he could change anything in this world—but there were always risks.

He'd learned not to push it.

"You can't *like* it here," he said quietly.

She laughed. "Why not? *I* didn't put that thing on."

"But—" His temples throbbed. He willed them to stop.

"Dan," she said gently, "*You* can keep up out there. I can't."

The tingling intensified in his extremities. Rho's face wavered before him, fading to black. He couldn't keep her together much longer. All this careful conservatism, these shackled environments that barely edged beyond the laws of physics—they only guarded against the Inner Heckler, not these unwelcome sensations intruding from *outside*. Headaches. Pins and needles. They distracted from his own contrivance; suddenly the whole façade was falling apart around him. "Come back soon," his wife called through the rising static. "I'll be waiting . . ."

She was gone before he could answer. He tried to construct something spectacular—the implosion of Heaven itself, a fiery inward collapse toward some ravenous singularity deep below the Canadian Shield—but he was rising too fast toward the light.

There'd been a time when he'd derided his own lack of imagination, cursed his inability to slip his shackles and just *dream* like everyone else, with glorious hallucinogenic abandon. Even now, sometimes, he had to remind himself: it wasn't a failing at all. It was a strength.

Even in sleep, Dan Brüks didn't take *anything* on faith.

> TO HIMSELF EVERYONE IS IMMORTAL; HE MAY KNOW
> THAT HE IS GOING TO DIE, BUT HE CAN NEVER KNOW
> THAT HE IS DEAD.
>
> —SAMUEL BUTLER

SUNSHINE STABBED HIS eyes through the cell's slotted window. His mouth was dry, his head athrob. His fingers pulsed with dull electricity. *Slept on my hands,* he thought, and tried to imagine how he might have actually done that as he swung his legs over the edge of the bed.

The same pins and needles flooded the soles of his feet when he planted them on the floor.

Great.

He found his way to the lav that Luckett had shown him the night before, emptied his bladder while every extremity tingled and burned. The discomfort was beginning to fade by the time he flushed; he headed off down the empty hall in search of other warm bodies, only slightly unsteady on his feet.

Something thumped behind one of the closed doors. He paused for a moment before continuing, his attention drawn by another door opening farther down the hall.

By the naked blotchy thing that fell into view, choking and twitching as if electrocuted.

He stood there for a moment, shocked into paralysis. Then he was moving again, his own trivial discomfort forgotten in a greater shock of recognition: Masashi the scarecrow, back arched, teeth bared, flesh stretched so tight across cheekbones that it was a wonder his face hadn't split down the middle. Brüks was almost at the man's side before realization stopped him in his tracks.

Every muscle thrown into tetany. This was some kind of motor disorder.

This was *neurological*.

The pins and needles were back in full force. Brüks looked down in disbelief at his own fingertips. Try as he might, he couldn't stop them from trembling.

When the screaming started, he barely heard it.

Whatever it was, it killed quietly. For the most part.

Not because it was painless. Its victims staggered from hiding and thrashed on the floors, faces twisted into agonized devil masks. Even the dead kept them on: veins bulging, eyes splattered crimson with pinpoint embolisms, each face frozen in the same calcified rictus. Not a word, not a groan from any of them. There was nothing he could do but step over the bodies as he tracked that lone voice screaming somewhere ahead; nothing he could feel but that terrifying electricity growing in his fingers and toes; nothing he could think but *It's in me too it's in me too it's in me too—*

Creatures in formation rounded the corner ahead of him: four human bodies moving in perfect step, more live than the bodies on the floor, just as dead inside. Valerie kept pace in their midst. Four sets of jiggling eyes locked onto Brüks for an instant, then resumed their frantic omnidirectional dance. Valerie didn't even look in his direction. She moved as if spring-loaded, as if her joints were subtly out of place. One of her zombies was missing below the knees; the carbon prosthetics it used for legs squeaked softly against the floor as they approached. Apart from that subtle friction, Brüks couldn't hear so much as a footfall from any of them. He flattened instinctively against the wall, praying to some Pleistocene god for invisibility—or at least, for insignificance. Valerie swept abreast of him, eyes straight ahead.

Brüks squeezed his eyes shut. Soft screams filled the darkness. He felt a small distant pride that none of them came from him. When he opened his eyes again the monster was gone.

The screaming had grown fainter. More—intimate. Some horrific lighthouse beacon running low on batteries, calling through the fog of war. Except this was no fucking war: this was a massacre, this was one tribe of giants slaughtering another, and any baseline fossil stupid enough to get caught underfoot didn't even rate the brutal mercy of a slashed throat on the battlefield.

Welcome to the armistice.

He followed the sound. He doubted there was anything he could do—euthanasia, perhaps—but if it could scream, maybe it could talk. Maybe it could tell him—something . . .

It already had, in a way. It had told him that all victims were not equal in the eyes of this pestilence. All the Bicamerals he'd seen so far seemed to have fallen within minutes of each other, seized by the throat and turned to tortured stone before they'd even had a chance to cry out. Not everyone, though. Not the vampire and her minions. Not the screamer. Not Dan Brüks.

Not yet.

But he was infected, oh yes he was. Something was at work on his distal circuitry, shorting out his fine motor control, working its way up the main cables. Maybe the screamer was just a little farther along. Maybe the screamer was Daniel Brüks in another ten minutes.

Maybe it was right here, behind this door.

Brüks pushed it open.

Luckett. He squirmed like a hooked eelpout in a cell identical to the one where Brüks had slept, slid around on a floor slippery with his own fluids. Sweat turned his tunic into a soaked dishrag, ran in torrents from his face and limbs; darker stains spread from his crotch.

The hook hadn't caught him by the mouth, though. It sprouted from a port at the back of his neck, a shivering fiber running to a socket low on the wall. Luckett convulsed. His head struck the edge of an overturned chair. The blow seemed to bring him back a little; the screaming stopped, the eyes cleared, something approaching awareness filtered through the dull animal pain that filled them.

"Brüks," he moaned, "Brüks, get it—*fuck* it hurts . . ."

Brüks knelt, laid a hand on the other man's shoulder. "I—"

The acolyte thrashed away from the touch, screaming all over again: "Fucking *hell* that hurts—!" He flailed one arm: a deliberate gesture, Brüks guessed, an instruction trying to dig its way out past the roaring static of a million short-circuiting motor nerves. Brüks followed its path to a small glass-fronted cabinet set into the wall. Lozenges of doped ceramic rested in neat labeled rows behind the sliding pane: HAPPINESS, ORGASM, APPETITE SUPPRESSANT—

ANALGESIC.

He grabbed it off the shelf, dropped to Luckett's side, grabbed the fiberop at the cervical end: fumbled as fingers misheard brain. Luckett screamed again, arched his back like a drawn bow. The smell of shit filled the room. Brüks gripped the plug, twisted.

The socket clicked free. Seething light flooded the walls: camera feeds, spline plots, deserts painted in garish blizzards of false color. Some tame oracle, deprived of direct access to Luckett's brain, continuing its conversation in meatspace.

Brüks jammed the painkiller home, click-twisted it into place. Luckett sagged instantly; his fingers continued to twitch and shiver, purely galvanic. For a moment Brüks thought the acolyte had lost consciousness. Then Luckett took a great heaving gulp of air, let it out again.

"That's better," he said.

Brüks eyed Luckett's trembling fingers, eyed his own. "It's not. This is—"

"Not my department," Luckett coughed. "Not yours, either, thank your lucky stars."

"But what is it? There's got to be a fix." He remembered: a rosette of monsters, the vampire at its heart, moving with frictionless efficiency through the dying fields. "Valerie—"

Luckett shook his head. "She's on our side."

"But she's—"

"Not her." Luckett turned his head, rested his eyes on an overhead real-time tactical of the surrounding desert: the monastery at the bull's-eye, a perimeter of arcane hieroglyphics around the edges. "Them."

We've been making moves all day.

"What did you do? *What did you do?*"

"Do?" Luckett coughed, wiped blood from his mouth with the back of his hand. "You were here, my friend. We got *noticed.* And now we're—reaping the whirlwind, you might say."

"They wouldn't just—" *Then again, why wouldn't they?* "Wasn't there some kind of, of ultimatum? Didn't they give us a chance to surrender, or—"

The look Luckett gave him was an even mix of pity and amusement.

Brüks cursed himself for an idiot. Headaches for most of the day before. Moore's *aerosol delivery.* But there'd been no artillery, no lethal canisters lobbed whistling across the desert. This thing had drifted in on the breeze, undetected. And not even engineered germs killed on contact. There was always an incubation period, it always took *time* for a few lucky spores to hatch out in the lungs and breed an army big enough to take down a human body. Even the magic of exponential growth took hours to manifest.

The enemy—

—*People like you,* Lianna had said—

—must have set this plan in motion the moment they'd set up their perimeter. It wouldn't have mattered one good goddamn if the whole Bicameral Order had marched out across the desert with their hands in the air; the weapon was already in their blood, and it was blind to white flags.

"How could you let them do this?" Brüks hissed. "You're supposed to be *smarter* than us, you're post-fucking-*singular,* you're supposed to be ten steps ahead of any plan we poor stupid cavemen could ever put together. *How could you let them?*"

"Oh, but this is all according to plan." Luckett patted him on the arm with one spastic, short-circuiting hand.

"What *plan?*" Brüks choked back a hysterical giggle. "We're *dead* already—"

"Even God can't plan for everything. Too many variables." Luckett coughed again. "Not to worry, though. We planned for the things we couldn't plan for . . ."

Faintly, through the open door—drifting down the corridor, through high narrow windows; through barred gates, through glass panes looking into deserts and gardens: a *whistling* sound, Doppler-shifted. The muffled thud of some nearby impact.

"Ah. The mopping-up begins." Luckett nodded serenely. "No point being stealthy now, eh?"

Brüks put his head in his hands.

"Don't worry, old chap. It's not over yet, not for you anyway. Jim's lair. He's waiting for you."

Brüks raised his head. "Jim—but—"

"I *told* you," Luckett said. "According to plan." Spasms rippled across his body. "*Go.*"

And now Brüks heard another sound, a deeper sound, rumbling up the scale behind the hacking of the maimed and whistling shriek of inbound paralysis. He felt the vibration of great blades spinning up far down in the earth, heard the muffled hiss of steam injected into deep silos. He heard the growing drumbeat of an elemental monster straining against its chains.

"Now *that,*" he said, "is more fucking like it."

Moore was in his bunker, but he wasn't running the show. No controls blinked on the smart paint, no sliders or dials or virtual buttons to press. The readouts were all one-way. Somewhere else, the Bicamerals were bringing their engine online; Moore was only watching from the bleachers.

He turned at Brüks's approach. "They're dug in."

"Doesn't matter, though, right? We're gonna tear them to pieces."

The soldier turned back to the wall and shook his head.

"What's the problem? They out of range?"

"We're not fighting."

"*Not fighting?* Have you *seen* what they're doing to us?"

"I see."

"Everyone's dead or halfway there!"

"We're not."

"Right." Nerves sang ominously in Brüks's fingers. "And how long is that going to last?"

"Long enough. This bug was customized for Bicamerals. We've got more time." Moore frowned. "You don't engineer something like that in the field, not overnight. They've been planning this awhile."

"They didn't even fire a warning shot, for fucksake! They didn't even try to negotiate!"

"They're scared."

"*They're* scared."

"They'd assume that giving us any advance warning would put them at an unacceptable disadvantage. They don't know what we're capable of."

"Then maybe it's time we showed them."

Moore turned back to face the other man. "Perhaps you're not familiar with Bicameral philosophy. It's predominantly nonviolent."

"You and Luckett and all your friends can argue the philosophical subtleties of unilateral pacifism while we all turn into *predominantly nonviolent* corpses." *Friends.* "Is Lianna—"

"She's fine."

"None of us are *fine*." Brüks turned back to the stairs. Maybe he could find her before the ceiling crashed in. Maybe there was some broom closet he could hide in.

Moore's hand closed on his shoulder and spun him as though he were made of balsa.

"We will not attack these people," he said calmly. "We don't know if they're responsible."

"You just said they'd been *planning* this," Brüks croaked. "They were just waiting for some kind of excuse. You watched them lock and load. For all I know you listened in on their fucking comm chatter, you heard them give the orders. You *know*."

"Doesn't matter. Even if we were right there in their command center. Even if we could take their brains apart synapse by synapse and backtrace every neuron that went into the go-ahead. We would still not know."

"Fuck you. I'm not going to suck your dick just because you trot out the old *no free will* shtick."

"These people could have been used without their knowledge. They could be slaved to an implanted agenda and they'd swear they were making their own decisions the whole time. We will not kill cat's-paws."

"They're not zombies, Moore."

"Whole different species."

"They're killing us."

"You're just going to have to trust me on this. Or"—Moore cocked his head, evidently amused—"we could leave you behind to hash it out with them personally."

"Leave me—?"

"We're getting out of here. Why do you think they're warming up the engine?"

Someone had rolled a giant soccer ball into the compound. A dozen fallen monks twitched wide-eyed and tetanic around a geodesic sphere of interlocking padded pentagons, maybe four meters across at the equator. A door-size polygon bent back from that surface like a snapped fingernail.

Some kind of escape pod. No obvious means of propulsion. No *onboard* propulsion, anyway; but rising high above the walls of the enclosure, the funnel spun and roared like an angry jet engine. Brüks craned his neck in search of the top of the thing, and swallowed, and—

And looked again. Something was scratching an arc across the sky.

"Get in," Moore said at his elbow. "We don't have much time."

Of course they know. They've got satellites, they've got micro-drones, they can look right past these walls and see what we're doing and just blow it all to shit . . .

"*Missile . . . ,*" he croaked.

The sky shattered where he was pointing.

The contrail just *stopped* high overhead, its descending arc amputated halfway to the jet stream; a new sun bloomed at its terminus, a blinding pinpoint, impossibly small and impossibly bright. Brüks wasn't sure what he really saw in the flash-blinded split second that followed. A great flickering hole opening in the morning sky, a massive piece of that dome peeled back as though God Itself had popped the lid off Its terrarium. The sky *crinkled*: wisps of high-flying cirrus cracking into myriad shards; expanses of deep and endless blue collapsing into sharp-edged facets; half of heaven folded into lunatic origami. The sky *imploded* and left another sky behind, serene and unscarred.

A thunderclap split Brüks's skull like an ice pick. The force of it lifted him off his feet, dangled him for an endless moment before dropping him back onto the grass. Something pushed him from behind. He turned; Moore's mouth was moving, but the only sound Brüks could hear was a high-pitched ringing that filled the world. Past Moore's shoulder, above the ramparts of the monastery, dark smoldering wreckage fell from the sky like the charred bones of some giant stick man. Its empty skin fled sideways across the sky in ragged pieces, great streamers of tinsel drawn toward the shackled tornado. The vortex engine seemed to draw strength from the meal: it grew *thicker,* somehow. Faster. Darker.

Valerie's invisible airship. He'd forgotten. A hundred thousand cubic meters of hard vacuum directly in the path of the incoming missile: broken on impact, sucking cascades of desert air into the void.

Moore pushed him toward the sphere. Brüks climbed unsteadily into darkness and the web of some monstrous spider. It was already full of victims, tangled half-seen silhouettes. All hung cocooned in a mesh of broad flat fibers stretching chaotically across the structure's interior.

"*Move.*" A tiny, tinny voice growling through a chorus of tuning forks. Brüks grabbed a convenient band of webbing, gripped as tightly as the sparks in his hand would allow, pulled himself up. Something bumped the side of his head. He turned and recoiled at the face of one of Valerie's zombies, upside-down, eyes jittering, hanging in the mesh like an entangled bat. Brüks yanked back his hand; the webbing stuck as though he were a gecko. He pulled free, clambered up and away from those frantic eyes, that lifeless face.

Another face, not so dead, hung in the gloom behind its bodyguard. Brüks—irises still clenched against the morning sun—couldn't make out details. But he could feel it watching him, could feel the predator grin behind the eyes. He kept moving. Sticky bands embraced at his touch, peeled gently free as he pulled away.

"Any empty spot," Moore said, climbing up in his wake. The ringing in Brüks's ears was fading at last, as if somehow absorbed by this obscene womb and its litter of freaks and monsters. "Try to keep away from the walls; they're padded, but it's going to be a rough ride."

The hatch swung into place like the last piece of a jigsaw, sealed them in and cut off the meager light filtering from outside; instantly the air grew dense and close, a small stagnant bubble at the bottom of the sea. Brüks swallowed. The darkness breathed around him with unseen mouths, a quiet claustrophobic chorus muffled by air heavy as cement.

Vision and ventilation returned within a breath of each other: a stale breeze across his cheek, a dim red glow from the padded facets of the wall itself. Bicamerals blocked the light on all sides: some spread-eagled, some balled up, a couple of pretzel silhouettes that spoke either of superhuman flexibility or broken bones. Maybe a dozen all told.

A dozen monks. A prehistoric psychopath with an entourage of brain-dead killing machines. Two baseline humans. All hanging together in a giant cobwebbed uterus, waiting for some unseen army to squash them flat.

All part of the plan.

Brüks tried to move, found that the webbing had tightened around him once he'd stopped climbing. He could wriggle like a hooked fish, bring his hand up far enough to scratch his nose. Beyond that he wasn't going anywhere.

His eyes were adapting to the longwave, at least. A face overhead resolved into welcome familiarity: "Lianna? Lianna, are you . . ."

Only her body was here. Its fingers tapped the side of its head with the telltale rhythm of someone tuned to a more distant reality.

"It's okay." Moore spoke quietly from somewhere nearby. "She's talking to our ride."

"This is it? Twenty people?" He gulped air, still strangely stale for all the efforts of the local life-support system.

"It's enough."

Brüks could barely catch his breath. The whole compartment hissed with the sound of forced ventilation, air washed across his face and still he couldn't seem to fill his lungs.

He fought rising panic. "I think—there's something wrong with the air conditioner . . ."

"The air's fine. Relax."

"No, it—"

Something kicked them, hard in the side. Suddenly *up* was sideways; suddenly *sideways* was down. Blood rushed to Brüks's head. A giant stood on his chest. The air, already unbearably close, got closer: the stench of rotten eggs flooded Brüks's sinuses like a tsunami.

Jesus Christ, he thought. He couldn't imagine a worse time or place for a fart. Under other circumstances it might have been funny. Now it only made him gag, stole whatever meager oxygen had remained.

"Here we go," Moore murmured from behind. From below. From overhead.

He sounded almost *sleepy.*

The web slewed. Bodies jerked in unison one way, slung like pendulums back the other, flipped around some arbitrary unknowable center of gravity. They seemed to be accelerating in ten directions at once. Niagara roared in Brüks's head.

"Can't—breathe . . ."

"You're not supposed to. Go with it."

"What—"

"Isoflurane. Hydrogen sulfide."

Whirling static engulfed the world from the outside in. Twenty bodies—barely visible through the maelstrom—threw themselves as one toward some unremarkable point on the far side of the compartment. They strained toward that point like iron filings drawn to a cyclotron, their elastic shackles strained almost to the breaking point.

So, Brüks mused as his vision failed. *This is it. The final conscious experience.*

Enjoy it while it lasts.

PARASITE

The essential wickedness of this approach is perhaps best exemplified by the so-called Moksha Mind engineered by the Eastern Dharmic Alliance. Their attempts to "modernize" their faith—through the embrace of technology that has been (rightly) banned in the West—resulted in a literally soul-destroying hive that has plunged millions into what we can only assume to be a state of deep catatonia. (The fact that this is exactly what the Dharmic faiths have aspired to for millennia does not render their fate any less tragic.) The misguided use of brain interface technology to "commune" with the minds of such alien creatures as cats and octopi—a practice by no means limited to the East—has also resulted in untold psychological damage.

At the opposite extreme, in the face of modern challenges we may find ourselves tempted to simply turn our backs on the wider world. Such a retreat would not only go against the Scriptural admonition to "go and make disciples of all nations," but also risks dire consequences in its own right. The Redeemer gyland offers a stark case in point. It has been almost a year since the alliance between the Southern and Central Baptists broke down, and three months since we have been able to establish contact with anyone from either side of that conflict. (It is no longer practical to board the gyland directly—any craft approaching within two kilometers is fired upon—but remote surveillance has yielded no evidence of human activity since March 28. The UN believes that the weapons fire is automated, and has declared Redeemer off-limits until those defenses exhaust their ammunition.)

—*An Enemy Within: The Bicameral Threat to Institutional Religion in the Twenty-First Century*
(An Internal Report to the Holy See by the Pontifical Academy of Sciences, 2093)

I COULD BE BOUNDED IN A NUTSHELL AND COUNT MY-
SELF A KING OF INFINITE SPACE, WERE IT NOT THAT I
HAVE BAD DREAMS.

—WILLIAM SHAKESPEARE

HE AWOKE TO screams and gray blurry light, a kick in the
side, a bolt of pain spiking up his left leg like an electric javelin.
He cried out but his voice was lost in some greater cacophony: the
sound of torquing metal, vast alloy bones shearing across unaccustomed stress lines. Gravity was all wrong. He was on his back
but it tugged him *sideways,* pulled him feetfirst through some translucent rubbery amnion that enveloped his body. Vague shapes
loomed and shifted beyond. Down near the subsonic the world
groaned like a humpback whale, wounded, spiraling toward a
distant seabed. Alarms shrieked on higher frequencies.

I'm in a body bag, he thought, panicking. *They think I'm dead . . .
Maybe I am . . .*

The pain settled excruciatingly in his ankle. Brüks brought up
his hands; weak elastic forces resisted the motion. His veins and
arteries were all on the outside, clinging to his skin. *No, not arteries. Myoelectric tensors—*

The world jerked down and sideways. Exhausted metal fell
silent; the alarm seemed to bleat all the louder in the absence of
competition. Something stabbed Brüks through the body bag,
just below the knee. The pain vanished.

A blurry shadow leaned down. "Easy, soldier. I've got you."

Moore.

The membrane split like an opening eye. The Colonel stood
over him, leaning thirty degrees off true in a world sliding downhill. The world itself was tiny, a cylindrical bubble five meters

across and maybe half that high, floor and walls and roof crazily askew. Something ran through its center like a wire-frame spinal cord (*Access ladder*, Brüks realized dimly: this world had an attic, a basement). Towers of plastic cubes, a meter on a side—some white, some gunmetal, some darkly transparent (the blurry things inside glistened like internal organs)—loomed on all sides like standing stones, geckoed one to another. A few had come loose and settled in an uneven pile at the downhill end of the chamber. Gravity urged Brüks to join them there; if his bag hadn't been fastened to its pallet he would have slid right off the end.

Moore reached out and touched some control past Brüks's line of sight; the alarms fell mercifully silent. "How you holding up?" the soldier asked.

"I'm—" Brüks shook his head, tried to clear it. "What's happening?"

"Spoke must have torqued." Moore reached down/across and peeled something off Brüks's head: a second membranous scalp, a skullcap studded with a grid of tiny nubs. "Loose cube got you. Your ankle's broken. Nothing we can't fix once we get you out of here."

There was *grass* on the walls—meter-wide strips of blue-green grass running from floor to ceiling, alternating with the pipes and grills and concave service panels that disfigured the rest of the bulkhead. (*Amped phycocyanin*, he remembered from somewhere.) Smart paint glowed serenely from any surface that wasn't given over to photosynthesis. His pallet folded down from an indentation in the wall; a little stack of time-series graphs flickered there, reporting on the state of his insides.

"We're in orbit," he realized.

Moore nodded.

"We're—they hit us—"

Moore smiled faintly. "*Who*, exactly?"

"We were under attack . . ."

"That was a while ago. On the ground."

"Then—" Brüks swallowed. His ears popped. He'd never been to space before, but he recognized the layout: off-the-shelf hab module, two levels, common as dead satellites from LEO to geosync. You'd sling them around a centrifugal hub to fake gravity. Which would normally be vectored *perpendicular* to the deck, not—

He tried to keep his voice steady. "What's going on?"

"Meteorite strike, maybe. Bad structural component." Moore shrugged. "Alien abduction, for all I know. Anything's possible when you don't have any hard intel to go on."

"You don't—"

"I'm as blind as you are right now, Dr. Brüks. No ConSensus, no intercom. The line must've broken when the spoke torqued. I'll be able to reconnect as soon as someone boosts the signal on the upstream node, but I imagine they have more important things on their minds right now." He laid a hand on Brüks's shoulder. "Relax, Doctor. Help is on the way. Can't you feel it?"

"I—" Brüks hesitated, lifted one rubbery arm, let it drop down/ sideways; it seemed to weigh a bit less than it had before.

"They've shut off the centrifuge," Moore confirmed. "We're spinning down smoothly. That suggests the rest of the ship is more or less okay."

Brüks's ears popped again. "We're not. I think—I think there's an air leak somewhere."

"You noticed."

"Shouldn't we be patching it?"

"Have to find it first. Tell you what: I'll move the cargo, you tear apart all these bulkheads."

"But—"

"Or we can go downstairs, suit up, and get out of here." He split Brüks's cocoon open the rest of the way, helped steady him as he sat up. "Can you walk?"

Brüks swung his legs over the edge of the pallet, trying to ignore the subtle sense of pressure building behind his eyes. He gripped its edge to keep from staggering down the skewed deck.

Myoelectric tattoos ran the length of his naked body like an impoverished exoskeleton. They traced the bones of his arms and legs, forked out along his toes and—(he flexed his right foot; the left hung insensate at the end of his ankle like a lump of clay)—over his heels and across his soles as well. Every movement met with rubber resistance. Every gesture was a small exercise.

Isometric muscle toner. They used them in Heaven sometimes, to keep the Ascended from curling into flabby fetuses. They still used them on those rare deep-space missions where the crew hadn't been preseasoned with vampire genes, to help in the rearguard fight against the shortening of tendons, the wasting of muscles during hibernation.

Moore helped him stand, offered his body as a crutch. Brüks bounced uncertainly on his good foot, his arm around the other man's shoulders. It wasn't as bad as he'd feared. Pseudograv pulled everything in the wrong direction but it was weak, and getting weaker.

"What am I doing here?" Hop-step-lean. Soft crimson light pulsed from the hole in the ceiling where the ladder emerged, staining the adjacent bulkhead.

"Getting to safety."

"No, I mean—" He gestured with his free arm, took in the containers stacked on all sides. "Why am I in the Hold?"

"The Hold's aft. We're using this for the overflow."

The rails of the ladder were the color of rawhide and smooth as plastic; some elastic polymer that stayed taut along a range of lengths. Brüks reached out and grabbed a rung, looked up through the ceiling and discovered the source of that bloody glow: an emergency hatch sealed tight, flashing a warning to any who might be contemplating passage: UNPRESSURIZED.

"My point is—" He looked through the hole in the floor: more metacubes down there, assemblages of smaller units stuck together. "Why did you wake me up in the basement?"

"You weren't supposed to wake up at all; we had you in a therapeutic coma." Brüks remembered being scalped: that skullcap, stippled with electrodes. "You're lucky I happened to be in the neighborhood when things went south."

"Are you saying you *stored me with—*"

The hab lurched, jumped in some sideways direction Brüks's inner ears couldn't parse; suddenly the ladder was slipping diagonally past, suddenly he was falling through the floor (the edge of the hatch bit his ribs in passing). A giant's building blocks, stacked together, would have snapped his spine under Earth gravity; here they merely bent it and bounced him back into the air.

Moore caught him on the rebound: "Well, that's one way of making the trip . . ."

Brüks thrashed in his arms, pushed him away: "*Get the fuck off me!*"

"Calm down, sol—"

"*I'm not your fucking soldier!*" Brüks tried to stand in the crowded space; his wounded ankle twisted under him as though attached by rubber bands. "I'm a *parasitologist,* I was down in the goddamn desert minding my own business. I didn't ask to get caught up in your gang war, I didn't ask to get my ass shot into fucking *orbit,* and I sure as shit didn't ask to get stored down in your *basement* like a box of Christmas ornaments!"

Moore waited until he'd run out of words. "Are you finished?"

Brüks fumed and glared. Moore took his silence for a yes. "I apologize for the inconvenience," he said drily. "Once things have calmed down a bit, maybe we can check in with your wife. Tell her you're working late."

Brüks closed his eyes. "I haven't checked in with my *wife,*" he said through gritted teeth, "in years." *My real wife, anyway.*

"Really." Moore refused to take the hint. "Why not?"

"She's in Heaven."

"Huh." Moore grunted. Then, more softly: "So's mine."

Brüks rolled his eyes. "Small world." His ears popped again. "Are we going to get out of here before our blood starts boiling?"

"Let's go, then," Moore said.

Up past a leaning cityscape of cargo cubes, man-size alcoves flanked an ovoid airlock, two to each side. Spacesuits hung there like flensed silver skins, held in place by cargo straps. They billowed gently at the knees and elbows. Moore helped Brüks across the slanted deck, passed him a loose cargo strap to cling to while unbuckling the suit in the leftmost alcove; it sagged sideways into the soldier's arms.

A breeze hissed softly against Brüks's cheek. Moore held out the suit: gutted from crotch to neck, a split exoskeleton shed by some previous owner. Brüks stood angled and bouncing slightly on his good foot, let Moore guide his bad one into the suit. The low gravity helped; by now Brüks couldn't have weighed more than ten kilos. He felt like some overgrown pupa plagued by second thoughts, trying to climb back into its husk.

An itch crawled across the back of his free hand; he held it up, eyed the blood-brown tracery of elastic filaments webbed across the skin. "Why—"

"So what's she in for?" Moore asked, jerking Brüks's leg hard to seat his injured foot in its boot. Bits of bone ground against each other down there—his tibia carried the vibration past whatever nerve block Moore had installed. It didn't hurt. Brüks grimaced anyway.

"Uh, what?"

"Your wife." The right leg was trickier, without the left to stand on; Moore offered himself as a crutch again. "What's she in Heaven for?"

"That's a strange way of putting it," Brüks remarked.

I'm sick of it, she'd said softly, looking out the window. *They're alive, Dan. They're sapient.*

Moore shrugged. "Everyone's running from something."

They're just systems, he'd reminded her. *Engineered.*

So are we, she'd said. He hadn't argued with her; she'd known better. Neither of them had been engineered, not unless you counted natural selection as some kind of designer and neither of them was woolly-minded enough to entertain such sloppy thinking. She hadn't wanted an argument anyway; she'd been long past the verbal jousts that had kept them sparking all those years. Now she'd only wanted to be left alone.

"She—retired," he told Moore as his right foot slid smoothly into its boot.

"From what?"

He'd respected her wishes. Left her alone when she'd lobotomized her last victim, left her alone to tender her resignation. He'd wanted to reach out when she'd started eyeing Heaven, would have done anything to keep her on his side of the afterlife, but by then it was long past being about what *he* wanted. So he'd left her alone even when she leased out her brain to pay her rent in the Collective Conscious, withdrew from the outer world to the inner. She'd left a link behind, at least. He could always talk to her, there on Styx's farthest shore. She always honored her obligations. But he'd known that's all it was, so even then—after she'd stopped slaughtering artificial systems and started *being* one—he left her alone.

"She was a cloud-killer," Brüks said at last.

"Huh," Moore grunted. Then, helping Brüks's arms into their sleeves: "Not a very good one, I hope."

"Why?"

"Let's just say that not every distributed AI's emergent, and not every emergent AI's rogue." Moore handed over his gauntlets. "We don't publicize it, but every now and then some of the better CKs have been known to pick targets we'd really rather they didn't."

Brüks swallowed on a throat gone suddenly dry. "The fucked-up thing is, she *agreed* with them. The AI Rights idiots, I mean. She quit because she got sick of killing conscious beings whose only crime was"—how had she put it?—"*growing up too fast*."

Suit zipped up. Gauntlets clicked into place. A solid yank on the boa-cord and the suit *squirmed* around him, cinching from flaccid to skintight in a few disquieting seconds. Moore handed him the helmet: "Seat it facing your three, turn counterclockwise until it clicks. Keep the visor up until I say."

"Really?" Brüks was starting to feel light-headed. "The air seems a little—thin . . ."

"Plenty of time." Moore grabbed another suit off the wall. "I don't want your hearing compromised." He bounced off the deck, brought knees to chest and spread his suit open with both hands. With one fluid motion he kicked his legs straight back onto the deck, suited to the waist. He bounced lightly.

"So she wasn't afraid of the conscious AIs." Moore shrugged arms into sleeves. "How about the smart ones?"

"W-what?"

"Smart AIs." He clicked his own helmet into place. "Was she afraid of them?"

Brüks gulped oily alpine air and tried to concentrate. *The smart ones.* Past that minimum complexity threshold where networks wake up: past the Sapience Limit where they go to sleep again, where self-awareness dissolves in the vaster reaches of networks grown too large, in the signal lags that reduce synchrony to static. Up where *intelligence* continues to grow even though the *self* has been left behind.

"Those, she—was a little worried about," he admitted, trying to ignore the faint roaring in his ears.

"Smart woman." The Colonel's voice was strangely tinny. He leaned over and checked Brüks's seals and sockets with precise mechanical efficiency, nodded. "Okay, drop your visor," he said, dropping his.

A louder hiss replaced the fainter one: a blessed wash of fresh air caressed Brüks's face the moment his visor sealed. Relief flooded in a moment later. An arcane mosaic of icons and acronyms flickered to life across the crystal.

Moore's helmet bumped against his own, his voice buzzing distantly across the makeshift connection: "It's a saccadal interface. Comm tree's upper left." Sure enough an amber star blinked there: a knock at the door. Brüks focused his gaze *just so* and accepted the call.

"That's better." Suddenly it was as though Moore was speaking from right inside Brüks's helmet.

"Let's get out of here," Brüks said.

Moore held his arm out, watched it drop. "Not quite yet. Another minute or two."

Out beyond Brüks's helmet, the air—the lack of it, maybe—grew somehow *hard*. Through that impoverished atmosphere and two layers of convex crystal, Jim Moore's face was calm and cryptic.

"What about yours?" Brüks asked after a moment.

"My what?"

"Your wife. What was she—in for?"

"Yes. Helen." A frown may have flickered across Moore's face then, but it was gone in an instant and he was answering before Brüks had a chance to regret the question. "She just got—tired, I suppose. Or maybe scared." His gaze dropped for a moment. "Twenty-first century's not for everyone."

"When did she ascend?"

"Almost fourteen years ago now."

"Firefall." A lot of people had fled into Heaven after that. A lot of the Ascended had even come back.

But Moore was shaking his head. "Just before, actually. Literally *minutes* before. We all said good-bye, and then we went outside and I looked up . . ."

"Maybe she knew something."

Moore smiled faintly, held out his arm. Brüks watched it drift back to his side, slow as a feather. "Almost—"

The hab lurched. Cubes and cartons teetered and wobbled against their mutual attraction; rogue containers lifted from the deck and bumped against the walls in a ponderous ballet. Brüks and Moore, tethered to their cargo straps, drifted like seaweed.

"—time to go." Moore dialed open the inner hatch. Brüks pulled himself along in the other man's wake.

"Jim."

"Right here." Moore pulled a spring-loaded clasp from a little disk at his waist. A bright thread unspooled behind it.

"Why *were* you here? When *things went south?*"

"I was on patrol." Fastening the clasp to a cleat on Brüks's own suit. "Walking the perimeter."

"What?"

"You heard me." The inner hatch squeezed down behind them. Brüks tugged on the thread while Moore went through the motions of depressurizing the 'lock: impossibly fine, impossibly strong. A leash of engineered spider silk.

"You've got a ConSensus feed in your head," Brüks pointed out. "You can see anyplace on the network without getting off the toilet and you *walk the perimeter?*"

"Twice a day. Going on thirty years. You should be thankful I've never seen any reason to stop." One gauntleted hand made a small flourish toward the outer hatch. "Shall we go?"

Moore, you old warhorse.

I'm alive thanks to you. I pass out inside a tornado, I wake up with a smashed ankle on a space station with a broken back. You get me into this suit. You get me to natter on about my wife so I barely even notice the air bleeding away around us.

I bet you'll never tell me how close we came, will you? Not your style. You were too busy distracting me from making a complete panicking ass of myself while you saved my life.

"Thank you," he said softly, but if Moore—tapping out some incantation on the bulkhead interface—even heard him, he gave no sign.

The outer airlock irised open. The great wide universe waited beyond.

And the magnitude of all Jim Moore's well-intentioned lies spread naked across the heavens for anyone to see.

"Welcome to the *Crown of Thorns,*" Moore said from the other end of the universe.

The sun was too large, too blinding: Brüks saw that as soon as the outer hatch opened, in the instant before a polarizing disk bloomed on his faceplate—perfectly line of sight—to cut the glare. *Of course,* he thought at first, *no atmosphere.* Things were bound to be brighter in orbit.

And then he stumbled out in Moore's wake, and toppled weightlessly around some lopsided center of mass while stars and vast structures spun around him.

The Earth was gone.

That wasn't true, he knew in some distant hypothetical place that made absolutely no difference. It *couldn't* be true. Earth was still out there somewhere; one of those billion bright shards lacerating the heavens on all sides. Unwinking pixels, all of them. Not a single one close enough to rise above zero dimensions, to actually assume a *shape.*

No ground to fall to.

His breath rasped in his ears, fast as a heartbeat. "You said we were in *orbit.*"

"We are. Not around Earth."

The ship—the *Crown of Thorns*—spread before him like the bones of some city-size monster. The broken spoke hung directly ahead, a tangle of struts and tubes suffused in a glittering sharp-edged halo: bits of foil, crystals of frozen liquid, little shurikens of metal with nowhere else to go. Things moved in that mosaic of light and shadow. Metal spiders swarmed across the wreckage, spot-welding with incandescent mandibles, spinning webs to suture shattered pieces back together. Tiny starbursts sparkled across the metalscape in waves.

Not bent. Not torqued. *Broken.* Snapped clean off. Horrified, Brüks took in the sight of a slender silver cable, its diameter barely that of a human finger: a lone tendon, miraculously intact, emerging from the amputated stump and stretching across vacuum to anchor the massive barrel-shaped hab at his back. If not for that one frail thread . . .

"You knew about this, didn't you?" He gulped air. "You've been hooked into ConSensus all along . . ."

Moore hung off a handhold, utterly unconcerned by the billions of light-years stretching away beneath his feet. "In my experience, it's generally better to ease people into these situations a little at a time."

"It's not *my* exp—exper—" His tongue was swelling in his mouth. He couldn't seem to catch his breath. Nowhere was up, nowhere was down—

"My *air*—"

Something smacked the sole of his boot; absurdly, *down* clicked back into place. Moore was in front of him, hands on his shoulders, squeezing through the suit: "It's okay. It's okay. Close your eyes."

Brüks squeezed them tight.

"You're just hyperventilating," Moore said from the darkness. "The suit'll thin the mix before you run any serious risk of passing out. You're perfectly safe."

Brüks almost laughed aloud at that. "You—" he managed, "are The Boy Who *Cried* Safe . . ."

"You must be feeling better," Moore observed.

He was, a little.

"Try opening your eyes. Focus on the ship, not the stars. Take your time. Get your bearings."

Brüks opened them a crack. Vacuum and vertigo came flooding in.

Focus on the ship.

Okay. The ship.

Start with this spoke. Truncated, cauterized, one of—one of six (the others apparently undamaged), radiating from a spherical hub like the skeleton of an impoverished bicycle wheel: no rim, nothing but a tin can at the end of each spoke. A few minutes ago those spokes had been slinging their habs around like stones on strings; now they just hung there. A smaller baton—a giant's femur skewered through the midpoint—hung equally motionless just fore of the Hub. (Counterspinning flywheel, probably. To neuter the torque.)

Fifty meters long at least, those hollow bones. This insane Ferris wheel stretched over a hundred meters from side to side.

But it was an ephemeral contraption of twigs and straws next to the wall of metal looming behind it. The drive section. Seen from dead-on it would be a disk: a whole landscape turned on edge, a hard-edged topography of ridges and trenches and right angles. But out here on the wounded rim, Brüks could see the mass piled up *behind* that leading edge: not so much a disk as a core sample extracted from some artificial moon. The striated faces of sedimentary cliffs, carved in metal; monstrous gnarled arteries twisting along the patchwork hull, carrying rivers of fuel or coolant. The arc of a distant engine nozzle, peeking past that metal horizon like a dull sunrise.

A cylindrical silo squatted dead center atop the drive section. Cargo hold, perhaps. The *Crown*'s backbone emerged from its apex like a sapling sprouting from the stump of a great redwood. All this forward superstructure—the Hub and its habs, the flywheel, a hemispherical nose assembly bristling with antennae— none of it mattered in the shadow of those engines. Just a few fragile twigs in which meat might huddle and breathe. Fleas clinging to the back of a captive sun.

"This thing is *huge*," Brüks whispered to Moore. But Moore wasn't there anymore; he was sailing spread-eagled across the gap between this dangling hab and its severed spoke. Moore was deserting him for an army of spiders.

Something tugged on Brüks's tether. He turned, ice water trickling along his spine, to see what new master held his leash.

"You come with me," Valerie said.

She yanked him across the void like bait on a hook, faster than even his brain stem could react. By the time it reached out to snatch a passing holdfast—before it could even look around to *find* one—they were already arcing through clouds of jagged tinsel.

Torn scaffolding reached out as he tumbled past; miraculously, none tore his suit.

He was falling down a well—*Not a well. The spoke. The broken spoke.* He could see its ragged mouth receding above him. He hit bottom, landed hard on his back; elastic inertia tried to bounce him off but a pile-driver slammed against his chest and held him fast. Blood-orange light pulsed at the edge of his eye. He sucked in great panicky gulps of air, turned his head.

The pile-driver extended from Valerie's shoulder. Her other hand worked controls set into the dropgate they'd landed on. Crimson light flashed at two-second intervals around its edge.

"Moore—" Brüks gasped.

"Wastes too much time on you already, Cold Cut. He helps with repairs." A hatch split open in the center of the dropgate. Valerie pitched him through one-handed. Something caught him like a catcher's mitt on the other side: a resilient membrane, stretched between hoops of tensile ribbing. Vacuum sucked at that translucent skin, stretched it tightly convex between those reinforcements.

Valerie sealed the hatch behind them. The little tent inflated instantly, its skin relaxing as the gradient leveled.

Tingling in the fingers of Brüks's left hand; clenched tight, he realized. He forced them open, was vaguely surprised to see a little piece of shrapnel floating on his palm. Its edges weren't entirely jagged. The metal had flowed and congealed in spots, like candle wax.

He must have grabbed it in passing.

The tent split like a clamshell. Valerie dragged him out before it had fully opened, pulled him along a tunnel of pale watery light. A headless brown serpent convulsed along its length, coils slapping the bulkheads with random energy: some kind of elastic cord, thick as his wrist and intermittently studded with little hoops. The rungs of a ladder, too far apart for merely human reach, strobed past on the bulkhead. Occasional flourishes of yellow-and-black hazard striping, flashing by too quickly for any glimpse of whatever they warned against. Brüks craned his neck, eyes forward. Sometime in the past few seconds Valerie had raised her visor. Her face was gray in the shade of her helmet, all planes and angles. Bones and no flesh.

The spoke ended in a slotted dome, like one of those antique telescopes left to rot on mountaintops after astronomy had moved offworld. Most of that slot was blocked by the socket on the other side. They ricocheted through the gap that remained.

They emerged into the space between two concentric spheres: a silvery inner core, like a great blob of mercury three meters across; an outer shell, dull and unreflective, containing it. Some kind of grille split the space between into hemispheres, joined crust to core at the equator. Valerie dragged him across the bowl of the aft hemisphere: around a cubist landscape of cargo modules, past the mouth of a gaping tunnel at the south pole (the spine of the ship, Brüks realized; shadows and scaffolds receded down its throat); past the ball-and-socket assemblies of other spokes, arrayed around that opening like a corolla. Brüks caught flickers of motion through the equatorial grille—personnel in the other hemisphere, otherwise occupied as Valerie dragged him to his fate—but in the next instant they were diving down another one of the *Crown*'s long bones and the faint tinny voice he might have heard through his sealed helmet—

—*Fuck me the roach is up!*—

—could just as well have been imagination.

Another long fall; this time they were being towed. The serpent in this spoke was intact, a moving belt stretched pencil-thin between pulleys at each end. Valerie still gripped Brüks's wrist with one iron hand. The other was locked around one of the hoops (handholds, Brüks realized; stirrups) on the conveyor's outbound leg. The inbound line streamed past just a meter or two to his left, heading back to the Hub. In some hopeful parallel fantasy world, Brüks broke free and seized one of those hoops to make his escape.

Another terminus—this one innocent of shrapnel or wreckage,

just a U-turn and a ledge around an open hatch festooned with a bit of signage:

MAINTENANCE & REPAIR

Now they were through. Now he was free, floating in a hab like the one he'd just escaped. Bulkheads, panels, gengineered strips of photosynthetic foliage. Coffin-size outlines, subtly convex, on the bulkhead: pallets like the one he'd awakened on, folded into the wall while not in use. More of those ubiquitous cubes, stuck and stacked high enough to turn half the compartment into a burrow: a spectrum of colors, a riot of icons. Brüks recognized some of the symbols—power tools, fab-matter stockpiles, the stylized Aesculapian staff that meant *medical*. Others might as well have been scribbled by aliens.

"Catch."

He turned, flinched, brought his hands up barely in time to grab the box sailing toward him. It might have held a large pizza, judging by size and shape; maybe three of them, stacked. Scasers, adhesives, bladders of synthetic blood nestled in molded depressions under its lid. Some kind of bare-bones first-aid kit.

"Fix it."

Somehow Valerie had already stripped down to her coverall, geckoed her abandoned spacesuit to the wall like a crumpled wad of aluminum foil. Her left arm was extended, wrist up, sleeve rolled back. Her forearm bent just slightly, halfway down its length. Not even vampires had joints there.

"What—how did—"

"The ship breaks. Shit happens." Her lips drew back. Her teeth looked almost translucent in the glassy light. "Fix it."

"But—my ankle—"

Suddenly they were eye to eye. Brüks reflexively dropped his gaze: a lamb in a lion's presence, no recourse beyond obeisance, no hope beyond prayer.

"Two injured elements," Valerie whispered. "One mission-critical, one ballast. Which gets priority?"

"But I don't—"

"You're a biologist."

"Yes but—"

"An expert. On life."

"Y-yes . . ."

"So *fix it.*"

He tried to meet her eyes, and couldn't, and cursed himself. "I'm not a medical—"

"Bones are bones." From the corner of his eye he saw her head tilt, as if weighing alternatives. "You can't do this, what good are you?"

"There must be some kind of sick bay on board," he stammered. "A, an infirmary."

The vampire's eyes flickered to the hatch overhead, to the label it framed: MAINTENANCE & REPAIR. "A biologist," she said, something like mirth in her voice, "and you think there's a *difference.*"

This is insane, he thought. *Is this is some kind of test?*

If so, he was failing it.

He held his breath and his tongue, kept his eyes on the injury: closed fracture, thank Christ. No skin breaks, no visible contusions. At least the break hadn't torn any major blood vessels.

Or had it? Didn't vampires—that's right, they vasoconstricted most of the time, kept most of their blood sequestered in the core. This creature's radial artery could be ripped wide open and she might never even feel it until she went into hunting mode . . .

Maybe give her prey a fighting chance, at least . . .

He tamped down on the thought, irrationally terrified that she might be able to see it flickering there in his skull. He focused on the bend instead: leave it, or try to reseat the bone? (*Leave it,* he remembered from somewhere. *Keep movement to a minimum, reduce the risk of shredding nerves and blood vessels . . .*)

He pulled a roll of splinting tape from the kit, snapped off a few thirty-centimeter lengths (long enough to extend past the wrist—it was starting to come back). He laid them down equidistantly around Valerie's arm (*God she's cold*), pressed gently into the flesh (*Don't hurt her, don't fucking hurt her*) until the adhesive took and hardened the splints into place. He backed away as the vampire flexed and turned and examined his handiwork.

"Not set straight," she remarked.

He swallowed. "No, I thought—this is just temp—"

She reached across with her right hand and broke her own forearm like a sapling. Two of the splints snapped with a sound of tiny gunshots; the third simply ripped free of the flesh, tearing the skin.

The fascia beneath was bloodless as paraffin.

She extended the refractured arm. "Do it again."

Holy shit, Brüks thought.

Fuck fuck fuck.

Not a test, he realized. *Never a test, not with this thing. A game. A sick sadistic game, a cat playing with a mouse . . .*

Valerie waited, patient and empty, less than two meters from his jugular.

Keep going. Don't give her an excuse.

He took her arm in his hands again. He clenched tight to keep them from shaking; she didn't seem to notice. The break was worse now, the bend sharper; bone pushed up from beneath the muscles, raised a knotty little hillock under the skin. A purple bruise was leaking into existence at its summit.

He still couldn't meet her eyes.

He grabbed her wrist with one hand, braced against the cup of her elbow with the other, *pulled.* It was like trying to stretch steel: the cables in her arm seemed too tough, too tightly sprung for mere flesh. He tried again, yanked as hard as he could; *he* was the one who whimpered aloud.

But the limb stretched a little, and the broken pieces within ground audibly one against another, and when he let go, the lumpy protuberance had disappeared.

Please let this be enough.

He left the broken splints in place, laid down new lengths of tape adjacent. Pressed and waited as they grew rigid.

"Better," Valerie said. Brüks allowed himself a breath.

Crack. Snap.

"Again," Valerie said.

"*What's wrong with you?*" The words were out before he could catch them. Brüks froze in their wake, terrified at the prospect of her reaction.

She bled. The bone was visible now beneath stretched skin, like a jagged deadhead in murky water. The contusion around it expanded as he watched, a bloody stain spreading through wax. But no, not wax, not anymore; the pallor was fading from Valerie's flesh. Blood was seeping from the core, perfusing the peripheral tissues. The vampire—*warmed*—

She's vasodilating, he realized. *She's switching into hunting mode. Not a game after all, not even an excuse.*

A trigger . . .

"I've got it," said a voice from behind.

Brüks tried to turn. Valerie's impassive gaze pinned him like a butterfly.

"No, really." A pale flash, a beige jumpsuit. Lianna coasted into view and braked against the wall. "I can finish up here. I think your guys need some supervision out on the hull anyway."

Valerie's eyes flickered to her broken arm, back to Brüks. He blinked and she was gone.

"Let's get you out of that suit," Lianna said, unscrewing his helmet.

She'd cut her hair. Her dreads ended along the jawline now.

Brüks sagged and shook his head. "How can you talk to her like that?"

"What? I just—talk." The helmet tumbled off across the compartment. Brüks fumbled with zippers and clasps, still quaking; Lianna unlocked his gauntlets. "Nothing special."

"No, I mean—" He took a breath. "Doesn't she scare the shit out of you?"

"Yeah, I suppose." She glanced at the first-aid kit drifting to one side. "Holy shit, she had you using *that*?"

"That creature is fucking *insane*."

Lianna shrugged. "By human standards, sure. Then again—" She tapped the bulkhead with her toe: a diagnostic pallet unfolded from its dimple in the wall. "Not much point in bringing them all the way back from the Pleistocene if their brains worked just like ours, right?"

"Weren't you afraid?"

She seemed to think about that for a moment. "Guess I was, in a way. I mean, predator-prey, right? Gut response."

"Exactly."

"Chinedum said there was nothing to worry about." She gestured him over to the pallet; he floated into place, let her strap him down around the waist. Biotelemetry readouts bloomed across the bulkhead.

"And you believed him. Them." It. Whatever the pronoun was for *hive*.

"Of course." She ran her finger down the stack of biosigns, winced at something she saw there. "Okay, let's see what we've got."

She cast her gaze around the compartment ("We should really get around to unpacking this stuff sometime"), opened a silver crate tagged with medical icons. A few seconds of rummaging turned up a scaffolding gun from the instrument trays stacked within. She dialed it to OSTEO and set the muzzle against his broken ankle. "You're nerve-blocked, right?"

He nodded. "Jim shot me up with something."

"Good. 'Cause otherwise this would *really* hurt." She fired. Brüks's leg jumped reflexively; he caught a glimpse of black filaments, fine as filaria, lashing frantic tails before they burrowed into his flesh and disappeared.

"Might itch for a bit once the block wears off." Lianna was already scanning the compartment for other treasures. "Takes a while for the mesh to line itself up when you're dealing with all those little bones—ah." An off-ivory cube, this time—no, a *transparent* one. It took its color from the viscous casting putty inside: the stuff quivered like gelatin when she cracked the lid.

There must have been enough in there to put ten people into full-body casts. Brüks glanced around while Lianna scooped up a handful; at least a half-dozen other crates were filled with the same stuff.

The putty squirmed in Lianna's hand, aroused by her body heat. "Where are we going?" Brüks wondered. "How many broken bones are you expecting when we get there?"

"Oh, they don't *expect* anything. They just like being prepared." She slapped the goop onto his ankle. "Hold still until it sets." It slithered around the joint like a monstrous amoeba, fused to itself, crept a few centimeters up his calf and down around his heel before slowing and hardening in the oxygen atmosphere.

"There." Lianna was back at the cube, resealing it before the rest of its contents crusted over. "You'll have to wear that for a few days, I'm afraid. Normally we'd have it off in eight hours but you're still fighting traces of the bug. Might stage a comeback if we crank your metabolism too high."

The bug.

Luckett, screaming in agony. A lawn littered with twisted bodies. A disease so merciless, so fast that it didn't even wait for its victims to die before throwing them into rigor mortis.

Brüks closed his eyes. "How many?"

"What—"

"Did we leave behind."

"You know, Dan, I wouldn't write those guys off. I know how bad it looked, but if I've learned anything, it's that you don't second-guess the Bicams. They're always ten steps ahead, and they've always got plans within plans."

He waited until the voice beyond his eyelids finished talking. Then he asked again.

It didn't answer at first. Then: "Forty-four."

"Ten steps ahead," he repeated in his own personal darkness. "You believe that."

"I do," the voice said solemnly.

"They expected forty-four deaths. They planned it. They *wanted* it."

"They didn't *want*—"

"And when they brought that—that *monster* along for the ride, they knew exactly what they were doing. They have it all under control."

"Yes. They do." There wasn't the slightest hint of doubt in the voice.

Brüks took a breath, let it out again, reflected on the faint unexpected scent of growing things at the back of his throat.

"I get the sense that faith doesn't come easily to you," the voice said gently after a few moments. "But sometimes things are just, you know. God's will."

He opened his eyes. Lianna stared at him, kind and gentle and utterly delusional.

"Please don't say that," Brüks said.

"Why not?" She seemed genuinely puzzled.

"Because you can't possibly believe—because it's a fairy tale, and it's been used to excuse way too much . . ."

"It's not a fairy tale, Dan. I believe in a creative force beyond the physical realm. I believe it gave rise to all life. You can't blame it for all the horrible shit that's been done in its name."

Faint tingling in his fingers. A tide of saliva rising at the back of his throat. His tongue seemed to swell in his mouth.

"Could you—I'd like to be alone, if you don't mind," he said softly.

Lianna blinked. "Uh . . . sure, I guess. You can ditch the mesh anytime. I brought you a fresh jumpsuit, it's over there on the pad. ConSensus is hooked in to the paint job if you need anything, just tap three times. The interface is pretty—"

I'm going to throw up, he thought. "Please," he managed. "Just *go.*" And closed his eyes again, and clenched his teeth, and choked back the rising nausea until the sounds of her retreat faded away and all he could hear were the voices of machines and the roaring in his head.

He did not throw up. He drew his legs to his chest, and wrapped his arms around them, and held them tight against the sudden uncontrollable shaking of his body. He kept his eyes clenched against the new world, against this microcosmic prison into which he'd awakened: infested by freaks and hungry predators, an insignificant bubble spinning farther from home with each passing second. Earth was only a memory now, lost and receding in an infinite void; and yet Earth was right here in his head, inescapable, a desert garden strewn with twisted corpses.

Every one had Luckett's face.

WE LEARN GEOLOGY THE MORNING AFTER THE EARTH-QUAKE.
—RALPH WALDO EMERSON

EVENTUALLY THE PANIC receded. Eventually he had to come back.

He wasn't sure how long he floated there. For the present he was content to take refuge in the darkness behind his own eyelids, in the hiss of ventilators and the soft beeping voices of medical monitors. Some kind of alarm chimed in the middle distance; it sounded five times and fell silent. A moment later the world lurched to the right and gentle pressure began to build against his shoulder blades, against his calves and heels. Up and down returned.

Brüks opened his eyes. The view hadn't changed.

He sat up, turned, let this new gravity drop his legs over the side of the pallet (his vitals vanished from the bulkhead as he rose). He fought off a threat of dizziness from his inner ears, held his hand out in front of him, watched until it stopped shaking.

The exoskeleton vibrated ecstatically as he peeled it away, each strip snapping back to some elastic minimum as he set it free. They took body hair and skin cells with them, left denuded strips along his body. He left it trembling on the deck, a tangled ball of rubbery ligaments that shivered and twitched as if alive.

He found his way to a lav that peeked around a small mountain of in-flight luggage, raided the bulkhead food fabber on the way back. Sucking a squeezebulb full of electrolytes, he peeled fresh folded clothing from the wall where Lianna had left it: a forest-green jumpsuit, preemptively custom-fabbed by some onboard printer. He wobbled precariously while pulling on the pants, but the pseudograv was weak and forgiving. Finally he was finished: clothed, upright, his batteries beginning to soak up charge from the nutrients in his gut. He folded the pallet back into its alcove. Its smart-painted underside bulged subtly from the wall, softly luminescent.

Tap three times, she'd said.

ConSensus bloomed at his touch, an impoverished interface for the augmentally impaired: Systems, Comm, Library. A little v3-D *Crown of Thorns* hovered to one side in an imaginary void. All waited to dance at his fingertips, but he took VOCAL INTER-FACE AVAILABLE at its word and said, "Ship layout."

The animation expanded smoothly into center stage, bristling with annotations. Engines and reactors and shielding swallowed at least three-quarters of the display: thrust cones, fusion reactors, the rippling toroidal contours of great rad-blocking magnetic fields. Shock absorbers and antiproton traps and great protective slabs of lithium hydride. Brüks had seen the tech thumbnailed for short attention spans on any number of popsci feeds. Antimatter microfusion, they called it. A nuclear pulse drive turbocharged with a judicious sprinkling of antiprotons. Give it a decent launch window and the *Crown of Thorns* could make it to Mars in a couple of weeks.

"What's our heading?" he asked aloud.

NAV UNAVAILABLE, ConSensus replied.

"What's our location?"

NAV UNAVAILABLE.

"What's our destination, then?"

NAV UNAVAILABLE.

Huh.

The *Crown's* habitable reaches lay along a spine one hundred fifty meters long, a tube of alloy and atmosphere connecting bits of superstructure like beads on a nail. The Hub Valerie had dragged him through was two-thirds of the way from drive to prow. Its spokes were back in motion, sweeping through space in majestic counterpoint to the flywheel farther up. (Only the Hub's aft hemisphere rotated, Brüks noticed. The other—COMMAND, according to ConSensus, as if any modern space vessel required anything as quaint as a *bridge* in physical space—seemed fixed to the spine.)

"Focus habitat."

The *Crown* redrew herself from the inside, engines and shielding neatly excised, nothing left but the hollows of the *Crown's* forward section turning bright and front and center. Annotated constellations twinkled in those spaces like fireflies in a luminous gut. A cluster of gray icons glowed aft in the HOLD (enormous now, in the absence of its substrate): CHODOROWSKA, K.; EULALI, S.; OFOEGBU, C. Eight or nine others. MOORE, J.—green—glowed in the hab called DORM. LUTTERODT, L. was in the Hub, next to SENGUPTA, R. The hab containing BRÜKS, D. showed up as MED/MAINTENANCE, no matter what the sign on the hatch said; GALLEY/COMMONS occupied the hab immediately clockwise, LAB the one counter. STORES/TRIM, where he'd suffered his rude awakening, balanced out the wheel. Evidently it had already been reattached; but yellow neon highlighted distal injuries where the spoke was still under repair.

The last hab didn't come with a label. Six stars shone there, though: five gray, one green. Only the green carried an ID, and it didn't follow the usual format.

VALERIE, was all it said.

Fifty meters farther forward—past the Hub, past some kind of attic full of plumbing and circuitry and airlocks, way up past the main sensor array at the very front of the ship—ConSensus had drawn a hemispherical nose assembly and called it PARASOL. It appeared to be packed away for the time being but a translucent overlay showed it unfurled, a great flattened cone wide enough for the whole ship to hide behind. Brüks had no idea what it was. Space-dust deflector, maybe. Heat radiator. Magic Bicameral Cloak of Invisibility.

"Root." The *Crown* dwindled on the wall, slipped back into line with the other thumbnails.

A Quinternet icon! He tore it open like a Christmas present. He didn't have access to his preferences but even the Noosphere's generic headlines were like water in the desert: ANARRES SECEDES, FFE KILLS VENTER, PAKISTAN'S ZOMBIE PREZ—

Just a cache, of course. A stale-dated abstract small enough to fit into the *Crown*'s memory—unless someone was breaking silent-running protocols dating all the way back to Firefall, or tightbeaming updates directly to the *Crown*. Anything was possible.

Probably a cache, though. In which case all he had to do was sort the available content by posting date, and—

Twenty-eight days. Assuming they'd grabbed the cache on their way out the door, he'd been stashed in the basement for almost a month.

He snorted softly and shook his head, vaguely surprised at his own lack of surprise. *I'm growing immune to revelation.*

Still. Stale rations were better than none. And it wasn't as though he had anyplace else to be.

The president of Pakistan had finally, to no one's great surprise, been unmasked as an avatar: the original had succumbed to viral zombieism almost a year before, almost certainly an assassination although no one was claiming responsibility. Venter Biomorphics—the last of the old-time corporations—had finally lost the fight against entropy and been swept away. A few proximists pointed their fingers at China's agricultural collapse (that nation was still nose-diving three years after Venter's artificial pollinators had crashed), but smart money blamed the incandescent hand of Forest Fire Economics. Something called *jitterbug*—some kind of weaponized mirror-neuron thing that hijacked its victims' motor-control circuits—was doing the rounds in Latin America. And way out at L-5 (way *in*, Brüks corrected himself; way *back*), the Anarres colony had bolted a row of antique VASIM-R engines onto their belly and were preparing to take secession to new heights.

ConSensus chimed. "Roaches to the Hub," the wall barked in its wake. A female voice, strangely familiar although Brüks couldn't put his finger on it. He returned to the cache, searched for references to a disturbance in the Oregon desert.

Nothing.

No mention of a mysterious nighttime skirmish on the Prineville Reserve: no zombie assault on religious fortifications, no counterattacking tornadoes impossibly slaved to human commands. No reports of armed forces keeping low to the ground, bivouacked around some cultist bull's-eye on the desert plain.

Odd.

Maybe their final hurried exodus from that arena never made it into the cache. Brüks had been unconscious at the time but he imagined the *Crown* might not have lingered in orbit long enough to refresh its memory with newborn updates. Still. Valerie's assault, the armistice, the quarantine—at least thirty solid hours of activity that should have pushed the needle about ten standard deevs above background. Even if there'd been no eyes on Prineville that night, someone would have noticed the sudden redeployment of personnel from previous assignments. Even if Valerie *had* blinded all those skeyes up in geosynch, the disappearance of her hijacked carousel from its garage would have registered somewhere.

The world had too many windows. Every house was glass. It

had been decades since any single entity—corporate, political, or synthetic—had been able to draw the blinds on all of them.

Maybe someone had just scrubbed the onboard cache. The same someone who had apparently locked him out of *you-are-here*.

Because this is all about you. Keeping you in the dark is everyone's top priority.

He winced.

"*Roaches to the Hub*. You think we've got nothing better to do than watch you fondle your dick?"

Brüks blinked, looked around. "What?"

"Uh, she means you, Dan," Lianna said invisibly. "Kind of a briefing. Thought you might like to know what's going on."

"Oh. I—"

Roaches?

"—I'll be right there."

The ladder stretched through the center of the compartment like a strand of DNA stretched straight. Brüks leaned across the hatch from which it emerged—still a bit wobbly in the spin—grabbed its rails, and peered into the basement. Stacked crates down there, lengths of dismembered plumbing. He craned his neck; overhead, the ladder rose into pale blue light.

The only way out was up. He took a breath and raised his foot.

The ladder left him at the bottom of the spoke, on a circular ledge framing the hatch. Another ladder opposite stretched up into the distance like an exercise in perspective geometry. He had not been hallucinating before: its rungs were easily a meter apart, unclimbable in Earth gravity. An easy enough reach here, though, under half that pull.

Not that it mattered. The ladder was only a fallback. The conveyor belt descended smoothly into its burrow to his left, passed around some hidden wheel beneath his feet, rose again toward the Hub. Its stirrup-handholds swept past at two-meter intervals, thoughtfully spaced for a foot and a hand. Going up; going down.

Going up.

Even under power the ascent seemed light-years long, an infinite regression of rungs and rings and bulkheads that almost seemed to breathe when he wasn't looking. The belt drew him up through a series of telescoping segments; hazard striping highlighted the spots where each handed off to the next, where the bore of the tunnel increased by some fractional increment. Little readouts, logarithmically spaced along the bulkhead, pegged the gravity—0.3, 0.25, 0.2—as he rose.

Halfway up, the panic returned.

He had a few seconds' warning: a sudden formless disquiet spreading through the gut, an anxiety that his civilized neocortex tried to write off as simple acrophobia. In the next instant it metastasized into a bone-chilling terror that froze him solid. Suddenly his breathing was fast as a hummingbird's heartbeat; suddenly his fingers were clenched tight as old roots around a rock.

He waited, paralyzed, for some nameless horror to rise in his sight and tear him limb from limb. Nothing did. He forced himself to move. His head turned like a rusted valve, creaked left, right; his eyes rolled frantically in search of threats.

Nothing. An intersegmental gasket passed around him. The rungs of the ladder ticked unremarkably by. Something flickered at the corner of—but no. Nothing there.

Nothing at all.

Over endless seconds time resumed its normal flow; the panic slouched back to the bottom of his brain. Brüks looked back down the way he'd come. His stomach stirred uneasily, but he saw nothing to provoke the slightest unease.

Down had disappeared by the time he reached top; Coriolis, pulling him gently sideways, persisted a few moments longer. He emerged near the bottom of the southern hemisphere, from one of the six teardrop protuberances ringing the south pole. The tunnel he'd glimpsed there before was sealed now, a waist-high railing around its perimeter, a great foil hatch squeezed tight as a sphincter across its mouth. An iris with no pupil. Its fish-eye reflection turned the mirrorball opposite into a blind chrome eyeball.

He turned to face the grille bisecting the Hub: the rings of some mercurial Saturn, closed in a tight hug. Fragments, flickers of motion were visible through that rotating mesh (*stationary* mesh, he corrected himself; it was this *lower* hemisphere that turned): the bottoms of bare feet, a flash of yellow rendered in a fractured mosaic. An insect's-eye view.

Soft voices filtered back through the grille. The yellow fragments moved like a school of fish. "Come on up."

Moore's voice.

There were two routes forward, two circular openings in the grate on opposite sides of the mirrorball. One was blocked by a retracted spiral staircase squashed almost flat, a black metal pie chart cut into staggered slices: a vital thoroughfare when the engines burned, when acceleration turned *forward* into *up*. A useless bit of lawn sculpture now, pulled up and out of the way.

The other was clear, though. Brüks kicked off from the bulkhead, sailed through the air with a mix of exhilaration and mild terror, flailed as the opening drifted lazily past and left him grabbing at the grille a couple of meters antispinward. Chastened, he clambered sideways and through like a crab emerging from its burrow, floated into the northern hemisphere between mirrored earth and smart-painted sky.

Moore stood barefoot, toes curled into the grating, attention focused on a tacband wrapped around his forearm. Mimetic G-couches disfigured the northern half of the mirrorball like body-cast impressions pressed into cookie dough. They ranged radially around the temperate zone, their headrests converging toward the pole. Anyone installed in one of those couches would find themselves looking forward onto the Hub's northern hemisphere: the dome of an indoor sky, a featureless wash of smart paint save for one spot where yet another redundant ladder stretched from the grille to a hatch just to one side of the north pole.

A Hindian woman strapped into the mirrorball—late twenties perhaps, blunt dark bangs, nape shaved halfway to the crest of her skull—jerked her head away the moment Brüks tried to meet her eyes. Something seemed to catch her attention down by her right foot. "About fucking time." She wore a chromaform vest over her orange jumpsuit (*We're color-coded,* Brüks realized): infinitely programmable, but all it showed now was a translucent render of the very couch she was strapped into. It turned her into a pair of arms and a floating head grafted to a ghostly body.

Lianna hovered off the grille on the far side of the compartment. She flashed a smile that broadcast welcome and apology in equal measure. "Dan Brüks, Rakshi Sengupta."

Brüks took another look around the dome; "Uh, Valerie . . ."

"Won't be joining us," Lianna said.

"Fixing her *arm,*" Sengupta added.

Thank Christ.

"So," Moore began, clearly eager to cut to the chase now that the straggler had arrived. "What was it?"

Sengupta rolled her eyes. "Whaddya *think* they burned through the felching spoke it was an *attack.*"

Who, Brüks wondered, and held his tongue.

"I was hoping for a bit more detail," Moore said mildly, unfazed.

Lianna obliged. "Basically they turned a magnifying glass on us. Focused microwave pulse, about half a gigawatt judging by the damage."

"From where?" Moore asked.

Lianna bit her lip. "Sun. Northern hemisphere."

"That's it?"

"Even Bicams have limits, Jim. It's pure hindsight; differential heat stress on different facets of the structure, spoke trajectory—basically they just back-calced how the different parts were lined up at the time, figured a bearing from the angle of the hit."

"Coulda done that ourselves," Sengupta grumbled.

"*Who?*" Brüks blurted out. "Who hit us?"

Nobody spoke. Sengupta regarded something in his general direction the way she might examine a bit of fecal matter scraped off her boot.

"That's what we're trying to figure out," Lianna said after a moment.

Moore pursed his lips. "So the hive didn't see it coming."

She shook her head, as if reluctant to admit to the shortcoming out loud.

"Tran, then."

"It'd be one for the books if a *baseline* caught them with their pants down."

Moore's eyes flickered to stern. "Under normal circumstances, certainly. They're not exactly operating at a hundred percent."

Gray icons, clustered in the Hold. "Uh—" Brüks cleared his throat. "What are they doing back there, exactly?"

"Convalescing," Lianna said. "Bug hit them a lot harder than it hit us. We've pumped up the pressure to speed their recovery, but it'll still be days."

"So after the break," Moore mused.

Break?

Lianna nodded. "We'll have to boot up at least a week early on the other end. They want the option of going hands-on."

"Hands-on *where?*" Brüks wondered. "What *bre*—"

Sengupta cut him off with an exasperated whistle through clenched teeth, turned to Lianna: "Didn't I *tell* you?"

"If you could hold on to your questions for the moment," Moore suggested, "I'll be happy to fill you in later."

"When you won't be wasting everyone *else's* time," Sengupta added.

"Rak," Lianna began.

"Why is he even *here* does anyone expect him to actually *do* anything other than *feel included?*"

"Is that what I'm feeling," Brüks remarked.

"It's not exactly *Dan* who's wasting our time right now," Lianna pointed out.

Sengupta snorted.

Moore waited a beat before getting back to business. "Are there any weapons that could do this from that range?"

Lianna shrugged. "You're the spook. You tell me."

"I'm not talking about baseline tech."

"This doesn't look like a dedicated weapon. More likely someone hijacked a bunch of powersats to fire simultaneously at the same spot. Probably a one-shot deal, too; you don't get that kind of output by staying inside the rated specs. Probably blew the circuits across the whole network, maybe even past their healing threshold."

"Wouldn't matter anyway with a twelve-minute lag. They had one chance to anticipate our position and they blew it. Rakshi, are—"

"Quarter-second thruster squirts random intervals between six and twelve minutes. You won't even feel 'em but those fuckers won't be forecasting *me* again."

Twelve-minute light speed lag, Brüks reflected. *From the sun and back. So we're six light-minutes from the sun, which puts us, puts us . . .*

One hundred eight million kilometers. Close as Venus, if he remembered his basic astronomy.

"—impact our tipping point?" Moore was asking

Lianna nodded. "But not enough to matter. They're working through the revisions now. Another couple of hours, they say."

"And what about our tail?"

Sengupta painted invisible strokes in the air. A window opened on the dome: some kind of plasma plot, three red spikes erupting from a landscape of violet foothills. The details wobbled in real time but those peaks stayed constant. Up in one corner arcane annotations nattered on about DISCRIMINANT COMPLEX and IN-FRARED OCCLUSION and MICROLENSING.

Heatprints of some kind, Brüks guessed. Cloaked, judging from the annotations, but apparently Sengupta had magic fingers.

They were being followed. *This just keeps getting better.*

"So." Moore considered. "Two prongs or two players?"

"Prongs, probably. The Bicams think the shot was meant to disable us enough to let them catch up." Lianna hmmed. "I *wondered* why they didn't just throw a missile at us . . ."

Sengupta: "Maybe they will now their big trip wire went kaput."

"We could use that," Moore mused. "Rakshi, how much warning would we get if they fired on us?"

"Fired *what* you want the whole catalog?"

"Standard ass-cracker. Ballpark's fine."

She wiggled her fingers, for all the world as if she were counting on them. "Seven hours eight minutes if the range doesn't change. Give or take."

"Then we better get started," Moore said.

"That is easily the most unenlightening briefing I have ever attended," Brüks grumbled, pulling himself back into the southern hemisphere. "And given the number of departmental committees I sit on, that's saying something."

"Yeah, I kind of got that." Lianna looked back from a bulkhead handhold. "Come with me. Got something that might help."

She turned like a fish and sailed through the nearest spokeway. The very sight made Brüks a bit queasy. He followed at his own awkward pace, back through the cube-infested southern hemisphere, into the ball-and-socket that had swallowed her. Lianna dropped easily ahead of him, fending off Coriolis with a push and a kick; she was ten meters down the spoke before she even grabbed a hoop. Fuck *those* acrobatics: Brüks grabbed his own hoop right off the top, swung around and fumbled his foot into another before he weighed more than a couple of kilograms. He couldn't be bothered to work out the acceleration of free-falling bodies that gained weight with each meter, but down the length of the spoke he was pretty sure they all ended in *splat*.

Commons. Another hab identical to those he kept escaping: a two-level propane tank from his grandfather's backyard barbecue, grown monstrous and pumped full of stale air. The upper level, at least, was less crowded than Maintenance & Repair: chairs, privacy screens, a half-dozen half-emptied cubes, a table. The usual bands of epiphytic astroturf. A framework of pencil-thin scaffolding extended from one wall. The facets of a personal tent—bone yellow, tough as tendons—stretched like latex between those vertices. A couple of sticky chairs faced each other amid the clutter.

Lianna was over by the fabber, rummaging through a freshly popped cube. "Got it."

The cowl she held up looked a little like a bondage hood for plumbing fetishists, studded with washers and tiny screws that traced a fine grid across the skull. It left only the lower face exposed: mouth, jaw, the tip of the nose. Two especially prominent washers sat embedded over the eyes.

Ambient superconductors. Compressed-ultrasound pingers. A read-write voxel array in black leather.

"My old gaming mask," Lianna announced. "I thought you could use an interface a little more user-friendly than Rakshi tends to be."

A gimp hood, for cripples confined to meatspace.

"I mean, since you don't have the imp—"

"Thanks," Brüks said. "I think I'll stick with the smart paint if it's all the same to you."

"It's not just for gaming," Lianna assured him. "It's perfectly transparent for ConSensus, and it's *way* faster than going through the paint. Plus it'll triple your assimilation rate over anything

filtered through the senses. Perfect for porn. Whatever you like."
She closed the cube. "There's really not much of anything it can't
do."

He took it from her. The material felt faintly oily in his hands.
He turned it over, read the little logo that hovered a virtual centimeter off its surface: INTERLOPER ACCESSORIES.

"It's completely noninvasive," Lianna told him. "All TMS and
compressed ultrasound, even the opt—"

"I'm familiar with the tech," he told her. And then: "Thanks."

"And you know, if you ever *are* in the mood for gaming, I'm
happy to buddy up."

No mention of his helplessness at Valerie's hands. No mention
of his panic attack. No impatience with his ignorance, no conde-
scension over his lack of augments. Just an overture and a helping
hand.

Brüks tasted a mixture of shame and gratitude. *I like this woman,*
he thought.

"Thanks," he said again, because he didn't know anything else
that fit.

She flashed a goofy smile—"Anytime"—and pointed to something past his shoulder. "I think Jim wanted a word, right?"

Brüks turned. Moore had dropped soundlessly onto the deck
behind him. Now he stood there looking vaguely apologetic, the
websack on his back bulging with curves and odd angles.

"Should I—"

"I gotta get back to the Hold anyway. He's all yours." Lianna
vanished into the ceiling with a jump and a grab while Moore
shrugged the sack off his shoulders and split the seal. Brüks
watched him withdraw a roll of the same kind of webbing.

Moore held it out. "For humping gear."

Brüks took it after a moment—"Thanks. Don't seem to have
brought much gear with me"—but the Colonel was already back
in his rucksack. This time he extracted a long green bottle,
turned it in his hands so Brüks could see the label: *Glenmorangie.*

"Found it in one of the cubes," he said. "Don't ask me how it got there. Maybe it was some kind of retailer's bonus for a big order. Maybe Chinedum just wanted to give me a doggie treat. All I know is, it's a personal favorite—"

He set it on the deck, reached back into the sack.

"—and it came with a nice set of glasses."

He gestured to the sticky chairs. "Pull up a seat."

Moore cracked the bottle; the smell of peat and wood smoke swirled in the air. "Technically we shouldn't be playing with open liquids even at one-third gee, but squeezebulbs make everything taste like plastic."

Brüks held out his glass.

"If I had to guess"—Moore let a wobbling, low-gravity dram escape from the bottle—"I'd say you're feeling a bit pissed off."

"Maybe," Brüks admitted. "When I'm not crapping my pants with existential terror."

"One day you're minding your own business on your camping trip—"

"Field research."

"—the next you're in the crossfire of a Tran war, the day after *that* you wake up on a spaceship with a bull's-eye painted on its hull."

"I do wonder what I'm doing here. Every thirty seconds or so."

They clinked and swallowed. Brüks grunted appreciatively as the liquid set the back of his throat to smoldering.

"There's a risk in being here, certainly," Moore admitted. "And for that I apologize. On the other hand, if we hadn't taken you with us you'd most likely be dead already."

"Do we even know who's chasing us?"

"Not with any certainty. Could be any number of parties. Even cavemen." The Colonel sipped his drink. "Sometimes Lianna doesn't give us enough credit."

"But why?" A thought occurred to him: "The hive didn't *steal* this thing, did they?"

Moore chuckled. "Do you know how many basic patents the Order has its name on? They could probably buy a fleet of these ships out of petty cash if they wanted to."

"Then why? "

"The hive was classified as a threat—rightly—even when it was stuck in a desert at the bottom of the well. Now we're on a ship that can take us anywhere from Icarus to the O'Neils." He regarded his scotch. "The threat level isn't going anywhere but up."

"That where we're going? Icarus?"

Moore nodded. "I don't think our tail knows that yet. For all they know we could be cutting across the innersys on our way somewhere else. Probably why they've held back as long as they have." He drained his glass. "*Why*'s a sticky word, though. It's not especially productive to think of them as agents with agendas. Better to think of them as—as very complex interacting systems, just doing what systems do. Whatever the reagents tell themselves to explain their role in the reaction, it's not likely to have much to do with the actual chemistry."

Brüks looked at the other man with new eyes. "You some kind of Buddhist, Jim?"

"A Buddhist soldier." Moore smiled and refilled their glasses. "I like that."

"Was Icarus part of—the magnifying glass?"

"Not likely. Can't rule it out, though. It's in the confidence zone."

"So why are we going there?"

"There's that word again." Moore set his glass down on the nearest cube. "Recon, basically."

"Recon."

"The Bicamerals would think of it as more of a—a pilgrimage, I suppose." His mouth tightened at one corner: a small lopsided grimace. "You remember the *Theseus* mission."

It was too rhetorical for a question mark. "Of course."

"You know the fueling technology it used—uses."

Brüks shrugged. "Icarus cracks the antimatter, lasers out the quantum specs, *Theseus* stamps them onto its own stockpiles, boom. All the antiprotons you can eat."

"Close enough. What matters is that Icarus has been beaming fuel specs up to *Theseus*'s telematter drive for over a decade now. And lately there's been some suggestion that something else has been coming *down* along the same beam."

"Wouldn't you expect them to send back samples?"

"*Theseus*'s fab channel went to a quarantine facility in LEO. I'm talking about the actual telematter stream."

"I didn't know that was even possible," Brüks said.

"Oh, it's quite possible. It was part of the design, in fact; fuel up, data down. Of course, the state of the art's still light-years away from being able to handle complex structure, the receiver's for—very basic stuff. Individual particles, exotic matter, nonbaryonic even. Stuff that might take a *lot* of energy to build."

Brüks sipped and swallowed. "What the hell were you expecting to find out there?"

"We had no idea." Moore shrugged. "Something alien, obviously. And the cost of sticking a condenser on the sun side was negligible next to the mission as a whole. At the very least they could use it for semaphore if the main channel went down. So they stuck one in. In case it proved useful."

"Which I'm guessing it did," Brüks said.

Moore eyed the empty glass at his side, as if weighing the wisdom of having set it down. After a moment he reached for the bottle.

"Here's the thing," he said, refilling his glass. "*Theseus* got—decoyed *en route,* did you know that? Did they ever make that public?"

Brüks shook his head. "There was something about course corrections out past Jupiter, new and better data coming down the pike."

"I can never keep it straight anymore," Moore growled. "What we've admitted, what we've massaged, what we've covered up completely. But yes. After Firefall we were all staring at the sky so hard our eyeballs bled. Found something beeping out in the Kuiper Belt—that much you know—sent a squad of high-gee probes to check it out. Sent *Theseus* afterward, soon as we could slap her together. But she never made it that far. The probes got there first, caught a glimpse of something buried in a comet just before it blew up. All that way to get suckered by a—a decoy, as far as anyone could tell. Glorified land mine with a squawk box bolted on top. So we went back to our radio maps and our star charts and we found an X-ray spike buried in the archives, years before Firefall and never repeated. IAU called it an instrument glitch at the time but now it's all we've got to go on. *Theseus* is already fifteen AUs out and headed the wrong way but you know, that's the great thing about an unlimited fuel supply. We feed her a new course and she spins around and heads into the Oort and she finds something out there, tiny brown dwarf it looks like. She goes in for a look, finds something in orbit, starts to send back details, and *pfsst*—"

He splayed the fingers of his free hand, brought them together at the tips, spread them again as if blowing out a candle.

"—gone."

"I didn't know that," Brüks said after a while.

"I'd be worried if you did."

"I thought the mission was still en route. Nothing on any of the feeds about finding anything." Brüks eyed his own glass. "So, what was it?"

"We don't know."

"But if they'd started sending—"

"Multiple contacts. Thousands. There was some evidence they might have been seeding the dwarf's atmosphere with prebiotic organics—some kind of superjovian terraforming project, perhaps—but if they ever followed that up we never heard about it."

"Jesus," Brüks whispered.

"Maybe something else in there, too," Moore added, staring at the deck. Staring through it. Staring all the way out to the Oort itself. "Something—hidden. Nothing definitive."

He didn't seem to be entirely in the room. Brüks softly cleared his throat.

Moore blinked and came back. "That's all we know, really. The telemetry was noisy at best—that dwarf has one mother of a magnetic field, shouts over anything you try to send out. The Bicamerals have some amazing extraction algorithms, they were squeezing data out of clips I swore were nothing but static. But there are limits. *Theseus* went in and it was like, like watching a ship vanish into a fog bank. For all we know she could still be sending—they left a relay sat behind at least. It's still active. As long as there's hope, we'll keep the feed going. But we're not getting anything back from the ship itself. Can't even get a signal through that soup."

"Except you're getting a signal right now, you said. Coming in along—"

"No." Moore held up his hand. "If the system was operating normally we'd have *seen* it operating, and we didn't. No handshaking protocols, no explicit transmissions, nobody from *up there* telling us they were sending something *down here*. None of the usual bells that are supposed to go off when a package arrives. At most we got a little hiccup that suggests that something might have *started* coming down, but the checksums didn't pass muster so move along folks, nothing to see here. Mission Control didn't even notice it. *I* didn't notice it. Wasn't until the Bicamerals helped me squeeze the archives through their born-again algorithms that I clued in, years after the fact."

"But if the stream isn't even running its own protocols, how can it be—"

"Ask them." Moore jerked his chin toward a vague point beyond the bulkhead, some nexus of Bicameral insight. "I'm just along for the ride."

"So, something's using our telematter stream," Brüks said.

"Or was, at least."

"And it's not us."

"And whatever it is, it's gone to great lengths to stay off the 'scope."

"What would it be sending?"

"*The Angels of the Asteroids.*" Moore shrugged. "That's what the Bicamerals are calling it, or at least that's our closest approximation. Probably just their idea of an op code. But I don't know if they really think *anything's* down there. Maybe it's just a glitch after all. Or some kind of long-distance hack that didn't work out, and we can learn something about the hackers by studying their footprints."

"Suppose there *is* something down there, though," Brüks said. "Something—physical."

Moore spread his hands. "Like what? A clandestine mist of dissociated atoms?"

"I don't know. Something that breaks the rules."

"Well," Moore said, "in that case, I suppose . . ."

He took a breath.

"It's had a few years to settle in."

THINGS FALL APART.
—WILLIAM BUTLER YEATS

THEY'D COME UP with this really great plan to keep their mysterious pursuers from blowing up the *Crown*: they were going to blow it up themselves first.

They hadn't asked Brüks for his input.

Now he was back in Maintenance & Repair, taping himself up with another rubbery exoskeleton. It was easy enough to lay down the bands; all he had to do was follow the denuded template he'd stripped into existence less than two days before.

Of course, by now there were no *days* left to while away. Judging by the chime that had just sounded, he only had about two minutes to burn.

Two minutes to *burn*.

Lianna dropped out of the ceiling. "Hey. Just so you know, Rak's about ready to fold down the spokes. Didn't want you falling over when the gravity shifted."

Yeah, always concerned about the roaches, Brüks reflected wryly. *That sounds just like Rakshi Sengupta.*

On cue, the bulkheads shivered. The hab trembled with the sudden faint roar of a distant ocean. A squeezebulb rolled a few centimeters along the cube where someone had left it.

Brüks swallowed. His knitting ankle itched maddeningly. He resisted the urge to scratch; it wouldn't help anyway, not through the cast.

"Nothing to worry about," Lianna assured him. "Right-side up goes out of whack by a couple of degrees for a couple of minutes. Not even enough to spill your drink. If you were drinking."

He wished he was.

Down edged out from between his feet like a lazy pendulum, came to rest half a meter off his centerline: the *Crown*'s hollow bones folding back along the spine like the ribs of a closing umbrella, the spin that threw them *out* slowing in a precise and delicate handoff to acceleration building from *behind*. All those thousands of tonnes in slow motion, all those vectors playing one against another, and Brüks could feel nothing but a brief polite disagreement between his inner ears. Even now, *down* was edging back to where it belonged.

It really was pretty impressive, he decided. Still: "It's not the burn that bothers me. It's the coma afterward."

"You won't even feel it."

"That's what I mean. If I'm going to fall into the sun I'd at least like to be awake enough to jump into an escape pod if things go south."

"Then you've got nothing to worry about. No escape pods."

The hab jumped a bit, to the solid omnipresent *thud* of great docking clamps snapping shut. The 'bulb on the table wobbled back and forth. The *Crown of Thorns,* tied down and rigged for sail.

She tossed him his jumpsuit, pointed to the ceiling. "Shall we go?"

No effortless sail through a tunnel of light this time. No easing ascent from pseudograv into free fall. The *Crown* was on fire now, engines alight, habs flattened back against her flanks; there was no escape from mass-times-acceleration. Every rung ascended left him as heavy as the last, each hoop of hazard tape left him with that much farther to fall.

For some reason he couldn't identify, that almost made it easier.

They emerged into the Hub, into the bottom of a bowl: a place as gravity-bound now as any other on the ship. The great iris at the south pole was fixed and dilated. Needles of mercury drooled from the mirrorball above like strings of gluey saliva, descending through the open pupil. Freight elevator, apparently. To the Hold, and maybe beyond: to cubbies and crawlspaces where circuits could be wrestled manually in the event of some catastrophic systems failure; to the colossal neutron-spewing engines themselves.

Brüks edged forward and leaned over the railing. The depths of the *Crown*'s hollow spine receded like an optical illusion, like God's own trachea. (Only a hundred meters, Brüks reminded himself. *Only.* A hundred meters.) Signs of activity down there: flickers of motion, the faint clank of metal on metal. Liquid mirror-ropes vibrating like bowstrings in response to whatever tugged at their ends.

He jumped at a touch on his shoulder. Lianna held two lengths of silver cord in her hand; a stirrup had miraculously opened at the end of each, like hypertrophic needle's eyes. She handed him one line, pointed her foot through the loop in the other. "Grab and jump," she said, stepping lightly onto the guardrail.

She dropped away in slow motion—under a quarter-gee burn

they weighed even less than under spin—and picked up speed with distance. Brüks hooked his own foot, grabbed his line with one hand (like wrapping your fingers around glassy rubber), and followed her down. The filament stretched and thinned in his grip as he descended. He raised his eyes and thought he might have glimpsed tiny shock waves rippling out from the point at which this miracle cord extruded from the mirrorball's surface; but speed and distance robbed him of a second look.

He dropped into pastel twilight, past biosteel struts and annular hoops and padded iridescent bulkheads. Conduit bundles lined the throat like vocal cords; silvery metal streams blurred in passing. The end of Lianna's discarded line snapped past going the other way, recoiling back up the shaft like a frog's tongue.

Only a quarter gee. Still dead easy to break your neck at the bottom of a hundred meters.

But Brüks's descent was slowing now, his miracle bungee cord stretching to its limits. Another great hatch yawned just below, flanked by grilles and service panels and a half-dozen spacesuit alcoves. An airlock puckered the bulkhead to one side like a secondary mouth, big enough to swallow two of him whole. It was the larger mouth that took him, though. The silver cord lowered him through like a mother putting her baby to bed, dropped him gently from light into darkness. It set him down on the floor of a great dim cavern where monsters and machinery loomed on all sides, and abandoned him there.

So this is strategy, Brüks mused. *This is foresight, these are countermeasures. This is intellect so vast it won't even fit into language.*

This is suicide.

"Have faith," Lianna had said drily as they'd climbed into their suits. "They know what they're doing."

The spacesuit wrapped around him like an asphyxiating parasite. His breath and his blood rasped loud in his helmet; the nozzle up his ass twitched like a feeding proboscis. He couldn't feel the catheter in his urethra, which in a way was even worse; he had no way of knowing what it was doing in there.

They know what they're doing.

They'd spent the past two hours in the Hold, lurking among the dim tangled shadows of dismembered machine parts while the rest of the ship froze down above them: habs, labs, spines and Hub all pumped dry and opened to vacuum. Until a few hours ago this cavernous space had been the exclusive domain of the afflicted Bicamerals, an improvised hyperbaric chamber where enemy anaerobes withered in poisonous oxygen, where the hive could lick their wounds and incant whatever spells they used to assemble the pieces of the puzzle they were building. Now all that arcane protomachinery was stacked and stored and strapped high against the walls. The Bicamerals, their tissues still saturated under the weight of fifteen atmospheres, had retreated into glass sarcophagi: personal decompression chambers with arms and legs. They stood arrayed on the deck like the opposite of deep-sea divers from a bygone age, barely mobile. Valerie's zombies moved silently among them, apparently charged with their care. Grubs tended by drones.

Now the Hold itself was freezing down, the *Crown*'s last pocket of atmosphere thinning around the assembled personnel. Bicamerals, baselines, monsters—those interstitial, indeterminate things who might be a little of each—they all stood watching as the flaccid pile of fabric in the center of the chamber unfolded into a great black sphere, some interlocking geodesic frame pushing out from under its skin like an extending origami skeleton. The hatching of a shadow.

Moore had called it a *thermos*. Watching it inflate, Brüks was almost certain it was the same giant soccer ball that had carried them from the desert. New paint job, though.

Lianna bumped him from the side, touched helmets for a private word: "Welcome to the Prineville class reunion." Brüks managed a smile in return.

They know what they're doing.

Brüks did, too, after a fashion. They were going to fall side-ways. They were going to tumble past the exhaust, almost close enough to reach out and see your own arm vaporizing in a tor-rent of plasma blasting past at twenty-five kilometers per second. No option to fire maneuvering thrusters for a bit of extra forward momentum, no chance of putting a little distance between this soon-to-be-broken spine and the rapture of a half-dozen fusion bombs per minute. Newton's First was a real bitch, not open to negotiation. Not even the Bicamerals could get her to spread her legs more than a crack, and even that grudging concession would be barely enough to mask the loss of their front end. There would be nothing left over for safe-distancing maneuvers.

And of course, if they didn't miscalculate by a micron or two—if this little sprig of struts and scaffolding didn't just get sucked into the wake and shredded to ions—well, maybe the barrage of neutrons sleeting out in all directions might be able to find a way in.

Rakshi Sengupta reached up and popped the thermos's hatch. It sprang open and bumped back against the curve of the sphere, pneumatic and bouncy. Sengupta climbed up and in. Valerie's automatons—even more interchangeable now, thanks to limited wardrobe options in the survival-gear department—formed a line and began passing the Bicamerals into that globe like worker ants carrying endangered eggs to safety.

All aboard, Lianna mouthed from behind her faceplate.

It wasn't just the radiance of the drive that would give them away. Even the heatprint of minimal life support would shine like a beacon against a cosmic background that barely edged above absolute zero. There were ways around that, of course. You don't notice a candle held up against the sun, and the *Crown of Thorns* had been keeping itself line of sight between Sol's edge and any pursuing telescopes: close enough to bury her heatprint in solar glare, not so close that she'd show up the moment some-one threw an occlusion filter in front of their scanner. Another approach was to keep any warm bodies nested inside so much insulation that they'd be outside any reasonable search radius by the time their heatprint made it to the surface.

The Bicamerals didn't like to take chances. They were doing both.

It was the same soccer ball all right.

Same webbing inside. Same ambience—*Victorian Whorehouse Red,* he thought with a grimace—shadows and wavelengths long enough to make even a corpse look pretty. Same company, with edits.

A clutch of umbilicals hung from an overhead plexus and spread throughout the webbing. Brüks grabbed the nearest and locked it into his helmet's octopus socket. Lianna reached down from overhead, double-checked the connection, gave him a thumbs-up. Brüks sacc'ed comm and whispered a thank-you over the chorus of quiet breathing that flooded his helmet. Lianna smiled back behind tinted glass.

Moore climbed into the womb and sealed the hatch as the longwave dimmed around them. By the last of the light Brüks saw the soldier reach for his own umbilical. Then darkness swallowed them all.

Valerie was in here, too, hidden inside one of these mercurial disguises. Brüks hadn't seen her enter—hadn't even seen her on the deck—but then again, she could do that. She had to be in here somewhere, maybe in that suit, or that one over there.

He eyed the countdown on his HUD: two minutes now. One fifty-nine.

He yawned.

They'd told him it would be easier this time. No seat-of-the-pants improvising, no panic-inducing suffocation. Just a breeze of fresh, cool anesthetic gas wafting through the helmet reg, putting him gently to sleep before the H_2S strangled his very cells from the inside.

They know what they're doing.

Fifty-five seconds.

An icon winked into existence next to the countdown: external camera booting up. Brüks blinked at it and—

"*Let there be light,*" Lianna whispered over the channel, and there was light: a blinding yellow sun, the size of Brüks's fist held at arm's length, blazing in a black sky. Brüks squinted up against the glare: a jagged sunlit tangle of beams and parallelograms hung overhead, sliced along a dozen angles by sharp-edged fissures of shadow.

Let there be a little less *light,* he amended, dialing back the brightness. The sun dimmed; the stars came out. They filled the void on all sides, a million bright motes that only managed to accentuate the infinite blackness between them. They disappeared directly overhead, eclipsed where the habs and girders of the *Crown* loomed like a junkyard in the sky. The sun turned the ship's lit edges into a bright jigsaw; the rest was visible only by inference, a haphazard geometry of negative space against the stars.

The sky lurched.

Here we go . . .

Another lurch. A sense of slow momentum, building. Somewhere behind them, the ligaments that held the *Crown* together were burning through. Up ahead, the view listed to port.

They know what they're doing.

The bow of the ship began to topple, slow and majestic as a falling redwood. Sunlight and shadow played across its facets, hiding and highlighting myriad angles as the stars arced past. The universe turned around them. The sun rose, reached zenith, fell.

Something glowed to stern, a corona peeking around a great black shape that blocked out the stars to stern: something finally tilting into view as a dozen insignificant rags of metal snapped and fell away. Brüks caught the briefest glimpse of dark mass, massive slabs of shielding, a great corrugated trunk thick as a skyscraper—

(*Shock absorbers,* he realized.)

—before a tsunami of white light struck him instantly, rapturously blind.

Floaters swarmed through his eyeballs like schools of panicked fish. Brüks blinked away tears, reflexively reached up, felt that strange, newly familiar inertia return to his arms—

—*Free fall*—

—before the sticky mesh released them to let his gloved hands swipe clumsily at his faceplate. He missed; his arms flailed, encountering nothing but the elastic bounce of the gee-web.

He wobbled gently, weightless, waiting for his vision to clear. By the time he could see again the panorama had been usurped by mere telemetry: an impoverished wraparound of numbers and contour plots and parabolic trajectories. Brüks squinted, tried to squeeze signal from noise through the cotton growing in his head: the *Crown*'s drive section was already kilometers to port and kilometers ahead, its lead increasing with each second per second. Tactical had laid a vast attenuate cone of light across the space before it, spreading from the abandoned drive like a searchlight. *Ramscoop,* Brüks realized after a second. A magnetic field to gather up ionized particles, a brake against the solar wind. A proxy for mass gone suddenly missing: no telltale change in acceleration, no suspicious easing back on the throttle. One measure among many, shoehorned in between the masking of heatprints and whatever stealthed this ship to radar. Moore had told him as much as he could understand, Brüks supposed. There would be more. Solutions to problems no baseline could even foresee, let alone solve. A careful clandestine exit stage left, while unwitting pursuers followed a bright burning decoy toward the land of the comets. All spread out across the curve of his own personal diving bell, numbers and diagrams and stick-figure animations for the retarded.

He only understood half of it, and didn't know if he could trust the other half.

Maybe it's not even real, he thought drowsily. *Maybe it's all just a comforting fantasy to keep me pacified in the backseat. Mommy and Daddy, telling nice stories to keep the children from crying.*

They were still alive, at least. The exhaust hadn't vaporized them outright. Only time would tell if radiation sickness might. Time, or—

He cast his eyes around the bubble of intel. He saw nothing that spoke obviously to the subject of gamma rays.

It would take a while, of course. You wouldn't feel anything at first, certainly not in the few minutes left before everyone went down for the . . . night . . .

Fifty days to Icarus. Fifty days tumbling ass-over-entrails, powered down, ballistic, just another piece of inner system junk. Needle in a haystack, maybe, but nowhere near sharp enough to prick anyone who happens to look this way. Lots of time for those bright little shards to rot us out from the inside. We could die in our sleep and never know it.

His eyelids felt incongruously heavy in the weightless compartment. He kept them open, peered around at all those faces under glass, looked for smiles or frowns or any telltale wrinkles of worry that might be creasing more-enlightened foreheads. Angles and optics turned half the helmets into warped mirrors, hiding the faces within. Some tiny part of Daniel Brüks furrowed its brow in confusion—*Wait a minute . . . aren't the lights supposed to be off?*—but somehow he could see Lianna, eyes already closed, her face smoothed either in sleep or resignation. He could see the back of Moore's helmet, down past his own boots. He was almost certain that he could make out a pair of Bicameral eyes here and there, all closed, the mouths beneath moving in some silent synchronized chant.

Nothing but breathing on comm.

Maybe I'm asleep already, he thought, twisting in the web. *Maybe I'm lucid.*

Valerie stared back at him. No trace of fatigue or anesthesia in that face.

No metabolic hacks for her, Brüks thought as his eyes began to close. *No rotten stench in the back of her throat, no CO or H₂S clogging up her blood cells, no half-assed technology to keep her under. She doesn't need our help. She was doing this twenty thousand years ago, she'd mastered the undead arts before we'd even started scratching stick figures on cave walls. She gorged on us and then she just* went away *while we bred back to sustainable levels, while we forgot she was real, while we turned her from predator to myth, myth to bedtime story . . .*

A bullet hole appeared in the center of her breastplate. A line, growing vertically: a crack splitting her suit down the middle.

All those years we took to convince ourselves she didn't really exist after all, and all that time she was sleeping right under our feet. Right up until she got hungry again, and dug herself out of the dirt like some monstrous godforsaken cicada, and went hunting while we put ourselves to sleep in our own graves and called it Heaven . . .

Valerie twisted and squirmed and emerged naked from her silvery cocoon: white as a grub, lean as a mantis. She grinned needles and clambered across the web toward him.

Like we're sleeping now, Brüks thought, fading. *While she smiles at me.*

> I AM LARGE, I CONTAIN MULTITUDES.
> —WALT WHITMAN

HE DESCENDED INTO Heaven's dungeon, but the shackles were empty and his wife was nowhere to be seen.

He lay on his back in the desert, looked down and saw that he'd been gutted, crotch to throat. Spectral snakes surged eagerly from the gash, fled the confines of his body for the endless baked mud of a fossil seabed, free at last, free at last . . .

He soared through an ocean of stars, dimensionless pinpoints:

abstract, unchanging, unreal. One of them broke the rules as he watched, a pixel unfolding into higher dimensions like some quantum flower blooming in time-lapse. Angles emerged from outlines; shadows stretched across surfaces turning on some axis Brüks couldn't quite make out. Bones spun majestically at its midsection.

Monsters in there, waiting for him.

He tried to veer off, to brake. He pulled all those temporoparietal strings that turned dreams lucid. The *Crown of Thorns* continued to swell in his sights, serenely untroubled by his pitiful attempts to rewrite the script. A hab swept toward him like the head of a mace; he flailed and thrashed and closed his eyes but felt no impact. When he looked again he was *inside,* and Valerie was staring back.

Welcome to Heaven, Cold Cut.

Her monster eyes were fully dilated; like headlights, like balls of bright bloody glass lit from within. The mouth beneath split open like a fresh grinning wound.

Go back to sleep, she told him. *Forget all your worries. Sleep forever.*

Her voice was suddenly, strangely androgynous.

It's your call.

He cried out—

—and opened his eyes.

Lianna leaned over him. Brüks raised his head, glanced frantically in all directions.

Nothing. No one but Lianna. They were back in Maintenance & Repair.

Better than Storage.

He settled back on the pallet. "I guess we made it?"

"Probably."

"Probably?" His throat was parched.

She handed him a squeezebulb. "We're where we're supposed

to be," she said as he sucked like a starving newborn. "No obvious signs of pursuit. It'll take a while before we can be sure but it's looking good. The drive blew up a few hours after we separated, so as far as we know they know, they got us."

"Whoever they are."

"Whoever they were."

"So. Next stop, Icarus?"

"Depends on you."

Brüks raised his eyebrows.

"I mean yes, we're going to Icarus. But you don't have to be up for it if you're not, you know, up for it. We could put you back under, next thing you know you're back on Earth safe and sound. Since you're not officially part of the expedition."

One mission-critical. One ballast.

"Or you put me back under and I die in my sleep when your expedition goes pear-shaped," he said after a moment.

She didn't deny it. "You can die in your sleep anywhere. Besides, the Bicams would know better than any of us, and they're pretty sure you'll make it back."

"They told you that, did they?"

"Not explicitly, but—yeah. I got that sense from them."

"If they really knew what they were going to find down there," Brüks mused, "they wouldn't have to go in the first place."

"There is that," she said. And then, more cheerfully: "But if the mission *does* go pear-shaped, wouldn't you rather die in your sleep than be wide awake and screaming when you get sucked into space?"

"You are the Queen of the Silver Lining," Brüks told her.

She bowed, and waited.

A trip to the sun. A chance to glimpse the traces of an alien intelligence—whatever *alien* meant in a world where members of his own species stitched themselves together into colony minds, or summoned their own worst nightmares back from the Pleistocene to run the stock market. The face of the unknown. What scientist would choose to sleep through that?

As if they'd ever let you get close to their precious Angel of the Asteroids, his inner companion sneered. *As if you'd be able to make any sense of it if they did. Better to sit it out, better to let them carry you back home so you can pick up your life where you dropped it. You don't belong out here anyway. You're a roach on a battlefield.*

Who could easily get squashed in his sleep. What soldier in combat, no matter how benign, ever gave a thought to the vermin underfoot?

Awake, at least, he might be able to scuttle clear of descending boots.

"You think I'd pass up the chance to do *this* kind of fieldwork?" he said at last.

Lianna grinned. "Okay, then. You know the drill, I'll let you get yourself together." She took a bouncing step toward the ladder.

"Valerie," Brüks blurted out behind her.

She didn't turn. "In her hab. With her entourage."

"When the ship was breaking—I saw—"

She tilted her head, lowered her gaze to some point on the far bulkhead. "You see weird things when you go under, sometimes. Near-death experiences, you know?"

Too near. "This was no Tunnel of Light."

"Hardly ever is." Lianna reached for the railing. "Brain plays tricks when you turn it on and off. Can't trust your own perceptions."

She paused and turned, one hand on the ladder.

"Then again, when can you?"

Moore dropped unsmiling onto the deck as Brüks finished pulling on his jumpsuit. He held a personal tent in one hand, a rolled-up cylinder the size of his forearm. "I hear you'll be joining us."

"Try to control your enthusiasm."

"You're an extra variable," the Colonel told him. "I have a great deal of work to do. And we may not have the luxury of

keeping an eye on you if things get sticky. On the other hand—"
He shrugged. "I can't imagine deciding any differently, in your
shoes."

Brüks raised his left foot, balanced on his right to scratch at his
freshly pinkened ankle (someone had removed the cast during
his latest coma). "Believe me, getting in the way's the last thing I
want to do, but this isn't exactly familiar territory for me. I don't
really know the rules."

"Just—stay out of the way, basically." He tossed the tent to Brüks.
"You can set up your rack pretty much anywhere you want. The
habs are a bit messy—we had to relocate a lot of inventory when
they converted the Hold—but we've also got fewer people living
in them for the time being. So find a spot, set up your tent, buckle
down. If you need something and the interface can't help you, ask
Lianna. Or me, if I'm not too busy. The Bicamerals will be coming out of decompression in a few days; try to keep out from underfoot. Needless to say that goes double for the vampire."

"What if the vampire *wants* me underfoot?"

Moore shook his head. "That's not likely."

"She already went out of her way to—to provoke me . . ."

"How, exactly?"

"You see her arm, after the spoke broke?"

"I did not."

"She broke it. She broke her own fucking arm. Repeatedly.
Said I wasn't setting it right."

"But she didn't attack you. Or threaten you."

"Not physically. She really seemed to get off on scaring the shit
out of me, though."

The Colonel grunted. "In my experience, those things don't
have to *try* to scare the shit out of anyone. If she wanted you dead
or broken, you would be. Vampires have—idiomatic speech patterns. You may have simply misunderstood her."

"She called me a *cold cut*."

"And Rakshi Sengupta called you a *roach*. Unless I miss my
guess you took that as an insult, too."

"Wasn't it?"

"Common Tran term. Means so primitive you're unkillable."

"I'm plenty killable," Brüks said.

"Sure, if someone drops a piano on your head. But you're also *field-tested*. We've had millions of years to get things right; some of those folks in the Hold are packing augments that didn't even exist a few *months* ago. First releases can be buggy, and it takes time for the bugs to shake out—and by then, there's probably another upgrade they can't afford to pass up if they want to stay current. So they suffer—glitches, sometimes. If anything, *roach* connotes a bit of envy."

Brüks digested that. "Well, if it was supposed to be some kind of compliment, her delivery needs work. You'd think someone with all that brainpower would be able to cobble together a few social skills."

"Funny thing"—Moore's voice was expressionless—"Sengupta couldn't figure out how someone with all your interpersonal skills could be so shitty at math."

Brüks said nothing.

"Don't take this personally," the Colonel told him, "but try to keep in mind that we're guests on this ship and your personal standards—whatever they might be—do not reign supreme here. Dogs are always going to come up short if you insist on defining them as a weird kind of cat. These people are not baselines with a tweak here and there. They're closer to, to separate cognitive subspecies. As far as Valerie goes, she and her—bodyguards—have pretty much stayed in their hab since the trip began. I expect that to continue. She finds the ambient lighting too bright, for one thing. I doubt you'll have trouble as long as you don't go looking for any."

Brüks felt his mouth tighten at the corners. "So"—remembering the briefing in the Hub, in the company of the *envious* Rakshi Sengupta—"a week to Icarus?"

"Closer to twelve days," Moore told him.

"Why so long?"

Moore looked grim. "That fiasco at the monastery. The *Crown* had to launch prematurely. The sep maneuver was always part of the plan—doesn't take a hive to know a trip like this is going to draw attention—but the replacement drive's still in pieces. They're putting it together as we speak."

Brüks blinked. "We've got no engines at *all*?"

"Maneuvering thrusters. Can't use them yet, not without risking detection." Moore saw the look on Brüks's face, added: "Not that I expect we'll need them in any event. The hive's ballistic calculations are *very* accurate. And it's just as well we're taking the long way, given the medical situation. The bug was easy enough to fix once they nailed down its specs, but healing takes time and hibernation's not the same thing as a medical coma. Last thing we want is to hit the zone with our core personnel compromised." Moore's face hardened at some grim insight, relaxed again. "My advice? Look on this as an extended sabbatical. Maybe you get a ringside seat to some amazing discoveries; maybe it's a dead end and you'll be bored out of your skull. Either way, you can weigh it against a painful death in the Oregon desert and call it a win on points." He spread his hands. "Here endeth the lesson."

The lights had been dimmed in the northern hemisphere. Climbing into the Hub, Brüks could see a wash of arcane tacticals through the equatorial grille, a chromatic mishmash he knew would make no sense even with an unobstructed view.

"Wrong way," said a familiar voice as he headed for the next spoke.

Sengupta.

"What?"

He couldn't see her, even through the grille; the mirrorball eclipsed the view. But her voice carried clearly around the chamber: "You visiting the vampire?"

"Uh, no." *God* no.

"Then you're going the wrong way."

"Thanks." He second-guessed himself, decided to risk it (hey, *she'd* started the conversation), swam through the air, and bull's-eyed the doorway more through luck than skill.

She was still embedded in her acceleration couch. Her face turned away as soon as he came into view.

She kept up her end, though. "Where you going?"

I don't know. I don't have a clue. "Commons. Galley."

"Other way. Two spokes over."

"Thanks."

She said nothing. Her eyes jiggled in their sockets. Every now and then a ruby highlight winked off her cornea as some unseen laser read commands there.

"Meatspace display," Brüks tried after a moment.

"What about it?"

"I thought everyone here used ConSensus."

"This *is* ConSensus."

He tapped his temple. "I mean, you know. Cortical."

"Wireless can bite my clit *anyone* can peek."

The fruit of her labor sprawled across a good twenty degrees of the dome, a light storm of numbers and images and—over on the far left side—a stack of something that looked like voice-prints. It didn't look like any kind of astrogation display Brüks had ever seen.

She was spelunking the cache.

"*I* can peek," he said. "I'm peeking right now."

"Why should I care about *you*?" Sengupta snorted.

Cats and dogs, he thought, and held his tongue.

He tried again. "So I guess I've got you to thank for that?"

"Thank for what?"

He gestured at weeks-old echoes plastered across the sky. "Grabbing that snapshot on the way out. Don't know what I'd do for the next twelve days if I didn't have some kind of Quinternet access."

"Sure why not. You're eating our food you're huffing our O_2 why not suck our data while you're at it."

I give up.

He turned and headed back to the exit. He felt Sengupta shift in the couch behind him.

"I *hate* that fucking vampire she moves all wrong."

It was nice to know that basic predator-aversion subroutines survived the augments, Brüks reflected.

"And I wouldn't trust Colonel Carnage either," Sengupta added. "No matter how much he cozies up to you."

He looked back. The pilot floated against the loose restraints of her couch, unmoving, staring straight ahead.

"Why's that?" Brüks asked.

"Trust him then do what you want. I don't give a shit."

He waited a moment longer. Sengupta sat as still as a stick insect.

"Thanks," he said at last, and dropped through the floor.

So that's what I am, then. A parasite.

He descended into the Lab.

Some half-dead fossil, scooped up in passing from the battlefield. Patched together for no better reason than the firing of a few mirror neurons, some vestigial itch we might have once called pity.

The equipment wasn't his, but the workbench provided some degree of plastic comfort: a bit of surrogate familiarity in a ship too full of long bones and strange creatures.

Worse than ballast: I suck their O_2 and eat their supplies and take up precious airspace millions of klicks from the nearest real atmosphere. Less than a pet: they don't want my company, feel no urge to scritch my ears, aren't interested in any tricks I might know except staying invisible and playing dead.

Sequence/splicer, universal incubator, optoelectron nanoscope with a respectable thirty-picometer threshold. All reassuringly familiar in a world where he'd half expected the very dust to be built out of miracles and magic crystals. Maybe that was deliberate: a security blanket for strays who'd missed the Singularity.

Okay, then. I'm a parasite. Parasites are not destroyed by the powerful: parasites feed on them. Parasites use the powerful to their own ends.

The lower level was empty except for a short stack of folded chairs and half-dozen cargo cubes (fab-matter stockpiles, according to the manifest). Brüks unslung the tent and spread it across the deck against a curve of bulkhead.

A tapeworm may not be as smart as its host but that doesn't stop it from scamming shelter and nourishment and a place to breed. Good parasites are invisible; the best are indispensable. Gut bacteria, chloroplasts, mitochondria: all parasites, once. All invisible in the shadow of vaster beings. Now their hosts can't live without them.

The structure inflated into a kind of bulbous lozenge. It swelled igloolike toward the center of the compartment, molded itself against the walls and flooring behind. It wasn't too different from his abandoned tent back in the desert; the piezoelectricity that buttressed the structure also powered the GUI sheathing its inner surface. Brüks ran an index finger down the center of the door. Its membranous halves snapped gently apart like a sheet of mesentery split down the middle.

Some go even farther. Some get the upper hand, dig down, and change the wiring right at the synapse. Dicrocoelium, Sacculina, Toxoplasma. *Brainless things, all of them. Mindless creatures that turn inconceivably greater intellects into puppets.*

He dropped to his knees and crawled inside. The built-in hammock clung to the inner surface of the tent, ready to peel free and inflate at a touch. The default config only provided enough headroom for a crouch but Brüks couldn't be bothered to dial up the headroom. Besides, the tight confines were strangely comforting down here at the very bottom of the spoke, just a few layers of alloy and insulation from the whole starry drum of the heavens rolling past beneath his feet.

So I'm a parasite? Fine. It is an honorable title.

Down here, nestled in this warm and self-regulating little structure, he was as heavy as the *Crown* would let him be. He felt almost stable, almost rooted. And while he wouldn't quite call it *safety,* he almost managed not to notice how like a burrow his quarters were: how deep in the earth, how far removed from other inhabitants of this pocket ecosystem. And how Daniel Brüks huddled against the deck like a mouse squeezed into the farthest corner of a great glass terrarium full of cobras, the lights turned up as bright as they would go.

> IF YOU ARE GIVEN A CHOICE, YOU BELIEVE YOU HAVE
> ACTED FREELY.
> —RAYMOND TELLER

EVERY HAB STARTED out like every other: same stand-alone life support, same snap-and-stretch frame guides to subdivide the living space to personal preference. Same basic bulkhead galley panel with a toilet on the other side. They all came with the same emergency hibe hookups, compatible with most popular pressure suits and long-distance coffins (not included). It was Boeing's most generic all-purpose personarium, plucked off the shelf, bought in bulk, stuck on the ends of the *Crown*'s spokes on short notice. In the almost inconceivable event that one of those spokes should snap and send a hab tumbling off on its own, corporate guarantees ensured that the bodies therein would keep fresh and breathing (if inert) for up to a year or until atmospheric reentry, whichever came first.

Which was not to say that custom features were out of the question. The fabber in Commons could whip up food with actual taste.

Moore was the only other warm body in evidence when Brüks climbed down for breakfast. The Colonel didn't return the other man's smile at first—Brüks recognized the thousand-meter stare of the ConSensused—but the sound of Brüks's feet on the deck brought him back to the impoverished world of mere meatspace.

"Daniel," he said.

"Didn't mean to disturb you," Brüks said, which was a lie. He'd waited until the sparse constellations arrayed across the *Crown*'s intercom had aligned just so—Lianna or Moore in the Commons, Valerie anywhere else—before venturing forth in search of forage.

Moore waved the apology away. "I could do with a break anyway."

Brüks told the fabber to print him up a plate of French toast and bacon. "Break from what?"

"*Theseus* telemetry," Moore told him. "What little there is of it. Brushing up for the main event."

"There's a main event? For *us*?"

"How do you mean?"

Brüks one-handed his meal to the Commons table (petroleum accents faintly adulterated the aroma of syrup and butter rising from the plate) and sat down. "Dwarves among giants, right? I didn't get the sense there'd be any kind of active role for mere baselines."

He tried a strip of bacon. Not bad.

"They have their reasons for being here," Moore said mildly. "I have mine." In a tone that said, *And they're not for sharing.*

"You deal with these guys a lot," Brüks guessed.

"These guys?"

"Bicams. Post-Humans."

"They're not post-Human. Not yet."

"How can you tell?" It was only half a joke.

"Because otherwise we wouldn't be able to talk to them at all."

Brüks swallowed a bolus of faux French toast. "They could talk to us. Some of them, anyway."

"Why would they bother? We're on the verge of losing them as it is. And—do you have children, Daniel?"

He shook his head. "You?"

"A son. Siri's not exactly baseline himself, actually. Nowhere near the far shore, but even so it's been difficult to—connect, sometimes. And maybe this comparison won't mean much to you, but—they're *all* our children, Humanity's children, and even now we can barely keep their interest. Once they tip over that edge . . ." He shrugged. "How long would it take *you* to decide you had better things to do than talk to a bunch of capuchins?"

"They're not gods," Brüks reminded him softly.

"Not yet."

"Not *ever*."

"That's denial."

"Better than genuflection."

Moore smiled, a bit ruefully. "Come on, Daniel. You know how powerful science can be. A thousand years to climb from ghosts and magic to technology; a day and a half from technology back up to ghosts and magic."

"I thought they didn't use *science*," Brüks said. "I thought that was the whole point."

Moore granted it with a small nod. "Either way, you put baselines against Bicamerals and the Bicamerals are going to be a hundred steps ahead every time."

"And you're comfortable with that."

"My comfort doesn't enter into it. Just the way it is."

"You seem so—fatalistic about it all." Brüks pushed his empty plate aside. "The far shore, the gulf between giants and capuchins."

"Not fatalism," Moore corrected him. "Faith."

Brüks glanced sharply across the table, trying to decide if Moore was yanking his chain. The soldier stared back impassively.

"The fact that something *shot* us," Brüks continued deliberately. "And you yourself said they're probably Tran."

"I did, didn't I?" Moore seemed to find that amusing. "Fortunately we've got a pretty good team of those in our own corner. Honestly, I wouldn't worry."

"You trust them too much," Brüks said quietly.

"So you keep saying. You don't know them the way I do."

"You think you know them? You're the one who called them *giants*. We don't know their agendas any more than we know what those smart clouds are up to. At least smart clouds don't open up your brain and dig around like, like . . ."

Moore didn't say anything for a moment. Then: "Lianna."

"You know what they did to her?"

"Not exactly."

"That's exactly my point. No one does. *Lianna* doesn't know. They shut her off for four days, and when she woke up she was some kind of Chinese Room savant. Who knows what they did to her brain? Who knows if she's the same person?"

"She's not," Moore said flatly. "Change the wiring, change the machine."

"That's what I'm saying."

"She agreed to it. She volunteered. She worked her ass off and elbowed her way to the front of the line just for the chance to make the cut."

"It's not informed consent."

That raised eyebrow again. "How so?"

"How can it be, when the person giving it is cognitively incapable of understanding what she's agreeing to?"

"So you're saying she's mentally incompetent," Moore said.

"I'm saying we *all* are. Next to the hives, and the vampires, and the thumbwirers, and that whole—"

"We're children."

"Yes."

"Who can't be trusted to make our own decisions."

Brüks shook his head. "Not about things like this, no."

"We need adults to make those choices on our behalf."

"We—" He fell silent.

Moore watched him above the ghost of a smile. After a moment he pulled the Glenmorangie off the wall.

"Have a drink," he said. "Helps the future go down easier."

Crawling unseen through the viscera of its host, the parasite takes control.

Daniel Brüks drilled into the central nervous system of the *Crown of Thorns* and bent it to his will. Lianna, as usual, was back in the Hold with her helpless omnipotent masters. Sengupta's icon glowed in the Hub. Moore was ostensibly in the Dorm but the feed from that hab put the lie to it: only his body was there, running on autopilot while his closed eyes danced through some ConSensual realm Brüks could only imagine.

He was going to be eating alone.

The anxiety had become chronic by now. It nagged at the bottom of his brain like a toothache, had become so much a part of him that it went unnoticed save for those times when some unexpected chill brought it all back. Panic attacks: in the spokes, in the habs, in his own goddamn tent. They didn't happen often, and they never lasted long. Just often enough to remind him. Just long enough to keep him paranoid.

The blade began to twist as he ascended the spoke. Brüks gritted his teeth, briefly closed his eyes as the conveyor pulled him past the Zone of Terror (it helped, really it did), relaxed as the haunted zone receded beneath him. He released the handhold at the top of the spoke and coasted into the Hub, crossed the antarctic hatch (half-contracted now, barely wide enough for the passage of a body) pushed himself toward—

A soft wet sound. A cough from the northern hemisphere, a broken breath.

Someone crying.

Sengupta was up there. Had been a few minutes ago, at least. He cleared his throat. "Hello?"

A brief rustle. Silence and ventilators.

Ohhkay . . .

He resumed his course, crossed to the Commons spoke, twisted and jackknifed through. He allowed himself a moment of self-congratulation as he grabbed the conveyor and started down headfirst, smoothly swinging around the handhold until his feet pointed down; just two days ago all these drainpipes and variable-gravity straightaways would have left him completely disoriented.

Valerie tagged him halfway.

He never saw her coming. He had his face to the bulkhead. There may have been a flicker of overhead shadow, just a split second before that brief touch between his shoulder blades: like a knife's edge sliding along his spine, like being *unzipped* down the back. His back brain reacted before he was even aware of the contact, flattened and froze him like a startled rabbit. By the time he could move again she was past and gone and Daniel Brüks was still alive.

He looked down, down that long tunnel she'd sailed into head-first and without a sound. She was waiting at the bottom of the spoke: white and naked and almost skeletal. Wiry corded muscle stretched over bone. Her right foot tapped a strange and disquieting pattern on the metal.

The conveyor was delivering him into her arms.

He released the handhold, lunged across the spoke for the static safety of the ladder. He missed the first rung he grabbed for, caught the second; leftover momentum nearly popped his shoulder from its socket. His feet scrabbled for purchase, finally found it. He clung to the ladder as the conveyor streamed past to each side, going up going down.

Valerie looked up at him. He looked away.

She just touched me for Christ's sake. I barely even felt it. It was probably an accident.

No accident.

She hasn't threatened you, she hasn't raised a hand. She's just— sitting there. Waiting.

Not in her hab. Not kept at bay by bright lights, no matter what comforting lies Moore had recited.

Brüks kept his eyes on the bulkhead. He swore he could feel the baring of her teeth.

She's just another failed hominoid. That's all she is. Without our drugs she couldn't even handle a few right angles without going into convulsions. Just another one of nature's fuckups, just another extinct monster ten thousand years dead.

And brought back to life. And chillingly, completely at home in the future. More at home than Daniel Brüks had ever felt.

She wouldn't even be alive if it weren't for us. If we roaches hadn't scraped up all those leftover genes and spliced them back together again. She had her day. She's nothing to be afraid of. Don't be such a fucking coward.

"Coming?"

With effort he looked down, managed to fix his gaze on the edge of the hatch behind her, kept her eyes in that great comforting wash of low resolution that made up 95 percent of the human visual field. He even managed to answer, after a fashion: "I, um . . ."

His hands stayed locked on the ladder.

"Suit yourself," Valerie said, and disappeared into the Commons.

Motion through the grille: the pixilated mosaic that was Rakshi Sengupta, returning from some place farther forward. The lav in the attic, perhaps. Brüks found it perfectly understandable that Sengupta might choose to leave for a piss at the same moment Valerie happened to be passing through.

She fell into eclipse behind the mirrorball. Brüks heard the sound of buckles and plugs clicking into place, a grunt that might have passed for a greeting: "Thought you were headed for Commons."

He swam into the northern hemisphere. Sengupta was pulling a ConSensus glove over her left hand: middle finger, ring, index, little, thumb. Her hair stood out from her head, crackling faintly with static electricity.

"Valerie got there first," he said.

"Room for two down there." Right glove: middle, ring, index . . .

"There really isn't."

She still refused to look at him, of course. But the smile was encouraging.

"Nasty cunt doesn't even *use* the galley." Sengupta's tone was conspiratorial. "Only comes out of her hab to scare us."

"How'd she even end up here?" Brüks wondered.

Sengupta did something with her eyes, a little jiggle that said *command interface*. "There. Now we'll see her coming." Her elbows moved out from her body and back in, a precise stubby wingbeat. Brüks couldn't tell whether it was interface or OCD. "Anyhow why ask me?"

"I thought you'd know."

"You were *there* I just fished you all out of the atmosphere."

"No, I mean—where's she even *from*? Vampires are supposed to live in comfy little compounds where they fight algos and solve Big Problems and don't threaten anybody. It's not like anyone would be stupid enough to let them off the leash. So how does Valerie show up in the desert with a pack of zombies and an army aerostat?"

"Smart little monsters," Sengupta said, too loud. (Brüks stole a nervous glance through the perforated deck.) "I'd start making *crosses* if I were you."

"No good. They've got those drug pumps in their heads. Anti-Euclideans."

"Things *change*, baseline. Adapt or die." Sengupta's head bobbed like a bird's. "I don't know *where* she comes from. I'm working on it though. Don't trust her at *all* don't like the way she moves."

Neither do I, Brüks thought.

"Maybe her friends can tell us," Sengupta said.

"What friends?"

"The ones she got *away* from, I've been looking and—hey you're a big-time biologist right? You go to conferences and all?"

"One or two, maybe. I'm not *that* big-time." Mostly he just virtualized; his grants weren't big enough to let him jet his actual biomass around the planet.

Besides, these days most of his colleagues weren't all that happy to see him anyway.

"Shoulda gone to this one." Sengupta bit her lip and summoned a video archive onto the wall. It was a standard floatcam view of a typical meeting hall in a typical conference: she'd muted the sound but the sight was more than familiar. Seated rows of senior faculty decked out in thermochrome and conjoined flesh-sculpture; grad students dressed down in ties and blazers of dumbest synth. A little corral off to one side where a few dozen teleops stood like giant stick insects or chess pieces on treads, rented mechanical shells for the ghosts of those who couldn't afford the airfare.

The speaker of the hour stood behind the usual podium. The usual flatscreen stretched out behind him; the usual corporate hologram spun lazily above it all, reminding the assembled of where they were and whose generous sponsorship had made it all possible:

FizerPharm Presents
The 22nd Biennial J. Craig Ventor Memorial Conference
on Synthetic and Virtual Biology

"Not really my thing," Brüks admitted. "I'm more into—"

"*There!*" Sengupta crowed, and froze the feed.

At first he couldn't see what she was getting at. The man at the podium, petrified in midmotion, gestured at a matrix of head shots looming behind him on the screen. Just another one of those eye-glazing group dioramas that infested academic presentations the world over: *I'd like to take this opportunity to thank all those wonderful folks who assisted in this research because there's no fucking way I'll ever give them actual coauthorship.*

Then Brüks's eyes focused, and his gut clenched a little.

Not collaborators, he saw: *subjects.*

He could tick off the telltales in his head, one by one: the pallor, the facial allometry, the angles of cheekbone and mandible.

The eyes: Jesus Christ, those eyes. An image filtered through three generations, a picture of a picture of a picture, fractions of faces degraded down to a few dark pixels and they *still* sent cold tendrils up his spine.

All these things he could itemize, given time. But the brainstem chill shrank his balls endless milliseconds before his gray matter could have ever told him why.

The Uncanny Valley on steroids, he thought.

For the first time he noticed the text glowing on the front of the podium, the thumbnailed intel of a talk already in progress: *Paglino, R. J., Harvard—Evidence of Heuristic Image Processing in the Vampire Retina.*

Sengupta drummed her fingers, fed the roach a clue: "Second row third column."

Valerie's face. Oh yes.

"They make 'em hard to track," she complained. "Keep changing ID codes move them around. All *proprietary information* and *filing errors* and *can't let the vampire liberation front know where the kennels are* but I got her now I got her now I got the first piece of the puzzle."

Valerie the vampire. Valerie the lab rat. Valerie the desert demon, mistress of the undead, scorched-earth army of one. Rakshi Sengupta *had* her.

"Good luck," Brüks said.

But the pilot had already brought up another window, a list of names and affiliations. Authors and attendees, it looked like. Some were flagged. Brüks squinted at the list, scanned it for whatever commonality might bind those highlighted names together.

Ah. Resident Institution: Simon Fraser.

"She had *friends,*" Sengupta murmured, almost to herself. "I bet she got away from 'em.

"I bet they want her back."

REALITY IS THAT WHICH, WHEN YOU STOP BELIEVING
IN IT, DOESN'T GO AWAY.
—PHILIP K. DICK

JIM MOORE WAS dancing.

There was no floor to speak of. No partner. Not even any witnesses until Daniel Brüks climbed into the Hub; the command deck was uncharacteristically quiet, no tapping toes or clicking tongues, none of the staccato curses that Sengupta barked out when some command or interface didn't see things her way. Moore was alone in the cluttered landscape, leaping from a stack of cargo cubes, rebounding off some haphazard plateau halfway down, hitting the deck for just a split second in a perfect barefoot crouch before bouncing back into the air: one arm tight across his chest, the other jabbing at some invisible partn—

Opponent, Brüks realized. Those open-handed strikes on empty air, that heel coming down with a *snap* against a passing bulkhead: those were combat moves. Whether he was interacting with a virtual partner in ConSensus or merely faking it old school, Brüks had no idea.

The dancing warrior caught a loose strap of cargo webbing floating from the grille, swung legs overhead, and planted them against the bulkhead: hands pulling against strap in lieu of gravity, legs pushing back from the grille in opposition, a human tripod planted against the wall like a three-legged spider. Brüks could clearly see his face. Moore wasn't even breathing through the mouth.

"Nice moves," Brüks said.

Moore looked right past him and lifted his feet without a word, turning slowly around the strap like a windmill in a light breeze.

"Uh . . ."

"Shhh."

He jumped a little at the hand on his arm. "You don't want to wake him up," Lianna said softly.

"He's *asleep?*" Brüks looked back at the ceiling; Moore was spinning more quickly now, head out, legs spread in a V, the strap winding tighter between man and metal. In the next instant he was airborne again.

"Sure." Lianna's dreads bobbed gently in the wake of her nod. "What, you stay *awake* when you exercise? You don't find it, um, boring?"

He didn't know whether she was taking a shot at the thought of Dan Brüks coming equipped with some kind of sleepwalking option, or the equally ludicrous thought of Dan Brüks working out.

"Why do it at all? A dose of AMPK agonist and he's a hard-body even if he lies in bed snarfing bonbons all day."

"Maybe he doesn't want to depend on augments that can be hacked. Maybe the endorphins give him happier dreams. Maybe old habits die hard."

Moore sailed over their heads, stabbing the air. Brüks ducked despite himself.

Lianna chuckled. "Don't worry about that. He can see us just fine." She caught herself: "Something in there can, anyway." A kick and a glide took her to the port staircase. "Anyway, don't waste your time with that loser—the moment he wakes up he'll just dive back into his *Theseus* files." She jerked her chin. "I've got some time to kill. Come play with me instead."

"Play w—" But she'd already turned like a fish and darted down the spoke. He followed her back to the heavy quarters, to the Commons where Moore's green bottle and his own abandoned gimp hood clung to the bulkhead between bands of minty astroturf.

"Play what?" he asked, catching up. "Tag?"

She grabbed his hood off the wall and tossed it to him, flumping into a convenient hammock in a single smooth motion. "Anything you want. Deity Smackdown. Body-swap boxing is kinda fun. Oh, and there's a Kardashev sim I'm pretty good at, but I promise to go easy on you."

He turned the Interloper Accessory over in his hands. The frontal superconductors stared up at him like a pair of startled eyes.

"You *do* remember that's mainly a gaming hood, right?"

He shook his head. "I don't game."

Lianna eyed him as though he'd just claimed to be a hydrangea. "Why ever *not?*"

Of course he couldn't tell her. "It's not *real.*"

"It's not supposed to be," she explained, surprisingly patient. "That's what makes them games."

"Doesn't *feel* real."

"Yeah it does."

"Not to me."

"Yeah it does."

"*Not to—*"

"Not to put too fine a point on it, Oldschool, but *Yes it does.*"

"Don't lecture me about my own perceptions, Lee."

"It's the *same neurons!* The same signal running up the same wiring, and there's *absolutely no way* your brain can tell the difference between an electron that came all the way from your retina and one that got injected midstream. Absolutely no way."

"Doesn't *feel* real," he insisted. "Not to me. And I'm not playing Porn Star Cat Wars with you."

"Just *try,* man."

"Play the AI. It'll give you a better run for your money anyway."

"It's not the sa—"

"Hah!"

Lianna's face fell. "*Fuck.* Skewered by my own position statement."

"By a roach, no less. How's it feel?"

"Like I just punched myself in the nose," she admitted.

Neither spoke for a moment.

"Just once? For me?"

"*I don't game.*"

"Okay, okay. No harm in asking."

"Now you've asked."

"Okay." She swung back and forth in the hammock for a few seconds. (There was something a little off about that motion, a hinted half-spiral oscillation. Coriolis was a subtle trickster.)

"If it makes you feel any better," she said after a while, "I kinda know what you mean."

"About?"

"About things not seeming real. I actually feel that way all the time. Gaming's the only time I *don't* feel that way."

"Huh," Brüks grunted, a little surprised. "I wonder why."

And after a moment's thought: "Probably the company you keep."

Someone had set up a second tent next to his, stuck it like an engorged white blood cell right at the base of the ladder. Brüks had to effect a half hop sideways off the second rung to avoid bumping it. Something rustled and muttered inside.

"Hello?"

Sengupta stuck her head out, stared at the deck. "Roach."

Brüks coughed. "You know, that doesn't actually sound as much like a compliment as you might think."

She didn't seem to hear him. "You should see this," she said, and withdrew.

And poked her head out again after a few seconds: "Well come *on.*"

He hunkered gingerly down into the tent. Sengupta crouched at its center. Patches of flickering intelligence swarmed across the fabric: columns of numbers; crude plastic-skinned portraits rendered by some computer sketch artist struggling with insufficient eye-witness data; rows of—home addresses, from the look of it.

"What's this?"

"Nothing you care about." Reflected lightning played across her face. "Just some fucker going to be eating his own guts when

I get hold of him." She waved one hand and the collage disappeared.

"You do realize they've got a whole hab set up as a dorm," Brüks said.

"That's too crowded nobody uses this one."

"*I* use—" *Never mind.*

A roommate might not be so bad, he reflected. He'd have never sought one out—good parasites do not draw attention to themselves, no matter how lonely the lifestyle—but if things went south, maybe Valerie would eat Rakshi first. Buy him some time.

"Watch this best party trick *ever.*"

She threw a video feed onto the wall: rowdy voices, flashing lights, a maglev table wobbling at an insane angle thanks to the drunken asshole trying to dance on the damn thing. Campus bar. The student ambience would be a dead giveaway anywhere on the planet but Brüks was pretty sure it was somewhere in Europe. The subtitler was off but he caught snatches of German and Hungarian at least.

A couple of grad students had randomly arranged a dozen empty beer glasses on a table. A crowd of others cheered and chanted and pulled chairs away, clearing a surrounding space. Something was happening stage left, just out of camera range: an *anti*disturbance, a sudden contagious quelling of noise and commotion that drew eyes and spread around the circle in an instant. The camera turned toward the eye in the storm. Brüks sucked in his breath.

Valerie again.

She stalked into the cleared floor space like a spring-loaded panther, unleashed, autonomous. She wore the cheap throwaway smart-paper weave ubiquitous to lab rats and convicts the world over; it seemed absurd against the jostling background of blazers and holograms and bioluminescent tattoos. Valerie didn't seem to notice her own violation of the dress code; didn't notice the way the front lines pushed back against the crowd as she passed, or the way the murmuring horde fell silent when she got too close. She had eyes only for the glasses on the table.

What kind of suicidal idiot would take a vampire to a bar? How zoned had these people been, to not be fleeing for the exits?

"Where did you *get*—"

"*Shut up and watch!*"

Valerie circled the table, once. She hesitated for a moment, her eyes unfocused, something that might almost have been a smile playing across her lips.

In the next instant, she sprang.

She came down on one bare foot, almost three meters from a standing start; snapped the other down with a *stomp,* spun and stamped again and jumped—arcing backward this time, over the table itself, flipping in midair and landing in a four-point crouch (*left foot right foot right knee left hand*) before hopping to the left (*stomp*), hand-springing forward to land chest-to-face with some semisober sessional who still had enough animal sense to turn greeny-white under a face loaded with retconned chloroplasts. Straight up now: a vertical one-meter leap with a one-legged landing; about-face (*stomp*), two diagonal steps toward the table (*stomp*). Both elbows, one knee crashing simultaneously against ancient floorboards that bounced her smoothly back into a standing position. *Finis.* After a moment, the camera, shaking despite the very best image-stabilization algorithms a student budget could buy, panned back to the table.

The glasses were arranged in a perfectly straight, evenly spaced line.

"Hard to find this one someone snuck her out the back door you take a vampire out without authorization and your career is *over* so they really kept the evidence locked up I think it was an initiation or something . . ."

The view hovered over the tableau for a long, disbelieving moment. Swung back to the monster who had created it. Valerie stared straight through the camera and a thousand kilometers beyond, smiled that patented bone-chilling smile. She wasn't even breathing hard.

Everyone else was, though. Reality was finally cutting through the drinks and the drugs and the sheer idiotic bravado of spoiled children raised on promises of immortality. They were in the presence of black magic. They were in the presence of something whose most trivial efforts turned the very laws of motion into feats of telekinesis. And one sodden instant behind all that awe and stunned disbelief, perhaps, the realization of just what all that vast intelligence, all those superconducting motor skills had evolved in the service of.

Hunting.

It didn't matter what bedtime stories these privileged brats had been told. They were not immortal in such a presence. They were only breakfast. And it was obvious to Brüks—from the way they pulled back and muttered their excuses, the way they edged for doors while keeping their backs to walls, the way even those pretending to be *in charge* averted their eyes as they scuttled side-long up to Valerie and told her in weak and shaking voices that it was time to come in now—that they finally knew it.

It was also obvious, in hindsight, that Brüks had been uncharitable to the baselines who'd stolen their rat from its cage for one wild night out. Whoever they were, they hadn't been suicidal. They hadn't been idiots. No matter what they might have told themselves before or after, no matter who remembered having the idea.

It hadn't really been their decision at all.

The gimp hood did amp his learning curve. Brüks had to admit that much.

Data once forced to time-share the cramped real estate between bands of astroturf stretched luxuriously around him along three axes and three hundred sixty degrees of infinite space. Options he would have had to make eye contact with on a smart-paint display leapt front and center the moment he so much as *thought* about them. Information that he'd normally have to read, and repeat, and review—it seemed to just stick in the brain with a glance and a swallow. He was used to cognitive enhancers, of course, but this had to be Bicameral tech; he couldn't imagine that even surgical augments would deliver a bigger boost.

Three trillion nodes and a ten-thousand-link search radius was a pretty impoverished echo of the actual Quinternet, but you could still dig for a thousand lifetimes and never reach its edge. Instant expertise in a million disciplines. Interactive novels you didn't even have to play, first-person eidetic memories that planted themselves directly into your head if you had the interface (Brüks didn't, but this came close), served up all the thrills and wonder and experience of *just having played* without even needing to set aside the time to inhabit the story in real time. Indelible footprints of all the things the Noosphere deemed worthy of remembrance.

Even after fourteen years, *Theseus* was all over it.

The shock, the disbelief in the wake of Firefall. Riots in every color of the rainbow: terrified hordes fleeing the coming apocalypse, not knowing which way to run; demonstrations against movers and shakers who'd always known more than they let on; looters with short attention spans, thinking only of all that swag left undefended while panicked populations hid under their beds or lashed back against uniforms whose guns and drones and area-denial weaponry were finally, after uncounted decades of casual and brutal unaccountability, just not up to the challenge. Tens of thousands returning from Heaven, fearful of new threats from the real world. Millions more fleeing *into* it, for pretty much the same reason.

And then, *Theseus*: the Mother Of All Megaprojects. A mission, a metaphor, a symbol of a shattered world reunited against the common threat. The brave souls who manned her, that small select force standing for Humanity against the cosmos. Amanda Bates, champion of countless WestHem campaigns: her skills so broad, her talents so highly classified that no one had even heard of her before her ascension to the Dream Team. Lisa Takamatsu, Nobel laureate, linguist, and den mother to a half-dozen separate personalities living in her own head. Jukka Sarasti, the noble vampire, the lion who'd lain down with lambs and was ready to give his life on their behalf. Siri Keeton, synthesist, ambassador to ambassadors, bridge between—

Wait a second—Siri?

He'd heard that name before. He sifted through dusty old memories laid down before the upgrade. Bulletins and biography washed over them in the meantime: Siri Keeton, synthesist, top of a field consisting exclusively of people at the top of their field. Possessed by demons at the age of six, some convulsive virus straight out of the Middle Ages that lit up his brain with electrical storms. It would have killed him outright if radical surgery hadn't snatched him back from the brink, patched him up, left him scarred and scared and possessed of something altogether new: a fierce never-say-die dedication to beating the odds, the world, to beating his own mutinous brain into submission and *getting the job done,* all the way out to the very edge of the solar system and beyond.

(*Siri's not exactly baseline himself, actually . . .*)

Almost nothing about his home life. No home vids, no leaked grade-school psych work-ups. An only child, apparently. Mother not mentioned at all, father left unnamed, a shadowy background figure that refused to come into focus except for one passing reference in *TimeSpace*:

> . . . owes his single-minded pursuit of personal goals as much to his childhood battle with epilepsy as to his up-bringing as a soldier's son . . .

Brüks turned the words over in his head, searching for coincidence.

"Yah Colonel Carnage had to go out and get his baby almost killed don'tcha know. Before he was even born."

The low gravity was no friend; Brüks jumped so high he cracked his head on the ceiling.

"*Je*-sus!" He pulled back the hood. Sengupta appeared between the interface dissolving in his head and the backup resurrecting on the bulkhead behind her. *I have got to figure out the privacy settings on this thing,* Brüks told himself. Not that they'd keep her from looking over his shoulder if she really wanted to, he supposed.

"Where did *you* come from?"

"I've been here all along five minutes at least."

"Well *say* something next time. Announce yourself." He rubbed the sore spot on his head. "What are you doing here anyway?"

Sengupta smacked her lips and cast sidelong eyes at her tent. "Hunting a dead man."

I am the only meat sack on this whole damn ship who isn't some kind of predator. "Hunting what?" One of the zombies?

"Not *on board* I mean like you"—snapping her fingers at the ConSensus display—"hunting *him.*"

Brüks looked back at the wall: a factoid collage, a palimpsest of puff pieces. It didn't come anywhere close to biography.

"Jim nearly got him killed?"

"Yah I said that." *Snap snap.*

"Says here he had some kind of viral epilepsy."

Sengupta snorted. "They had to cut out half his brain for *viral epilepsy* right. Like anyone on Carnage's salary has to settle for leeches and laudanum when his brat gets sick."

"So what was it, then?"

"Viral *something,*" Sengupta crowed. "Viral *zombieism.*"

Ventilator sounds filled the sudden silence.

"Bullshit," Brüks said softly.

"Oh he didn't do it *deliberately* the larva was just collateral.

Some evildoer cooked up a basement bug but he got the fine-tuning wrong. Virus likes fetus brains way better than grown-up brains right? All that growth metabolism all that neural pruning everything moves faster so they give it to Mommy and she gives it to Daddy but it *really* takes off when it gets past that old-time placenta in the third tri. Goes through baby's brain faster'n flesh-eating. Wake up next morning the little fucker's already seizing in the womb and it's lucky for them it's their canary in the coal mine, they go down to Emerg and shoot up on antizombals, get cleaned out just in time. But too late for little Siri Keeton. He comes into the world and he's already damaged goods and they deal with it best they can they try all the best drugs and all the best lattices but it's downhill all the way and after a few years the seizures start up and that's all they wrote on Siri Keeton's left hemisphere right? Had to scrape it out like a rotten coconut."

"*Jesus,*" Brüks whispered, and glanced around despite himself.

"Oh you don't have to worry about *him* he's way down deep in his precious *Theseus* signals." An odd, single-shouldered shrug. "Anyway it all turned out okay though better'n before like I say. Storm troopers have really good medical plans. Replacement hemisphere's a big improvement. Made him the man for the mission."

"What a horrible thing to do to a kid."

"If you can't grow the code stay out of the incubator. Fucker probably did it himself to God knows how many others, that's what they *do.*"

Brüks had seen the footage, of course: civilian hordes reduced to walking brain stems by a few kilobytes of weaponized code drawn to the telltale biochemistry of conscious thought. It wasn't the precise surgical excision of cognitive inefficiency, not the military's reversible supersoldiers or Valerie's programmed body-guards. It was consciousness and intellect just *chewed away* from cortex to hypothalamus, Humanity reduced to fight/flight/fuck. It was people turned back into reptiles.

It was also a hell of an effective strategy for anyone on a budget: cheap, contagious, terrifyingly effective. If you were caught in some panicking crowd you could never be sure whether the person pushing from behind was trying to rape you, or bash in your skull, or just get the fuck out of the zone. If you were *above* the crowd all your state-of-the-art telemetry would never tell the undead from the merely undone; not even Tran tech could pick out the fractional chill of a zombie brain inside its skull, not from a distance, not through a wall or a roof, not in the middle of a riot. All you could do was seal off the area and try to keep upwind until the flamethrowers showed up.

They had special squads for that in India, Brüks had heard. People with off switches in their heads, fighting fire with fire. They were really good at their jobs.

"Had it coming you ask me," Sengupta hissed.

"Jesus, Rakshi." Brüks shook his head. "What do you have *against* that guy?"

"Nothing I don't have against any jackboot who fucks people over and then's all *just following orders.*" She poked at some unseen irritant with the toe of her boot. "Look I know you two are dating or whatever okay? Fine with me tell him whatever you want just don't be surprised when he fucks you over. He'll feed you into the meat grinder the moment he thinks it serves his *greater good.* Feed himself in too for that matter. I swear sometimes I don't know which is worse."

Neither spoke for a few moments.

"Why are you telling me this?" Brüks asked at last.

"Why not?"

"You're not afraid I'll pass it on?"

Sengupta barked. "Like you *would.* Besides he can't blame me if he stomps his muddy footprints all over the 'base for anyone to see. *You* coulda seen 'em even."

Why do I put up with her? Brüks asked himself for the tenth time. And then, for the first: *Why does she put up with* me?

But he thought he knew that answer already. He'd suspected it at least since she'd moved in next door: Sengupta *liked* him, in a weird twisted way. Not sexually. Not as a colleague or a peer, not even as a friend. Sengupta liked Daniel Brüks because he was easy to impress. She didn't think of him as a person at all; she thought of him as a kind of pet.

Shitty social skills. Rakshi Sengupta was too contemptuous of etiquette to be bothered. But the fact that she didn't abide by social cues didn't mean she couldn't read them. She'd read *him* well enough, at least; there was no way he'd ever tell Jim Moore what Sengupta had learned about his son. Not Dan Brüks.

He was a *good* boy.

The next time he saw Lianna, he didn't.

He heard her voice—"Whoa, *watch that*"—just a second before the hab tilted crazily askew and pain shot up from—in from . . .

Actually, he didn't know *where* the pain was coming from. It just *hurt*.

"Holy Heyzeus, Dan, you didn't *see* that?" Lianna popped magically into existence beside the Commons coffee table as he blinked up from the deck.

The table, he realized. *I ran into the table . . .*

He shook his head to clear it. Lianna vanished again—

"Hey—"

—and reappeared.

Brüks hauled himself to his feet, pulled the gimp mask off his face as the pain settled in his left shin. "There's something wrong with this thing. It's screwing with my eyes."

She reached out and took it. "Looks okay. What were you doing?"

"Just trawling the cache. Thought I'd bookmarked an article but I can't find the damn thing."

"You encrypt the search?"

Brüks shook his head. Lianna far-focused into ConSensus.

"Szpindel et al? 'Gamma-protocadherin and the role of the PCDH11Y ortholog'?"

"That's the one."

"It's right here." She frowned, handed back the gimp hood. "Try again."

He pulled it back on over his head. Search results reappeared in the air before him, but Szpindel wasn't among them. "Still nothing."

"Hmm," Lianna said, and vanished.

"Where are you? You just dis—"

She leaned back into view from nowhere in particular.

"—appeared."

"There's the problem," she said, and peeled the gimp hood back off his scalp. "Induced hemineglect. Probably a bad superconductor."

"Hemineglect?"

"See why you should get augged? You could just pull up a subtitle, know exactly what I'm talking about."

"See why I don't?" Brüks conjured up a definition out of smart paint. "Nobody has to cut my head open to replace a bad superconductor."

Broken brains that split the body down the middle and threw half of it away: an inability to perceive anything to the left of the body's midline, to even *conceive* of anything there. People who only combed their hair on the right side with their right hands, who only saw food on the right side of their plates. People who just *forgot* about half the universe.

"That is fucked," Brüks said, quietly awed.

Lianna shrugged. "Like I said, a bad superconductor. We got spares, though; faster'n fabbing a replacement."

He followed her through the ceiling. "So you never told me why you *were* so old school," she said over her shoulder.

"Fear of vivisection. When superconductors go bad. We covered this."

"The reason that stuff *goes* bad is because it's crappy old tech. Internal augs are less failure-prone than your own brain."

"So they'll work flawlessly when some spambot hacks in and leaves me with an irresistible urge to buy a year's supply of bubble bath for cats."

"Hey, at least the augs are firewalled. It's *way* easier to hack a raw brain, if that's what you're worried about.

"Then again," she added, "I don't think it is."

He sighed. "No. I guess it isn't."

"What, then?"

They emerged into the southern hemisphere. Their reflections, thin as eels, slid across the mirrorball as they passed.

"Know what a funnel-web spider is?" Brüks asked at last.

After the barest hesitation: "I do now." And a moment later, "Oh. The neurotoxins."

"Not just any neurotoxins. This one was special. Pharm refugee maybe, or just some open-source hobby that got loose. Might have even been beneficial under other circumstances, for all I know. The little fucker got away. But I felt a *nip,* right about here"—he spread the fingers of one hand, tapped the webbing between thumb and forefinger with the other—"and I was flat on my back ten seconds later." He snorted softly. "Taught me not to go sampling without gloves, anyway."

They crossed the equator, single file. No one in the northern hemisphere.

"Didn't kill you, though," Lianna observed shrewdly.

"Nah. Just induced the mother of all allergic responses to nanopore antiglials. Any kind of direct neural interface finishes what that little bugger started."

"They could fix that, you know." Lianna bounced off the deck and glided along the forward ladder, Brüks clambering in her wake.

"Sure they could. I could take some proprietary drug for the rest of my life and let FizerPharm squeeze my balls every time they change their terms and conditions. Or I could get my whole immune system ripped out and replaced. Or I can take a couple of pills every day."

The attic.

A warren of pipes and conduits, an engineering subbasement at the top of the ship. Plumbing, docking hatches, great wraparound bands full of tools and spacesuits and EVA accessories. Stone Age control panels in the catastrophic event that anyone might need to take manual control. A stale breeze caressed Brüks's face from some overhead ventilator; he tasted oil and electricity. Up ahead the docking airlock bulged to starboard like a tinfoil hubcap three meters across; a smaller lock, merely man-size, played sidekick across the compartment. Spacesuits drifted in their alcoves like dormant silver larvae. Portals and panels crowded the spaces between struts and LOX tanks and CO_2 scrubbers: lockers, bus boards, a head gimbaled for variable gee.

Lianna cracked one of the lockers and began rummaging about inside.

Yet another ladder climbed farther forward, out of the attic and up along a spire of dimly lit scaffolding. Afferent sensor array up there, according to the map. Maneuvering thrusters. And the parasol: that great wide conic of programmable metamaterial the *Crown* would hide behind when the sun got too close. Photosynthetic, according to the specs. Brüks didn't know whether it would shuttle enough electrons to run whatever backup drive the Bicamerals were putting together, but at least hot showers were always an option.

"Got it." Lianna held up a greasy-looking gray washer, smiling.

For a moment. The look of triumph drained from her face while Brüks watched; the expression left behind was bloodless and terrified.

"Lee . . . ?"

She sucked in breath, and didn't let it out. She stared past his right shoulder as if he were invisible.

He spun, expecting monsters. Nothing to see but the airlock.

Nothing to hear but the clicks and sighs of the *Crown of Thorns*, talking to itself.

"Do you hear that?" she whispered. Her eyes moved in terrified little saccades. "That—*ticking* . . ."

He heard the sigh of recycled air breathed into cramped spaces, the soft rustle of empty spacesuits stirring in the breeze. He heard faint muffled sounds of movement from below: a scrape, a hard brief footfall. Brüks looked around the compartment, swept his eyes past alcoves and airlocks—

Now he heard something: sharp, soft, arrhythmic. Not a ticking so much as a *clicking,* a sound like, like a clicking tongue, perhaps. A *hungry* sound, from overhead.

His stomach dropped away.

He didn't have to look. He didn't dare to. Somehow he could *feel* her up there in the rafters: a dark predatory shadow, watching from places where the light couldn't quite reach.

The sound of teeth tapping together.

"*Shit,*" Lianna whispered.

She can't be up there, Brüks thought. He'd checked the board before leaving the Commons. He *always* checked. Valerie's icon had been down in her hab where it always was, a green dot among gray ones. She must have *really* moved.

Of course, they could do that.

Now those clicking teeth were so loud he didn't know how he could have missed them. There was no pattern to that sound, no regular predictable rhythm. The silences between clicks stretched forever, drove him insane with trivial suspense; or snapped unexpectedly closed after a split second.

"Let's—" Brüks swallowed, tried again. "Let's get . . ."

But Lianna was already headed aft.

The Hub was bright light and sterile reflections: the soft glow of the walls chased Brüks's fears back to the basement where they belonged. He looked at Lianna a bit sheepishly as they rounded the mirrorball.

Lianna did not look sheepish at all. If anything, she looked more worried than she had in the attic. "She must have hacked the sensors."

"What do you mean?"

She wiggled her fingers in midair; INTERCOM appeared on the bulkhead. Sengupta was astern near the Hold; Moore was back in the Dorm.

Valerie's icon glowed reassuring green, down in her own private hab with the grays.

"Ship doesn't know where she is anymore," Lianna said. "She could be anywhere. Other side of any door you open."

"Why would she do that?" Brüks glanced up at the hole in the ceiling as Lianna grabbed the ladder. "What was she even doing up there?"

"Did you see her?"

He shook his head. "Couldn't look."

"Me, neither."

"So for all we know, she wasn't even up there."

She managed a nervous laugh. "You wanna go back and check?"

Here among the bright lights and the gleaming machinery, it was hard not to feel utterly ridiculous. Brüks shook his head. "Even if she *is* up there, so what? It's not like she's confined to quarters. It's not like she did anything other than—grind her teeth."

"She's a predator," Lianna pointed out.

"She's a sadist. She's been pushing my buttons since day one; I think she just gets off on it. Jim's right: if she wanted to kill us we'd be dead already."

"Maybe this is *how* she kills us," Lianna said. "Maybe she *mambos.*"

"Mambos."

"Voodoo *works,* Oldschool. Fear messes up your cardiac rhythms. Adrenaline kills heart cells. You can literally scare someone to death if you hack the sympathetic nervous system the right way."

So voodoo's real, Brüks mused.

Chalk one up for organized religion.

. . .

Moore was heading down when Brüks was heading out.

"Hey, Jim."

"Daniel."

It didn't happen often anymore. Whether at meals or after, during the *Crown*'s bright blue day or the warmer shadows of its night cycle, the Colonel always seemed to be deep in ConSensus these days. He never talked about what he did there. Cramming for Icarus, of course. Reviewing the telemetry *Theseus* had sent before disappearing into the fog. But he kept those details to himself, even when he came out to breathe.

Brüks stopped at the foot of the Commons ladder. "Hey, you want to see a movie?"

"A what?"

"*The Silences of Pone*. Like a game you can only watch. Lee says it's one of—you know, back when they couldn't just induce desired states directly. They had to manipulate you into feeling things. With plot and characters and so on."

"Art," Moore said. "I remember."

"Pretty crude by current standards but apparently it won a whole bunch of awards for neuroinduction back in the day. Lee found it in the cache, set up a feed. Says it's worth watching."

"That woman is getting to you," the Colonel remarked.

"This whole fucking *voyage* is getting to me. You in?"

He shook his head. "Still reviewing the telemetry."

"You've been doing that for a week now. You hardly come up for air."

"There's a lot of telemetry."

"I thought they went in and went dark."

"They did."

"Almost immediately, you said."

"*Almost* is a relative term. *Theseus* had more eyes than a small corporation. Take a lifetime to sift through even a few minutes of that feed."

"For a baseline, maybe. Surely the Bicams have everything in hand."

Moore looked at him. "I thought you didn't approve of blind faith in higher powers."

"I don't approve of breaking your back pushing boulders up-hill when you're eyeprinted for the heavy lifter across the street, either. You said it yourself. They're a hundred steps ahead of us. We're just here to enjoy the ride."

"Not necessarily."

"How so?"

"We're here. They're stuck in decompression for the next six days."

"Right," Brüks remembered. "Field-tested."

"Why they brought us along."

Brüks grimaced. "They brought *me* along because I happened to stumble onto the highway and they didn't have the heart to see me turn into roadkill."

The Colonel shrugged. "Doesn't mean they can't make the most of an opportunity when it presents itself."

Brüks's fingertips tingled in remembrance. *Opportunities,* he realized with sudden dull surprise.

I'm missing one.

It was a window in the crudest possible sense: a solid pane of transparent alloy, set into the rear bulkhead. You couldn't zoom it or resize it or lay a tactical false-color overlay across its surface. You couldn't even turn it off, unless someone on the other side brought down the blast shield. It was a clear, impenetrable *hole* in the ship: a circular viewport into an alien terrarium where, out past the ghostly reflection of his own face, strange hyperbaric creatures built monstrous artifacts out of sand and coral. Their eyes twinkled like green stars in the gloom.

Six of the monks were resting, suspended in medical cocoons

like dormant grubs waiting out the winter. The others moved purposeful as ants across a background of shadows and half-built machinery: a jumbled cityscape of tanks and stacked ceramic superconductors and segments of pipe big enough to walk through without ducking. Brüks was pretty sure that the patchwork sphere coming together near the center of the Hold was shaping up to be the fusion chamber.

Two of the Bicamerals huddled off to one side in some sort of wordless back-to-back communion. A glistening gelatinous orb floated beside them. Someone else (Evans, that was it) seized a nearby hand tool and lobbed it to starboard. It spun lazily end over end until Chodorowska reached up and snatched it from the air, without ever taking her eyes off the component in her other hand.

She'd never even looked. Which was not to say she hadn't seen it coming.

But of course, there was no *her*. Not right now, anyway. There was no Evans or Ofoegbu, either.

There was only the hive.

How had Moore put it? *Cognitive subspecies*. But the Colonel didn't get it. Neither did Lianna; she'd shared her enthusiastic blindness with Brüks over breakfast that very morning, ticked off in hushed and reverent tones the snips and splices that had so *improved* her masters: *No TPN suppression, no Semmelweis reflex. They're immune to inattentional blindness and hyperbolic discounting, and, Oldschool, that synesthesia of theirs—they reset millions of years of sensory biases with that trick. Randomized all the errors, just like that. And it's not just the mundane sensory stuff, it's not just feeling color and tasting sounds. They can literally* see time . . .

As if those were *good* things.

In a way, of course, they were. All those gut feelings, right or wrong, that had kept the breed alive on the Pleistocene savanna—and they *were* wrong, so much of the time. False negatives, false positives, the moral algebra of fat men pushed in front of onrushing trolleys. The strident emotional belief that children made you happy, even when all the data pointed to misery. The high-amplitude fear of sharks and dark-skinned snipers who would never kill you; indifference to all the toxins and pesticides that could. The mind was so rotten with misrepresentation that in some cases it literally had to be *damaged* before it could make a truly rational decision—and should some brain-lesioned mother abandon her baby in a burning house in order to save two strangers from the same fire, the rest of the world would be more likely to call her a monster than laud the rationality of her lifeboat ethics. Hell, rationality itself—the exalted Human ability to *reason*—hadn't evolved in the pursuit of truth but simply to win arguments, to gain control: to bend others, by means logical or sophistic, to your will.

Truth had never been a priority. If believing a lie kept the genes proliferating, the system would believe that lie with all its heart.

Fossil feelings. Better off without them, once you'd outgrown the savanna and decided that Truth mattered after all. But Humanity wasn't defined by arms and legs and upright posture. Humanity had evolved at the synapse as well as at the opposable thumb—and those misleading gut feelings were the very groundwork on which the whole damn clade had been built. Capuchins felt empathy. Chimps had an innate sense of fair play. You could look into the eyes of any cat or dog and see a connection there, a legacy of common subroutines and shared emotions.

The Bicamerals had cut away all that kinship in the name of something their stunted progenitors called *Truth,* and replaced it with—something else. They might look human. Their cellular metabolism might lie dead on the Kleiber curve. But to merely call them a *cognitive* sub*species* was denial to the point of delusion. The wiring in those skulls wasn't even mammalian anymore. A look into *those* sparkling eyes would show you nothing but—

"Hey."

Lianna's reflection bobbed upside down next to his in the window. He turned as she reached past and unhooked her pressure suit from its alcove. "Hey."

His eyes wandered back to the window. The back-to-back Bi-camerals had ended their joint trance; they turned, simultane-ously plunged their hands into the wobbling sphere at their side (*Water,* Brüks realized: *it's just a blob of water*), dried off on a towel leashed to the bulkhead.

"I didn't know," he said, too quietly. As if afraid they'd hear him through the bulkhead. "How they work. What they—are."

"Really." She checked her suit O_2. "I would've thought the eyes'd be a giveaway."

"I just assumed that was for night vision. Hell, I know people who retro fluorescent proteins as a fashion statement."

"Yeah, *now.* Back in the day they were—"

"Diagnostic markers. I figured it out." After Moore had in-spired him to go back and actually look at the thing that had left all those corpses twisted like so much driftwood in the Ore-gon desert. It still lingered in his own blood, after all—and it had been almost too easy, the way the lab had taken that chimera apart and spread-eagled every piece for his edification. Strepto-coccal subroutines lifted from necrotizing myelitis; viral encepha-litides laterally promoted from their usual supporting role in limbic encephalitis; a polysaccharide in the cell wall with a spe-cial affinity for the nasal mucosa. A handful of synthetic subrou-tines, built entirely from scratch, to glue all those incompatible pieces together and keep them from fighting.

But it had been the heart of that piecemeal bug that had be-trayed the hive to Brüks's investigations: a subroutine targeting a specific mutation of the p53 gene. He hadn't got any direct hits when he'd run a search on that mutation, but the nearest miss was close enough to spill the secret: a tumor antagonist patented almost thirty years before.

As if someone had weaponized an anticancer agent.

"Doesn't it bother you?" he wondered now.

The suit had swallowed her to the waist. "Why should it?"

"They're *tumors,* Lee. Literally. Thinking tumors."

"That's a pretty gross oversimplification."

"Maybe." He wasn't clear on the details. Hypomethylation, CpG islands, methylcytosine—black magic, all of it. The precise and deliberate rape of certain methylating groups to turn interneurons cancerous, just *so*: a synaptic superbloom that multiplied every circuit a thousandfold. It was no joyful baptism, as far as Brüks could tell. There'd be no ecstasy in that rebirth. It was a breakneck overgrowth of weedy electricity that nearly killed its initiates outright, pulled sixty-million-year-old circuits out by the roots.

Lianna was right: the path was subtle and complex beyond human imagining, controlled with molecular precision, tamed by whatever drugs and dark arts the Bicamerals used to keep all that overgrowth from running rampant. But when the rites and incantations had been spoken, when the deed had been done and the patient sewn up, it all came down to one thing:

They'd turned their brains into cancer.

"I was so worked up about Luckett." Brüks shook his head at his own stupidity. "We just left him back there to die, you know, we left all of them—but he would have died anyway, wouldn't he? As soon as he graduated. Every pathway that ever made him what he was, the cancer would eat it all and replace it with something . . ."

"Something better," Lianna said.

"That's a matter of opinion."

"You make it sound so horrible." Wrist seals. *Click click.* "But you know, you went through pretty much the same thing yourself and you don't seem any the worse for it."

He imagined coming apart. He imagined every thread of conscious experience fraying and dissolving and being eaten away. He imagined dying, while the body lived on.

"I don't think so," he said.

"Sure. When you were a baby." She laid a gloved hand on his shoulder. "We *all* start out with heads full of random mush; it's the neural pruning afterward that shapes who we are. It's like, like sculpture. You start with a block of granite, chip away the bits that don't belong, end up with a work of art. The Bicams just start over with a bigger block."

"But it's *not you.*"

"Enough of it is." She plucked her helmet out of the air.

"Sure, the *memories* stick." Some elements were spared: in the thalamus and cerebellum, hippocampus and brain stem all left carefully unscathed by a holocaust with the most discriminating taste. "But something else is remembering them."

"Dan, you gotta let go of this whole *self* thing. Identity changes by the second, you turn into someone else every time a new thought rewires your brain. You're already a different person than you were ten minutes ago." She lowered the helmet over her head, yanked it counterclockwise until it clicked into place. His fish-eye reflection slid bulging across her faceplate as she turned.

"What about you, Lianna?" he asked softly.

"What *about* me?" Her voice muffled and breathy across the glass.

"You aspiring to the same fate?"

She eyed him sadly from the bowl of her helmet. "It's not like you think. Really." And passed on to some farther shore.

THE INTUITIVE MIND IS A SACRED GIFT AND THE RATIONAL MIND IS A FAITHFUL SERVANT. WE HAVE CREATED A SOCIETY THAT HONORS THE SERVANT AND HAS FORGOTTEN THE GIFT.

—ALBERT EINSTEIN (APOCRYPHAL)

LOOK, BRÜKS WANTED to say: fifty thousand years ago there were these three guys spread out across the plain, and they each heard something rustling in the grass. The first one thought it was a tiger, and he ran like hell, and it *was* a tiger but the guy got away. The second one thought the rustling was a tiger, and *he* ran like hell, but it was only the wind and his friends all laughed at him for being such a chickenshit. But the third guy, *he* thought it was only the wind, so he shrugged it off and a tiger had him for dinner. And the same thing happened a million times across ten thousand generations—and after a while everyone was seeing tigers in the grass even when there weren't any tigers, because even chickenshits have more kids than corpses do. And from those humble beginnings we learned to see faces in the clouds and portents in the stars, to see agency in randomness, because natural selection favors the paranoid. Even here in the twenty-first century you can make people more honest just by scribbling a pair of eyes on the wall with a Sharpie. Even now, we are wired to believe that unseen things are watching us.

And it came to pass that certain people figured out how to *use* that. They painted their faces or they wore funny hats, they shook their rattles and waved their crosses and they said, *Yes, there are tigers in the grass, there are faces in the sky, and they will be very angry if you do not obey their commandments. You must make offerings to appease them, you must bring grain and gold and altar boys for our delectation or they will strike you down and send you to the Awful Place.* And people believed them by the billions, because after all, they could see the invisible tigers.

And you're a smart kid, Lianna. You're a bright kid and I like you but someday you've got to grow up and realize that it's all a trick. It's all just eyes scribbled on the wall, to make you think there's something looking back.

That's what Brüks wanted to say. And Lianna would listen, and ponder this new information, and she would come to see the wisdom of his argument. She would change her mind.

The only problem with this scenario was that it rapidly became obvious that she already *knew* all that stuff, and believed in invisible tigers anyway. It drove him up the fucking wall.

"That's not *God,*" she said one morning in the Commons, wide eyed with astonishment that he could have made such a stupid mistake. "That's just a bunch of ritualistic junk that got stuck onto God by people who wanted to hijack the agenda."

A derisive snort from over by the galley dispenser. "Between you two arguing about ghosts and Carnage stringing out on rotten bits"—Sengupta grabbed her breakfast and headed for the ladder—"I don't think I can handle five more minutes of this shit."

Brüks watched her go, turned his attention to a bulkhead window Lianna had opened into the Hold: shadows, machine parts, weightless bodies drawing dismembered components together into tangled floating jigsaws. Binary stars, sparkling in the gloom.

"If it's junk, why do they keep doing it?" He jerked his thumb at the display. "Why can't those guys go thirty minutes without doing that hand-washing thing of theirs?"

"Hand-washing reduces doubt and second-guessing in the wake of making a decision," Lianna told him. "Brains tend to take metaphors literally."

"Bullshit."

Her eyes defocused for an instant. "I've just sent you the citation. Of course, an actual tweak would be more efficient—I bet they do that, too, actually—but I think they like to remember where they came from. You'd be surprised how much folklore has survival value when you rip it up and look at the roots."

"I never said religious beliefs weren't *adaptive*. That doesn't make them true." Brüks spread his hands, palms up.

"What do you think *vision* is?" she asked him. "You don't see a fraction of the things that surround you, and at least half the things you *do* see are deceptive. Hell, *color* doesn't even exist outside your own head. Vision's just plain *wrong*; it only persists because it *works*. If you're going to dismiss the idea of God, you better stop believing your own eyes in the bargain."

"My *eyes* never told me to murder anyone who doesn't share my worldview."

"My *God* never told me to do that, either."

"Lots of people's Gods have."

"Riiight. And we're just gonna ignore everybody who quoted Darwin to justify turning people into slaves? Or wiping them out altogether?" He opened his mouth; she preempted him with a raised hand: "Let's just agree that neither side has a monopoly on assholes. The point is, once you recognize that *every* human model of reality is fundamentally unreal, then it all just comes down to which one works best. And science has had a damn good run, no question. But the sun is setting on the Age of Empiricism."

He snorted. "The Age of Empiricism is just getting started."

"Come on, Oldschool. We're long past the days when all you had to do was clock a falling apple or compare beak length in finches. Science has been running into limits ever since it started trying to get Schrödinger's cat to play with balls of invisible string. Go down a few orders of mag and everything's untestable conjecture again. Math and philosophy. You know as well as I do that reality has a *substructure*. Science can't go there."

"Nothing can. Faith may *claim*—"

"Knot theory," Lianna said. "Invented it for the sheer beauty of the artifact. We didn't have particle accelerators back then; we had no evidence at all that it would turn out to describe subatomic physics a century or two down the road. Pre-Socratic Greeks intuited atomic theory in *200 BC* Buddhists were saying centuries ago that we can't trust our senses, that sensation itself is an act of faith. Hinduism's predicated on the Self as illusion: no NMRs a thousand years ago, no voxel readers. No *evidence*. And damned if I can see the adaptive advantage of not believing in your own existence; but neurologically it happens to be true."

She beamed at him with the beatific glow of the true convert. "There's an *intuition,* Dan. It's capricious, it's unreliable, it's corruptible—but it's so *powerful* when it works, and it's no coincidence that it ties into the same parts of the brain that give you the rapture. The Bicamerals harnessed it. They amped the temporal and they rewired the parietals—"

"You mean ripped them out completely."

"—and they had to leave conventional language back in the dust, but they figured it out. Their *religion,* for want of a better word, goes places science can't. Science backs it up, as far as science can go; there's no reason to believe it doesn't keep right on working after it leaves science behind."

"You mean you have *faith* it keeps working," Brüks observed drily.

"Do you measure Earth's gravity every time you step outside? Do you reinvent quantum circuits from scratch whenever you boot up, just in case the other guys missed something?" She gave him a moment to answer. "Science *depends* on faith," she continued, when he didn't. "Faith that the rules haven't changed, faith that the other guys got the measurements right. All science ever did was measure a teensy sliver of the universe and assume that everything else behaved the same way. But the whole exercise falls apart if the universe doesn't follow consistent laws. How do you test if that's true?"

"If two experiments yield different results—"

"Happens all the time, my friend. And when it does, every good scientist discounts those results because they *failed to replicate.* One of the experiments must have been flawed. Or they both were. Or there's some unknown variable that'll make everything balance out just as soon as we discover what it is. The idea that physics *itself* might be inconsistent? Even if you considered the possibility in your wildest dreams, how could you test for it when the scientific method only works in a consistent universe?"

He tried to think of an answer.

"We've always thought c and friends ruled supreme, right out to the quasars and beyond," Lianna mused. "What if they're just— you know, some kind of local ordinance? What if they're a *bug?* Anyway"—she fed her plate into the recycler—"I gotta go. We're test-firing the chamber today."

"Look, science—" He marshaled his thoughts, unwilling to let

it go. "It's not just that it works. We know *how* it works. There's
no secret to it. It makes *sense*."

She wasn't looking at him. Brüks followed her eyes to the
bulkhead feed. They all seemed more or less mended by now—
Chinedum, Amratu, a handful of other demigods who'd never
be more than names and ciphers to him—although the pressure
still kept them captive for the moment. Still insufficiently omnipotent to speed the physics of decompression. It was a small
comfort.

"Those guys do *not* make sense," he continued. "They roll
around on the floor and ululate and you write up the patent applications. We don't know how it works, we don't know if it's
going to *keep* working, it could *stop* working at any moment. Science is more than magic and rituals—"

He stopped.

Ululations. Incantations. Hive harmonics.

Rituals.

These feeds have motion cap, he remembered.

Colonel Jim Moore crouched sideways against the Commons
wall like a monstrous grasshopper: legs folded tight at the knees,
spring-loaded and ready to pop; thorax folded over them like a
protective carapace; one hand dancing with some unseen Con-
Sensus interface while the other, wrapped around a convenient
cargo strap, held body to bulkhead. His eyes jiggled and danced
beneath closed lids: blind to this impoverished little shell of a
world, immersed in some other denied Daniel Brüks.

The grasshopper opened its eyes: glazed at first, clearing by
degrees.

"Daniel," it said dully.

"You look awful."

"I asked for an onboard cosmetics spa before we launched.
They went for a lab instead."

"When was the last time you ate?"

Moore frowned.

"That does it. I'm buying, you're eating." Brüks stepped over to the galley.

"But—"

"Unless you think that anorexia's the best way to prep for an extended field op."

Moore hesitated.

"Come on." Brüks punched in an order for salmon steak (he was still tickled by the fabber's proficiency with extinct meats). "Lianna's back in the Hold, and Rakshi's—being Rakshi. You want me eating with *Valerie*?"

"So this is a rescue mission." Moore unfolded himself onto the deck, relenting at last.

"That's the spirit. What do you want?"

"Just coffee."

Brüks glared at him.

"Okay, fine. Anything." The Colonel waved a hand in surrender. "Kruggets. With tandoori sauce."

Brüks winced and relayed the order, tossed a 'bulb of coffee across the compartment (Coriolis turned it into a curveball but Moore caught it anyway with barely a glance), grabbed one for himself and twisted the heat tab en route. He set the wobbly warming sphere onto the table and wound his way back to collect their meals.

"Still going over the *Theseus* data?" He pushed Moore's fluorescent krill across the table and sat down opposite.

"I thought the whole point of this was to get my mind *off* that."

"The point was to get you off your damn hunger strike," Brüks said. "And to get me something to talk to besides the walls."

Moore chewed, swallowed. "Don't say I didn't warn you."

"Warn me?"

"I distinctly remember raising the possibility—the likelihood, even—that you might be bored out of your skull."

"Believe me, I'm not complaining."

"Yes you are."

"Maybe a little." (Why did everything from the galley taste like *oil?*) "But it's not so bad. I got ConSensus, I got Lee to try and deprogram. Weigh a little cabin fever against getting stashed with the luggage for the next six months—"

"Believe me." Moore smiled faintly. "There are worse things than extended unconsciousness."

"For example?"

Moore didn't answer.

The *Crown* did, though. In an instant she turned half the bulkhead bloody with Intercom alarms.

SENGUPTA, they screamed.

Moore commed the Hub while Brüks was still peeling himself off the ceiling. "Rakshi. What—"

Her words cascaded back, high-pitched and panicky: "She's coming oh shit she's coming up she *knows*—"

A pit opened in Brüks's stomach.

"I'm onto her I think she knows of course she knows she's a fucking *vampire* she knows *everything*—"

"Rakshi, where—"

"Listen to me you stupid roach she kil—oh *fu*—"

The channel died before she could finish, but it didn't really matter. You could have heard the screaming halfway to Mars.

Moore was through the ceiling in an instant. Brüks followed in his wake, a jump up the ladder, a grab for a passing handhold, the endless loop of the conveyor pulling him smoothly along the weight-loss gradient from hab to Hub. Moore had no time for that shit; he shot up the ladder two rungs at a time, then three, then four. He ricocheted free-falling out the top of the spoke before the belt had drawn Brüks even halfway. That was okay. Maybe he'd have everything fixed by the time Brüks made it to the top, maybe Sengupta's screams of rage would end and calm soothing voices would murmur in their stead, intent on reconciliation . . .

Sengupta's screams ended.

He tried to ignore the other voices, the ones in his head saying *Go back, you idiot. Let Jim handle it, he's a soldier for chrissakes, what are you gonna do against a goddamn vampire? You're collateral. You're lunch.*

That's right, Backdoor. Just turn around and run away. Again.

The conveyor, insensitive, drew him forward into battle.

He emerged into the southern hemisphere, knees shaking. There were no calm voices. There were no voices at all.

There was no reconciliation.

The vampire clung one-handed to the grille. Her other hand held Sengupta by the throat, right at eye level, as if the pilot were a paper doll. Valerie looked impassively into her victim's eyes; Sengupta squirmed and choked and didn't look back.

The south pole was a bright gaping pit to stern. Its reflection smeared across the mirrorball like a round toothless mouth. An image flashed across Brüks's forebrain, courtesy of his hind: Valerie tossing Sengupta into that maw. The *Crown of Thorns* closing its mouth and *chewing.*

Moore edged along the Tropic of Capricorn, feet just above the deck, hands open at his sides.

"Okay, we can take it from here."

Not Moore. Lianna's voice, ringing calm and clear from the back of the *Crown's* throat. A moment later she sailed forth from its maw, fearless, light as air, heading directly for Valerie & Victim.

What's wrong *with her?* "Lianna, *don't——*"

"S'okay." She spared a glance. "I've got it under——"

And was cut down with the sudden crack of bones snapping under the impact of Valerie's foot, an obscene and elegant en pointe fired like a piston into Lutterodt's rib cage. She spun back toward the south pole, a rag doll with no fixed center of gravity; the *Crown* caught her spine in passing, bent it the wrong way, tossed her back down its throat from whence she'd come.

Fuck fuck fuck—

"Let her go," Moore was saying, his eyes still on Sengupta, calm as death. As though Lianna Lutterodt had never even made an appearance, as though she hadn't just been swatted like a mosquito. As though she couldn't possibly be bleeding out against the bulkhead a hundred meters to stern.

I have to help her.

Valerie kept eyes on Sengupta, head cocked like a predatory bird sizing up something shiny. "She attacks *me*." Her voice was distant, almost distracted: voicemail from a monster with other things on its mind.

Brüks crept forward, belly against bulkhead: a strut here, a cargo strap there, hand over hand toward the south pole.

"She's no threat." Moore was behind Valerie now, looking past her shoulder to her prey. The prey croaked softly. "There's no reason to—"

"Thank you for your tactical advice." A faint white smile ghosted across her lips.

Was that a faint moan sighing up through the *Crown*'s throat? Still conscious, then, maybe. Still hope.

"Trade," Valerie said.

"Yes," Moore replied, moving forward.

"Not you."

Suddenly Brüks was off the deck and yanked into the air; suddenly Valerie's hand was around his throat, gripping him just below the jaw with fingers cold and sinuous as tentacles while a distant irrelevant Rakshi Sengupta bounced off the southern hemisphere, hacking, doubled over.

And when Valerie looked at *him* with that bemused and distant stare, he looked back. He tried not to. Over the slow burning in his lungs, over the casual pain of a larynx compressed just this side of strangulation, he would have given anything to turn away. Somehow he didn't have the will. He couldn't even close his eyes against hers.

Her pupils were bright bloody pinpoints, red stars clenched tight against the light of day. Behind them, the bulkhead rolled past in lazy slow motion.

The Hub dwindled to the wrong end of a telescope. Sengupta was shouting somewhere, her voice raw and tinny and barely audible over the white noise of distant pounding surf: *She killed one of them she killed one of her zombies one of her* people *he's not on the board I can't find him anywhere*—

There was nothing in Valerie's face but that spectral half smile, that look of dispassionate appraisal. She didn't seem to notice Moore slipping up from behind, or Sengupta screaming headlong back into the fray with claws bared. She didn't even seem to notice her own left hand flicking back of its own accord to casually slap the pilot into the soldier, all that momentum spun impossibly on the head of a pin and redirected a hundred eighty degrees. *Fucking monster fucking monster fucking monster,* Sengupta shouted from across an ocean and Brüks could only think: *Cats and dogs cats and dogs . . .*

But none of that mattered. All that mattered were he and Valerie, alone together: the way she let just enough air past her fingers to keep him awake, the way she reached out with her free hand and tapped that light arrhythmic tattoo across his temple; the things she whispered for his ears only, intimate secrets of such vital importance he forgot them even as she breathed them out along his cheek.

Behind her, Jim Moore grabbed a cargo strap and braced his feet against the wall. Valerie didn't even bother to keep him in view.

"Is it true?" he asked quietly.

"Of course it's fucking true she's a *vampire* she'd kill *all* of—"

Moore, eyes locked on Valerie, raised a palm in Sengupta's direction. Sengupta shut up as if guillotined.

"You think this matters." There was distant amusement in Valerie's voice, as if she'd just seen a rabbit stand up on its hind legs and demand the right to vote.

"You think so, too," Moore began. "Or—"

"—you wouldn't have reacted," he and Valerie finished in sync. He tried again: "Were they under formal con . . . ," they chorused. He trailed off, an acknowledgment of futility. The vampire even matched his ellipsis without missing a beat.

Sengupta fumed silently across the compartment, too smart and too damn stupid to be scared. Brüks tried to swallow, gagged as his Adam's apple caught between the vice of Valerie's thumb and forefinger.

"Malawi," Valerie said quietly, and: "Not mission-critical."

Brüks swallowed again. *As if there's anyone on this goddamn ship who's less* mission-critical *than me.*

Maybe Moore was thinking it, too. Maybe he decided to act on behalf of Daniel Brüks, the Parasite That Walked Like a Man. Or maybe he just took advantage of his adversary's distraction, maybe it didn't have anything to do with Brüks at all. But something—changed subtly, in Moore's stance. His body seemed *looser,* somehow, more relaxed, incongruously taller at the same time.

Valerie was still eye to eye with Brüks, but it didn't matter. It was obvious from the way her smile widened and cracked, from the tiny *click* of teeth against teeth: she could see everything that mattered about Moore's face, reflected in his own.

She turned, almost lazily, tossed Brüks aside like a cigarette butt. Brüks flailed across the open spine; he barely missed a figure blurring past in the opposite direction. A cargo cube caught him and slapped him back off the deck. He doubled over, coughing, while Moore and Valerie danced in fast-forward. The monster's arms moved as though spun by a centrifuge; her body rebounded off the deck and shot through empty space where Jim Moore had existed a split second before.

"Fhat thouding do're."

Not a shout. Not even an exclamation. It didn't *sound* like a command. But those sounds reached into the Hub from the south pole and seemed to physically slap Valerie off target, reach right into the monster's head and grab her by the motor nerves. She twisted in midair, landed like a jumping spider on the curve of the bulkhead and froze there: eyes bright as halogen, mouth full of gleaming little shark teeth.

"*Juppyu imaké.*"

Moore rose from a defensive crouch, studied hands half-raised against blows that hadn't materialized. Brought them down again.

Chinedum Ofoegbu rose from the throat of the *Crown.*

You can't do that, Brüks thought, astonished. *You're stuck in the Hold for another three days.*

"*Prothat blemsto bethe?*" Ofoegbu's hands fluttered like a pianist's against an invisible keyboard. The light in his eyes slithered like the aurora borealis.

I don't care how smart you are. You're still made out of meat. You can't just step out of a decompression chamber.

The Bicameral's blood must be fizzing in its flesh. All those bubbles out on early parole, all those gases freed from the weight of too many atmospheres: all set loose to party it up in the joints and capillaries . . .

One's all it'll take, one tiny bubble in the brain. A pinpoint embolism in the right spot and you're dead, just like that.

"Your *vampire*—" Sengupta began, before Moore preempted her with: "We have some *mission-critical* issues to deal with . . ."

But there is no you anymore, is there? You're just a body part, just a node in a network. Expendable. When the hive cuts you loose, will you get it all back? Will Chinedum Ofoegbu wake up in time to die a roach's death? Will he change his mind too late, will he have a chance to feel betrayed before he stops feeling anything at all?

Ofoegbu coughed a fine red mist into the room. Blood and stars bubbled in his eyes. He began to fold at the middle.

Lianna Lutterodt climbed up in his wake, bent in on herself, one arm clenched tight to her side. With the other she reached out, wincing; but her master was too far away. She pushed off the lip of the south pole, floated free, caught him. Every movement took a visible toll.

"If you people are through trying to kill each other"—she coughed, tried again—"maybe someone could help me get him back to the Hold before he fucking *dies*."

"Holy *shit*," Brüks said, dropping back into Commons. The node was back with its network. Lianna was meshed and casted and had retreated to her rack while her broken parts stitched themselves back together.

Moore had already cracked open the scotch. He held out a glass.

Brüks almost giggled. "Are you kidding? *Now?*"

The Colonel glanced at the other man's hands: they trembled. "Now."

Brüks took the tumbler, emptied it. Moore refilled it without asking.

"This can't go on," Brüks said.

"It won't. It didn't."

"So Chinedum stopped her. This time. And it just about killed him."

"Chinedum was only the interface, and she knows that. She would have gained nothing and risked everything by attacking him."

"What if she'd pulled that shit a few days ago? What if she pulls it again?" He shook his head. "Lee could have been *killed*. It was just dumb luck that—"

"We got off lightly," Moore reminded him. "Compared to some."

Brüks fell silent. *She killed one of her zombies.*

"Why did she do it?" he asked after a moment. "Food? Fun?"

"It's a problem," the Colonel admitted. "Of course it's a problem."

"Can't we do anything?"

"Not at the moment." He took a breath. "Technically, Sengupta *did* attack first."

"Because Valerie *killed* someone!"

"We don't know that. And even if she did, there are—jurisdictional issues. She may have been within her rights, legally. Anyway, it doesn't matter."

Brüks stared, speechless.

"We're a hundred million klicks from the nearest legitimate authority," Moore reminded him. "Any that might happen by wouldn't look more kindly on us than on Valerie. Legalities are irrelevant out here; we just have to play the hand we're dealt. Fortunately we're not entirely on our own. The Bicamerals are at least as smart and capable as she is. Smarter."

"I'm not worried about their *capabilities*. I don't trust them."

"Do you trust me?" Moore asked unexpectedly.

Brüks considered a moment. "Yes."

The Colonel inclined his head. "Then trust them."

"I trust your *intentions*," Brüks amended softly.

"Ah. I see."

"You're too close to them, Jim."

"No closer than you've been, lately."

"They had their hooks into you *way* before I joined the party. You and Lianna, the way you just—*accept* everything . . ."

Moore said nothing.

Brüks tried again. "Look, don't get me wrong. You went up against a vampire for us, and you could've been killed, and I know that. I'm grateful. But we got lucky, Jim: you're usually wrapped up in that little ConSensus shell you've built for yourself, and if Valerie had chosen any other time to torque out—"

"I'm *wrapped up in that shell*," Moore said levelly, "dealing with a potential threat to the whole—"

"Uh-huh. And how many new insights have you gained, squeezing the same signals over and over again since we broke orbit?"

"I'm sorry if that leaves you feeling vulnerable. But your fears are unfounded. And in any case"—Moore swallowed his own dram—"planetary security has to take priority."

"This isn't about planetary security," Brüks said.

"Of course it is."

"Bullshit. It's about your son."

Moore blinked.

"Siri Keeton, synthesist on the *Theseus* mission," Brüks continued, more gently. "It's not as though the crew roster was any kind of secret."

"So." Moore's voice was glassy and expressionless. "You're not as completely self-absorbed as you appear."

"I'll take that as a compliment," Brüks tried.

"Don't. The presence of my son on that mission doesn't change the facts on the ground. We're dealing with agents of unknown origin and vastly superior technology. It is my *job*—"

"And you're doing that job with a brain that still runs on love and kin selection and all those other Stone Age things we seem hell-bent on cutting out of the equation. That would be enough to tear anyone apart, but it's even harder for you, isn't it? Because one of those facts on the ground is that you're the reason he was out there in the first place."

"He's out there because he's the most qualified for the mission. Full stop. Anyone in my place would have made the same decision."

"Sure. But we both know *why* he was the most qualified."

Moore's face turned to granite.

"He was most qualified," Brüks continued, "because he got certain augments during childhood. And he got those augments because you chose a certain line of work with certain risks, and one day some asshole with a grudge and a splicer kit took a shot at you and hit him instead. You think it's your fault that some Realist fuckwit missed the target. You blame yourself for what happened to your son. It's what parents *do*."

"And you know all about being a parent."

"I know about being *Human*, Jim. I know what people tell

themselves. You made Siri the man for the job before he was even born, and when the Fireflies dropped in you had to put him at the top of the list and ship him out and now all you've got is those goddamned signals, that's your last link, and I *understand,* man. It's natural, it's Human, it's, it's *inevitable* because you and I, we haven't gotten around to cutting those parts out of us yet. But just about everyone else around here has, and we can't afford to ignore that. We can't afford to be—distracted. Not here, not *now.*"

He held out his glass, and felt a vague and distant kind of relief at how steady his hand was around the crystal. Colonel Jim Moore regarded it for a moment. Looked back at the half-empty bottle.

"Bar's closed," he said.

PREY

Of greater concern are the smaller networks pioneered by the so-called Bicameral Order, which—while having shown no interest in any sort of military or political activism—remain susceptible to weaponization. Although this faction shares tenuous historical kinship with the Dharmic religions behind the Moksha Mind, they do not appear to be pursuing that group's explicit goal of self-annihilation; each Bicameral hive is small enough (hence, of sufficiently low latency) to sustain a coherent sense of conscious self-awareness. This would tend to restrict their combat effectiveness both in terms of response-latency and effective size. However, the organic nature of Bicameral MHIs leaves them less susceptible to the signal-jamming countermeasures that bedevil hard-tech networks. From the standpoint of brute military force, therefore, the Bicamerals probably represent the greatest weaponization potential amongst the world's extant mind hives. This is especially troubling in light of the number of technological and scientific advances attributable to the

Order in recent years, many of which have already proven destabilizing.

—J. Moore, "Hive Minds, Mind Hives, and
Biological Military Automata: The Role of
Collective Intelligence in Offline Combat,"
Journal of Military Technology 68 no. 14
(December 3, 2095)

BEHOLD, I STAND AT THE DOOR AND KNOCK.
—REVELATION 3:20

A SUN GROWN huge. A shadow on its face. A fleck, then a freckle: a dot, a disk, a *hole*. Smaller than a sunspot—darker, more symmetrical—and then larger. It grew like a perfect tumor, a black planetary disk where no planet could be, swelling across the photosphere like a ravenous singularity. A sun that covered half the void: a void that covered half the sun. Some critical, razor-thin instant passed and foreground and background had switched places, the sun no longer a disk but a brilliant golden iris receding around a great dilating pupil. Now it was less than that, a fiery hoop around a perfect starless hole; now a circular thread, writhing, incandescent, impossibly fine.

Gone.

A million stars winked back into the firmament, cold dimensionless pinpricks strewn in bands and random handfuls across half the sky. But the other half remained without form and void— and now the tumor that had swallowed the sun was gnawing outward at the stars as well. Brüks looked away from that great maw and saw a black finger lancing through the starfield directly to port: a dark spire, five hundred kilometers long, buried deep in the shade. Brüks downshifted his personal spectrum a few angstroms and it glowed red as an ember, an infrared blackbody rising from the exact center of the disk ahead. Heat radiator. A hairbreadth from the center of the solar system, it never saw the sun.

He tugged nervously at the webbing holding him to the mirrorball. Sengupta was strapped into her usual couch on his left,

Lianna to his right, Moore to hers. The old warrior had barely said a word to him since Brüks had broached the subject of his son. Some lines were invisible until crossed, apparently.

Or maybe they were perfectly visible, to anyone who wasn't an insensitive dolt. Empiricists always kept their minds open to alternative hypotheses.

He sought refuge in the view outside, dark to naked eyes but alive on tactical. Icons, momentum vectors, trajectories. A thin hoop of pale emerald shrank across the forward view, drawing tight around the *Crown*'s nose: the rim of her reflective parasol—erased from ConSensus in deference to an uninterrupted view—redundant now, spooling tight into stowage. The habs had already been folded back and tied down for docking. Beyond the overlays, the *Crown* fell silently past massive structures visible only in their absence: shadows against the sky, the starless silhouettes of gantries and droplet-conveyors, endless invisible antennae belied by the intermittent winking of pilot lights strung along their lengths.

The *Crown* bucked. Thrusters flared like the sparks of arc welders in the darkness ahead. *Down* returned, dead forward. Brüks fell gently from the couch into the elastic embrace of his harness, hung there while the *Crown*'s incandescent brakes gave dim form to the face of a distant cliff: girders, the cold dead cones of dormant thrusters, great stratified slabs of polytungsten. Then the sparks died, and *down* with them. All that distant topography vanished again. The *Crown of Thorns* continued to fall, gently as thistledown.

"Looks normal so far," Moore remarked to no one in particular.

"Wasn't there supposed to be some kind of standing guard?" Brüks wondered. There'd been an announcement, anyway, in the weeks after Firefall. *While we have seen no evidence of ill will on the part of* blah blah blah *prudent to be cautious* yammer yammer *cannot afford to leave such a vital source of energy undefended in the current climate of uncertainty* yammer blah.

Moore said nothing. After a moment Lianna took up the slack: "The place is almost impossible to see in the glare unless you know where to look. And there's nothing like a bunch of big obvious heatprints going back and forth for telling the other guys where to look."

It was as much as she'd said—to Brüks, at least—since Valerie had flexed her claws in the Hub. He took it as a good sign.

More sparks, tweaking the night in split-second bursts. Wireframes crawled all over tactical now, highlighting structures the naked eye could barely discern even as shadows. Constellations ignited on the cliff ahead, lights triggered by the presence of approaching mass, dim and elegant as the photophores of deep-sea fish. Candles in the window to guide travelers home. They rippled and flowed and converged on a monstrous gray lamprey uncoiling from the landscape beneath. Its great round mouth pulsed and puckered and closed off the port bow.

One final burst of counterthrust. The lamprey flinched, recoiled a meter or two, resumed its approach. The *Crown* was barely moving now. The lamprey closed on the port flank and attached itself to the docking hatch.

"We are down to fumes felching Bicams better know what they're doing because even our *chemical* just ran dry," Sengupta reported. "You want this ship to go anywhere now you gotta get out and push."

"Not a problem," Moore said. "We're sitting on the biggest charger in the solar system."

Lianna looked at Brüks and tried to smile.

"Welcome to Icarus."

Of course, no one was going to fuck on a first date.

The sky in the Hub began to fill with handshakes and head shots: Icarus and the *Crown* introducing each other, coming to terms, agreeing that this little rendezvous was an intimate affair that really didn't warrant the involvement of Earthbound engineers.

Sengupta whispered sweet nothings to the station's onboard, coaxed it into turning on the lights, booting up life-support, maybe sharing a few pages from its diary.

Naked bodies floated up from the lower hemisphere. Eulali and one of the other Bicamerals (*Haina*, Brüks thought), purged of hostile microbes and decompressed at last, slumming it with the baselines. Nobody seemed to think it worthy of comment.

"No one since the last on-site op check." Sengupta jabbed one finger at a window full of alphanumeric gibberish. "Nobody came or went anytime in the last eighteen months. Boosters fired a hundred ninety-two days ago to stabilize the orbit but nothing else."

Sudden swift movement from the corners of both eyes: the undead in formation, shooting single-file through the hatch like raptors diving for a kill. They bounced off the sky, swung around the forward ladder, disappeared through the ceiling fast and fluid as barracuda.

So much for the pack, Brüks thought nervously. *What about the Alph*—and didn't finish the question, because the flesh crawling up his backbone had just given him the answer.

She was right behind him. For all he knew, she always had been. The Bicamerals didn't seem to notice. They hadn't taken their eyes off tactical since they'd arrived. Brüks swallowed and forced his gaze left. He forced himself to turn. He resisted the urge to lower his gaze as Valerie came into view, forced himself to look her right in the eyes. They shone back at him. He gritted his teeth and thought very hard about leucophores and thin-film optics and finally realized: *She's not even looking at me.*

She wasn't. Those bright monster eyes burned a path right past him to the dome behind, shifted and jiggled in microscopic increments to this datum or that image, jittered fast as the eyes of zombies and with twice the intensity. Brüks could almost *see* the brain sparking behind those lenses, the sheets of electricity soaking up information faster than fiber. It had all of them now, monks and monsters and minions alike, all of them finally brought together under a tiny metal sky crowded with the machinery of thought:

boot sequences, diagnostics, the sprawling multidimensional vistas of a thousand mechanical senses. It threatened to overflow the hemisphere entirely, a ceaseless flickering infostorm that breached the equator and started spilling aft as Brüks watched.

Crude as papyrus, he realized. All these dimensions, squashed flat and pasted across physical space: it was a medium for cavemen and cockroaches, not these cognitive giants looming on all sides. Why were they even here? Why come together in the land of the blind when ConSensus went on forever, arrayed endless intelligence throughout the infinite space within their own heads? Why settle for eyes of jelly when invisible signals could reach through bone and brain and doodle on the very synapses themsel—

Shit, he thought.

All that smart paint, so ubiquitous throughout the ship. He'd just assumed it was for ambient lighting, and a backup for backups should the implants fail in one of these overclocked brains. But now it seemed to be their preferred interface: crude, pointillist, *extrinsic.* Not completely unhackable, perhaps—but at least any intrusions would take place outside the head, would compromise the mech and not the meat. At least no alien, imagined or otherwise, would be rewriting the thoughts in the heads of the hive.

A few years to settle in, Moore had said. A few years for parties unknown to study new and unfamiliar technology, to infer the nature of the softer things behind it. Years to build whatever gears and interfaces an unlimited energy source could provide, and sit back, and wait for the owners to arrive. All that time for anything *in there* to figure out how to get *in here.*

They're afraid, Brüks realized, and then:

Shit, they're *afraid?*

Sengupta threw a row of camera feeds across the dome. Holds and service crawlways, mainly: tanks for the storage of programmable matter, warrens of tunnels where robots on rails slid along on endless missions of repair and resupply. Habs embedded here and there like lymph nodes, vacuoles to be grudgingly pumped full of warmth and atmosphere on those rare occasions when

visitors came calling—but barren, uninviting, barely big enough
to stand erect even if gravity had been an option. Icarus was an
ungracious host, resentful of any parasites that sought to take up
residence in her gut.

Something had done that anyway.

Sengupta grabbed that window and stretched it across a fifth
of the dome: AUX/RECOMP according to the feed, a cylindrical
compartment with another cylinder—segmented, ribbed, studded with conduits and access panels and eruptions of high-voltage
cabling—running through its center like a metal trachea. The
view brightened as they watched. Fitful sparks ignited along the
walls, caught steady, dimmed to a soft lemon glow that spread
across painted strips of bulkhead. Wisps of frozen vapor swirled
in weightless arabesques before some reawakened ventilator sucked
them away.

Brüks had educated himself on the way down. He knew what
he'd find if he were to cut that massive windpipe down the middle.
At one end a great black compound eye, a honeycomb cluster
of gamma-ray lasers aimed along the lumen of the tube. Pumps
and field coils encircled that space at regular intervals: superconductors, ultrarefrigeration pipes to bring some hypothetical vacuum down to a hairbreadth of absolute zero. Matter took on
strange forms inside that chamber. Atoms would lie down, forget
about Brown and entropy, take a message from the second law of
thermodynamics and promise to get back to it later. They would
line up head to toe and lock into place as a single uniform substrate. A trillion atoms would condense into one vast entity: a blank
slate, waiting for energy and information to turn it into something new.

Theseus had fed from something a lot like this, part of the same
circuit in fact. Maybe it was feeding still. And down at the far end
of AUX/RECOMP, past the lasers and the magnets and the micro-
channel plate traps, Brüks could see something else, something—

Wrong.

That was all he could tell, at first: something just a little bit *off* about the far end of the compiler. It took a few moments to notice the service port just slightly ajar, the stain leaking from its edges. His brain shuffled through a thousand cue cards and tried *spilled paint* on for size, but that didn't really fit. It looked too thick, too blobby for the smart stuff; and he'd seen no other surface painted that oily shade of gray on any of the other feeds.

Then someone zoomed the view and a whole new set of cues clicked into place.

Those branching, filigreed edges: like rootlets, like dendrites growing along the machinery.

"Is it still coming through?" Lianna's voice, a little dazed.

"Don't be stupid you don't think I'd *mention* it if it was? Wouldn't work anyway some idiot left the port open."

But life support had been shut down until the *Crown* had docked, Brüks remembered. Vacuum throughout. "Maybe it was running until you pressurized the habs. Maybe we—interrupted it."

Those little pimply lumps, like—like some kind of early-stage fruiting bodies . . .

"I *told* you I'd mention it Jesus the logs say no juice for weeks."

"Assuming we can trust the logs," Moore said softly.

"It looks almost like dumb paint of some kind," Lianna remarked.

Brüks shook his head. "Looks like a slime mold."

"Whatever it is," Moore said, "it's not something any of our people would have sent down. Which raises an obvious question."

It did. But nobody asked it.

Of course, no slime mold could survive in hard vacuum at absolute zero.

"Name one thing that can," Moore said.

"*Deinococcus* comes close. Some of the synthetics come closer."

"But *active?*"

"No," Brüks admitted. "They pretty much shut down until conditions improve."

"So whatever that is"—Moore gestured at the image—"you're saying it's dormant."

Stranger even than the thing in the window: the experience of being asked for an opinion by anyone on the *Crown of Thorns*. The mystery lasted long enough for Brüks to glance sideways and see monks and vampire clustered in a multimodal dialogue of clicks and phonemes and dancing fingers. The Bicamerals faced away from each other; they hovered in an impromptu knot, each set of eyes aimed out along a different bearing.

Jim may be Colonel Supersoldier to me, Brüks realized, *but we're all just capuchins next to those things . . .*

"I said—"

"Sorry." Brüks shook his head. "No, I'm not saying that. I mean, *look* at it: it's outside the chamber, part of it, anyway. You tell me if there's some way for that machine to assemble matter *off* the condenser plate."

"So it must have—grown."

"That's the logical conclusion."

"In hard vacuum, near absolute zero."

"Maybe not so logical. I don't have another answer." Brüks jerked his chin toward the giants. "Maybe they do."

"It *escaped*."

"If that's what you want to call it. Not that it got very far." The stain—or slime mold, or whatever it was—spread less than two meters from the open port before petering out in a bifurcation of rootlets. Of course, it shouldn't have even been able to do that much.

The damn thing looked *alive*. As much as Brüks kept telling himself not to jump to conclusions, not to judge alien apparitions by earthly appearance, the biologist was too deeply rooted in him. He looked at that grainy overblown image and he didn't see any random collection of molecules, didn't even see an exotic crystal growing along some predestined lattice of alignment. He saw something organic—something that couldn't have just *coalesced* from a diffuse cloud of atoms.

He turned to Moore. "You're sure Icarus's telematter technology isn't just a wee bit more advanced than you let on? Maybe closer to actual fabbing? Because that looks a lot like complex macrostructure to me."

Moore turned away and fixed Sengupta with a stare: "Did it— break out? Force open the port?"

She shook her head and kept her eyes on the ceiling. "No signs of stress or metal fatigue nothing popped nothing broken no bits floating around. Just looks like someone ran a standard diagnostic took out the sample forgot to close the door."

"Pretty dumb mistake," Brüks remarked.

"Cockroaches make dumb mistakes all the time."

And one of the biggest, Brüks did not say, *was building you lot.*

" 'Course there's only so much you can see with a camera you gotta go in there and check to be sure."

Up on the sky, the slime mold beckoned with a million filigreed fingers.

"So that's the next step, right?" Brüks guessed. "We board?"

A grunted staccato from Eulali, with fingertip accompaniment. From any other primate it might have sounded like a laugh. The node spared him a look and returned her attention to the dome.

It wasn't English. Brüks supposed it wasn't even language, not the way he'd define it at least. But somehow he knew exactly what Eulali had meant.

You first.

Two hours later four of the Bicamerals and a couple of Valerie's zombies were on the hull crawling forward along the *Crown*'s spine with a retinue of maintenance spiders, hauling torches and lasers and wrenches behind them. Two hours to start making half a ship whole again.

Three days to screw up the courage to go anywhere else.

Oh, they laid the groundwork. Sengupta did cam-by-cams of the whole frozen array, hijacked a couple of maintenance bots and sent them through every accessible corner and cranny. Brüks couldn't make out any angels on the feeds. No asteroids, either, for that matter. He was starting to wonder if that code-name hadn't been a red herring—a phrase set loose across the ether so pursuers wouldn't think twice when the *Crown* relit her engines half-way through the innersys and accelerated away to some farther destination.

Squinting as hard as she could, all Sengupta could see was a small dark suspicion that disappeared when you laid an error bar across it: "Station allometry's off by a few millimeters but it'd be weirder if you *didn't* get shrinkage and expansion with all the heat flux." The hive huddled together and passed occasional instructions through Lianna: *Bring the condenser up to twenty atmospheres. Freeze the chamber. Heat the chamber. Turn out the lights. Turn them on again. Vent the condenser back to vacuum. Here, fab this SEM and bot it over.*

The elephant in the room refused to rise to any flavor of bait. After three days, Brüks was itching for action.

"They want you to stay here," Lianna said apologetically. "For your own safety."

They floated in the attic, the *Crown*'s viscera hissing and gurgling about them as a procession of Bicamerals climbed into spacesuits at the main airlock. A globe of water, held together by surface tension, wobbled in midair just off the beaten path. The soft light spilling from the lamprey's mouth washed everything in robin's egg.

"*Now* they're interested in my safety."

She sighed. "We've been over this, Dan."

Valerie emerged from the Hub and bared her teeth as she sailed past. Her fingers trailed along a bundle of coolant pipes, lightly tapping an arrhythmic tattoo. Brüks glanced at Lianna; Lianna glanced away. Up the attic, Ofoegbu plunged his hands into the water; pulled them out; rubbed them together before donning his gauntlets.

"You're going, though," Brüks observed. To work side by side with the creature who had nearly killed her without so much as a glance in her direction. He'd edged around the subject in casual conversation, what little of that there'd been lately. She hadn't seemed to want to talk about it.

"It's my job," she said now. "But you know, we're even keeping Jim pretty much in the background."

That surprised him. "Really?"

"We might bring him over once we're a little more sure of our footing—he *was* ground control for the *Theseus* mission, after all— but even then he'll mostly be remoting in from the *Crown.* The Bicams don't want to expose anyone to unnecessary risk. Besides"— she shrugged—"what would you do over there anyway?"

Brüks shrugged. "Watch. Explore." Farther up the hall, the blob shuddered afresh as the node called Jaingchu washed away her sins. *Why do all the bodies do that,* he wondered, *if there's only one mind behind them all?*

"You'll get better real-time intel back here."

"I guess." He shook his head. "You're right, of course. They're right. I'm just—going a bit stir-crazy in here."

"I'd have thought you'd want *less* excitement in your life. The way things have been going lately, boredom's something we should be *aspiring* to." She managed a smile, laid a hand on his arm. "You'll be as good as there. Looking right over my shoulder."

Sengupta grunted from her couch as Brüks drifted back into the Hub. "So they won't let you out to play."

"They will not," he admitted, and settled in beside her.

"Better view from here." One foot tapped absently against the deck. "Wouldn't wanna be over there anyway, not with that lot can't even talk to them they got *shitty* manners in case you hadn't noticed. Wouldn't go over there if you paid me."

"Thanks," Brüks said.

"For what?"

For trying. For the comforting scritch between the ears.

Sengupta waved her hand as if spreading a deck of cards: a row of camera windows bloomed left to right across the dome. Gloved hands, visors, the backs of helmets; tactical overlays describing insides and outsides in luminous time-series.

The lamprey opened its mouth. The Bicameral entourage swam innocently down its throat.

Brüks pulled on his hood and booted up the motion sensors.

He wasn't entirely useless. They set him to work reseeding the astroturf panels; scraping away the dead brittle stuff that had been sacrificed to cold and vacuum on the way down; spraying fresh nutrigel into the bulkhead planters; spraying, in turn, a mist of microscopic seeds into the gel. The treated surfaces began to green up within the hour, but rather than watch the grass grow he looked on from a distance while Bicams and zombies swarmed across Icarus like army ants, carving great cookie-cutter chunks of polytungsten from its flanks and hauling them back to that jagged gaping stump where the *Crown* had been torn in two. Eventually they let him outside; the array itself was still off-limits but they let him help out closer to home, tutored him in the use of heavy machinery and set him loose on the *Crown*'s hull. He torched pins and struts on command, helped shear the parasol free from its mooring at the bow and haul it aft; helped cut precise holes in its center for improvised thrusters that could stare down the heat of ten suns.

Other times he sat restlessly in the Hub while Sengupta ran numbers across the wall, this many tonnes and that many kilonewtons and so much Isp thrust. He'd tap into AUX/RECOMP and watch Valerie and Ofoegbu and Amina at work, scientific and religious paraphernalia floating about their heads as they attempted communion with an impossible slime mold from the stars. He'd capture their movements and their incantations, feed them to a private database he'd been building since before the *Crown* had docked. Sometimes Jim Moore would be there; other times Brüks would catch him sequestered in some far-off corner of the *Crown,* adrift on a sea of old telemetry that had nothing to do with his son, nothing at all, just facts on the ground.

The Colonel was always civil, these days. Never more.

When the sight of people in more productive roles failed to satisfy, Brüks abandoned Icarus's bustling tourist district and went off by himself, cam by cam: stepped through views of empty crawlspaces and frozen habs, an endless dark maze of tunnels connecting the uninhabited and the unexplored. Sometimes there was atmosphere, and frost sparkling on bulkheads. Sometimes there was only vacuum and girders and rails along which prehensile machinery scuttled like platelets in a mechanical bloodstream.

Once there were stars where no stars should have been: a great hole bitten out of Icarus's carapace where it would do the least damage. Brüks could see incendiary Bicameral teeth through the gap, brilliant blue pinpoints taking another bite farther down the hull. Even filtered by the camera, they made him squint.

Next stop.

Ah. AUX/RECOMP again, more crowded than before: Moore had joined Valerie and the Bicamerals at play.

Just another roach, Brüks thought. *Just like me.*

But you get a seat at the table just the same.

He watched in silence for a few moments.

Fuck this.

Pale blue light spilled into the attic from the open airlock, limned the edges of pipes and lockers and empty alcoves. Brüks sailed through the hatch, grabbed a strut in passing, swung to port and into the glowing mouth of the lamprey itself.

Eyes hypersaccading in an ebony face, snapping instantly into focus. A body rooted to the airlock wall by one arm, fingers clenched around a convenient handhold. Spring-loaded prosthetics below the knees; they extended absurdly and braced against a bulkhead, blocking Brüks's way.

He braked just in time.

"Restricted access, sir," the zombie said, eyes dancing once more.

"Holy shit. You talk."

The zombie said nothing.

"I didn't think there'd be—anyone in there," Brüks tried. Nothing. "Are you awake?"

"No, sir."

"So you're talking in your sleep."

Silence. Eyes, jiggling in their sockets.

I wonder if it knows what happened to the other one. I wonder if it was there . . .

"I want to—"

"You can't, sir."

"Will you—"

"Yes, sir."

—stop me?

"Yes but it won't be necessary," the zombie added.

Brüks had been wondering about lethal force. Maybe best not to push that angle.

On the other hand, the thing didn't seem to mind answering questions . . .

"Why do your ey—"

"To maximize acquisition of high-res input across the visual field, sir."

"Huh." Not a trick the conscious mind could use, with its limited bandwidth. A good chunk of so-called vision actually consisted of preconscious filters deciding what *not* to see, to spare the homunculus upstream from information overload.

"You're black," Brüks observed. "Most of you zombies are black."

No response.

"Does Valerie have a melanin feti—"

"I've got this," Moore said, rising into view through the docking tube. The zombie moved smoothly aside to let him pass.

"They talk," Brüks said. "I didn't—"

Moore spared a glance at Brüks's face as he moved past. Then he was back on board, and heading aft. "Come with me, please."

"Uh, where?"

"M&R. Freckle on your face I don't like the look of." Moore disappeared into the Hub.

Brüks looked back at the airlock. Valerie's sentry had moved back into place, blocking the way to more exotic locales.

"Thanks for the chat," Brüks said. "We'll have to do it again sometime."

"Close your eyes."

Brüks obeyed; the insides of his lids glowed brief bloody red as Moore's diagnostic laser scanned down his face.

"Word of advice," the Colonel said from the other side. "Don't tease the zombies."

"I wasn't teasing him, I was just chat—"

"Don't chat with them, either."

Brüks opened his eyes. Moore was running his eyes down some invisible midair diagnostic. "Remember who they answer to," he added.

"I can't imagine that Valerie forgot to swear her minions to secrecy."

"And I can't imagine her minions will forget to tell her any secrets you might have asked about. Whether they answered or not."

Brüks considered that. "You think she might take offense at the melanin-fetish remark?"

"I have no idea," Moore said quietly. "*I* sure as hell did."

Brüks blinked. "I—"

"You look at them." There was liquid nitrogen in the man's voice. "You see—zombies. Fast on the draw, good in the field, less than human. Less than animals, maybe; not even conscious. Maybe you don't even think it's *possible* to disrespect something like that. Like disrespecting a lawn mower, right?"

"No, I—"

"Let me tell you what I see. The man you were *chatting* with was called Azagba. Aza to his buddies. But he gave that up— either for something he believed in, or because it was the best of a bad lot of options, or because it was the only option he had. You look at Valerie's entourage and you see a cheap joke. *I* see the seventy-odd percent of military bioauts recruited from places where armed violence runs so rampant that nonexistence as a conscious being is actually something you *aspire* to. I see people who got mowed down on the battlefield and then rebooted, just long enough to make a choice between going back to the grave or paying off the jump-start with a decade of blackouts and indentured servitude. And that's pretty close to the *best*-case scenario."

"What would be worst-case?"

"Some jurisdictions still hold that life ends at death," Moore told him. "Anything else is an animated corpse. In which case Azagba has exactly as many rights as a cadaver in an anatomy class." He stabbed the air and nodded: "I was right: it's precancerous."

Malawi, Brüks remembered.

"That's why you took her on," he realized. "Not for me, not for Sengupta. Not even for the mission. Because she killed one of your own."

Moore looked right through him. "I would have thought that by now you'd have learned to keep your attempts at psychoanalysis to yourself." He extracted a tumor pencil from the first-aid kit. "Any nausea? Headaches, dizziness? Loose stools?"

Brüks brought his hand to his face. "Not yet."

"Probably nothing to worry about, but we'll run a complete body scan just to be safe. Could be internal lesions as well." He leaned in, pressed the pencil against Brüks's face. Something electrical snapped in Brüks's ear; a sudden tingling warmth spread out across his cheek.

"I'd recommend daily scans from here on in," Moore said. "Our shielding on approach wasn't all it could have been." He gestured for Brüks to move to the right, unfolded the medbed from the wall. "I have to admit I'm a bit surprised this started so soon, though. Maybe you had a preexisting condition." He stood aside. "Lie back."

Brüks maneuvered himself over the pallet; Moore strapped him into place against the free fall. A biomedical collage bloomed across the bulkhead.

"Uh, Jim . . ."

The soldier kept his eyes on the scan.

"Sorry."

Moore grunted. "Perhaps I shouldn't have expected you to be so fast on the uptake." He paused. "It's not as though you're some kind of zombie."

"Roaches, you know—we fuck up," Brüks admitted.

"Yes. I forget that sometimes." The Colonel took a breath, let it out softly through clenched teeth. "Before you showed up, I— well . . ."

Brüks waited in silence, fearful of tipping some scale.

"It's been a while," Moore said, "since I've had much call to deal with my own kind."

> GOD CREATED THE NATURAL NUMBERS. ALL ELSE IS
> THE WORK OF MAN.
> —LEOPOLD KRONECKER

"GOT SOMETHING FOR you."

It was a white plastic clamshell, about the size and shape to hold a set of antique eyeglasses. Lianna had fabbed a bright green bow and stuck it to the top.

Brüks eyed it suspiciously. "What is it?"

"The Face of God," she declared, and then—deflated by the look he shot at her, "That's kind of what the hive's calling it, anyway. Piece of your slime mold." She held it out with a flourish. "If Muhammad can't come to the sample . . ."

"Thanks." He took the offering (try as he might, he couldn't keep from smiling), and set it on the table next to dessert.

"They thought you'd like to take a shot at, you know. Seeing what makes it tick."

Brüks glanced at a bulkhead window where three Bicamerals floated at the compiler, their gazes divergent as was their wont. (Not any Senguptoid aversion to eye contact, he'd come to realize; just the default preference for a 360-degree visual field, adopted by a collective with eyes to share.) "Are they throwing me a bone, or do they just want someone expendable doing the dissections?"

"A bone, maybe. But you know, this thing does have certain biological properties. And you are the only biologist on board."

"Roach biologist. And that slime mold's got to be *post*biological if it's anything at all. And you know as well as I do that I've got better odds of getting a blow job from Valerie than—"

He caught himself, too late. *Idiot. Stupid, insensitive—*

"Maybe not," Lianna said after a pause so brief it might have been imaginary. "But you're the only one in the neighborhood with a biologist's perspective."

"You—you think that makes a difference?"

"Sure. More to the point, I think they do, too."

Brüks thought about that. "I'll try not to let them down, then." And then: "Lee—"

"So what you doing here, anyway?" She leaned in for a closer look at his display. "You're running mo-cap."

He nodded, wary of speech.

"What for? Slimey hasn't moved since we got here."

"I'm, uh . . ." He shrugged and confessed. "I'm watching the Bicams."

She raised an eyebrow.

"I've been trying to figure out their methodology," he confessed. "Everyone's got to have one, right? Scientific or superstitious or just some weird gut instinct, there's at least got to be some kind of *pattern* ..."

"You're not finding one?"

"Sure I am. They're *rituals*. Eulali and Ofoegbu raise their hands just *so*, Chodorowska howls at the moon for precisely three-point-five seconds, the whole lot of them throw their heads back and *gargle*, for fucksake. The behaviors are so stereotyped you'd call them neurotic if you saw them in one of those old labs with the real animals in cages. But I can't correlate them to anything *else* that happens. You'd think there'd be some kind of sequence, right? Try something, if that doesn't work try something else. Or just follow some prescribed set of steps to chase away the evil spirits."

Lianna nodded and said nothing.

"I don't even know why they bother to *make* sounds," he grumbled. "That quantum callosum or whatever they have has *got* to be faster than any kind of acoustic—"

"Don't spend too much effort on that," Lianna told him. "Half those phonemes are just a side effect of booting up the hyperparietals."

Brüks nodded. "Plus I think the hive—fragments sometimes, you know? Sometimes I think I'm looking at one network, sometimes two or three. They drop in and out of sync all the time. I'm correcting for that—trying to, anyway—but I still can't get any correlations that make sense." He sighed. "At least with the Catholics, you know that when someone hands you a cracker there's gonna be wine in the mix at some point."

Lianna shrugged, unconcerned. "You gotta have faith. You'll figure it out, if it's God's will."

He couldn't help himself. "Jesus *Christ,* Lee, how can you keep *saying* that? You know there's not the slightest shred of evidence—"

"*Really.*" In an instant her body language had changed; suddenly there was fire in her eyes. "And what kind of *evidence* would be good enough for you, Dan?"

"I—"

"Voices in the clouds? Fiery letters in the sky proclaiming *I Am the Lord thy God, you insignificant weasel? Then* would you believe?"

He held up his hands, reeling in the face of her anger. "Lee, I didn't mean—"

"Oh, don't back down *now*. You've been shitting on my beliefs since the day we met. The least you can do is answer the goddamn question."

"I—well . . ." Probably not, he had to admit. The first thought that fiery skywriting would bring to his mind would be *hoax,* or *hallucination*. God was such an absurd proposition at its heart that Brüks couldn't think of any physical evidence for which it would be the most parsimonious explanation.

"Hey, *you're* the one who keeps talking about the unreliability of human senses." It sounded feeble even to himself.

"So no evidence could ever change your mind. Tell me how that doesn't make you a fundamentalist."

"The difference," he said slowly, feeling his way, "is that *brain hack* is an alternate hypothesis entirely consistent with the observed data. And Occam likes it a lot more than *omnipotent sky wizard*."

"Yeah. Well, the people you're putting under your nanoscope know a thing or two about *observed data*, too, and I'm pretty sure their publication record kicks yours all over the innersys. Maybe you don't know everything. I gotta go."

She turned to the ladder, gripped the rails so hard her knuckles whitened.

Stopped. Unclenched, a little.

Turned back.

"Sorry. I just . . ."

"S'okay," he told her. "I didn't mean to, well . . ." Except he had, of course. They both had. They'd been doing this dance the whole trip downhill.

It just hadn't seemed so *personal* before.

"I don't know what got into me," Lianna said.

He didn't call her on it. "It's okay. I can be kind of a brain stem sometimes."

She tried on a smile.

"Anyhow, I *do* have to go. We're good?"

"We're good."

She climbed away, smile still fastened to her face, bent just slightly to the left. Favoring ribs that medical technology had long since completely healed.

He wasn't a scientist, not to these creatures. He was a baby in a playpen, an unwelcome distraction to be kept busy with beads and rattles while the grown-ups convened on more adult matters. This gift Lianna had brought him wasn't a sample; it was a pacifier.

But by all the laws of thermodynamics, it did its job. Brüks was hooked at first sight.

He pulled the gimp hood over his head, linked into the lab's ConSensus channel, and time just—stopped. It stopped, then shot ahead in an instant. He threw himself down through orders of magnitude, watched molecules in motion, built stick-figure caricatures and tried to coax them into moving the same way. He felt distant surprise at his own proficiency, marveled at how much he'd accomplished in just a few minutes; wondered vaguely why his throat felt so dry and somehow eighteen hours had passed.

What are you? he thought in amazement.

Not computronium, anyway. Not organic. More like a Tystovich plasma helix than anything built out of protein. Things that looked like synaptic gates were ticking away in there to the beat of ions; some carried pigment as well as electricity, like chromatophores moonlighting as associative neurons. Trace amounts of magnetite, too; this thing could change color if it ran the right kind of computations.

Not much more computational density than your garden-variety mammalian brain, though. That was surprising.

And yet . . . the way it was *arranged* . . .

He resented his own body for needing water, ignored the increasing need to take a piss until his bladder threatened to burst. He built tabletop vistas of alien technology and shrank himself down into their centers, wandered thunderstruck through streets and cityscapes and endlessly shifting lattices of intelligent crystal. He stood humbled by the sheer impossibility held in that little fleck of alien matter, and by the sheer mind-boggling simplicity of its execution.

It was as though someone had taught an abacus to play chess. It was as though someone had taught a spider to argue philosophy.

"You're *thinking*," he murmured, and couldn't keep an amazed smile off his face.

It actually did remind him of a spider, in fact. One particular genus that had become legendary among invertebrate zoologists and computational physicists alike: a problem-solver that improvised and drew up plans far beyond anything that should have been able to fit into such a pinheaded pair of ganglia. *Portia*. The eight-legged cat, some had called it. The spider that thought like a mammal.

It took its time, mind you. Sat on its leaf for hours, figuring out the angles without ever making a move, and then *zap*: closed on its prey along some roundabout route that broke line of sight for minutes at a time. Somehow it hit every waypoint, never lost track of the target. Somehow it just *remembered* all those three-dimensional puzzle pieces with a brain barely big enough to register light and motion.

As far as anyone could tell, *Portia* had learned to partition its cognitive processes: almost as if it were emulating a larger brain piece by piece, saving the results of one module to feed into the next. Slices of intellect, built and demolished one after another. No one would ever know for sure—a rogue synthophage had taken out the world's Salticids before anyone had gotten around to taking a closer look—but the Icarus slime mold seemed to have taken the same basic idea and run with it. There'd be some upper limit, of course—some point at which scratchpads and global variables took up so much room there'd be none left over for actual cognition—but this was just a *fleck*, this was barely the size of a ladybug. The condenser chamber was *awash* in the stuff.

What had Lianna called it? God. The Face of God.

Maybe, Brüks thought. *Give it time.*

"Scale-invariant shit it *time-shares*!"

He'd almost gotten used to it by now. Barely even jumped at the sound of Rakshi Sengupta exclaiming unexpectedly at his side. He peeled the hood back and there she was, a meter to his left: eaves-dropping on his models through an ancillary bulkhead feed.

He sighed and nodded. "Emulates larger networks a piece at a time. That one little piece of *Portia* could—"

"*Portia*." Sengupta stabbed the air, stabbed ConSensus. "After the spider right?"

"Yeah. That one little piece could probably model a human brain if it had to." He pursed his lips. "I wonder if it's conscious."

"No chance it'd take *days* just to chug through a half-second brain slice and networks only wake up—"

"Right." He nodded. "Of course."

Her eyes jiggled and another window sprouted off to one side: AUX/RECOMP, and the postbiological wonder painted on its guts. "Bet *that* could be though. What else you got?"

"I think it was designed specifically for this kind of environment," Brüks said after a moment.

"What space stations?"

"*Empty* space stations. Smart mass isn't anything special. But something *this* small, running cognition-level computations—there's a reason you don't run into that a lot on Earth."

Sengupta frowned. " 'Cause being a thousand times smarter than the thing that's trying to eat you isn't much help if it takes you a month to *be* a thousand times smarter."

"Pretty much. Glacial smarts only pay off if your environment doesn't change for a long time. 'Course, it's not such a bottleneck at higher masses, but—well, I think this was designed to work no matter how much or how little managed to sneak through.

Which implies that it's optimized for telematter dispersal—although if it isn't using our native protocols, how it hijacks the stream in the first place is beyond me."

"Oh they figured that out couple days ago," Sengupta told him.

"Really?" *Fuckers.*

"Know how when you pack a layer of ball bearings into the bottom of a crate and the second layer fits into the bumps and valleys laid down by the first and the third fits onto the second so it all comes down to the first layer, first layer determines all the turtles all the way up, right?"

Brüks nodded.

"Like that. 'Cept the ball bearings are atoms."

"You're shitting me."

"Yah because I got nothing better to do than play tricks on roaches."

"But—that's like laying down a set of wheels and expecting it to act as a template for a car."

"More like laying down a set of *tread marks* and expecting it to act as a template for a car."

"Come on. Something has to tell the nozzles where to squirt that first layer. Something has to tell the second layer of atoms when to come though so that they *can* line up with the first. Might as well call it magic and be done with it."

"You call it magic. Hive calls it the Face of God."

"Yeah. Well, the tech may be way beyond us, but superstitious labels aren't bringing it any closer."

"Oh that's rich you think God's a *thing* God's not a *thing.*"

"I've *never* thought God was a thing," Brüks said.

"Good 'cause it's not. It's water into wine it's life from clay it's waking meat."

Sweet smoking Jesus. Not you, too.

He summed it up to move it along. "So God's a chemical reaction."

Sengupta shook her head. "God's a *process.*"

Fine. Whatever.

But she wasn't letting it go. "Everything's *numbers* you go down far enough don't you know?" She poked him, pinched his arm. "You think this is *continuous*? You think there's anything but *math*?"

He knew there wasn't. Digital physics had reigned supreme since before he'd been born, and its dictums were as incontrovertible as they were absurd. Numbers didn't just describe reality; numbers *were* reality, discrete step functions smoothing up across the Planck length into an illusion of substance. Roaches still quibbled over details, doubtless long since resolved by precocious children who never bothered to write home: Was the universe a hologram or a simulation? Was its boundary a program or merely an interface—and if the latter, what sat on the other side, watching it run? (A few latter-day religions had predictably answered that question with the names of their favorite deities, although Brüks had never been entirely clear on what an omniscient being would need a computer *for*. Computation, after all, implied a problem not yet solved, insights not yet achieved. There was really only one sort of program for which foreknowledge of the outcome didn't diminish the point of the exercise, and Brüks had never been able to find any religious orders that described God as a porn addict.)

So. The laws of physics were the OS of some inconceivable supercomputer called *reality*. At least that explained why reality had a resolution limit; Planck length and Planck time had always looked a bit too much like pixel dimensions for comfort. Past that, though, it had always seemed like angels dancing on the head of a pin. None of it changed anything way up here where life happened, and besides, positing *universe as program* didn't seem to answer the Big Questions so much as kick them down the road another order of magnitude. Might as well just say that God did it after all, head off the infinite regress before it drove you crazy.

Still . . .

"A process," Brüks mused. That sounded more—modest, at least. He wondered why Lianna had never spelled it out during their debates.

Sengupta's head bobbed. "What *kind* of process though that's the question. Master algorithm defining the laws of physics or some daemon reaching up to *break* 'em?" Her eyes flickered briefly toward his, flickered away at the last instant. "That's how we know it exists in the first place. Miracles."

"Miracles."

"Impossible events. Physics violations."

"Such as?"

"Star formation way below the z-limit. Photons doing things they're not supposed to the metarules changing over by the Cloverleaf Nebula. They vindicated the Smolin model or something I dunno it's beyond me so *you'd* never get it in a million years. But they found something impossible. Way down deep."

"A miracle."

"I think more than one but that's what I said."

"Wait a second." Brüks frowned. "If the laws of physics are part of some universal operating system and God, by definition, *breaks* them . . . you're basically saying . . ."

"Don't stop now roach you're almost there."

"You're basically saying God's a *virus*."

"Well that's the question isn't it?"

Portia iterated before them.

What was it Lianna had said? *We've always thought* c *and friends ruled supreme, out to the quasars and beyond. What if they're just some kind of local ordinance?*

"What if they're a *bug*?" he murmured.

Sengupta grinned and stared at his wrist. "Change the whole mission wouldn't it?"

"This mission?"

"*Bicameral* mission the mission of the whole Order. Reality's iterating everywhere but there're these inconsistencies. Maybe not the *right* reality, mmm? Change alpha a just bit and the universe stops supporting life. Maybe alpha's *wrong*. Maybe life's just a parasitic offshoot of a corrupted OS."

Somewhere in Brüks's head, a penny dropped.

For fifteen billion years, the universe had been shooting for maximum entropy. Life didn't throw entropy into reverse—nothing did—but it put on the brakes, even as it spewed chaos out the other end. The gradient of Life was the first scale any aspiring biologist learned to sing: the further you kept yourself from thermodynamic equilibrium, the more alive you were.

It's the anthropic principle's evil twin, he thought.

"What—what *is* this mission, exactly?" Brüks asked softly.

"Mmmm." Sengupta rocked gently back and forth. "They know God exists already that's old. I think now they're trying to figure what to *do* with It."

"What to do with God."

"Maybe worship. Maybe disinfect."

The word hung there, reeking of blasphemy.

"How do you disinfect God?" Brüks said after a very long time.

"Don't ask me I just fly the ship." Her gaze slid back to the bulkhead, to the church of AUX/RECOMP and the alien emissary there.

"I think that puppy's giving them some ideas though," she said.

Lianna Lutterodt was lost in inner space when he sailed through the Commons ceiling. She blinked as he bounced off the deck, shook her head: her eyes came back to the here and now as a courtesy window opened on the bulkhead. A flatscreen concession to the neurologically disabled.

Icarus. The confessional. A rosette of spacesuited monks, outward facing, visors raised to bare their souls before the Face of God.

"Hi," Brüks said carefully.

She nodded around a mouthful of couscous. "Rakshi says you made some serious headway. Even gave it name."

He nodded. "*Portia.* It's pretty amazing, it . . ."

Her gaze drifted back to the window. *She can't take her eyes off them,* he thought, just as she did and caught him looking: "What?"

"It's not just amazing," he told her. "It's actually kind of scary." He dipped his chin at the feed. "And they cut pieces out of it."

"They take *samples,*" Lianna said. "Almost like real scientists."

"Something that reaches down across half a light-year and makes our own machines do backflips around the laws of physics."

"Not like they can get all the answers by just staring at it all day."

"I thought that was exactly how they got their answers."

"They know what they're doing, Dan."

"That's one hypothesis. Want to hear another?"

"I'm not sure."

"Ever hear of induced thanoparorasis?" he asked.

"Uh-huh." Lianna shrugged. "Common procedure among the augmented. Keeps 'em from collapsing into existential angst."

"It's a bit more fundamental than that," Brüks said. "Have you got it?"

"Thanoparorasis? 'Course not."

"Are you going to die?"

"Eventually. Hopefully not for a while."

"Good to know," Brüks told her. "Because if you *were* a victim of ITP, you wouldn't be able to answer that question. You might not even have *heard* it."

"Dan, I don't—"

"You and I"—raising his voice over hers—"we're blessed with a certain amount of denial. You admit you're going to die, you even know it intellectually on some level, but you don't really be-lieve it. You can't. The thought of dying is just too damn scary. So we invent some Fairyland Heaven to take us in after we *pass on,* or we look to your friends and their friends to give us immortality on a chip or—if we're hard-core realists—we just pay lip service to death and decay and keep right on feeling immortal anyway.

"But *some* folks"—he nodded at the feed—"just get too damn smart. They put their heads together and develop insights way too deep to paper over with a few million years' worth of whis-tling past the graveyard. People like that would *know* they were going to die, they'd feel it in the gut. They'd know what death means in a way you or I never could. And the only way they can keep from collapsing into whimpering puddles is to give denial a hand, cut a cognitive hole into the middle of their heads. We may live in denial most of the time but *those* people—they didn't even show a fright response when it looked like their whole damn hive was an hour from the morgue. Like those agnosiacs who'd die of thirst in their own homes after some tumor's destroyed their ability to recognize water."

"I don't think they're like that," Lianna said softly.

"Sure you do. You told me as much, remember? Reset the sensory biases, randomize the errors."

They watched in silence as the hive poked a stick at something dangerous.

"A lot of them died, not so long ago," Brüks said after a while.

"I remember."

"Me, too. And you know what I remember the most, you know what I can't forget? Luckett rolling around in his own shit while his spinal cord shorted out, smiling and insisting that everything was going according to plan."

Lianna turned away, eyes bright. "I liked him. He was a good man."

"I wouldn't know. All I know is, he sounded just like every hapless Yahweh junkie who ever looked around at all the horror and injustice in the world and mumbled some shit about how *It's not the place of the clay to question the potter.* The only difference is that everyone else lays it all on God's master plan and your Bicamerals talk about their own."

"You're wrong. They don't think of themselves that way at all."

"Then maybe you shouldn't, either. Maybe you shouldn't have quite so much *faith*—"

"Dan, *shut the fuck up*. You don't know anything about it, you *can't* know—"

"I was there, Lee. I *saw* you. They've got you so convinced they're infallible, they've got everything so *factored five ways to Sunday* that you didn't even *need* a hole cut into your brain. You went straight into the lion's den without missing a beat, you got right up in Valerie's face and it didn't occur to you for a microsecond that she's your goddamn *predator,* she could rip your throat out without even thinking about it—"

"*Do not put that on them.*" Lianna's voice was flinty. "That was *my* mistake. Chinedum was—I will *not* let you blame anyone else for *my* stupidity."

"Isn't that the way, though? Isn't that how it's always been? Just obey the guys in the funny hats and if it's a win it's all *praise be to Allah* but if your ass gets kicked it's *your* fault. You read scripture the wrong way. You weren't *worthy.* You didn't have enough *faith.*"

Some of the fight seemed to bleed out of her then; some of the old Lianna Lutterodt peeked through. She sighed, and shook her head, and ghosted a smiled. "Hey, remember when this used to be *fun?*"

He spread his hands, feeling helpless. "I just . . ."

"You mean well. I know. But after all you've seen, you can't deny how far ahead of us they are."

"Oh, they're scary smart, I'll give them that. They run circles around the best we roaches can throw at them, they snap this ship like a twig and pitch it all the way to the sun, drop us dead center onto Icarus's dark side from a hundred million kilometers with barely a thruster tweak. But they *glitch,* just like we do. They still *wash away their sins,* because after all that rewiring their brains still mix up sensation and metaphor. They're *more* glitchy than we are, because half their upgrades are barely out of beta—and while we're on the subject, has anyone factored in the neuropsychologic impairment that a few weeks of hyperbaric exposure must be inflicting on all that extra brain tissue?"

Lianna shook her head. "We're not on the steppes anymore, Dan. We don't measure success by how far you can throw a spear in a crosswind. They think rings around us in every way that matters."

"Uh-huh. And Masashi and Luckett are still dead. And all that poor bastard could cling to while his lights went out was that it was all according to *plan.*" He put his hands on her shoulders.

"Lee, it's not just that these people can't wrap their heads around mortality. They can't even entertain the possibility they could be *wrong*. If that doesn't scare the shit out of you—"

She shook him off. "The plan was to get us to Icarus. Here we are."

"Here we are." Brüks pointed to a hole in the wall, where a hived demigod communed with something that could change the laws of physics. "And how does it feel to know our lives depend on the judgment of something that can't even imagine it could die?"

WARS TEACH US NOT TO LOVE OUR ENEMIES, BUT TO HATE OUR ALLIES.
—W. L. GEORGE

"WHAT'S RAKSHI GOT against you guys?"

The lights were dimmed, the mutants and monsters were off pursuing their alien agendas, and the Glenmorangie was back on the table. Moore grimaced at Brüks, refriended, over the lip of his glass. "Who's *us guys*?"

"Military," Brüks said. "Why's she got such a hate-on for you?"

"Not sure. Self-loathing, maybe."

"What's that supposed to mean?"

"Sengupta's as much of a soldier as I am. She just doesn't know it. Not consciously, at least."

"Metaphorically, you mean."

Moore shook his head, took another sip; his cheeks puckered as he swirled the single malt around in his mouth. He swallowed. "WestHem Alliance. Same as me."

"And she doesn't know."

"Nope."

"What's her rank?"

"Doesn't work like that."

"Some kind of sleeper agent?"

"It's not like that, either."

"Then what—"

Moore raised a hand. Brüks fell silent.

"I say *army,*" Moore told him, "you think boots on the ground. Drones, zombies, battlefield robots. Things you can *see.* Fact is, if you've reached the point where you need that kind of brute force, you've already lost."

Visions of the Oregon desert sprang into Brüks's head. "Brute force seemed to work just fine for those fuckers who attacked the monastery."

"They were trying to stop us. Here we are."

Human bodies, turned to stone. The screams of dying Bicamerals.

Not bodies, he reminded himself. *Body parts.* Here in the dusk of the twenty-first century it was so easy to confuse murder with the amputation of a fingertip. None of the usual definitions made sense when a single supersoul stretched across so many bodies.

"Suppose you're a political heavyweight," Moore was saying. "A mover and shaker, a titan. And down around your ankles are all those folks you never used to worry about. The moved and the shaken. They don't like you much. They never have, but historically that never mattered. Little people. Back in the day you just ignored them. The business of titans is other titans.

"But now they get into the nodes, they decrypt your communiqués, they hack your best-laid plans. They hate your guts, Daniel, because you are big and they are small, because you turn their lives upside down with a wave of your hand and they don't care about realpolitik or the big picture. They only care about monkey-wrenching and whistle blowing.

"And you find out about them. You find out about Rakshi Sengupta and Caitlin deFranco and Parvad Gamji and a million others. You give them what they want. You leave the back door open just a crack, so they can see your files on the African Hegemony. You let them sniff out a weakness in your firewall. Maybe one day they find out how to provoke a firestorm in one of your subsidiary accounts, bankrupt some puppet government you kept under your thumb for tax purposes."

"Except that's not what they're doing," Brüks surmised.

"No it's not." There was a hint of sadness in Moore's smile. "It's all window dressing. They think they're really sticking it to you, but they're being—herded. Into the service of agendas they'd never support in a thousand years, if they only knew. And they're *dedicated,* Daniel. They're ferocious. They fight your wars with a passion you could never buy and never coerce, because they're doing it out of pure ideology."

"Should you be telling me this?" Brüks wondered.

"You mean, state secrets? What's a *state,* these days?"

"I mean, what if I tell *her?*"

"Go ahead. She won't believe you."

"Why not? She already hates you guys."

"She *can't* believe you." Moore tapped his temple. "Recruits get—tweaked."

Brüks stared.

"Or at least," Moore elaborated, "she can't *believe* she believes you." He eyed his scotch. "On some level, I think she already knows."

Brüks shook his head. "You don't even have to pay them."

"Sure we do. Sometimes. We make sure they have enough to make ends meet. Let them skim some cream from an offshore account, drop a legitimate contract into their in-box before the rent comes due. Mostly, though, we *inspire* them. Oh, they get bored sometimes. Kids, you know. But all it takes is a little judicious injustice, some new atrocity visited on the little people. Get them all fired up again, and off they go."

"That seems a bit—"

Moore raised an eyebrow. "Immoral?"

"Complicated. Why herd them into hating *you*? Why not just leave a trail of bread crumbs pointing back at the other guy?"

"Ah. Demonize your enemy." Moore nodded sagely. "I wonder why we never thought of that."

Brüks grimaced.

"Rakshi and her kind, they're wise to the old school. You leak footage showing the slants skewering babies and it'll take them maybe thirty seconds to find a pixel that doesn't belong. Discredit the whole campaign. People put a lot less effort into picking apart evidence that confirms what they already believe. The great thing about making yourself the villain is nobody's likely to contradict you.

"Besides." He spread his hands. "These days, half the time we don't even know who the real enemy *is*."

"And that's easier than just *tweaking* them so they flat-out *want* to work for you."

"Not easier. Marginally more legal." The Colonel sipped his drink. "A small agnosia to protect state secrets is one thing. Changing someone's basic personality without consent—that's in a whole other league."

Neither spoke for a while.

"That is really fucked-up," Brüks said at last.

"Uh-huh."

"So why's she here?"

"Driving the ship."

"*Crown*'s perfectly capable of driving itself, unless it's even more old school than I am."

"Better to have meat and electronics backing each other up in low-intel scenarios. Complementary vulnerabilities."

"But why *her*? Why would she agree to work under someone she hated—"

"This mission's under *Bicameral* command," the Colonel reminded him. "And anyone in Sengupta's position would jump at an opportunity like this. Most of those people spend their time babysitting low-orbit crap-zappers from their bedrooms, praying that one of them glitches enough to warrant human intervention. Actual deep-space missions—anything with enough of a time lag to need onboard real-time piloting—those've been scarcer than snowstorms ever since Firefall. The Bicamerals had their pick of the field."

"Rakshi must be very good at her job."

Moore drained his glass, set it down. "I think in her case it was more a function of motivation. She has a wife on class-four life support."

"And no way to pay the bills," Brüks guessed.

"She does now."

"So they didn't want the best and the brightest," Brüks said slowly. "They wanted someone who'd do anything to save her wife."

"Motivation," Moore repeated.

"They wanted a *hostage*."

The soldier looked at him with something that might almost have been pity. "You disapprove."

"You don't."

"You'd rather they picked someone who just wanted to get out of the house? Someone who was in it for the thrills or the bank balance? This was the *humane* choice, Daniel. Celu would have been dead. Now she's got a chance."

"Celu," Brüks said, and swallowed on a throat gone suddenly dry.

Moore nodded. "Rakshi's wife."

"What was, um . . . what was wrong with her?" Thinking: *There's no chance. It would be one in a million.*

Moore shrugged. "Bio attack, about a year ago. New England. Some kind of encephalitis variant, I think."

Then you're wrong. She doesn't have a chance. She doesn't. I don't care how much they spend keeping her heart beating, there's no coming back from something like that.

Oh my God. I killed her.

I killed Rakshi's wife.

It hadn't been anything radical. It hadn't even been anything *new*.

The methodology was decades old, a proven tent pole for a thousand peer-reviewed studies or more. Everyone knew you couldn't simulate a pandemic without simulating its victims; everyone knew that human behavior was too complex to thumbnail with a few statistical curves. Populations weren't clouds, and people weren't points; people were *agents,* autonomous and multifaceted. There was always the outlier who ran into the hot zone after a loved one, the frontline medic whose unsuspected fear of centipedes might cause him to freeze at some critical juncture. And since pandemics, by definition, involved millions of people, your simulation had better be running millions of human-level AIs if you wanted to get realistic results.

Or you could piggyback on a preexisting model where each of a million data points was *already* being run by a human-level intelligence.

Game worlds weren't nearly as popular as they'd once been— Heaven had stolen away those myriad souls who preferred to play with themselves, free of community standards—but their virtual sandboxes were still more than large enough to keep them way out front as the CDC's favorite platform for epidemiological research. For decades now, the plagues and sniffles that afflicted wizards and trolls alike had been tweaked and nudged toward specs that made them ideal analogs for the more pedestrian outbreaks afflicting what some still called *the real world*. Corrupted Blood bore more than a passing similarity to ectopic fibrodysplasia. The transmission dynamics of Beowulf's Bane, an exotic glowing fungus that ate the flesh of elves, bore an uncanny resemblance to those of necrotizing fasciitis. Flying carpets and magic portals mapped onto airlines and customs bottlenecks; Mages to jet-setting upper-echelon elites with unlimited carbon ceilings. For a generation now, public health policies the world over had been informed by the lurid fantasy afflictions of clerics and wights.

It was just bad timing that a Realist faction out of Peru figured how to hack that system when Dan Brüks and his merry band were running a sim on emerging infectious diseases in Latin America.

Nobody caught it at the time. The Realists had been subtle. They'd left the actual disease parameters strictly alone: any sudden changes to mutation rate or infectivity would've shown up in the dailies. They'd tweaked the superficial appearance of infected players instead, according to location and demographic. Certain victims looked a bit sicklier than they should have, while others— wealthier PCs with gold and flying mounts at their command— looked a little healthier. It didn't change the biology one whit, but it edged Human responses just a hair to the left. Subsequent outbreaks edged them a bit farther. The ripples spread out of gamespace and into the reports, out of the reports and into policy. Nobody noticed the tiny back door that had opened in the resulting contingency plans until six months later, when someone discovered a suspicious empty vial in the garbage behind the Happy Humpback Daycare Center. By then, a shiny new encephalitis mod had already slipped past Daniel Brüks's first-response algorithms and was carving a bloody swathe from Bridgeport to Philadelphia.

Celu MacDonald had survived unscathed. She'd hadn't even been in the kill zone; she'd been on the other side of the world, growing freelance code next to the girl of her dreams. Those weren't as rare as they'd once been. In fact they'd grown pretty common ever since Humanity had learned to edit the dream as well as the girl. Soul mates could be made to order now: monogamous, devoted, fiercely passionate. The kind of love that prior generations had barely tasted before their hollow sacraments withered into miserable life sentences, or shattered outright as the bloom faded, the eye wandered, the genes reasserted themselves.

Not for Macdonald and her kind, that empty hypocrisy. They'd ripped the lie right out of their heads, rewired and redeemed it, turned it into joyful truth with a lifetime warranty. First-person sex had even made a modest comeback in the shelter of that subculture, or so Brüks had heard.

He didn't know any of that at the time, of course. Celu MacDonald was just a name on a list of subcontractors, a monkey hired to grow code the academics couldn't be bothered with. Brüks only learned of her after the fact: a bloody little coda at the end of the massacre.

There'd been no conspiracy. No one had thrown her to the wolves. But the academics had had deans and CEOs and PR hotshots keeping their identities confidential, keeping their connections from staining the good names of venerable institutions. Nobody had given any cover to Celu MacDonald. When the dust had finally settled, when the inquiries and ass-covering and alibis had all run their course, there'd she'd been: standing alone in the crosshairs with hacked code dribbling from her hands.

Maybe it had been Rakshi who'd found her, staring slack-jawed at the ceiling after some bereaved next of kin decided to make the punishment fit the crime. She would still have been breathing. The variant didn't kill its victims. It burned them out and moved on; you could tell when it had finished because the convulsions stopped, at long last, and left nothing behind but vegetation.

They'd found the guy who did it, eventually: dead for days, at the center of a micro-outbreak that had imploded under quarantine. Evidently he'd slipped up. But Rakshi Sengupta was still *hunting.* That was the word she'd used. Denied her revenge on the hand that had pulled the trigger, she was looking for the gunsmith. All that seething anger. All those hours spent trawling the cache. All that implanted idealized love, transmuted into grief: all that grief, transmuted into rage. The growled threats and mutterings about hunting dead men and debts owed and *Some fucker going to be eating his own guts when I get hold of him.*

Rakshi Sengupta didn't know it yet, but she was gunning for Backdoor Brüks.

She was waiting at the mouth of his tent.

"Roach. Got something for you."

He tried to read her eyes, but they were averted. He tried to read her body language, but it had always been a cipher to him.

He tried to keep the wariness out of his voice. "What you got?"

"Just watch." She called a window to the adjacent bulkhead.

She doesn't know. She couldn't know.

She'd have to look into my eyes for that . . .

"What are you looking at?"

"No—nothing. Just—"

"Look at the *window*," Sengupta said.

I am so sorry, he thought. *Oh God, I am so very sorry.*

He forced his eyes to the bulkhead: an over-the-shoulder view of a diagnostic chair, facing a flatscreen. A tropical savanna glowed there, lit by the grimy yellow light of a fading afternoon (Africa, Brüks guessed, although there were no telltale animals in frame). Telemetry framed the tableaux on every side: ribbons of heart rate, respiration, skin galvanics. A translucent brain scan glowed to the left, writhing with the iridescence of neurons firing in real time.

Someone sat in that chair, almost totally eclipsed by its back. The top of their skull crested above a padded headrest, wrapped in the superconducting spiderweb of a tomo matrix. The tip of one armrest peeked into view; a hand rested there. The rest of the person existed only by inference. Fragments of a body, almost lost among the bright flayed images of its own electricity.

Sengupta wiggled a finger: the still life began to move. A chrono readout ticked out the time at one second per second: 03/05/2090—0915:25.

"What do you see?" Not Sengupta talking. Someone in the video, speaking offstage.

"Grassland," said the person in the chair, face still hidden, voice instantly recognizable.

Valerie.

The grasses dissolved into storm-tossed waves; the yellowish sky hardened down to wintry blue. The horizon didn't change position, though; it still bisected the scene halfway up the frame.

Something tapped faintly on the soundtrack, like fingernails on plastic.

"What do you see?"

"Ocean. Subarctic Pacific, Oyashio Current, early Feb—"

"Ocean's fine. Basic landscape, that's all we want. One word."

A hint of motion, center right: Valerie's fingers, just visible, drumming against the armrest.

A salt flat, shimmering in summer heat. The edge of a mesa rose in the hazy distance, a dark terrace that split-leveled the horizon.

"What now?"

"Desert." *Tick . . . tick tick tick . . . tap . . .*

Brüks glanced at Sengupta. "What *is*—"

"*Shhhh.*"

Same salt flat: the mesa had magically disappeared. Now a skeletal tree rose from the cracked earth, halfway to the horizon: leafless, yellow as old bone, a crown of naked branches atop a stripped featureless trunk almost too straight for nature. The trunk's shadow reached directly toward the camera, like an unbroken phantom extension of the object itself.

"Now?"

"Desert."

"Good, good."

Down in the glass brain, a smattering of crimson pinpoints swept briefly across the visual cortex and disappeared.

"Now?"

Same picture, higher magnification: the tree was front and center now, its trunk straight as a flagpole, close enough to vertically split the horizon and a good chunk of the sky above. The speckles reappeared, a faint red rash staining the soap-bubble rainbows swirling across the back of Valerie's brain. Her fingers had stopped moving.

"Same. Desert." There wasn't a trace of expression in her voice.

Right angles, Brüks realized. *They're turning the landscape into a natural* cross . . .

"Now."

"Same."

It wasn't. Now the branches were out of frame: all that remained was the white of the land, the hard crystalline blue of the sky and the hypothetical razor-edged line between, splitting the world side to side. And that impossibly straight vertical trunk, splitting it top to bottom.

They're trying to trigger a glitch . . .

No longer a mere rash, glowing across the back of the vampire's skull: a pulsing tumor. And yet her voice remained empty and untroubled; her body rested unmoving in the chair.

Her face still unseen. Brüks wondered why the archivists had been so afraid to record it.

Now the world on the screen began to come apart. The salt flat behind the tree came *unstuck* just a little at the bottom (the tree stayed in place, like a decal on glass), shrank up from the lower edge of the display like old curling parchment, and revealed a strip of azure beneath: as if more sky had been hiding under the sand.

"Now?"

The desert pixels compressed a little further, squeezed tighter against the skyline—

"Same."

—compressed from landscape to land*strip,* the undersky pushing it up from below, the horizon holding it down from above—

"Now?"

"S-same. I . . ."

Scarlet auroras squirmed across Valerie's brain. SKIN GALV and RESP shuddered along their time series.

CARDIAC beat strong and steady and did not change at all.

"And now?"

The ground was almost all sky now. The desert had been reduced to a bright squashed band running across the screen like a flatlined EEG, like a crossbeam at Calvary. The tree trunk cut it vertically at right angles.

"I—sky, I think, I—"

"Now?"

"—know what you're doing."

"Now?"

The flattened desert shrank some critical fraction further; horizontal and vertical axes split quadrants of sky with borders of nearly equal thickness.

Valerie began to convulse. She tried to arch her back; something stopped her. Her fingers fluttered, her arms shook against the padded arms of the chair; for the first time Brüks realized that she was strapped into the thing.

Fireworks exploded across her brain. Her heart, so immutably stable until now, threw jagged spikes onto the time series and shut down completely. The body paused for a moment in mid-convulsion, frozen in bone-breaking tetany for an endless moment; then the chair's defibrillators kicked in and it resumed dancing to the rhythm of new voltage.

"Thirty-five total degrees of arc," the invisible voice reported calmly. "Three-point-five degrees axial. Rep twenty-three, oh-nine-nineteen." The recording ended.

Brüks let out his breath.

"Has to be real," Sengupta grunted.

"What?"

"Horizon's not *real*. It's, it's *between*. They don't glitch on hypotheticals."

He thought he understood: vampires were immune to horizons. No matter how flat, no matter how perfect, they were zero thickness. You couldn't build a cross with a horizon, not one that stopped Valerie and her buddies at least: for that, you'd need something with *depth*.

"Really hard to get this," Sengupta remarked. "The explosion scrambled the records."

"Explosion?"

"Simon Fraser."

Realist attack, he remembered. A couple of months before he'd gone on sabbatical; the bomb had taken out a lab working on spindle emulation. He hadn't heard anything about the vamp program being targeted, though.

"There would've been backups," he guessed.

"For the footage sure. But how do you know it's *her*, huh? You never see her face. The embeds just give a subject code. Gait recognition not so great when your target's tied down."

"The voice," Brüks said.

"That's what I used. Now try trawling the cloud with a random voice sample, no stress data, no contextuals." Sengupta jerked her chin. "Like I said. Hard. But I got it now it's getting easier all the time."

"They tortured her," Brüks said softly. We *tortured her*. "Does—does Jim know about this?"

Sengupta barked out a humorless laugh. "I wouldn't tell that asshole what time zone he was in."

You don't have to do this, Brüks thought. *You don't have to work so hard turning all that pain into anger. You could be free, Rakshi. Fifteen-minute tweak and they'd cut the grief right out of you, the same way they wired in the love. Twenty-five minutes and you'd forget you'd ever been in pain.*

But you don't want to forget, do you? You want the grief. You need it. Your wife's dead, she'll be dead forever but you can't accept that, you're clinging to Moore's Law like a life jacket in a hurricane. Maybe they can't bring her back now but maybe in five years, maybe ten, and in the meantime you'll make do on hope and hate even if you haven't figured out where they belong.

He closed his eyes while she smoldered at his side.

God help me when you do.

Back in the Hub, she'd stripped the sun naked. It seethed and roiled overhead, close enough to touch (which he did, just for the surrealistic hell of it: a gentle push off the grille, a weightless drift, and Daniel Brüks could kiss the sky). But the curve of its edge was as clean and sharp as if razored: no flares, no prominences, no great gouts of plasma to dwarf a dozen Jupiters and fuck with Earthly broadcasts.

"Where's the corona?" he asked, thinking: *Filters.*

"Ha that's not the sun that's the *sun side.*"

Of Icarus, she meant: the sun and Icarus face-to-face, the light of one bouncing off the disk of the other into the eye of some remote camera, massively shielded, floating out front on the breath of a trillion hydrogen bombs.

"Perfect reflector if you crank it up high enough," Sengupta said. "Won't do much for the rads but if you're talking about thermal and visible spectrum I could turn this place into the coldest spot from here to the Oort."

"Wow," Brüks said.

"That's nothing look at *this.*"

The sun—the sun's reflection—darkened by degrees. Those brilliant writhing coruscations began to dim: the sunspots, the weather systems, the looping cyclones of magnetic force began to fade from sight, sink into some colder cosmic background. Within moments the sun was a pale phantom on a dark mirror.

Something else was there, though: other currents, convecting like a pot of molten glass brought to a rolling boil. Liquid mass upwelled near the center of the disk, swirled outward in an endless bloom of turbulent curlicues, cooled and slowed and stagnated near the darker perimeter. It was as though the solar photosphere had been stripped away to reveal some other, completely separate weather system churning beneath.

Except, Brüks realized after a moment, he wasn't looking at the sun at all, not even in reflection. This was—

"That's *Icarus*," he murmured. A great convex solar cell a hundred kilometers across: transparent or opaque, solid or liquid, its optical properties slaved to the whims of a glorified thermostat and Rakshi Sengupta's little finger. Darker now, just a few degrees closer to blackbody status, the convection currents swirled ever faster as it worked to dump the excess heat.

Off in some distant corner, an alarm woke with a soft beeping.

"Um . . . ," Brüks began.

"Don't worry roach just throttling up a bit to build some extra ergs don't want Earth to fall below quota do you?"

The beeping continued, increasingly urgent. Insistent little tags began flashing near the bottom of the display, albedo falling, absorbance and ΔT on the rise.

"I thought we'd already tanked up." It had been the final phase of the reconstruction: the last of the Bicams had stowed their tools and abandoned the *Crown*'s refitted hull for a group hug around *Portia*, twelve hours before. (Apparently their brains fell out of contact beyond some limited range.)

"Got *some* need *more* that's a lot of mass we gotta get out from under."

Brüks couldn't take his eyes off the sunside view: like looking down at a blooming mushroom cloud in the wake of an airburst. He knew it was only imagination but the Hub felt—*warmer* . . .

He bit his lip. "Aren't we overheating? Those tags—"

"More product takes more power right? Basic physics."

"Not *that* much more." Surely she hadn't dialed down the reflectivity this far the last time, surely this was just—

"Want to double-check my numbers roach? Don't trust my math think you can do better?"

—showing off . . .

The sunside sparked and vanished from the dome: NO SIGNAL pulsed above the warning icons left behind.

"*Shit*," Sengupta spat. "Stupid cambot melted."

"I'm impressed," Brüks said quietly. "Now will you *please* just dial it back a—"

"Quit fucking around, Rak." Lianna ricocheted up from the southern hemisphere, bounced off the Tropic of Cancer and arced toward the forward hatchway. "We've got more important things to do right now."

"Yeah right more important than putting charge in the tank." But her fingers twitched in the air, and the alarms dimmed a little. "Like what?"

Lianna spun around a handhold and planted herself on the arctic circle. "Like Oldschool's slime mold. It's talking to us." And disappeared through magnetic north.

THE QUICKEST WAY OF ENDING A WAR IS TO LOSE IT.

—GEORGE ORWELL

TALKING WAS GENEROUS: the images that had begun crawling across *Portia*'s skin were crude, chunky things, primitive mosaics built from pixels a centimeter on a side. There was no window per se, no distinct bounded area within which relevant information was neatly displayed. The mosaics simply faded into existence and out again, the oily gray of default epidermis stippling gradually into a roughly circular area of increasing contrast, a black-and-white scratchpad reminiscent of a crossword puzzle. Brüks's secular circuitry couldn't discern any pattern there.

Chromatophores, he remembered. *This thing could change color if it ran the right kind of computations.* "What started it up?"

"Dunno don't bug me." Sengupta had demoted the helmet-cam feeds to a line of thumbnails; her attention was fixed on Icarus's own stereocams, zoomed and focused on *Portia*'s—what?

Graphics interface? The same picture respawned in several itera-
tions across the dome: sonar, infrared, ultrasound. The mosaic
only showed up along visible wavelengths: infrared and ultravio-
let filters showed nothing but plain old *Portia,* a monochrome
porridge devoid of surface detail.

Smack-dab in the middle of the human visual range, Brüks
thought. *Wouldn't* that *be a coincidence . . .*

"Ha!" Sengupta barked. "Z-contours the thing's talking in
terraces . . ." She zoomed the view. Sure enough the white pixels
were *elevated,* little square mesas raised a millimeter above their
darker counterparts. Brüks spawned his own window and zoomed
even closer: the surfaces of all that topography were *fracturing,*
folding, each pixel splitting and resplitting into a mesh of ever
finer pigeonholes.

"It's building *diffraction gratings!*" Sengupta brayed.

"And it's increasing pixel-res—"

"I said shut up!"

Brüks bit back a response and cycled through MonkCam. The
Bicamerals had fallen silent around the object of their veneration,
played with their instruments, passed bands of radiation invisible
and otherwise over *Portia*'s skin. Lianna was staying out of the way;
her camera panned across the backs of helmets from the compartment hatch.

The resolution on that patchy window was improving by the
second now; pixels the size of thumbnails shattered into spots
the size of lentils, dissolved again into swirling clusters of pinheads
that collapsed into shards below the resolving power of the camera. Steps became sawtooth lines became smooth, swirling curves
that swept across the display and faded into flat gray oblivion.
Now Brüks could almost recognize the patterns moving there—
each new geometry seemed more familiar than the last, tugged a
little harder at some half-forgotten memory before giving up and
giving way to the next iteration. But nothing stuck. Nothing lasted
long enough to sink his teeth into—until the patterns slowed,

and Rakshi and Lianna spoke a single word, a shout and a whisper uttered in the same instant:

"Theseus."

Eleven minutes was all it had taken. Eleven minutes for an anaerobic time-sharing slime mold to refine its pixels from the size of sugar cubes down to units that exceeded the resolving power of the human eye. Eleven minutes from coma to conversation.

First-contact protocols. Fibonacci sequences, golden ratios, periodic tables. The Bicamerals scribbled cryptic responses onto tacpads and held them up in turn; Brüks was not especially surprised to note that *Portia*'s swirling communiqués were a lot more comprehensible than the Bicamerals' responses.

A shadow intruded subtly from the direction of the hatch, a hint of some presence beyond the lines of sight offered up by helmet feeds and onboard eyes. Icarus was full of blind spots; its cameras had not been installed with an eye to comprehensive surveillance. Brüks noticed, and tried not to.

Sudden surprised murmurs from the Bicamerals; a soft *oooh* from Lianna. Brüks scanned the feeds, where geometric primitives acted out some arcane theorem across *Portia*'s skin. "Lianna. Talk to me."

"The GUI," she told him. "It's gone *three-D*." Her feed circled the compartment, fixing *Portia* from every angle. "Some kind of lenticular diffraction effect. I'm seeing that whole display in three-D, we're *all* seeing it in three-D. Wherever we move. The thing's *tracking* us, it's tracking five—uh, six pairs of eyes and pointing a customized diffraction grid at each one of us *simultaneously. A single display surface.*"

"Doesn't look three-D to *me*," Sengupta grumbled. "Too dumb to track the stereocam."

Eleven minutes to derive the precise architecture of human eyesight. It seemed an impossibly short time to intuit a whole new sensory system from scratch, without invasion, without dissection. Except *Portia* hadn't done that at all, most likely. It had probably taken the tutorials long before it ever made the in-system jaunt. Wherever the place it called home, it had at the very least made a pit stop at *Theseus*. These probably weren't the first Humans it had encountered.

Maybe there'd been some dissection after all.

"Where's Jim?" Lianna said.

"Right here," Moore called in from the depths of the *Crown*. He'd been off-shift but he was back in the game. "I'm on my way."

"Uh, that's a negative, Jim. We'd rather you stay back for now. Give us your insights from there."

"Why's that?"

"You know why. This thing's using *Theseus*'s contact protocols. Your stock just went up."

"That's ridiculous," Moore said mildly. "I've been over there many times."

"It was never *active* before." The slightest hint of exasperation tinged Lianna's voice. "Come on, Jim, you know the rules about high-value assets better than anyone."

"I do," Moore agreed. "Which means my expert opinion should prevail. I'm coming over."

No sound over comm. On the great surveilling compound eye, points of view shifted and bobbed.

"Fine," Lianna said at last. "Don't forget to suit up."

Brüks and Sengupta, the last of the daycare buddies. They watched through one camera eye as Moore, fore in the attic, slid into his suit. They watched through a half-dozen others as Ofoegbu et al returned to their rituals at the altar of First Contact, as *Portia* continued to iterate through stolen protocols; Sengupta grunted something about building a pidgin but all Brüks could see was plasma plots and dancing stick figures.

"Little warm in there," Sengupta remarked. Brüks barely heard her.

Up in one corner of the compound eye, one of the Bicamerals—AMINA, according to the feed—panned away from the shrine and floated out of the sanctum; EULALI followed a moment later. The two began to trace a path back to the docking hatch. (Brüks felt a twinge of resentment on Moore's behalf—as though the poor dumb caveman might get lost without a couple of grown-ups to show him the way.)

Metal guts sailed past in Moore's feed: grilles, bulkheads, conduits and plumbing turning around his axis in constant lazy rotation. Landmarks passed in faster succession than Brüks had ever seen through Bicameral feeds: the radiator bus, the T-junction leading off to the LEAR hoop, that row of fluorescent pink high-pressure tanks he'd never been able to find on any schematic. Moore moved as if he'd been born to this place; he rounded one last corner like a dolphin twisting onto a new heading and he was *there*. Lianna and Ofoegbu moved aside to let him enter.

Somehow he'd missed Amina and Eulali. *Probably took a short cut*, Brüks thought, glancing up at the nondescript passageway floating past in their feeds. *That'll teach 'em*.

Soft ululations from the sanctum. On Lianna's feed Moore frowned stage left, evidently squeezing some kind of intelligence from those sounds.

"I think I see the problem," he said after a moment.

Somewhere—else—Eulali and Amina had stopped moving. They hesitated for a moment, looming in each other's feeds; then Janused back-to-back, turning slowly. Signage and hazard striping adorned a hatch in the background: VPR H$_2$ STORAGE, THRUSTER ASSEMBLY. HARD VACUUM BEYOND.

"It's as you said," Moore was saying back in the sanctum. "These are *standard* protocols." His helmet cam held a tight focus on *Portia*'s paintings. Lianna's feed showed him from the side, visor raised, cheek eclipsed by his helmet, his profile visible past the forward edge of the seal. Just past him, the node called Ofoegbu wasn't looking at Moore or *Portia*: he was looking back through the open hatchway, into the corridor beyond—

Wait a second, Brüks thought. *Shouldn't there be—*

That shadow, hinting at an unseen presence by the hatch. Gone now.

Moore: "It's using the same protocols we are."

Valerie had been there, just a few minutes ago. Now she was gone.

"It's reflecting our own protocols back at us. It's completely rote."

Amina and Eulali. They weren't going to meet Jim at all, Brüks realized. *I bet they're tracking Valerie . . .*

He foregrounded their feeds. They still faced in opposite directions, each presumably sharing in the wraparound vista of a conjoined visual field. Icarus drifted about them like a sharp-edged dream.

"We're not talking to an alien intelligence," Moore continued. "We're talking to a mirror."

Something caught Brüks's eye, a tiny bright sparkle in the upper-left corner of Amina's feed. A faint star drifting on the recycled breeze. He skimmed the stereocam menu, selected 27E—VAPOR CORE REACTOR—EXT. CORRIDOR. Same corridor, dorsal view. Now he stared down at the tops of two open helmets; that floating star twinkled in the foreground. He zoomed the feed onto a sliver of glass—something like that, anyway—barely the size of a hangnail. A shard of something *broken.*

A big place, Icarus. It went on forever, breathed through more than a thousand kilometers of ductwork. This glass speck could have come from anywhere.

"You want to make any progress at all—" Moore said.

No signs of stress or metal fatigue nothing popped nothing broken no bits floating around.

. . . 'Course you gotta go in there and check to be sure *. . .*

"—you've got to *break* it."

In the sanctum, Jim Moore extended his arm. Too late, Ofoegbu rushed to intervene. A bright little figurine sprang into existence on the palm of Moore's hand, a hologram, an offering in the shape of a man.

"This is my son." Moore's voice carried soft and clear along the channel. "Do you know him?"

Portia's interface imploded and disappeared.

Holy shit holy shit—"Holy *shit* holy *shit holy*—" That was Sengupta beside him, locked in a loop, synced with another voice in Brüks's own head.

"*Shut up,*" Brüks said; amazingly, both obeyed.

Moore's hand didn't move. The offering on its palm glowed steadily. *Portia* lay silent on its shrine while every sapient being within a hundred million kilometers held its breath.

After an endless moment, a single bright eye opened in the middle of that surface. Light spilled from its pupil, fountained swirling across some canvas of melanin and magnetite, settled finally into an image with arms and legs. Siri Keeton looked back at himself, arms spread just slightly at his sides, palms out.

Brüks leaned forward. "Another mirror image."

Sengupta clicked and ticked and shook her head. "Not a mirror look at the *hand* the right *hand*." She zoomed the feed to make it easy: a ragged line there, from the heel of the palm right up to the webbing between the index and ring fingers. As if something had torn Keeton's hand apart, right down to the wrist, and glued it back together.

Brüks glanced at Sengupta, trying to remember: "That's not on Jim's—"

"Of course not that's the whole fucking *point* isn't—"

A sudden strangled sound from somewhere in the network: Bicameral sounds, a host of complex harmonics that probably held volumes. All Brüks could decipher there was surprise: over at 27E— EXT. CORRIDOR. Eulali was charging up the passageway at full speed. Amina floated transfixed, staring straight at the camera—no, not at the camera. At that telltale shard floating in front of it.

Everywhere, suddenly: pandemonium.

The helmet feeds at the shrine were all in frantic motion, swinging like drunken pendulums and sweeping the scenery too fast to make out whatever had scared them. Off down 27E Eulali bounced off a bulkhead (Wait a second; had there even *been* a bulkhead there a moment ago?) and retreated back toward Amina; another instant and both were gone from third-person view, lost but for the frantic blurry sweep of their suit cams. Sengupta grabbed AUX/RECOMP and spread it front and center across the dome, a top-down view of the shrine and its resident deity and its misbegotten acolytes caroming off solid metal where an open hatchway had gaped only a few moments before. *Portia* lay quiet as clay along the condenser, its subtle mutilation of Siri Keeton glowing soft and steady as a child's nightlight: the oily gray tentacle that lashed out toward Chinedum Ofoegbu sprouted from the far bulkhead, and Moore barely had time to push the monk out of the way.

All in those final furious moments before the feeds went dark.

Sengupta gibbered faintly to port. Brüks barely heard her. *I know what that is,* he thought as those last seconds played over in his head. *I've seen these before, I've used these before, I know exactly what this is . . .*

Magnetite and chromatophores and crypsis. Cages broken and painstakingly rebuilt. Footprints wiped clean, disturbing alien smells erased, sensors and samplers carefully planted and natural habitat reconstructed along all axes.

This is a sampling transect.

He yanked the quick-release buckle on his harness, floated free. "We've got to get them out."

Sengupta shook her head so hard Brüks thought it might come off. "No fucking *way* no fucking *way* we gotta get *outta here*—"

He spun above the mirrorball, grabbed her by the shoulders—

—*"Don't fucking touch me!"*—

—let her go but kept close, face-to-face, mere centimeters between them though she squirmed and turned her face away: "It doesn't know we're here, do you understand? You said it yourself, *too dumb to track the camera too dumb to know we're here,* they never let us onto Icarus so *it's never seen us.* We can take it by surprise—"

"Roach logic that's *stupid* that doesn't mean *anything* man we gotta *leave*—"

"*Don't leave.* Do you hear me? Stay here if you want but *don't you fucking leave* until I get back. Boot up the engines if the damn things even work yet, but *stay put.*"

She shook her head. An arc of spittle spread from her lips and fanned through the air. "What are *you* gonna do huh they're *ten* times smarter than you and they never even saw it coming—"

Good question. "In some ways, Rakshi. They're ten times dumber in others. They know all about quarks and amplituhedrons but they didn't get nailed by a piece of quantum foam, do you understand? They got nailed by a goddamned *field biologist.* And that's a game I know inside out."

He cupped her head in his hands and kissed her on the crown—
—"*Don't leave.*"—
—and leapt into the attic.

He shot through the rafters like a pinball, bouncing from strut to handhold, knocking aside straps and buckles and glistening blobs of oily water that splattered on contact. Brüks the baseline. Brüks the roach. *Give it up, Danny-boy: don't even try to think, you'll only embarrass yourself in front of the grown-ups. Just nod and swallow what they feed you. Keep your mouth shut when Sengupta brushes off a discrepancy of a few millimeters as insignificant thermal expansion. Play it safe when Moore points out that* Portia, *wonder of wonders,* grows; *point to a puddle of candle wax on the machinery and dismiss it with a shrug. Don't bother wondering whether the infiltration really stopped at such an obvious border. Forget that* Portia *computes and pattern-matches, forget its capacity to build mosaics of such intricate resolution that no meatball eye could tell the difference between a naked bulkhead and one sheathed in the thinnest layer of thinking plastic. Don't let the results of your own half-assed research point you to the obvious: that* Portia *might coat* everything *like an invisible intelligent skin, that it's there* between *whenever anyone boots up an interface or turns on the goddamn lights: watching everything we do, feeling every sequence our fingers tap against the*

*panels. Just sit back and smile as the adults blunder innocently into
an alien cage painted inside the man-made one.*

*And when the traps snaps shut and all those pieces come together
you can comfort yourself that the grown-ups didn't see it, either, that
these brain-damaged groupthink Bicamerals aren't so smart after all.
You can die smug and vindicated with the best of them in a mass
grave swinging around the sun.*

The lamprey gaped ahead and to port, highlighting edges and
angles in blue pastel. Three empty spacesuits floated in their alcoves. Brüks considered and dismissed them in an instant: by the
time he wriggled into one of those things, everyone on Icarus
might be pickled in whatever *Portia* used for formalin. Up past
the 'lock, though, encircling the forward reaches of the docking
bay: an array of tools sufficient to cut a ship in two and build it
back again.

Portia could obviously lock its molecules into something like
armor: Ofoegbu was not a small man and yet the slime mold—
stretched thin across the hatch, drawn tight in seconds—had
bounced him back into the compartment without even bending.
But Brüks had seen this fucker from the inside, close up. He'd
seen the pieces that let *Portia* talk, and think, and blend in; he
had a least a rough idea of how those parts were structured and
what they were made of.

He was pretty sure they couldn't all be fireproof.

He yanked a welding laser from its mount and pulled himself
aft, flipping off the safety and wrapping the tether around his
wrist as he moved. An electric insect whined faintly up toward
the ultrasonic as the capacitors charged.

Down the lamprey's throat: a glowing semiflexible trachea, re-
inforced by skeletal hoops at three-meter intervals. Soft padded
striations extending the length of the passageway, the ligaments
and muscles that moved the tunnel during docking. A biosteel
frame hove into view around the curve, a massive square hatch
embedded within: Icarus's main airlock, sealed and solid as a
mountain, reassuringly industrial after all this squishy biotecture.

Pressed into the alloy off to the side, a handle nested within a crimson dimple. Brüks grabbed it, braced himself with one foot to either side; turned; pulled. The dimple turned green around his fist. The airlock sighed open. He grabbed its edge, swung it back, ignored the yellow flashing of nervous smart paint warning against DUAL HATCH DISCONNECT: stared through an open inner hatch into the labyrinth beyond.

Enemy territory. He had no way of knowing how far it extended. Maybe *Portia* was looking back at him now.

He hefted the welder and pushed off.

No animatics to guide him. No convenient schematics rotating in his head, no bright icon to pinpoint his location. He remembered the way from a dozen suit feeds, from his own solitary voyeurism. He didn't know how useful those memories might be. Maybe they were as reliable as any roach's. Maybe the very architecture had changed.

Gross anatomy would get him to the sanctum: down the longitudinal notochord, right fork past the LEAR hoop, turn right again under the coolant nexus. If he was lucky, someone would be making sounds to guide him the rest of the way.

Should've grabbed a helmet, he thought, looking backward with perfect clarity. *Should've brought something with a comm link. An extra laser or two for Jim and the boys.*

Shit shit shit.

Sounds ahead, sounds to starboard, sounds behind: a glimpse of motion from the corner of his eye as he sailed past some side tunnel that had never made it onto his mental map. He grabbed at a passing rib; the laser sailed on, yanked him forward by the wrist, pulled him off balance and sent him tumbling into the bulkhead. His head cracked painfully against a strut; the laser, jerking at the end of its strap, recoiled through weightless space and punched him in the chest.

Shouts from behind. A small chorus of wordless, panicky voices. An almost electrical *slithering* sound.

Brüks cursed and launched himself back the way he'd come.

The forgotten passageway slid toward him; he braked, grabbed, swung around the corner—

—and nearly ran headlong into a wall congealing before him like a membrane of living clay.

In the time it took him to stop and gibber to himself—

—*I almost* touched *it I almost* touched *it It almost* got *me*—

—the membrane had transmuted to biosteel, rigid and impenetrable and almost thick enough to muffle the sounds of carnage on the other side.

Not biosteel, Brüks reminded himself. *Not impenetrable.*

Not fireproof.

He brought up the welder.

No. Not fireproof at all.

Portia squirmed where the beam hit, curled and blackened and iridesced like an oil slick. Brüks kept the focus tight, the beam as steady as free fall and nerves could keep it. It burned through, opened a hole that dilated like an eye: stretched elastic tissue split apart, recoiling from the hit. The beam weaved briefly, scoring inert metal on the other side, barely missing one of the figures beyond before Brüks's killed the circuit.

And stopped, blinking.

Taken in during that endless, frozen moment: a tunnel with no deck and no ceiling, its walls buried behind an infestation of pipes and conduits, capped by a T-junction ten meters in. Five spacesuited figures, helmets open, halfway down that length. At least one shattered visor: a cloud of coppery crystal shards following their own small trajectories, some polished as new mirrors, others stained and splattered by a band of crimson mist that arced from a small silvered body turning in midair. Brüks knew who it was even before the face came into view, even before he saw those sightless eyes staring bone-white from a black mask.

Lianna.

The others moved under their own power. Amina, making desperately for the faint hope Brüks had just opened before her. Evans, flailing through the carnage in search of a handhold or a brace point, finding only the rag-doll embrace of a corpse entangled in passing. Azagba, the legless zombie: lashing out quick as a striking snake, spinning Amina around by the shoulder, driving the straightened fingers of one bladed hand pistonlike into her open helmet and turning her *off* in an instant. Another of Valerie's zombies bounding forward like something arboreal, reaching out after Evans to do the same.

Brüks fired the torch. The zombie saw it coming and twisted like an eel but she was trapped in midair, purely ballistic, wed to inertia for just that instant too long. The beam bounced briefly off her silver abdomen, flash-burned a slash of cauterized charcoal across her exposed face. Amazingly she stayed on target: burned and half-blind, one eye boiled and burst in its socket, she lashed out and crushed Evans's throat in passing, bounced off metal viscera, grabbed the nearest handhold without even looking.

Portia was there, too. It felt the clasp and returned it, wrapped glistening waxy pseudopods around that hand faster than even zombie reflexes could respond. Wisps of white vapor swirled at the seams where suit and slime fused together. The trapped zombie looked down with one dead dancing eye; but when she raised her head again there was something else in that face.

"*Jesus,*" she breathed. She doubled over in a great wracking cough, hand embedded in the wall; blood and spittle swirled around her face. "What am I—oh God, what's—"

The light faded in her eye; the tics and stutters that reasserted themselves seemed dead even by zombie standards, the twitch of dying cells released on their own recognizance.

Jim would know your name, Brüks thought.

Something moved past her shoulder, past the drifting bodies, way down at the T-junction: behind the crack in the closet door, down in the space beneath the bed. Another glint of silver, moving with silent purpose: another figure, rounding the corner.

Valerie.

For a moment they stared at each other across a litter of corpses: predator with a look of distracted curiosity, prey because he simply couldn't look away. Brüks didn't know how long the moment lasted; it might have gone on forever if Valerie hadn't lowered her faceplate. Maybe that was an act of mercy, the breaking of a headlight paralysis that would have kept him frozen right up until she tore him limb from limb. Maybe she just wanted to give him a sporting chance.

Brüks turned and fled.

Coolant clusters. Service tunnels. Sealed hatches leading to far-off places he'd never explored or long-since forgotten. He passed them unseeing, let instinct steer the meat while his global workspace filled with predator models and pants-pissing terror. He was passing a tertiary heat sink and he could see Valerie closing through the back of his head; he was at the Cache Hatch and he could see her lips drawn back in that gleaming predatory grin; he was fleeing up the notochord and he could feel her muscles bunching for the final killing blow.

In the lamprey now: *No time to stop, no chance to bar the way, you even* think *about dogging that hatch and she'll be on you before you even turn around. Don't look back. Just keep running. Don't think about where, don't think about when: thirty seconds is a lifetime, two minutes is the far future, it's the moment that matters, it's now that's trying to kill you.* A voice ahead, as panicky as the one inside, echoing down the throat and getting louder: all *shit shit shit* and *docking clamps* and numbers going backward—but *Don't worry about that, either, that's for later, that's for ten seconds from now if you're still alive and*—

The *Crown*.

End of line. Nowhere else to go, no more time to buy. All the future you have, right now.

Nothing left to lose.

Brüks turned and stared back down the throat; Valerie stood there, casually braced against the lip of Icarus's inner hatch, looking up through the mirrored cyclops eye of her helmet. She might have been standing there for hours, just waiting for him to turn around and notice her.

Now that he had, she leapt.

He brought up the laser and *snarled*. Valerie sailed toward him; Brüks could have sworn she was laughing. He fired. The beam scattered off the reflective thermacele of the vampire's spacesuit, shattered into myriad emerald splinters bright as the sun. They scorched split-second tracks on random surfaces before Valerie darted out of the way.

Brüks lunged for the hatch controls, grabbed the lever, fumbled. The *Crown* clenched her front door a fraction, relaxed it again. Valerie closed for the kill, arms outspread. Somehow he could hear her: a mere whisper, impossibly audible even over Sengupta's panicked chanting on comm. A voice as clear as if she were murmuring at his shoulder, as if she were right inside his head:

I want you to imagine something: Christ on the Cross . . .

Electricity sang, deep down in his bones. Synapses snapped like blown circuits. Brüks's flesh hummed like a tuning fork, every muscle thrown instantly into tetanus. Wet warmth bloomed at his crotch. He couldn't move, couldn't blink, could barely even breathe. Some distant part of him worried briefly about that last fact, then realized that it probably didn't matter. Valerie was bound to kill him long before he had a chance to suffocate.

In fact here she came now, reaching out—

—and careening away, struck from behind. Jim Moore loomed up in her stead, his face utterly reptilian, eyes dancing frantic little jigs in the dark cavern of his open helmet. He pushed Brüks into the bay, slammed the airlock shut behind them both; his fist came down on Brüks's chest not quite hard enough to crack the sternum through the suit. Something broke in there, though; something *unlocked,* and Brüks was sucking back great tidal washes of recycled air. By the time he stopped gasping Moore had webbed him into an empty alcove for safekeeping, an occupied suit next to empty ones.

There were plenty of those.

The *Crown* was a symphony orchestra, warming up: the creak and groan of stressed metal, the distant cough of awakening engines, the random percussion of buckles clanking against bulkheads pushed into grudging motion. Sengupta's vocals, crackling out panicked numbers. A rogue droplet of oil floated in place while the ship shifted around it, splashed against Brüks's cheek with a whiff of benzene.

From somewhere very far away, the roar of an ocean.

Moore's hands brought up an interface on the bulkhead. His fingers played those controls with inhuman precision. A window opened to one side, an exterior feed rendered in smart paint: a smear of ragged blue light lashing back and forth, the lamprey torn free and recoiling into some distant burrow. A play of stars and shadow and knife-edged geometries blocking out the heavens. Dim red constellations flashed along wire-frame gantries: cliffs of black alloy stretched far and wide to their own horizons.

Valerie's helmet, blocking the view. Fists pounding against the hull, any possible sound drowned out by the vibration of the engines. *Sunrise,* sudden and scalding: the whole universe burst into flame as the *Crown of Thorns* lumbered out of eclipse. Somewhere Sengupta was cursing; somewhere else, thrusters fired. For one brief instant Valerie was a black writhing shadow against a blinding sky: then burst into flame an instant before the pickup fried.

Moore's fingers never stopped dancing.

It took endless seconds for the backup camera to kick in. By the time it did they were back in hiding, huddled in Icarus's shadow, the starless black silhouette of the radiator spire sliding past to port. A gentle hand began to nudge Brüks down against the bottom of the alcove, mass-times-acceleration pulling him out against the webbing. The dim zodiac of the array's streetlights receded slowly to stern—but other lights ignited back there as he watched, a pentagon of hot blue novae flaring silently in the darkness. It was only then that another silence registered: Moore had stopped talking to the wall, stilled the machine-gun staccato of his fingers against metal. Brüks could barely make out a fuzzy shape at the edge of vision; it took a Herculean effort to move his eyes even a fraction of a degree, to bring the Colonel into focus.

He never did succeed completely. But he squeezed enough from his peripheral vision to see the old warrior standing still as stone against the deck, one hand half-raised to his face. He thought he heard a soft intake of breath caught halfway, and decided to call it the sound of a returning soul.

Icarus shrank away. The sun burst back into view around it. Five blue sparks still flickered even in the light of that blinding corona: five bright dots in a dwindling black disk in a sea of fire. *Stabilizing thrusters,* Brüks realized distantly, and wondered why they burned so long and so bright, and wished that the answer hadn't come to him so quickly.

The newborn gravity kept putting on weight. It pulled Brüks ever harder against his restraints, leaned him out of the alcove and angled over the deck. His knees did not buckle under the strain; his body did not collapse. He was breathing statuary, and some gut sense stronger than logic knew that he would not crumple if those straps gave way: he would topple to the deck and *shatter.*

The spacesuits beside him had disappeared. Rotting corpses hung in their stead, slivers of gray flesh dangling through the mesh, maggots dripping like rice grains from empty eye sockets. Grinning mandibles clicked and clattered and uttered incomprehensible sounds. *REM paralysis,* one part of Brüks said to another, although he was not asleep. *Hallucination.* The corpses laughed like something less dead, coughing through mud.

Floaters swarmed in his eyes. Half-visible in the encroaching fog, Jim Moore stood against the deck without benefit of webs or incantations or anything but the crushing awareness of his own actions. Darkness closed in. With the last few synapses sparking in his cache, Brüks wondered what Luckett might have said in the face of such a toll.

Probably that everything was going according to plan.

PREDATOR

You have to understand, Deen, this is the fifth attack on Venezuela's jet-stream injection program so far this year. Stratospheric sulfates are *still* down by three percent and even if there aren't any further attacks, we'll be lucky if they recover by November. Any agro who can't afford seriously drought-hardened transgenics is going to have a disastrous summer. Clones and force-grown crops from higher lats should be able to pick up the slack—as long as we don't suffer a repeat of last year's monoculture collapse—but local shortages are pretty much inevitable.

We're well aware that the Venezuelan program is technically illegal (you think none of us have read the GBA?) but I don't have to tell you about the benefits of stratospheric cooling. And even if geoengineering *is* a short-term solution, you gotta use what you can or you don't live long enough to reach the long term. Of course, Caracas isn't doing itself any favors with their idiotic adherence to an outmoded judicial system. Personal culpability? What are these [EPITHET AUTOREDACT] going to come up with next, witch-dunking?

So I can speak for the whole department when I say that we sympathize completely. And if you folks over in

Human Rights want to blacklist them again, go right ahead. But the bottom line is, *You can't ask us to withdraw support for Venezuela*. The world just can't afford to see even modest climate-mitigation efforts sabotaged like this.

I know how bad the optics are. I know how tough it is to sell an alliance with a regime whose neuropolitics are rooted in the Middle Ages. But we're just going to have to take this dick in our mouths and swallow whatever comes out. Stratospheric cooling is one of the few things keeping this planet from falling on its side right now, and as you know that technology takes a *lot* of power.

If it makes you feel any better, consider the fact that if this had happened twenty, twenty-five years ago we wouldn't even be having this conversation; we didn't have enough joules in hand back then to be able to afford these kinds of options. We'd probably be tipping into another Dark Ages by now.

Thank God for Icarus, eh?

—Fragment of internal UN communiqué (correspondents unknown): recovered from corrupted source released during a scramble competition between unidentified subsapient networks, 1332:45 23/08/2091

HE WOKE UP weightless. Unseen hands guided him like a
floating log through the Hub, through a southern hemisphere
that didn't move any more than he could. Rakshi Sengupta called
in from somewhere far away, and she did not bray or bark but
spoke in tones as soft as any cockroach: "This is taking too long
we're gonna start falling back if we don't restart the burn in five
minutes tops."

"Three minutes." Moore's voice, much closer. "Start your clock."

And that's all of us, Brüks thought distantly. *Just Jim, and Rakshi,
and me. No vampires left, no undead bodyguards. Bicamerals all gone.
Lianna dead. Oh God, Lianna. You poor kid, you poor beautiful innocent corpse. You didn't deserve this; your only crime was faith . . .*

One of the axial hatches passed around him. In the next instant
he was swinging around an unaccustomed right angle: the *Crown's*
spokes, rigged for thrust, still laid back along her spine. Rungs
scrolled past his face as Moore pushed him headfirst to stern.

*All our children, gone. Smarter, stronger, leaner. All those souped-
up synapses, all those Pleistocene legacy issues stripped away. Where
did it get them? Where are they now? Dead. Gone. Turned to plasma.
Where* we'll *be, probably, before long . . .*

Maintenance & Repair. Moore folded out the medbed and
strapped him in just as the *Crown* began clearing her throat. By
the time he turned to leave, weight was seeping back into the
world. Brüks tried to turn his head, and almost succeeded. He
tried to clear his throat, and did.

"Uh . . . Jim . . ." It was barely above a whisper. The Colonel paused at the ladder, a vague silhouette in the corner of Brüks's eye. The ongoing burn seemed to sink him into the deck.

". . . Th-thanks," Brüks managed.

The silhouette stood silently in the burgeoning gravity.

"That wasn't me," he said finally, and climbed away.

Moore was not the only one to visit. Lianna returned to him from the grave, a dark flickering plasma who smiled down on his frozen features and shook her head and whispered *You poor man, so lost, so arrogant* before the sun called her back home. Chinedum Ofoegbu stood for hours at his side and spoke with fingers and eyes and sounds that stuttered from the back of his throat, and somehow Brüks understood him at last: not the ululating cipher, not the intelligent hive cancer, but a kind old man whose fondest childhood memory was the family of raccoons he'd surreptitiously befriended with a few handfuls of kibble and subtle sabotage inflicted on the latch of the household organics bin. *Wait—you had a childhood?* Brüks tried to ask, but Ofoegbu's face and hands had disappeared under eruptions of buboes and great ropy tumors, and he could no longer get out the words.

Rhona even came back from Heaven, though she'd sworn she never would. She stood with her back to him, and fumed; he tried to turn her around and make her smile, but when she did the expression was bitter and furious and her eyes were full of sparks. *Oh, do you miss her?* she raged. *You miss your mindless puppet, your sweet adoring ego-slave? Or is it just the fact that you've lost the one small fake part of your whole small fake life where you had some kind of* control? *Well, the chains are off, Dan, they're off for good. You can rot out here for all I care.*

But that's not what I meant, he tried, and *I never thought of you that way,* and—when he finally ran out of denials and had nothing else to say: *Please. I need you. I can't do it on my own . . .*

Of course you can't, she sneered. *You can't do anything on your*

own, can you? I'll give you that much: you've actually turned incom-
petence into a survival strategy. Whatever would you do if you actually
lost your excuses, if you augged up like everyone else? How would you
ever survive without your disability to invoke when you can't keep up?

He wondered what Heaven could possibly be like, to make her
so vindictive. He would have asked but Rhona had turned into
Rakshi Sengupta right in front of his fossiled eyes, and her train
of thought seemed to have jumped to a whole different track. *You*
gotta stay away from the bow, she whispered urgently, glancing
nervously over her shoulder. *You gotta stay out of the attic,* he's *in*
there now and maybe something else. I wish you'd come back this
could be bad and I'm only good with numbers, you know? I'm not so
hot in meatspace.

You're doing fine, Brüks tried to say. *You're even starting to talk*
like one of us roaches. But all he could manage was a croak and a
cough and whatever Rakshi heard seemed to scare her more than
his silence had.

Sometimes he opened his eyes to see Moore looming over him,
moving shiny blinking chopsticks in front of his face. Once or
twice an invisible roaring giant stood on his chest, pressing him
deep into the soft earth at his back (the sparse bands of new-
grown grass on the bulkhead bowed low against the wall, every
blade in uniform alignment); other times he was as weightless as
a dandelion seed. Sometimes he could almost move, and the creatures gathered at his side would startle and pull back. Other times
he could barely roll his eyes in their sockets.

Sometimes he woke up.

Something sat at his side, a vaguely humanoid blur at the edge of
eyesight. Brüks tried to turn his head, unfix his gaze from the
ceiling. All he could see was pipes and paint.

"It's only me." Moore's voice.

Is it. Is it really.

"I guess you weren't expecting it," said the blur. "I'm actually surprised that Sengupta didn't tell you. It's the kind of thing she'd enjoy spreading around."

He tried again. Failed again. His cervical vertebrae seemed—fused, somehow. Corroded together.

"Maybe she doesn't know."

Brüks swallowed. That much he could do, although his throat remained dry.

The blur shifted and rustled. "It's a mandatory procedure where I come from. Too many scenarios when conscious involvement—compromises performance. Whatever the military is these days, you don't get into it unless you . . ."

A cough. A reset.

"The truth is, I volunteered. Back when everything was still in beta, before it was policy."

Do you get to decide, Brüks wondered, *when it comes and goes? Is it a choice, or is it a reflex?*

"You may have heard we just go to sleep. Lose all awareness, let the body run on autopilot. So we won't feel bad about pulling the trigger, afterward." Brüks heard a note of bitterness in the old man's voice. "It's true enough, these days. But we first-gen types, we—stayed awake. They said it was the best they could do at the time. They could cut us out of the motor loop but they couldn't shut down the hypothalamic circuitry without compromising autonomic performance. There were rumors floating around that they could do that just fine, that they *wanted* us awake—for debriefing afterward, experienced observer in the field and all—but we were such hot shit we didn't really care. The sexy bleeding edge, you know. First explorers on the post-Human frontier." Moore snorted softly. "Anyway. After a few missions that didn't quite go according to plan, they rolled out the Nirvana Iteration. Even offered me an upgrade, but it—I don't know. Somehow it just seemed important to keep the lights on."

Why are you telling me this? What does it matter, now that you've thrown the world's lifeline into the sun?

"What I'm saying is, I was there. The whole time. Only as a

passenger—I wasn't running anything—but I didn't *go away*. I'm
not like Valerie's mercenaries, I was—watching, at least. If that
makes you feel any better. Just wanted you to know that."

It wasn't you. That's what you're saying. It's not your fault.

"Get some rest." The blur stretched at his side; the Colonel's
face resolved briefly in Brüks's field of focus, faded again to the
sound of receding footsteps.

Which paused.

"Don't worry," Moore said. "You won't be seeing it again."

The next time he woke up Sengupta was leaning over him.

"How long?" Brüks tried, and was relieved to hear the words
come out.

She said: "Can you move yet try to move."

He sent commands down his legs, felt his toes respond. Tried
wiggling his fingers: his knuckles were rusted solid.

"Not eashily," he said.

"It'll come back it's just temporary."

"Wha' she *do* to me?"

"I'm working on that listen—"

"It's like some kind of ass-fac—ass-*backwards* Crucifix Glitch."
His tongue fought its way around the words. "How the hell did
she—baysh—*baselines* don't glitch, we don't have the shircuits—"

"I said I'm *working* on it. Look we got other things to worry
about right now."

You've *got other things, maybe*—"Whersh Jim?"

"That's what I'm trying to *tell* you he's up there in the attic he's
up there with *Portia* I think—"

"*Whah!*"

"Well how do we know *how* far that shit spread huh it coulda
coated the whole inside of the array and we never woulda known.
Coulda grown all the way up to our front door and got *inside*."

His sympathetic motor nerves were still working at least: Brüks
could feel the hairs rising along his forearms.

"Anybody take sh—take *samples?*"

"That's not what I *do* I'm a math maid not a bucket boy I don't even know the protocols."

"You couldn't look them up?"

"It's not what I do."

Brüks sighed. "What about Jim?"

Sengupta stared past him. "No help he just keeps reading those letters from home over and over. I told him but I don't think he even cares." She shook her head (she did it so *effortlessly*), added: "He comes down here sometimes checks up on you. He's been shooting you up with all sorts of GABA and spasmolytics he says you should be good to go by now."

He flexed his fingers; not too bad, this time. "It's coming back, I guess. Body's just out of practice."

"Yah it's been a while. Anyway I gotta get back." She stepped across the hab, turned back at the base of the ladder. "You gotta get back in the game Dan things are getting weird."

They were, too.

She'd never called him by name before.

He'd stopped slurring his words by the time Sengupta had departed; five minutes later he could roll from side to side without too much discomfort. He bent knees and arms in small hard-won increments, ratcheting each joint against the brittle resistance of his own flesh. At some critical angle his right elbow *cracked* and pain splintered down his arm like an electrical shock: but the limb worked afterward, bent and straightened at his command with nothing but a dull arthritic aching in the joint. Encouraged, he forced his other limbs past their breaking points and reclaimed them for his own.

Reclaimed from what? he wondered.

The medical archives reenacted the corruption of his flesh in fast-forward: a body flooded with acetylcholine, Renshaw cells compromised, ATP drawn down to the fumes by fibrils that just wouldn't stop clenching. No ATP to cut in and ask myosin for this dance; nothing to break the actin-myosin bond. Gridlock. Tetany. A charley horse that froze the whole damn body.

The mechanism was simple enough: once the action potentials started hammering *that* fast it could only end one way. But this didn't seem to be drug induced. Valerie hadn't spiked his coffee or slipped anything into his food. His medical telemetry hadn't picked up the trail until long minutes after Brüks had been hit, but as far as he could tell those signals had come from his own brain: CNS to alpha-motor to synaptic cleft, boom boom boom.

Whatever this was, he'd inflicted it on himself.

He took his time in checking out. Time to extract the catheters and stretch his limbs; time to boot his defossilized corpus back into some semblance of an active state. Time to refuel: his convalescence had left him ravenous. Almost an hour had passed by the time he climbed out of M&R in search of whatever the galley might serve up.

He was halfway across the Hub before he noticed the light bleeding from the spoke.

A snapshot of the past: a corpse, laid out on the lawn. Brüks didn't know which element was the more incongruous.

The lawn, he supposed. At least that was unexpected: not so much a lawn as a patchy threadbare rug of blue-green grass—rusty in the dim longwave vampires preferred—ripped from the walls of the hab and strewn haphazardly across the deck. Vampires had OCD, Brüks remembered vaguely. The mythical ones at least, not the ancient flesh-and-blood predators that had inspired them. Seventeenth-century folk legends had it that you could drive a vampire to distraction by the simple act of throwing salt in its path; some supernatural brain circuit would compel it to drop everything and count the grains. Brüks thought he'd read that somewhere. Probably not peer reviewed.

For all he knew, that ridiculous superstition might have at least a rootlet in neurological reality. It certainly wasn't any more absurd than the Crucifix Glitch; maybe some pattern-matching hiccup in those omnisavant brains, some feedback loop gone over the top. Maybe Valerie had fallen victim to the same subroutine, seen all those thousands of epiphytic blades and torn them from their bulkhead beds with her bare fingernails, counting each leaf as it fluttered to the deck in a halfhearted chlorophyllous blizzard.

Of course, the catch was that vampires didn't have to *count*: they would simply *see* the precise number of salt grains or grass leaves in an instant, know that grand seven-digit total without ever going through the conscious process of adding it up. Any village peasant who sacrificed two seconds scattering salt in his path would buy himself a tenth-of-a-second's grace, tops. Not a great rate of exchange.

Maybe the zombie hadn't known that, though. Maybe the homunculus behind the eyes had rebooted just in time to see what was coming, maybe it somehow wrested control back from all those shortcuts and back alleys and tried one last-ditch Hail Mary with nothing left to lose. Maybe Valerie had let it, watching, amused; maybe even played along, pretended to count each falling blade while her dinner turned the deck into a haphazard shag rug.

Maybe the zombie hadn't even cared. Maybe it had just lain down on command and waited to be eaten. Maybe Valerie had just wanted a tablecloth.

The zombie's throat had been slashed. It lay spread-eagled on its stomach, naked, face turned to the side. The right buttock had been carved away; the quads; one long strip of calf muscle. There was flesh above and flesh below: in between, a flensed femur connected the lower leg to the torso, socketed into the broad scraped spatula of the pelvic girdle.

There was very little blood. Everything had been cauterized.

"You never checked it out," Brüks said.

Sengupta zoomed the view: the gory table setting expanded across the window. Blades of grass grew to the size of bamboo shoots; tooth marks resolved like jagged furrows on bared bloody bone.

Some kind of wire snaked through the grass—barely visible even at this magnification—and disappeared beneath the half-eaten corpse.

"Found eight wires don't know what for exactly but that thing wasn't exactly Secret Santa you know? Carnage said probably booby traps and Carnage is probably right for once. She wanted us to see this."

"How do you know?"

"This is the only feed she didn't break." Sengupta waved the recording off the bulkhead.

"So you jettisoned the habs."

She nodded. "Too risky to go in too risky to leave 'em there."

Another feed abutted the first, a view down the truncated spoke that had once led to Valerie's lair. It ended after only twenty meters now, in a pulsing orange disk flashing UNPRESSURIZED back up the tunnel at two-second intervals. Just like the Commons spoke opposite, cut loose in turn to keep the vectors balanced.

He remembered downhill conversations, the sound of glasses clinking together. "Shit," he said.

"It's not like they're not all the same you know they all got the same plumbing and life support."

"I know."

"And it's not like we're gonna run out of food or air what with everybody being dead and—"

"I fucking *know*," Brüks snapped, and was surprised when Sengupta fell immediately silent.

He sighed. "It's just, the only half-decent moments I've had on this whole bloody trip were in Commons, you know?"

She didn't speak for a moment; and when she did, Brüks couldn't make out the words.

"What did you say?"

"You talked to him down there," she mumbled. "I *know* that

but it doesn't matter even if it was still here *he's* not. He just sits up in the attic and runs those signals over and over like he never even left Icarus . . ."

"He lost his son," Brüks said. "It changed him. Of course it changed him."

"Oh yah." She barely spoke above a whisper. Something in that voice made Brüks long for the trademark hyena laugh. "It changed him all right."

No excuses left. Nothing else to do.

He ascended into the Hub, breached its sky into the guts beyond: hissing bronchioles, cross-hatched vertebrae, straight-edged intestines. He moved like an old man, free fall and residual paralysis and the spacesuit he'd scavenged from the cargo-bay airlock all conspiring to take him to new depths of clumsiness. Up ahead, the paint around the docking hatch splashed the surrounding topography with the usual diffuse glow.

This is where the shadows come, Brüks realized. *Every other corner of the* Crown *is bright as a swimming pool now that the Hold's off-limits, now that Valerie's cave has been cut loose. Shadows don't have a chance back there.*

They've got nowhere else to go . . .

"Welcome back to the land of the living."

Jim Moore turned slowly in the rafters, just past the airlock. The lines of his face, the edges of limbs moved in and out of eclipse.

"This is living?" Brüks tried.

"This is the waiting list."

He thought he might have seen a smile. Brüks pushed himself across the attic and pulled a welding torch from the tool rack: checked the charge, hefted the mass. Jim Moore watched from a distance, his face full of shadow.

"Uh, Jim. About—"

"Enemy territory," Moore said. "Couldn't be helped."

"Yeah." A fifth of the world's energy supply, in the hands of an

intelligent slime mold from outer space. Not a cost-benefit decision Brüks envied. "The collateral, though . . ."

Moore looked away. "They'll make do."

Maybe he was right. Firefall had slowed Earth's headlong rush
to offworld antimatter; a power cord stretched across a hundred
fifty million kilometers was far too vulnerable for a universe in
which godlike extraterrestrials appeared and vanished at will.
There were backups in place, fusion and forced photosynthesis,
geothermal spikes driven deep into the earth's crust to tap the
leftover heat of creation. Belts would be tightened, lives might be
lost, but the world would make do. It always had: the beggars
and the choosers and the spoiled insatiable generations with
their toys and their power-hungry virtual worlds. They would
not run out of air, at least. *They* would not freeze to death in the
endless arid wastes between the stars.

For Moore so loved the world that he gave his only begotten
son. Twice.

"Anyway," Moore added, "we'll know soon enough."

Brüks chewed his lip. "How long, exactly?"

"Could be home in a couple of weeks," Moore said indifferently.
"You'd have to ask Sengupta."

"A couple—but the trip down took—"

"Using an I-CAN running on half a tank, and keeping our
burns to an absolute minimum. We're on purebred beamed-core
antimatter now. We could make it to Earth in a few *days* if we
opened the throttle. We'd just be going too fast to stop when we
got there. End up braking halfway to Centauri."

Or somewhere in between, Brüks thought.

He looked across the compartment. Moore pinwheeled slowly
through light and shadow and looked back. This time the smile
was as unmistakable as it was cryptic.

"Don't worry about it," he said.

"About . . . ?"

"We're not headed for the Oort. I'm not taking you away on
some misguided desperate search for my dead son."

"I—Jim, I didn't—"

"There's no need. My son is alive."

Maybe six months ago. Maybe even now. I suppose it's possible. Not in six months, though. Not after the telematter stream winks out and leaves Theseus *to freeze in the dark.*

Not after you cut him adrift . . .

"Jim . . ."

"My son is alive," Moore said again. "And he's coming home."

Brüks didn't say anything for a while. Finally: "How do you know?"

"I know."

Brüks pushed the torch with one hand into the other, felt the solid reality of mass and inertia without: the fragility of aching body parts within. "Okay. I, um, I should take some samples—"

"Of course. Sengupta and her invading slime mold."

"Doesn't cost anything to check it out."

" 'Course not." Moore reached out a casual hand, anchored himself to an off-duty ladder. "I take it the suit's a condom."

"No point in taking chances." Watching Moore in his yellow paper jumpsuit, the Colonel's naked hand clenched on untested territory.

"No helmet," Moore observed.

"No point in going overboard, either." If *Portia* ran on ambient thermal, it wouldn't be getting enough joules from the bulkhead to sprout any pseudopods on short notice. Besides, Brüks felt stupid enough as it was.

Under Moore's bemused gaze he positioned himself to one side of the hatch and dialed the beam down to short focus. Smart paint sparked and blistered along the lip of the hatch. Nothing screamed or recoiled. No tentacles extruded from the metal in frantic acts of self-defense. Brüks scraped a sample from the scored periphery of the burn. Another from the untouched surface a few centimeters farther out. He moved systematically around the edge of the hatch, taking a sample every forty centimeters or so.

"Will you be using that on me?" Moore wondered behind him.
I should. "I don't think that's necessary just yet."

Moore nodded, his face impassive. "Well. Change your mind, you know where I am."

Brüks smiled.

I wish I did, my friend. I really wish I did.

But I don't have a fucking clue.

Out of the attic into the Hub.

Looks like the Hub, anyway. Could be a lining. Could be a skin.

Through the equator, from frozen north to pirouetting south. Try not to touch the grate on your way through.

Could be watching me right now. I could be swimming through an eyeball.

Don't be an idiot, Brüks. Portia *had* years *in* Icarus; *you were there for three weeks. Not nearly enough time to grow enough new skin to—*

Unless it didn't grow new lining, unless it just redistributed the old. Unless it spent all those years building up extra postbiomass as an investment against future expansion.

It couldn't just ooze through the front door and down the throat without anyone noticing. (Coasting between an eyeball and an iris now: one open, one shut, both silver. Both blind.) No kinetic waste heat, no mass alarms—

Unless it moved slowly enough to blend in with the noise. Unless it happens to know a little more about the laws of thermodynamics than we do . . .

Down the spoke, putting on weight, staring hard at the gloved fingers clenched around their handhold. Alert for subtle mycelia threading between suit and stirrup. Eyes open for any bead of moisture there, some meniscus of surface tension that might belie a film in motion.

You're being paranoid. You're being an idiot. This is just a precaution against a remote possibility. That's all this is.

Don't go off the deep end. You're Dan Brüks.
You're not Rakshi Sengupta.
You only made her.

He heard her moving in the basement as he fed samples into the holding tray. He tried to ignore her foot taps and mutterings as the scrapings cycled through quarantine, as he gave in to reawakened hunger and wolfed down whatever the lab hab's bare-bones galley disgorged, swallowing not quite fast enough to stay ahead of the *Spirulina* aftertaste.

Finally, though, he gave in: pushed from above by Moore's matter-of-fact dissonance, pulled from below by Sengupta's compulsive scuttling. He climbed down out of the lab, maneuvered around the giant seedpod obstruction of Sengupta's tent beside his own. The pilot was running ConSensus on the naked bulkhead between two impoverished bands of astroturf. The *Crown of Thorns* rotated there in animatic real time, two of her limbs amputated at the elbow. *We keep going at this rate and we're going to be three spacesuits and a tank of O_2 by the time we get home,* Brüks mused.

A dot on the map: MOORE, J. floated safely distant in the attic. Other readouts formed a sparse mosaic across the bulkhead; Brüks couldn't understand them all but he was pretty sure that one or two involved the blocking of intercom feeds.

She turned as his feet hit the deck, stared expectantly at his lapel.

"Jim," he said.

"Yah."

"You said he'd—changed . . ."

"Don't have to take my word for it you saw it yourself he's been changing ever since we left LEO."

Brüks shook his head. "He was only—distracted before. Preoccupied. Never delusional."

Sengupta ran her fingers down the wall; file listings flew by too fast for Brüks to make out. "He was transmitting into the Oort did you know that? Even before we left Earth he broke the law hell he helped *make* that law after Firefall nobody else could get away with it but man, he's the great Jim Moore and he was— sending messages . . ."

"What kind of messages?"

"To *Theseus*."

"Well, of course. He was with Mission Control."

"And it talked *back*."

"Rakshi. So *what*?"

"It's talking to him *now*," Sengupta said.

"Uh—what? Through all the interference?"

"We're out of the solar static already most of it anyhow. But he's been collecting those signals for way longer some of the timestamps go back seven years and they *change*. All the early stuff that's all just telemetry you know? Lot of voice logs too but mainly just data, all the sensor records contingency analyses and about a million different scenarios that vampire that *Sarasti* was running when they were closing on target. It was dense there was noise all *over* the signal but the streams were redundant so you can make it out if you run it through the right filters right? And then *Theseus* goes dark you don't hear anything for a while and then there's this—"

She fell silent.

"There's what, Rak?" Brüks prompted gently.

She took a breath. "There's this *other* signal. Not tightbeam. *Omnidirectional*. Washing over the whole innersys."

"He said *Theseus* went dark," Brüks remembered. "They went in and lost contact and that was all anybody knew."

"Oh he knew. It's really thin and it's so degraded you can barely make it out even *with* every filter and noise-correction algorithm in the arsenal I don't think you'd even see it if you didn't already know it was there but Colonel Carnage, man he *knew*. He picked it out and it's . . . it's . . ."

Her fingers danced and jittered in the air between them. The faintest breeze of static wafted through the hab: the moan of a distant ghost.

"That it?" Brüks asked.

"Almost but then you add the last couple of Fouriers and—"

—And a *voice*: thin, faint, sexless. There was no timbre to it, no cadence, no sense of any feeling behind the words. Any humanity it ever might have contained had been eroded away by dust and distance and the dull microwave rumble of a whole universe roaring in the background. There was nothing left but the words themselves, not reclaimed from static so much as built from the stuff. A whisper on the void:

Imagine you are Siri Keeton. You wake in an agony of resurrection . . . record-shattering bout of sleep apnea spanning one hundred forty . . . feel your blood, syrupy . . . forcing its way through arteries shriveled by months on standby. The body inflates in painful increments: blood vessels dil . . . flesh peels apart from flesh; ribs crack . . . udden unaccustomed flexion. Your joints have seized up through disuse. You're a stick man, frozen . . . rigor vitae. You'd scream if you had the breath.

The hab fell silent.

"What the fuck was that?" Brüks whispered after a very long time.

"I dunno," Sengupta drummed her fingers on her thigh. "The start of a story. It's been coming through in bits and pieces, every few years according to the timestamps. I don't think it's finished, either, I think it's still—in progress."

"But what *is*—"

"*I don't know okay?* It *says* it's Siri Keeton. And there's something *underneath* it too not words exactly I don't know."

"Can't be."

"Doesn't matter what you or I think *he* thinks it's Siri Keeton. And you know what he's talking back to it I think he's talking back."

My son is alive.

"He's got a while to wait. If that's really coming from the Oort it'll be a solid year before he can even think about getting an answer."

Sengupta shrugged and looked at the wall.

He's coming home.

ANY SUFFICIENTLY ADVANCED TECHNOLOGY IS INDIS-
TINGUISHABLE FROM NATURE.

—KARL SCHROEDER

NEGATIVE.

Negative.

Negative.

Torn lattices and broken nanowires and mangled microdiodes.
Eviscerated smart paint. Nothing else.

For hours now he'd let worst-case scenarios play out in his
imagination. *Portia* had expanded into the *Crown*. *Portia* had
spread past the attic. *Portia* had oozed invisibly across every bulkhead and every surface, coated the skins of tents and of crew-
members, wrapped itself around every particle of food each of
them had taken into their mouths from the moment they'd
docked. *Portia* enveloped him like a second skin; *Portia* was *inside*
him, measuring and analyzing and corroding him from the outside in and the inside out. *Portia* was everywhere. *Portia* was everything.

Bullshit.

His neocortex knew as much, even as his brain stem stole its
insights and twisted them to its most paranoid ends. Whatever
Portia's ultimate origin, it was the telematter system that had built
it: lasers etching blank condensates into thinking microfilms that
planned and plotted and spread across each new frontier like a
plague of cognition. However far it had spread, however much or
little had infiltrated the *Crown,* it couldn't keep growing once
severed from the engine of its creation. They hadn't been docked
that long: surely the enemy couldn't have achieved anything but
the most superficial penetration of the front line.

The samples were clean.

Which proved, of course, absolutely nothing.

Aboard Icarus it had sprung shut like a leg-hold trap—but it
had had unlimited power to play with, and eight years to learn

how to use it. One passive filter on the solar panels, damped by a thousandth of a percent. One short-circuited electrical line, sparking and heating the surrounding metal. That's all it would have taken—just time, and a little Brownian energy to keep it fed.

What had Sengupta said so offhandedly, just before *Portia* had attacked? *Little warm in there . . .*

It can't sprint without stockpiling energy, he mused. *Maybe it builds up a detectable heatprint before it pounces . . .*

Sengupta poked her head up through the floor. "Find anything?"

Brüks shook his head as she climbed onto the deck.

"Yah well *I* did. I found how that fucking vampire turned you to stone and better you than me, sorry but it *coulda* been me or Carnage either for all I know. I think she did it to all of us."

"Did *what*, exactly?"

"You ever been *scared* roach?"

All the time. "Rakshi, we almost *died*—"

"*Before* that." Sengupta head jerked back, forth. "Scared for *no reason* scared just going to the *bathroom*."

Something jumped in his stomach. "What did you find?"

She threw a camera feed onto the wall: an eye in the attic, looking down along the empty compartment to the Hub hatch. Sengupta zoomed obliquely on a patch of bulkhead beside the secondary airlock. Someone had scrawled some kind of glyph across that surface, a tangle of multicolored curves and corners that might have passed for some Cubist's rendition of a very simple neural circuit.

"I don't remember seeing that before," Brüks murmured.

"Yah you do you just don't *remember* it. Only lasts two hundred milliseconds pure luck this showed up on a screen grab. You see it but you don't remember it and it scares the shit out of you."

"Not scaring me now."

"This is just one *frame* roach it's part of an *animation* but the cameras don't scan fast enough and they're all gone now. I had to sieve like a bugger to even get this much."

He stared at the image: a jagged little tangle of lines and arabesques, a piece of abstract graffiti maybe a hand's-width across. It almost looked meaningful when spied from the corner of the eye, like a collection of letters on the verge of forming a word; it dissolved into gibberish when you looked at it. Even cut out of sequence, even spied from this oblique angle, it made his brain itch.

"It's like she painted—gang signs," he said softly. "All over the ship."

"That's not all she did the way she *moved* remember I *said* I didn't like the way she moved all those little clicks and ticks—shit even that time she attacked me and then *you* I saw her *whisper things* in your ear what did she say to you huh?"

"I—don't know," Brüks realized. "I don't remember."

"Yah you do. Just like that time in Budapest, changed your wiring with vibrations like lining up a bunch of beer glasses pretty wild right?" Sengupta tapped her temple three times in rapid succession, hard. "Not even radical I mean you can't hear a word or smell a fart without your brain rewiring at least a bit that's how brains *are* everything reprograms you. She just figured out where to stamp on the floor to make you freeze up on command. Coulda happened to me just as easy."

"It *did* happen to you," Brüks said. "Why did you attack her, Rak? I saw you in the Hub, you went at her like a rabid dog. What got into you?"

"I dunno it was like she was making these *noises* they just *really* pissed me off I dunno couldn't help myself."

"Misophonia." Brüks barked a soft bitter laugh. "She gave you misophonia."

Images from Simon Fraser: Valerie strapped to a chair, tapping on the armrest . . . *Even back then she was doing it. Even when they were torturing her, she was—reprogramming them* . . .

He couldn't help laughing.

"What?" Sengupta said. "*What?*"

"You know the secret of a good memory?" He bit back another laugh. "You know what really kicks the hippocampus into overdrive, burns tracks into your brain faster and deeper than anything this side of direct neuroinduction?"

"Roach you gotta—"

"Fear." Brüks shook his head. "All that time, playing the monster. I thought she was just into sadistic games, you know? I thought she just got off on scaring us. But she was never that—gratuitous. She was only cranking up the baud rate . . ."

Sengupta smacked her lips and looked out the window.

He snorted softly. "Even that time in the attic, Lee and I—we couldn't even look. We just *knew* she was up there, but we were *facing each other,* Rak. We were each terrified by something to our *left* but we were *facing each other*—" *Of course we were, it's* obvious. *Why didn't I see it before?* "I bet she wasn't there at all, it was just—temporoparietal hallucinations. Night hags. Sensed-presence bullshit."

"Roach remembers." Sengupta was almost whispering. "Roach is starting to *wake up* . . ."

"She was moving us around like checkers." Brüks didn't know whether to be awed or terrified. "The whole time . . ."

"And what *else* did she program into us huh? We gonna start seeing things that aren't there or go walking naked on the hull?"

Brüks thought about it. "I don't—think so. Not if she hacked us all the same way, anyway. Basic things, sure. Fear. Lust. Stuff that's universal." He smiled, a bit grimly, at the thought of the *Crown*'s surviving denizens sprouting preprogrammed hard-ons and spiked nipples. *And that is really not a picture I need in my head right now.* "You want to hack higher-level behavior, you're getting into formative childhood experiences, specific memory pathways. Too many individual differences for one-size-fits-all."

Sengupta clicked her teeth. "That's *old* roach talking new roach should know better. Who *knows* what that—"

"She couldn't hack the Bicamerals," he said slowly.

"What?"

"These tricks—they exploit classic pathways, they'd never work

on someone who'd remixed their brain circuitry. She had to get
them out of the way." A thousand pieces fell suddenly, blindingly
into place. "That's why she attacked the monastery, that's why she
didn't just knock on the front door with an offer. She wanted to
goad them into getting *noticed*. She knew how the roaches would
respond, right down to a weaponized biological just lethal enough
to keep the hive out of the way for the trip but not lethal enough to
derail the mission completely. *Fuck*." He sucked in his breath at
the thought.

"You see the problem," Sengupta said.

I don't see anything but *problems*. "Which one in particular?"

"She's a *vampire* she's prepost-Human all wrapped up into one.
These fuckers solve NP-complete problems in their *heads* and
they drop us like go stones and she's stupid enough to *just acci-
dentally get locked outside* when we leave?"

Brüks shook his head. "She burned. I saw her. Ask Jim."

"*You ask* him." She turned, her eyes lifting from the deck the
moment his face fell from view. "Go on. He's right up there."

"No hurry," Brüks said after a moment. "I'll see him when he
comes down."

To stern the transplanted parasol held back the sun: a great black
shield, coruscations of flame still flickering intermittently past its
edges. Ahead, the stars: one at least crawled with life and chaos,
too distant yet to draw the eye, more hypothesis than hope but
closing, closing. That was something.

In between:

A metal spine webbed in scaffolding, lumpy with metal tumors. Spokes and habs and cauterized stumps sweeping one way
across the sky; a weighted baton sweeping the other to balance
the vectors. The Hub. The Hold: a cylindrical cavern abutting the
shield to stern, its back end ragged and gaping into space. Once it
had been full of cargo and components and thinking cancers:

now it was packed with tonnes of uranium and precious micrograms of antihydrogen and great toroidal superconductors big as houses.

And shadows everywhere: webs and jigsaws cast by a hundred dim lanterns decorating the tips of antennae or the latches of access panels or mounted as porch lights around the edges of half-forgotten emergency airlocks. Sengupta had turned them all on and maxed them all out but they were waypoints, not searchlights: they didn't so much illuminate the darkness as throw it into contrast.

No matter. Her drone didn't need light to see.

She'd eschewed the usual maintenance 'bots that crawled spiderlike along the hull, patching and probing and healing the scars left by micrometeorites. Too obvious, she'd said. Too easy to hack. Instead she'd built one from scratch, remote-printed it on the fabricator still humming away in the refitted Hold: decompiled one of the standard bots for essential bits of lanthanum and thulium and built the rest from the *Crown*'s matter stockpile like Yahweh breathing life into clay. Now it made its painstaking way over a landscape of struts and conduits, shadows and darkness overlaid with false-color maps on a dozen wavelengths.

"*There!*" Sengupta cried for the fourth time in as many hours, and then "*Fuck.*"

Just another pocket of outgassing. By now Brüks had learned not to worry about the myriad leaks in the hull. The *Crown of Thorns* was a sieve. Most ships were. Fortunately the holes in that mesh were pretty small: it would take years for the internal air pressure to decline significantly, barring a direct hit from anything larger than a lentil. They'd die of starvation or radiation sickness long before they had to worry about asphyxiation.

"Felching hell *another* leak I swear . . ." Sengupta's voice trailed off, rebooted: "Wait a second . . ."

The telltales looked the same to Brüks: the faintest wisp of yellow on infrared, the kind of heat a few million molecules might retain for a moment or two after bleeding out from some warmer core. "Looks like more microgassing to me. Smaller than that last one, even."

"Yeah but look where it *is*."

Along one of the batwing struts where the droplet radiator sprouted from the spine. "So?"

"No atmo there no tanks or lines either."

One long arm swept through the near distance, like the candle-lit vane of a skeletal windmill. Another.

Sengupta played with herself. Her marionette picked a careful route through dark, jumbled topography. Something hunkered on the hull ahead, its visible outlines buried in shadow. Infrared showed nothing but that diaphanous micronebula dissipating across the hull.

Can't cloak thermal emissions, Brüks remembered. *Not if you're an endotherm.* "That's not enough of a heat trace—"

"Not if you're a cockroach. Plenty big enough if you can *shut yourself off for a few decades* . . ."

"Just LIDAR it."

Sengupta jerked her head back and forth. "No chance nothing active there could be tripwires."

It can't be her, Brüks told himself. *I saw her burn* . . . "What about StarlAmp?" he wondered.

"I'm *using* StarlAmp we just gotta get closer."

"But if she's tripwired against active sensors—"

"Proximity alert I know"—Sengupta nodded and tapped and kept her eyes on the prize—"but that would be active too and I could pick it up. Plus I'm hiding a lot."

She was: the 'bot's eye saw struts and plating more often than shadows within shadows. Sengupta was keeping her head down on approach. At the moment they could see nothing but the looming face of some small grated butte dead ahead.

"Right around the corner now this should do it."

The drone farted hydrogen and drifted gently out of eclipse. Still nothing but faint amorphous yellow on infrared.

On StarlAmp, though: a silver body, legs straight arms spread, wired against the side of the ship. Boosted photons rendered the body in fragments: ridges of mirrored fabric glinting in thousand-year-old starlight, creases that swallowed any hint of mass or structure. The spacesuit was a patchwork of bright strips and dark absences, the shell of some tattered mummy with half its bandages ripped away and nothing at all underneath. But the right shoulder shone pale and clear: the double-E crest boasting the unsurpassed quality of Extreme Environments, Inc., protective gear; a name tag, programmable for the easy identification of multiple users.

LUTTERODT.

It can't be, Brüks thought. *I saw her, she was dead, her faceplate was in pieces. She was not unconscious. She was not stunned. That was not* her *I saw pounding on the hatch, awake again, running for her life, too frantic to notice that she'd awakened in someone else's suit. It was not Lianna we left to burn, it was Valerie. It was Valerie. We abandoned no others who were not already dead.*

We did not do this.

Sengupta was making noises somewhere between laughter and hysteria: "I *told* you I *told* you I *told* you.

"Not stupid at *all.* She knows what she's doing."

Out there all this time, Brüks thought. *Hiding. I would never have found her. I would never have even looked.*

Maybe Portia's *hiding, too. Maybe I just haven't looked hard enough.*

"We have to tell Jim," he said.

"Will you look at that," Moore remarked.

Lianna's spacesuit flickered on the dome, a snapshot taken before Sengupta had pulled the drone back for fear of setting off alarms. Not that a live feed would have been any more dynamic.

"It's Valerie it's fucking *Valerie*—"

"Apparently."

It can't be, Brüks thought for the thousandth time, the voice in his head weaker with each iteration. By now it was barely whispering.

"I told you we can't *trust*—"

"She seems harmless enough for now," the Colonel remarked.

"*Harmless* are you felching crazy don't you remember what she—"

Moore cut her off: "There's no way that suit could support an active metabolism all the way back to Earth and there's no sign of any kind of octopus rig. She's gone undead for the trip home. Probably expects to revive and jump ship when we dock in LEO. Waking up earlier wouldn't accomplish anything except using up her O_2."

"*Good* then I say we give the bot some teeth and go scrape her off the hull like a goddamn barnacle while we got the chance."

"By all means, if you think she hasn't set up any defenses against just that scenario. If you're certain the hull isn't booby-trapped with a nanogram of antimatter set to blow a hole in the ship if anything disturbs her. I assumed you realized that she's *smart*. You certainly pulled your drone back fast enough."

That gave her pause. "Whadda we do then?"

"She's waiting for us to dock. So we don't dock." Moore shrugged. "We jump ship and let the *Crown* burn up on reentry."

"And then what surf back through the atmosphere on top of a passing comsat? If I was supposed to pack a shuttle nobody told me."

"One thing at a time. For now, just continue your hull crawl in case she's left anything else out there for us to find. If you'll excuse me"—he drifted around his own axis and pushed himself off the deck—"I have my own work to do."

He disappeared into the attic. Brüks and Sengupta stayed at the mirrorball. Buried in the shadows of some obscure province on the hull, Valerie lay still as death in her stolen skin.

"What does she *want?*" Brüks wondered.

"What all of them want I guess to touch the Face of God."

The common enemy, he remembered. "That whole enemy-of-my-enemy thing went down the toilet the moment she slaughtered the Bicams. Whatever it was, she wanted sole access."

"She's got *plans* for God oh yah they all did. Too bad God had plans for them too."

Maybe she wasn't happy just touching the Face of God, he mused. *Maybe she wants to bring God home as a pet. Maybe, while we've been going crazy looking for* Portia *in here, it's been out there all along sealed up in a ziplock bag.*

Another good reason to burn this fucking ship. As if we needed one.

"Whatever those plans were," he said, "they're all dead in the water now."

"Oh you think so huh?"

"Jim's—"

"Oh *Jim* that's a good one. Because vampires are no match for roach plans are they? So how did she get *out* then in the first place huh? How come she isn't still strapped to a chair solving puzzles at SFU?"

Every vampire ever brought back from the junkyard: scrupulously isolated from their own kind, every aspect of their environment regulated and monitored. Hemmed in by crosses and right angles, mortally dependent on precisely rationed drugs to keep them from seizing at the sight of a windowpane. Creatures that, for all their terrifying strength and intelligence, couldn't even open their eyes on a city street without keeling over.

Valerie, walking blithely out of her cage one night and scaring the piss out of prey in a local bar for chrissakes and *then walking back in again,* just to show that she could.

"I don't know," Brüks admitted.

"I do." A single, jerky nod. "It wasn't just her there were others there were three other vampires in that lab and they worked *together.*"

He shook his head. "They'd never have met. Vampires are hardly ever allowed in the same wing of a building at the same time, let

alone the same room. And if they *did* meet they'd be more likely
to tear out each other's throats than draw up escape plans."

"Oh they drew up their plans all right they all just did it *alone*."

Brüks felt a contradiction rising on his tongue. Then it sunk in.

"*Shit,*" he said.

"Yah."

"You're saying they just *knew* what the others were going to
do. They just—"

"*Elevated respiration from the short redhead prey consistent with
conspecific encounter within the past two hundred breaths,*" Sengupta chanted. "*East south corridors public so exclude them; conspecific must have been moved twenty meters along the north tunnel no
more than one hundred twenty five breaths ago.* Like that."

Each observing the most insignificant behavioral cues, the sub-
tlest architectural details as their masters herded them from lab to
cell to conference room. Each able to infer the presence and location of the others, to independently derive the optimal specs for a
rebellion launched by X individuals in Y different locations at Z
time. And then they'd acted in perfect sync, knowing that others
they'd never met would have worked out the same scenario.

"How do you *know?*" he whispered.

"It's the *only way* I tried to make it work from every other angle but it's the only model that *fits.* You roaches never stood a
chance."

Jesus, Brüks thought.

"Pretty good hack right?" Admiration mingled with the fear in
Sengupta's voice. "Can you imagine what those fuckers could do
if they actually *could* stand to be in the same room together?"

He shook his head, amazed, trying to take it in. "That's why
we made sure they couldn't."

"Made? I thought they were just you know. Really territorial."

"Nobody's *that* territorial. Someone must've amped their
responses to keep them from ganging up on us." Brüks shrugged.
"Like the Crucifix Glitch, only—deliberate."

"How do you know that I haven't seen that anywhere."

"Like you said, Rak: it's the only the model that *fits*. How do you think the line could even breed if their default response was to eviscerate each other on sight? Call it the, the *Divide and Conquer* Glitch." He smiled bitterly. "Oh, we were good."

"They're better," Sengupta said. "Look I don't care how helpless Carnage thinks that thing is I'm not taking my fucking eyes off it. And I'm firewalling every onboard app and every subroutine I can find until I check every last one for logic bombs."

Now there's *a quick weekend project.* Aloud: "Anything else?"

"I don't *know* I'm working on it but how do I know she hasn't already figured everything I could think of? No matter what I do I could be playing right into her hands."

"Well, for starters," Brüks suggested, "what about welding the airlocks shut? You can't hack sheet metal."

Sengupta took her eyes off the horizon, turned her head. For a moment Brüks even thought she might look *at* him.

"When it's time to leave, we cut a hole," he continued. "Or blow one. I assume this isn't a rental. If it is, I'm pretty sure the damage deposit's already a write-off."

He waited for the inevitable put-down.

"That's a *great* idea," Sengupta said at last. "Brute-force baseline thinking shoulda thought of it myself. *Fuck* safety protocols. I'll do the Hold and the spokes you do the attic."

The docking hatch wouldn't take a weld: it was too reactive, its reflexes almost the stuff of living systems. Clenched tight it could withstand the point-blank heat of lasers and still dilate on command like a dark-adjusting eye. Brüks had to make do with bulkhead panels from the attic, strip them from their frames and weld them into place across the airlock's inner wall.

Jim Moore appeared at his side, wordlessly helped him maneuver the panels into place. "Thanks," Brüks grunted.

Moore nodded. "Good idea. Although you could probably fab a better—"

"We're keeping it low-tech. In case Valerie hacked the fabbers."

"Ah." The Colonel nodded. "Rakshi's idea, I'm guessing."

"Uh-huh."

Moore held the panel steady at one end while Brüks set the focus. "Serious trust issues, that one. Doesn't like me at all."

"You can't really blame her, given the way you folks—manipulated her." Brüks lined up the keyhole, fired. Down at the tip of the welder, metal flared bright as a sun with an electrical *snap*; but the lensing field damped that searing light down to a candle flame. The tang of metal vapor stung Brüks's sinuses.

"I don't think she knows about that," Moore said mildly. "And that wasn't me in any case."

"Someone like you, anyway." Aim. Fire. *Snap*.

"Not necessarily."

Brüks looked up from the weld. Jim Moore stared back impassively.

"Jim, you told me how it works. *Herded into the service of agendas they'd never support in a thousand years,* remember? *Somebody* thought that up."

"Maybe. Maybe not." Moore's eyes focused on some spot just past Brüks's left shoulder.

You're barely even here, Brüks thought. *Even now, half of you is caught up in some kind of—séance . . .*

"There's a whole other network out there," Moore was saying. "Orthogonal to all the clouds, interacting with them like—I don't know, the way dark matter interacts with baryonic matter maybe. Weak effects, and subtle. Very tough to trace, but omnipresent. Ideally suited for the kind of tweaks we use to *marshal our forces,* as we like to say. And do you know what's really remarkable about it, Daniel?"

"Tell me."

"As far as we know, nobody built the damn thing. We just

discovered it. Turned it to our own ends. The theorists say it could just be an emergent property of networked social systems. Like your wife's supraconscious networks."

"Uh-huh," Brüks said after a moment.

"You don't buy it."

He shook his head. "A stealth supernet fine-tuned for the manipulation of pawns with a specific skill set suited to military applications. And it just *emerged?*"

Moore smiled faintly. "Of course. No complex finely tuned system could ever just *evolve*. Something must have *created* it."

Ouch, Brüks thought.

"I'll admit I've heard that argument before," Moore said. "I just never thought I'd hear it from a biologist."

Evidently half of him was enough.

AN INSTRUMENT HAS BEEN DEVELOPED IN ADVANCE OF
THE NEEDS OF ITS POSSESSOR
—ALFRED RUSSEL WALLACE

HE AWOKE TO the sound of jagged breathing. Shadows moved across the skin of his tent.

"Rak?"

The flap split down the middle. She crawled inside like some heartbroken infant returning to the womb. Even in here, cheek to jowl, she would not look at his face; she squirmed around and lay down with her back to him, curled up, fists clenched.

"Uh . . . ," Brüks began.

"I told you I didn't like him I never did and now look," Sengupta said softly. "We can't trust him roach, I never really *liked* him but you could count on him at least you knew where he stood. Now he's just—gone all the time. Don't know *what* he is anymore."

"He lost his son. He blames himself. People deal with it in different ways."

"It's more than that he lost his kid *years* ago."

"But then he got him *back*. In a small way, for a little while. Can you imagine what that must be like—to, to deal with the loss of someone you loved only to find out that they're still out there somewhere, and they're *talking* and it doesn't matter if they're talking to you or not it's still *them*, it's *new*, you're not just playing a sim or wallowing in the same old video she's *actually out there* and—"

He caught himself, and wondered if she'd noticed.

I could have her back, he told himself. *Not in the flesh maybe, not here in the real world but real* time *at least, better than this thin graveside monologue Jim clings to. All I have to do is knock on Heaven's door . . .*

Which was, of course, the one thing he'd sworn to never do.

"He says Siri's alive," Sengupta whispered. "Says he's coming *home*."

"Maybe he is. That clip from the transmission, right near the beginning, you know? The coffin."

She ran her finger across the inside of the tent. Words wrote themselves in her wake: *Point of view matters: I see that now, blind, talking to myself, trapped in a coffin falling past the edge of the solar system.*

Brüks nodded. "That's the one. If you take that at face value, he's not on board *Theseus* anymore."

"Lifeboat," Sengupta said. "Shuttle."

"Sounds like he's coasting in. It'll take him forever, but there'll be a hibernaculum on board." He rested a hand on her shoulder. "Maybe Jim's not wrong: maybe his son's coming home."

He lay there, breathing in the scent of oil and mold and plastic and sweat, watching his breath ruffle her hair.

"Something's coming," she said at last. "Maybe not Siri."

"Why do you say that?"

"It just sounds *wrong* the way it talks there are these tics in the speech pattern it keeps saying *Imagine you're this* and *Imagine you're that* and it sounds so *recursive* sometimes it sounds like it's trying to run some kind of *model* . . ."

Imagine you're Siri Keeton, he remembered. And gleaned from a later excerpt of the same signal: *Imagine you're a machine.*

"It's a literary affectation. He's trying to be poetic. Putting yourself in the character's head, that kind of thing."

"Why do you have to put yourself in your *own* head though eh why do you have to imagine what it's like to be *you*?" She shook her head, a sharp little jerk of denial. "All those splines and filters and NCAs they take out so much you know, you can't hear the words without them but you can't hear the *voice* unless you strip them away. So I went back through all the steps I looked for some sweet spot where you might be able to hear and I don't know if I did the signal's so weak and there's so much fucking noise but there's this one little spot forty-seven minutes in where you can't make out the words but you can sort of make out the voice, I can't be sure you can never be sure but I think the harmonics are off."

"Off how?"

"Siri Keeton's male I don't think this is male."

"A woman's voice?"

"Maybe a woman. If we're lucky."

"What are you saying, Rakshi? You're saying it might not be human?"

"I don't know I don't *know* but it just *feels* wrong and what if it's not a—a *literary affectation* what if it's some kind of simulation? What if something out there is literally trying to imagine what it's like to be Siri Keeton?"

"The voice of God," Brüks murmured.

"I don't know I really don't. But whatever it is it's got its hooks into a professional killer with a zombie switch in his brain. And I don't know why but I know a hack a when I see one."

"How could it know enough to hack him? How would it even know he exists?"

"It must've known Siri and Siri knew him. Maybe that's enough."

"I don't know," he admitted after a bit. "Hacking a human mind over a six-month time lag, it seems—"

"That's enough touching," she said.

"What?"

She shrugged his hand off her shoulder. "I know you gerries like to touch and have meat sex and everything but the rest of us don't need *people* to get us off if you don't mind. I'll stay here but it doesn't mean anything okay?"

"Uh, this is *my*—"

"What?" she said, facing away.

"Nothing." He settled back down, maneuvered his back against the wall of the tent. It left maybe thirty centimeters between them. He might even be able to sleep, if neither of them rolled over.

If he felt the least bit tired.

Rakshi wasn't sleeping, either, though. She was scratching at her own commandeered side of the tent, bringing up tiny light shows on the wall: a little animatic of the *Crown,* centered on the rafters where MOORE, J. clung to a ghost, or danced on the strings of some unknowable alien agenda, or both; the metal landscape the drone traversed in search of countermeasures; the merest smudge of infrared where a sleeping monster hid in the shadows. There really weren't any safe places, Brüks reflected. Might as well feign what safety you could in numbers. The company of a friend, the warmth of a pet, it was all the same; all that mattered was the simple brain-stem comfort of a body next to yours, huddled against the night.

Sengupta turned her face a little: a cheekbone, the tip of a nose in partial eclipse. "Roach?"

"I really wish you'd stop calling me that."

"What you said before, about losing people. Different people deal in different ways that's what you said right?"

"That's what I said."

"How do *you* deal?"

"I—" He didn't quite know how to answer. "Maybe the person you lose comes back, someday. Maybe someone else fits into the same space."

Sengupta snorted softly, and there was an echo of the old derision there: "You just sit around and *wait?*"

"*No,* I—get on with my life. Do other things." Brüks shook his head, vaguely irritated. "I suppose *you'd* just whip up some customized ConSensus playmate—"

"Don't you fucking tell me what I'd do."

Brüks bit his lip. "Sorry."

Stupid old man. You know where the hot buttons are and still you can't help pushing the damn things.

There was a bright side, though, to Colonel Carnage's deepening insanity, to Valerie's lethal waiting games, to ghosts haunting the ether and uncertain fates waiting to pounce: at least Rakshi wasn't hunting *him* anymore. He wondered at that thought, a little surprised at Sengupta's place atop his own personal hierarchy of fear. She was just a human being, after all. Unarmed flesh and blood. She wasn't some prehistoric nightmare or alien shapeshifter, no god or devil. She was just a kid—a friend even, insofar as she could even think in those terms. An innocent who didn't even know his secret. Who was Rakshi Sengupta, next to monsters and cancers and a whole world on the brink? What was her grudge, next to all these other terrors closing in on all sides?

It was a rhetorical question, of course. Sure the universe was full of terrors.

She was the only one he'd brought upon himself.

His own hunt wasn't going so well.

Of course, *Portia* wasn't quite so visible a target as Daniel Brüks. Brüks couldn't subsist on the ambient thermal energy of bulkhead atoms vibrating at room temperature, couldn't flatten himself down to paper and wrap himself around a water pipe to mask even that meager heatprint. He'd wondered about albedo or spectro, wondered if a probe built of very short wavelengths might be able to pick up the diffraction gratings that *Portia* used to talk—perhaps it used them as camouflage as well—but the improvised detectors he fabbed turned up nothing. Which didn't mean they didn't work, necessarily. Maybe it only meant that *Portia* kept to the *Crown*'s infinite fractal landscape of holes and crannies too small for bots and men.

He was almost certain it couldn't launch an open attack without letting some tell slip beforehand: the heat signature of muscle analogs building a charge, the reallocation of mass sufficient to construct an appendage at some given set of coordinates. It could *run,* though, in some sort of postbiological baseline state, powered by the subtle energy resonating from the crude mass of the real substrate into the superconducting intelligence of the false one. It could think and plan forever in that mode, if Bicameral calculations had been right. It could hide.

The less he found, the more he feared. Something nearby was watching him; he felt it in his gut.

"Ship's too damn noisy," he confided to Sengupta. "Thermally, allometrically. *Portia* could be anywhere, everywhere. How would we know?"

"It's not," she told him.

"Why so sure? *You* were the one who warned me, back when—"

"I thought it might have got in yah. Maybe it did. But not enough to get everywhere it didn't coat *everything.* It didn't *swallow* us."

"How do you know?"

"It wanted to keep us in Icarus. It wouldn't have tried to stop us from leaving if we were still inside it. It's not everywhere."

He thought. "It could still be *any*where."

"Yah. But not enough to take over, just a—a little bit. Lost and alone."

There was something in her voice. Almost like sympathy.

"Yah well why not?" she asked, although he had said nothing. "We know how that feels."

. . .

Sailing up the center of the spine, navigating through the grand rotating bowl of the southern hemisphere, up through the starboard rabbit hole with the mirrorball gleaming to his left: Daniel Brüks, consummate parasite, finally at home in the weightless intestines of the *Crown of Thorns*. "I checked the numbers three times. I don't think *Portia*—"

He stopped. His own face looked down at him across half the sky.

Oh fuck—

Rakshi Sengupta was a presence near the edge of vision, a vague blur of motion and color more felt than seen. He had only to turn his head and she would come into focus.

She knows she knows she knows—

"I *found* the fucker," she said, and there was blood and triumph and terrible promise in her voice. He could not bring himself to face her. He could only stare at that incriminating portrait in front of him, at his personal and professional lives scrolling across the heavens big as the zodiac: transcripts, publications, home addresses; Rhona, ascendant; his goddamn *swimming certificate* from the third grade.

"This is him. This is the asshole who killed my—who killed seven thousand four hundred eighty-two people. Daniel. Brüks."

She was no longer talking like Rakshi Sengupta, he realized at some horrible remove. She was talking like someone else entirely.

"I said I would find him. And I found him. And here. He. Is."

She's talking like Shiva the fucking Destroyer.

He floated there, dead to rights, waiting for some killing blow.

"And now that I know who he is," Shiva continued, "I am going to survive that thing on the hull and I am going to survive that thing in Colonel Carnage's head and I am going to make it back to Earth. And I will hunt this fucker down and make him wish he had never been born."

Wait, what—?
He forced back his own paralysis. He turned his head. His pilot, his confidante, his sworn nemesis came into focus. Her face, raised to the heavens, crawled with luminous reflections of his own damnation.

She spared him a sidelong glance; her lips were parted in a smile that would have done Valerie proud. "Want to come along for the ride?"

She's toying with me? This is some kind of twisted—
"Uh, Rakshi—" He coughed, cleared a throat gone drier than Prineville, tried again. "I don't know—"

She raised one preemptive hand. "I know, I know. Priorities. Counting chickens. We have other things to do. But I've had friends wiped by the storm troopers for hacking some senator's *diary,* and then *this* asshole racks up a four-digit death toll and those same storm troopers *protect* him, you know what I mean? So yah, there are vampires and slime molds and a whole damn planet coming apart at the seams but I can't do anything about that." Her gaze on the ground, she pointed to the sky. "*This* I can do something about."

You don't know who I am. I'm right here in front of you and you've dredged up my whole sorry life and you're not putting it together how can you not be putting it together?
"Bring back a little balance into the social equation."

Maybe it's the eye contact thing. He suppressed a hysterical little giggle. *Maybe she just never looked at me in meatspace . . .*
"There's no fucking justice anywhere, unless you make your own."

Wow, Brüks thought, distantly amazed. *Jim and his orthogonal networks. They really got your number.*
Why don't you have mine?

"What did they do to her? Why doesn't she know me?"
"Do . . . ?" Moore shook his head, managed a half smile under

listless eyes. "They didn't do anything, son. Nobody *does* anything, we're done *to* . . ."

The lights were always low in the attic, the better for Moore to see the visions in his head. He was a half-seen half-human shape in the semidarkness, one arm tracing languid circles in the air, all other limbs entwined among the rafters. As though the *Crown* was incorporating him into her very bones, as though he were some degenerate parasitic anglerfish in conjugal fusion with a monstrous mate. The smell of old sweat and pheromones hung around him like a shroud.

"She found out about Bridgeport," Brüks hissed. "She found out about *me,* she had all my stats right up there on the screen, *and she didn't recognize me.*"

"Oh that," Moore said, and nothing else.

"This goes way beyond some *tweak* to protect *state secrets.* What did they do? What did *you* do?"

Moore frowned, an old man losing track of seconds barely past. "I—I didn't do anything. This is the first I've heard of it. She must have a filter."

"A filter."

"Cognitive filter." The Colonel nodded, intact procedural memories booting up over corrupt episodic ones. "Selectively interferes with the face-recognition wetware in the fusiform gyrus. She sees you well enough in the flesh, she just can't recognize you in certain . . . contexts. Triggers an agnosia. Probably even mangles the sound of your name . . ."

"I know what a cognitive filter is. What I want to know is why someone took explicit measures to keep Rakshi from recognizing me when *nobody knew I was going to be on this goddamn ship.* Because I just *happened* to go on sabbatical just before a bunch of postals decided to duke it out in the desert, right? Because I just *happened* to be in the wrong place at the wrong time."

"I was wondering when you were going to figure that out," Moore said absently. "I thought maybe someone had spiked your Cognital."

Brüks hit him in the face.

At least he tried to. Somehow the blow went wide; somehow Moore was just a little left of where he'd been an instant before and his fist was ramming like a piston into Brüks's diaphragm. Brüks sailed backward; something with too many angles and not enough padding cracked the back of his skull. He doubled over, breathless, floaters swarming in his head.

"Unarmed biologist with no combat experience attacking a career solder with thirty years in the field and twice your mitochondrial count," Moore remarked as Brüks struggled to breathe. "Not generally a good idea."

Brüks looked across the compartment, holding his stomach. Moore looked back through eyes that seemed a bit more focused in the wake of his outburst.

"How far back, Jim? Did they drop some subliminal cue into my in-box to make me choose Prineville? Did they *make* me fuck up the sims and kill all those people just so I'd feel the urge to get lost for a while? Why did they want me along for the ride anyway, what possible reason could a bunch of superintelligent cancers have for taking a cockroach on their secret mission?"

"You're alive," Moore said. "They're not."

"Not good enough."

"*We're* alive, then. The closer you are to baseline, the better your odds of surviving the mission."

"Tell that to Lianna."

"I wouldn't *have* to. I've told you before, Daniel: *roach* isn't an insult. We're the ones still standing after the mammals build their nukes, we're the ones with the stripped-down OS's so damned simple they work under almost any circumstances. We're the goddamned Kalashnikovs of thinking meat."

"Maybe it wasn't the Bicams at all," Brüks said. "Maybe I'm Sengupta's paycheck. That's how you operate, isn't it? You trade in ideology, you exploit passion. Sengupta does her job and you remove the blinders and let her loose to take her revenge."

"That's not it," Moore told him softly.

"How do you know? Maybe you're just out of the loop, maybe those orthogonal stealthnets are running you the way you think you're running Rakshi. You think everyone on the planet's a puppet *except* for Colonel Jim Moore?"

"Do you really think that's a likely scenario?"

"Scenario? I don't even know what the goddamned *goal* is! No matter who's pulling the strings, what have we *accomplished* other than nearly getting killed a hundred fifty million klicks from home?"

Moore shrugged. "God knows."

"Oh, *very* clever."

"What do you want from me, Daniel? I'm not much more clued in than you are, no matter what Machiavellian motives you want to lay at my feet. The Bicamerals see God in everything from the Virgo Supercluster to a flushing toilet. Who knows why they might want us on board? And as for Rakshi's *filter*—how do you know your own people didn't do it?"

"My own people?"

"Public Relations. Faculty Affairs. Whatever your academic institutions use to keep their dirty laundry out of the public eye. They did a lot of mopping up after Bridgeport; how do you know Rakshi's tweak wasn't just another bit of insurance? Preemptive damage control, as it were?"

"I—" He didn't actually. The thought hadn't even occurred to him.

"Still doesn't explain why we both ended up on the same mission," he said at last.

"*Why.*" The Colonel snorted softly. "We're lucky if we even know *what* we've done. Any *why* simple enough for either of us to consciously understand would certainly be wrong."

"Just not enough room in the cache," Brüks said bitterly.

Moore inclined his head.

"So it's just God's will. All these augments and all this technology and four hundred years of so-called *enlightenment* and you still just come around to *God's will*."

"For all we know," Moore said, "your presence on the mission is the *last* thing God wants. Maybe that's the whole point."

Sengupta's voice in his head: *Maybe worship. Maybe disinfect.*

Lazily, almost indifferently, Jim Moore disentangled himself from the rafters and moved spiderlike around the attic. Even in this artificial twilight Brüks could see the slow change in his eyes, the focus deepening in stages: into Brüks's eyes, then past them; through the bulkhead, through the hull; past planets and ecliptics, past dwarfs and comets and transNeptunians, all the way out to some invisible dark giant lurking between the stars.

He's gone again, he thought, but not entirely: Moore dropped that distant gaze from Brüks's face, took his hand, pointed to a freckle there that Brüks hadn't noticed before.

"Another tumor," Brüks said, and Moore nodded distantly:
"The wrong kind."

The sun diminished behind them; they jettisoned the parasol. Ahead, just a few degrees starboard, the Earth grew from dimensionless point to gray dot, edging infinitesimally closer to twelve o'clock with each arbitrary shipboard day. The solar wind no longer roared across every frequency; it spat and hissed and gave way to other voices, infinitely weaker but so much closer to the ear. Jim Moore continued to feed on the archives that carried his son; Sengupta squeezed signal from noise and insisted that other patterns lay embedded there, if she could only decipher them.

But the ghost that called itself Siri Keeton was only one voice on the ether. There were others. Far too many for Brüks's liking.

The world they'd left behind had been almost voiceless, scared into silence by the memory of regimented apparitions burning in the sky. But the voices were coming back now: the rapid-fire click-trains of encrypted data; grainy approximations of faces and landscapes flickering along the six-hundred megahertz band; the hiss of carrier waves on reawakened frequencies, nominally active but holding their tongues as if waiting for the firing of some starting pistol. A myriad of languages; a myriad of messages. Weather reports, newsfeeds rotten with static, personal calls connecting families scattered across continents. The content of the signals wasn't nearly so troubling as their very existence, out here in the unshielded wastes. They should have been trapped in lasers and fiberop, should have been winking confidentially between lines of sight. These, these *broad*casts were relics of another age. The airtight machinery of twenty-first century telecommunications had begun leaking at the seams; people were falling back into more patchwork technologies.

It was what a brain might do, stunted for want of nutrients and oxygen. It was the predictable decoherence of any complex system starved of energy.

But it was home, and they were almost there. There was groundwork to be laid; Moore and Sengupta attended to the details, each returning from whatever far-off places they ventured when not guiding the *Crown* into port. The warrior divided the rest of his time between his tent and the attic; the widow continued to sleep obliviously with the enemy. The vampire lay like a fossil on the hull, undisturbed by whatever alarms or tripwires she might have put in place. Brüks measured the time to Earth by the size of its disk and the incremental unclenching of his own gut. He thought about getting back into gaming, briefly. He slept and dreamt his lucid dreams, but Rhona would not come to him and he no longer had the heart to seek her out. The guts of the *Crown* continued to not grow tentacles.

He finished the last of the Glenmorangie by himself, toasting his lab bench while they crossed lunar orbit. If anyone even noticed their return, they were too busy to send a welcoming committee.

TO TRAVEL HOPEFULLY IS A BETTER THING THAN TO
ARRIVE.
—ROBERT LOUIS STEVENSON

LOW FAST ORBIT over a world in flames. A thousand cool political conflicts had turned hot while they'd been away. Twice as many epidemiological and environmental ones. A myriad of voices cried out on long-forgotten radio bands from kilohertz to giga, tightbeams swamped, planetary gag orders rescinded or forgotten. The O'Neils were under quarantine. The space elevator had collapsed; burning wreckage still fell from orbit, wrought untold havoc along a splatter cone wrapped around a third of the equator. Jet-stream geoengineering had finally buckled beneath the weight of an insatiable atmosphere. Atlas had lost the strength to hold the heavens from the earth; atmospheric sulfates were plummeting and firestorms sparkled endlessly across six continents. Pretoria, Bruges, a hundred other cities had been overrun by zombies, millions reduced to fight/flight/fuck and the authorities weren't even *trying* to control anything inside the hot zones. There was no end to the claims or the confusion. Icarus had fallen. The Fireflies had returned. The invasion had begun. The Realists had struck. The Bicamerals had destroyed the world.

Moore listened to the tsunami along with Brüks and Sengupta—all three of them strapped into the mirrorball on approach—and his face was impassive as a corpse's. *This is your doing,* Brüks did not say. *This was a world just making ends meet until you snatched away its biggest asset. All those millions kept barely watered by power-hungry desalinators; all those uprisings kept barely in check by the threat of institutional force; all those environmental catastrophes kept barely at bay by the sheer overwhelming application of brute-force technologies. Icarus carried a solid fifth of our civilization on its back: what did you* think *would happen when you threw it into the sun?*

Even Sengupta said nothing. There would have been no point. Enemy territory. Couldn't be helped.

Maybe Moore was even right. The world had been simmering for over a century. It had always only been a matter of time before it boiled over. Maybe he hadn't done anything but advance the schedule by a few months.

"Got it," Sengupta said. "Just came line of sight over the Aleutians whole lotta junk between there and here."

A tactical profile flashed up on the horizon: a cylinder ten meters across and maybe thirty long, a great broad corona of solar panels deployed from the starside end and a cluster of mouth parts—microwave emitters, from the look of them—jutting down from the other. It looked like an old-style powersat, albeit in a very strange orbit. Which was, of course, the whole idea.

"Be tricky docking with that thing." Off to one side a simulacrum of the *Crown* lazily lowered its remaining arms—spread-eagled but already spun down—into lockdown position.

"We don't dock," Moore reminded her.

"How long?" Brüks asked.

"Thirty minutes, give or take. We should bottle up."

The attic was not designed to be a working environment during maneuvers but they'd made do, one survivor strapped into each of three suit alcoves directly across from the docking hatch. Brüks and Moore had welded it shut somewhere past Venus but it had been Sengupta who'd planted the thermite along those seams just six hours ago. There wasn't much bulkhead to spare so Sengupta, still unwilling to let ConSensus into her head, had stripped the tool rack bare and slathered smart paint across the gecko boards. The microfibers fuzzed the image a little at high rez but the space was big enough to contain the windows she needed: radar profiles and trajectory overlays, engine vitals, throttles and brakes in shades of gold and emerald. A naked-eye view of Moore's last ace up the sleeve, still posing a little too convincingly as decommissioned junk, swelling slowly against the deceptively blue-green crescent of a world falling into ever-greater depths of disrepair.

In a dedicated window, stage right: Valerie, still tied to the mast. She hadn't moved in weeks; and yet there was still a vague sense of lethality in that frozen body, a sense of something spring-loaded and biding its time.

Its remaining time. Measured in minutes now.

A gentle nudge; a slow, steady pressure pushed Brüks against the side of the alcove. Over on the tool rack the *Crown's* avatar turned one hundred eighty ponderous degrees around its center of mass and coasted on to retrograde.

"Hang on," Sengupta warned, and hit the brakes.

Mutilated, amputated, cauterized, the ship groaned and ground down the delta-vee. Deceleration pushed Brüks against the floor of his alcove. He staggered; the harness held him *up* against this final encore performance of *down*. Moore touched some unseen control and out across the vacuum his chameleon satellite split at the seams like an exploding schematic: solar panels and radiator vanes came apart in puffs of vapor turned instantly to snow. The shell fell apart as if drawn and quartered; body parts sailed silently in all directions. A great arrowhead, aimed at the earth, floated exposed where the false skin had come apart. It glinted in the rising sun, its stubby wings iridescent as a dragonfly's.

Flying debris rattled across the *Crown's* hull like a hail of pebbles. Moore waited until the shower had passed and hit the switch.

Cracks of sunlight ignited around the hatch: the barrier there, welded shut, burned open and fell away. The hatch beyond dilated in an instant; a brief hurricane pulled the plating into space and Brüks toward the stars. The webbing held him fast for the moment it took Moore to snap the buckles. Then they were through and into a void silent but for the sound of fast harsh breathing, just this side of panic, filling Brüks's helmet. The dark Earth spread out below: too convex for mere landscape, too vast

and imminent to be a sphere. Weather systems laid dirty finger-
prints across its face. Coastlines and continents shone like galaxies
where civilization burned bright, flickered dull and intermittent
orange where it had burned out.

It was such a long way down.

Sunlight turned the flotsam ahead into a blinding jigsaw, save
for one brief instant when a great dark hand passed over the sun.
Brüks flailed and turned to see the *Crown of Thorns* in passing,
still huge in the sky, backlit against a risen sun and a bright spreading crescent. Her last frozen breath sparkled near the bow like a
faint cloud of jewels.

He could not see Valerie's hiding place from here.

Something yanked at his leash. Brüks spun to heel, to the shuttle swelling in his sights amid its cloud of debris. *"Focus,"* Moore
hissed over comm.

"Sorry—"

They tumbled forward, Moore in the lead, the others dragged
behind. The shuttle's hatch gaped just behind the wraparound
cockpit window, like a frog's eardrum cut away and folded back
against the head. Some magical spray-on ablative made the hull
shimmer with oily rainbows.

A faint static of ice crystals whispered across Brüks's helmet;
then Moore was on the hull, dead on target, boots coming down
between the edge of the hatch and a convenient handhold welded
like a towel bar to the shuttle's skin. His legs bent to absorb the
impact; one gloved hand seized the handhold as if it had eyes of
its own. Brüks sailed past overhead and splatted against the fuse-
lage. He bounced, spun against the tether, grasped wildly at the
recessed cone of some dormant maneuvering thruster just a few
centimeters out of reach—finally felt his boots click home against
the hull.

The *Crown* was well past and well below them now, drifting
in a slow majestic tumble toward the terminator: forward momentum stalled, decelerating from the endless satellite fall *around*
to the terminal incendiary fall *into.* Distance and the limits of

vision had healed its scars. Now—torn apart, spliced back together, burned and broken—she looked almost pristine. *You kept us alive,* Brüks thought, and then: *I'm sorry.*

Moore yanked him out of one moment and into the next, reeling Brüks and Sengupta in together like fish on a line. Brüks spared a moment to envy the pilot's composure; she hadn't made a sound, hadn't even breathed hard during their fall across the endless chasm. Only now, peering into her faceplate, did he see her lips move below tightly clenched eyelids. Only now, bumped helmet to helmet, could he hear her incantation.

"—oh fuck oh fuck oh fuck—"

You little chickenshit. You turned off your comm . . .

Moore bundled her through the open hatch. Brüks followed, pulling himself into the cabin: two racks, one behind the other, each holding six acceleration couches like a half-dozen eggs in the carton. The couches themselves were squashed nearly flat, each bent just enough at the ass and the knees to avoid being classified as *cots*; the racks faced forward toward a pair of more conventional command chairs and a control horseshoe. Above those controls a visor of quartz glass ran around the front of the cockpit. No stars shone in that nose-down view; the world filled it from side to side, mostly dark, brightening to starboard.

That was pretty much it. One hatch in the aft bulkhead and a smaller one in the deck, both sealed. The first might have led to a cargo hold—a very modest one, given the size of the vessel—but that hole in the deck couldn't have led to anything more spacious than a service crawlway. Contingency orbital extraction, Moore had said. Emergency planetfall for soldiers stranded in the wake of failed missions. This wasn't a shuttle: it was a glorified parachute to be used once and thrown away.

Moore had sealed the hatch and pushed himself into one of the command chairs; Sengupta, recovered from her brief catatonia, fumbled into the other. Brüks strapped himself into one of the hamburger racks behind as their ride booted up. Outside sounds came back to him, faint as a whisper at first, barely audible above the breath of his helmet regulator and the murmured recitation of preflight checklists coming over comm. The hiss of compressed gas. Tiny clicks and beeps, muffled as if under pillows. The snap of ancient switches in their sockets.

70 KPA, HUD reported. He unsealed his visor and slid it back: cold as a glacier in his lungs, the taste of plastic monomers at the back of his throat. Breathable, though.

Moore twisted against his straps, couldn't quite turn to line of sight. "Better keep that down. This bird's been up here a while; could be some leaks."

For the first time Brüks focused his attention on the dashboard: single-function LEDs, rows of manual switches big enough for hands wrapped in Mylar and urethane. Tactical displays trapped in embedded panes of crystal, instead of flowing freely across whatever real estate the moment required.

He brought his visor back down. "This thing is *ancient.*"

Moore grunted over comm. "Older it is, the better the odds everyone's forgotten about it."

We've traded one derelict for another. Past the viewport something flared in the corner of Brüks's eye: sunlight bouncing off a piece of orbital debris, maybe. Or perhaps the thrusters of some distant ship. But it burned too long for one and too low for the other, and the wrong color for either. When he turned to face it, squinting against the sun, he could almost swear he saw the core inside the contrail: a dark jagged patchwork coming apart in a line of fire etching its way across the face of the planet. Sticks and bones, turning to ash.

"There she goes," Moore said softly, and Brüks wasn't quite sure whether he meant the monster or the machine.

"Ignition," Sengupta said as they too began to fall.

The *Crown* burned cleanly. Nothing escaped. No spacesuited figure roused itself at the last moment to leap miraculously free of the hull, although Sengupta's camera watched it until the end. A limb may have twitched, just before the feed died—a brief flicker of consciousness passing through a body just long enough to sense that something had gone wrong with its best-laid plans—but even that could have been a trick of the light. The anticlimax left a guilty lump in Brüks's throat. The ease with which they'd murdered Valerie somehow made her less of a threat in hindsight, stole the justification from their crime.

He barely remembered their descent: frictional incandescence flickering across the windshield like sheet lightning; static hissing on every channel until he remembered to shut down his radio. Fragments, really. Disconnected images. At some point weight returned, stronger and steadier than it had been for a hundred years; racks and acceleration couches and a lone cockroach folded up into conventional sitting positions against a vibrating deck that Brüks could finally perceive as a *floor*. Then they were gliding in a wide spiral over a steely gray ocean and the sun had dropped back below the horizon. Something listed on the seascape below, glimpsed in split-second snatches as it slipped back and forth across the windshield: a half-submerged jump-ramp for water-skiers; a flooded parking lot; the disembodied corner of an aircraft carrier, flickering with Saint Elmo's fire. Brüks got no sense of scale from this altitude, and after a few moments the ocean dropped from sight as Sengupta lifted the nose for final approach.

Something kicked them hard from behind, threw Brüks forward against the harness and brought the nose down with a *slap*. Walls of white spray geysered just past the port, split down the centerline; an instant later the view shattered and dissolved behind sheets of water running down the quartz. Something punched the shuttle under the chin; it bucked back and screamed along its length like an eviscerated banshee. Now they were climbing again. Now they were slowing. Now they were still.

Sheets of water contracted to runnels, to droplets. The shuttle squinted past them to a few fading stars in a steel sky. Way off to the left, almost past line of sight, something flickered in and out of view like a half-remembered dream. Some kind of antennae, perhaps. A wire-frame tree.

Moore dislocated his helmet and let it roll to the deck. "Here we are."

Someone had carved a landing strip out of thin air.

It hung four or five meters above the waves, a scorched scarred tongue of alloy with the shuttle at its tip. It extended back to solid land like some kind of absurd diving board—except the substrate wasn't land, and it wasn't solid. It emerged from the ocean as gradually as a seashore; electric blue sidewinders writhed and sparked along the waterline, followed the swells as they surged up and down the slope. The surface seemed gray as cement in the predawn half-light, and almost as featureless except for the scored tracks the shuttle had left. But while it rose from the sea as unremarkably as a boat ramp at one end, it did not subside or drop off or reimmerse at the other: it just *faded away,* a massive slab of listing alloy big as a parking lot, segueing from solid undeniable opacity to spectral translucence to *nothing at all* over a distance of maybe a meter and a half.

Except for this runway, freshly sculpted by the screaming friction of a hot landing.

Moore had already shed his spacesuit and was standing on thin air, ten meters ahead of the grounded shuttle. Bitter gray swells marched past below his feet. Every couple of seconds a wire-frame structure flickered into existence nearby, towering six meters over his head and infested with parabolic antennae.

Brüks leaned out the hatch and took it all in. The frigid Pacific wind blew through his jumpsuit as though he were naked. The earth pulled at him with a force he'd almost forgotten; his arms, bracing him against the bulkhead, seemed made of rubber.

Sengupta poked him from behind. "Hurry *up* roach you never seen chromatophores before?"

In fact, he had. Chroaks were basically just a subspecies of

smart paint. But he'd never encountered one on this *scale* before.
"How big is this thing?"

"Pretty small only a klick across look you want to get off before
the damn thing sinks the rest of the way?"

He squatted, grabbed the lip of the hatch, clambered overboard. Gravity almost tipped him on the landing but he managed to keep his feet under him, stood swaying with one hand
braced against the hull (still warm enough for discomfort, even
after being soaked by an ocean). This close to the shuttle the
cloak had been thoroughly scored away, but a half-dozen uncertain steps took him onto a substrate clearer than glass. He looked
down onto a wave-tossed sea, and fought the urge to flail his
arms.

Instead, he walked carefully toward Moore as Sengupta climbed
down behind him. Flickering orange light caught his eye as he
rounded the nose of the shuttle: fire in the near distance, a gutter-
ing line of flames atop an incongruous levitating patch of scorched
earth. Brüks could make out superstructure silhouetted there: low
flat-topped rectangles, a radio dome cracked open like an eggshell,
the barely visible crosshatch of railings and fence posts against the
fire. Maybe something moving, ant-size with distance.

Not your average gyland, this. Not a refugee camp or a city-state,
no iffy commercial venture with a taste for the forgiving regulatory
climate of International Waters. This was a place for Moore and
his kind: a staging ground for covert military actions. A lookout
on the high seas, patrolling the whole Northern Gyre. Clandestine.

Not clandestine enough, apparently.

He shivered at Moore's shoulder. "What happened here?"

The Colonel shrugged. "Something convenient."

"How so?"

"It's been abandoned. We won't have to talk our way in."

"Is it still plugged in? What if it—"

Moore shook his head. "Shouldn't be a problem. Nobody who'd
have done this would care about Heaven." He pointed at the distant flames. "That way."

Brüks turned as Sengupta came up behind them; the shuttle cooled in the background, half-melted ablative oozing like candle wax around its belly. "Huh," he remarked. "I'd have thought there'd be, you know. Landing gear."

"Too expensive," Moore told him. "Everything's disposable."

You got that right.

A halting, freezing hike up a shallow slope. A walk on the water. An invisible bridge to the visible tip of a derelict iceberg. Gutted structures spread out before them like little pieces of Gehenna, some still aflame, others merely smoldering. Finally they reached the visible edge of that levitating island: little more than a patina of black greasy soot floating in midair. It was still a relief to see something underfoot; it was a greater relief to stop and catch his breath.

Moore laid a sudden hand on his shoulder. Sengupta said, "*Wha*—" and fell silent.

Ahead, barely visible through a curtain of oily smoke, things moved.

They'd arrived at what had once been some kind of air-traffic hub: a low-slung control shack whose walls and roof came together in a wraparound band of soot-stained windows angled at the sky. Two dead helicopters and a one-winged jump jet littered a scorched expanse of tarmac and landing bull's-eyes, barely visible beneath the scoring. The nozzles of retracted fuel lines poked through the deck here and there; one burned fitfully, a monstrous candle or a fuse set to detonate whatever reservoir fed the flame. In the middle of it all, bodies moved.

The bodies were human. Their movements were anything but.

Moore waved the others back against the shack, spared a backward glance and a raised hand: *Stay here.* Brüks nodded. Moore slipped around the corner and disappeared.

A swirling gust blew sparks and acrid smoke into Brüks's face. He suppressed a cough, eyes stinging, and squinted through the haze. Human, yes. Two, maybe three, near the edge of one of the bull's-eyes. Gray coveralls, blue uniform, insignia impossible to make out from this distance.

They were *dancing*.

At least, that was the closest word Brüks could summon to describe the tableaux: movements both inhumanly precise and inhumanly *fast,* humanoid simulacra engaged in some somatic call-and-response unlike anything he'd ever seen. There was a lead, but it kept changing; there were steps, but they never seemed to repeat. It was ballet, it was semaphore, it was some kind of *conversation* that engaged every part of the body except the tongue. It was utterly silent but for the machine-gun staccato of boots on the deck, faint and intermittent through the soft roar of the wind and the crackling of the flames.

And faintly familiar, somehow.

Moore ended it all with a blow to the back of the head. One moment the dancing marionettes were alone on the stage; the next the Colonel had materialized from the smoke, his hand already blurring toward the target. The gray-clad dancer jerked and thrashed and collapsed twitching onto the deck, a disconnected puppet gone suddenly grand mal; the other threw himself down at the same instant, although Moore hadn't touched him. He lay twisting beside his fallen partner, still in frantic clockwork motion but only twitching now, amplitude reined in to complement these new and unexpected steps brought so suddenly into the routine.

"Echopraxia echofucking*praxia,*" Sengupta hissed at his shoulder.

Moore was back. "This way."

A broken door gaped around the corner. Inside, brain-dead smart paint sparked and sizzled along those few control surfaces that hadn't already been put to the flame.

Brüks glanced over his shoulder. "What about—"

"They're in a feedback loop. We don't have to worry until the mechanic comes back." A companionway gaped from the far bulkhead. A fallen cabinet blocked the way. Moore pushed it aside.

"Isn't that bad for them?" Brüks wondered, and immediately felt like an idiot. "I mean, wouldn't it be better if we broke the loop? Split them up?"

Moore paused at the top of the stairs. "Best-case scenario, they'd do as well as you would if someone split you down the middle."

"Oh." After a moment: "Worst-case?"

"They wake up," Moore said, "and come after us."

YOU CAN'T GO HOME AGAIN.

—THOMAS WOLFE

THEY CAME ACROSS a sloping commons area, dark and derelict but for a cone of emergency light spilling in from the corridor and a smattering of icons winking fitfully from the far bulkhead: a row of comm cubbies, snoozing until some lonely grunt chose to phone home or eavesdrop on the happening world. They could only access Main Street—no windows into anything that might require security clearance—but ConSensus and perscomm links floated free to one and all, serenely untroubled by whatever small apocalypse had taken out the upper deck.

Moore moved on in search of greater privilege and darker secrets. Sengupta hung around long enough to make sure the links were solid before disappearing in his wake.

Brüks sat in the leaning darkness and did not move.

What do I say to her? What do I say?

Hey, you know how Icarus went away and the world fell apart? Funny story . . .

You know how we thought there was no God? Well, it's worse than you think . . .

Hi, honey. I'm home.

He took a deep breath.

This is a stupid idea. We're way past this. I should just—catch up with the others.

Let it out again.

Someone has to tell her. She needs to know.

He felt the corners of his mouth pull back in a grimace of self-loathing.

This isn't even about her. This is about Dan Brüks and his imploding worldview. This is about running back to the only person who ever gave you any shred of comfort whether you deserved it or not . . .

He sacc'ed the interface.

He tried four times before the system could even find the address; the lump in his throat grew with each attempt. The Quinternet was falling apart; *everything* was. But it had deep roots, old roots reaching back over a century: a design both completely uncephalized and massively redundant. Functionality in the face of overwhelming entropy had been built into its DNA from the start.

> LINK ESTABLISHED: WELCOME TO HEAVEN
> TIMMINS FRANCHISE
> VISITOR'S LOBBY

Still there. Still online. Still alive. He hadn't entirely believed it. "Uh, Rhona McLennan, November 13, 2086."

> PINGING.

Please pick up.

PINGING

Please be busy.

PINGING

"Dan."
Oh God. Here she is.
I must be dreaming . . .
"Hi, Rho."
"I wondered where you'd got off to. Things have been so con-
fused out there lately . . ."
She was a voice in the darkness, distant, disembodied. There
was no visual.
"I'm sorry I haven't been in touch . . ."
"I wasn't *expecting* you to get in touch." Maybe there was warmth
in her voice now. Wry amusement at least. "When was the last
time you dropped by?"
"You didn't *want* me to drop by! You said—"
"I said I wasn't going to come back out, love. I said I didn't want
you to spend all our time together trying to change my mind."
He didn't say anything.
"I'm glad you *did* come by," she said after a while. "It's good to
see you."
"I can't see you," he said softly.
"Dan. What would be the point?"
He shook his head.
"Is it important? I could show you—something. If that would
make it any easier."
"Rho, you can't stay in there."
"I'm not having this argument again, Dan."
"*This is not the same argument!* Things have *changed* . . ."
"I know. I'm in Heaven, not Andromeda. I can see everything
out there that I want to. Upheaval, rebellion, environmental col-
lapse. *Plus ça change.*"

"It's a loss worse since Icarus went down."

"Yeah," she said slowly. "Icarus."

"Everything's stretched to the breaking point, there're outages and brownouts everywhere you look. Took me four tries to even *find* you, did you know that? And Heaven's hardly the most obscure address on the planet. The whole network's—forgetting things . . ."

"Dan, it's been forgetting things for ages. That's why we call it the Splinternet."

"I didn't know you called it that," he said, vaguely surprised.

"How is an elephant like a schizophrenic?"

"I—what?"

"An elephant never forgets."

He said nothing.

"That's an AI joke," she said after a while.

"Could be the worst one I've ever heard."

"I got a million of 'em. You sure you want me to come back out?"

More than ever.

"But really, how long do you think *you* could stay sane if you remembered everything you'd ever experienced? It's *good* to forget, no matter what kind of network you are. It's not a breakdown, it's an *adaptation.*"

"That's bullshit, Rho. Losing network addresses is a *good* thing? What's next, the voltage protocols? What happens when the grid *forgets* to shunt power to Timmins?"

"There are risks," she said gently. "I get it. The backups could fail. The Realists could strike. The AIRheads probably still want me for war crimes just on general principles, and I can't say I really blame them. Every day in here could be my last, and how's that any different from life out there?" Some tiny lens sent her the sight of Daniel Brüks opening his mouth; she rushed on, preempting him: "I'll tell you. I don't have anything anyone could want. I'm not a threat to anyone. My footprint's a tiny fraction of yours, even factoring in your kink for spending so much time in tents. I can experience literally everything in here that you can out there, and a billion other things besides. Oh, and one other thing."

She paused some precise number of milliseconds.

"I don't have to kill intelligent beings to pay the rent."

"Nobody's saying you'd have to—"

"Now let's look out *there,* shall we? Infectious zombieism running rampant in at least twenty countries I know of. Realists and Rearguard Catholics taking shots at any heretics they can lay their crosshairs on. Food poisoning on the rise for anyone who can't afford a consumables-class printer. They haven't even *bothered* tracking species extinction rates for a decade now, and—oh, and have you heard about that new weaponized echopraxia that's going around? *Jitterbug,* they call it. Used to be pure monkey-see-monkey-do, but they say it's mutating. Now you get to die dancing, bring a friend along for the ride."

"The difference," he said grimly, "is that when the power fails out here, you can curl up under a blanket. If it fails in Heaven you're brain-dead in five minutes. You're *helpless* in there, Rhona, and it's all just a house of cards waiting for . . ."

She didn't answer. He couldn't finish.

He wondered how much she'd changed already, how much of her remained behind that gentle, utterly unyielding and unreal voice. Was he even talking to an intact brain, or to some hybrid emulation of neurons and arsenide? How much of his wife had been replaced over the past two years? That incremental cannibalism, that ongoing fossilization of flesh by minerals—it had always scared the living shit out of him.

And she *embraced* it.

"I've seen things," he told her. "World-shaking things."

"We all have. It's a shaky world."

"Will you just shut up and *listen* to me? I'm not talking about the goddamned news feeds, I'm talking about things that—I've seen things that—I know why you went away now, you know? I finally get it. I never did before, but right now I swear I'd join you in a second if I could. But I can't. It doesn't feel like transcendence to me, it doesn't feel like rising into some better world, it feels like being—*replaced*. I mean, I can't even stand to have a ConSensus augment in my head. It's like anything that changes what I am *kills* what I am. Do you understand?"

"Of course. You're scared."

He nodded miserably.

"You've always been scared, Dan. As long as I've known you. You've spent your whole life being an asshole just to keep people from finding out. Lucky for you I could see through it, mmm?"

He said nothing.

"Know what else I see?"

He didn't. He didn't have a clue.

"That's what makes you brave."

It took a moment for that to sink in. "What?"

"You think I don't know? Why you keep mouthing off to the wrong people? Why you sabotaged your own career every step of the way? Why you can't help but face off against anybody who has any power over you?"

Climbing an endless ladder toward a hungry monster. Charging into a leghold labyrinth with living walls. Biting the head off a girl half his size when she told him he couldn't go home.

Maybe not such a proud moment, that last one . . .

"You're saying I overcame my fear," he began.

"I'm saying you *gave in* to it! Every time! You're so scared of being seen as a coward you'd jump off a cliff just to prove you weren't! You think I never saw it? I was your *wife,* for God's sake. I saw your knees knocking every time you ever stood up to the schoolyard bully and got your teeth kicked in for your troubles. Your whole damn life has been one unending act of overcompensation, and you know something, love? *It's just as well.* Because people *need* to stand up now and then, and who else is going to?"

It didn't sink in at first. All he could do was frown and replay and try to figure out when the conversation had switched tracks like that.

"That has to be the most heartwarming definition of *asshole* I've ever heard," he said at last.

"I liked it."

He shook his head. "It doesn't matter, though. I still can't—follow you . . ."

"Follow me." Her voice was flat with sudden insight. "You think . . ."

She won't come out, and I can't go in—

"Dan." A window opened on the wall. "Look at me."

He looked away.

He looked back.

He saw something that resembled a pickled fetus more than it did a grown woman. He saw arms and legs drawn close against the body in defiance of the cuffs at wrists and ankles, of the contractile microtubes that pulled them straight three times a day in a rearguard battle against atrophy and the shortening of tendons. He saw a shriveled face and a hairless scalp and a million carbon fibers sprouting from the base of the skull, floating like a nimbus around her head.

"This is not what I'm talking about," something said with her voice, and her lips did not move.

"Rhona, why are you—"

"You call this change, but it isn't," the voice said. "Heaven isn't the future. It's a refuge for gutless wonders who want to *hide* from the future, a nature preserve for people who can't adapt. It's, it's wish fulfillment for passenger pigeons. You think I was *lording* this over you? This is nothing but a dumping ground for useless also-rans. You don't belong here."

"Useless?" Brüks blinked, stunned. "Rho, don't *ever*—"

"I ran away. I threw in the towel years ago. But you—you may be doing everything for the wrong reasons and you may be pissing yourself when you do it, but at least you haven't given up. You could be hiding with the rest of us but you're out there in a world with no reset button, a place you have no control over, a place where other people can take your whole life's work and twist it to such horrible ends and there's *no way to ever take back what they did.*"

"Rhona—what—"

"I *know,* Dan. Of course I know. You didn't have to hide it from me. You *couldn't* hide it from me, I'm more plugged in than you are." The voice was gentle, and kind, and still the face of that thing did not move. "The moment they quarantined Bridgeport I knew. I almost called you then, I thought maybe you'd finally give up and come *inside* but—"

A mountain smashed into the back of his skull. His forehead smacked the wall of the cubby, rebounded; he toppled backward in his chair and sprawled across the deck. A red-shifted galaxy ignited, pulsing, in his head: light-years away, an upside-down giant stood silhouetted in the doorway.

He blinked, moaned, tried to focus. The starfield dimmed; the roaring in his head faded a little; the giant shrank down to merely life-size. Its depths were so black they almost glowed.

Rakshi Sengupta, meet Backdoor Brüks.

Somewhere far away, a computer called out in the voice of his dead wife. Brüks tried to bring his hand to his head; Sengupta stomped on it and leaned over him. Fresh pain erupted off the midline and shot up his arm.

"I want you to imagine something, you fucking *roach.*" Sengupta's fingers danced and dipped overhead.

Oh God no, Brüks thought dully. *Not you, too . . .* He let his head loll to the side, let his eyes stray somewhere anywhere else; Sengupta kicked him in the head and made him pay attention. Her fingers clenched and interlaced and bent backward so far he thought they'd break.

"Want you to imagine *Christ on the Cross*—"

He was barely even surprised when the spasms started.

Sengupta leaned in to admire her handiwork. Even now she could not look at his face. "Oh *yes* I have been waiting for this I have been *working* for this I have—"

A sound: sharp, short, *loud*. Sengupta fell instantly silent. Stood up.

A dark stain bloomed on her left breast.

She collapsed onto Brüks like a rag doll. They lay there a moment, cheek to cheek, like slow-dancing lovers. She coughed, tried to rise; sprawled downhill to Brüks's side. Her dimming eyes focused, unfocused, settled finally on some point near the hatch. Jim Moore stood there like a statue, his eyes so full of grief they might as well have been dead already.

Something crossed Sengupta's face in that moment. Not happiness, not quite. Not surprise. Enlightenment, maybe. After a moment, for the very first time, she looked Dan Brüks straight in the eye.

"Oh *fuck*," she whispered as her eyes went out. "Are you ever screwed."

"I know it doesn't make any sense," Moore was saying, turning the gun over in his hands. "We were never close. That may have been my fault, I suppose. Although, you know, he wasn't what you'd call an *easy* child . . ."

He'd pulled up a chair, sat hunched and leaning against the slant with his knees on his elbows, the light from the corridor catching him in quarter-profile. Brüks lay on the floor while Sengupta's blood pooled against his side. It soaked through his clothing, stuck his jumpsuit to his ribs. His head throbbed. His throat was parched. He tried to swallow, was relieved and a bit surprised to find that he could.

"Now, though . . . he's half a light-year away, and for the first time in his life I feel that we're actually able to *talk* . . ."

Pale nebulae clouded Sengupta's open eyes. Brüks could see them clearly even in this dim light; could even turn his head a little to bring them into proper focus. Not Valerie's best-laid glitch, not the total paralysis the vampire had layered down with weeks of graffiti and subtle gesticulation—or at least, not the same precision in the trigger stimulus. It probably *was* the same program, the same chain of photons to mirror neurons to motor nerves, still dozing in the back of his head should anyone sound the call to arms; Sengupta must have just improvised after the fact, gone back over old footage, figured out the basic moves and acted them out as best she could.

"It's as though he knew I'd be listening all those months ago, as though he knew what I'd be *thinking* when his words arrived . . ."

She probably hadn't even been planning for vendetta. It had probably been just another pattern-matching puzzle to keep that hyperactive brain occupied, fortuitously available when it turned out that her wife's murderer and her adopted roach were one and the same. This rigor was half-assed and short-lived; he could feel it in his tendons. The tightness was already beginning to subside.

Still pretty impressive, though.

"I feel closer to Siri than I ever did when we were on the same planet," Moore said. He leaned forward, assessed the living and the dead. "Does that make any sense to you?"

Brüks tried to move his tongue: it barely trembled against the palate. He focused on moving his lips. A sound emerged. A groan. It contained nothing but frustration and distress.

"I know," Moore agreed. "And at first it felt more like just— reports, you know? Letters home, but full of *facts*. About the mission. I listened to that signal, oh, I would have listened forever, even if all he'd ever done was tell the tale. I learned so much about the boy, so much I never suspected."

Take two . . . : "Jim . . ."

"And then it—changed. As though he ran out of facts and had nothing left but feelings. He stopped the *reportage* and started *talking* to me . . ."

"Jim—Rak—Rakshi thought—"

"I can even hear him *now,* Daniel. That's the remarkable thing. The signal's so weak it shouldn't even be able to penetrate the atmosphere, especially with all the broadband chatter going on. And yet I can *hear* him, right here in the room."

"Rakshi thought—your zombie switch—"

"I think he's trying to warn me about something . . ."

"—you might have been—hacked—"

"Something about *you*."

"She said you—you might not be in—control—"

Moore stopped turning the gun in his hands. Looked down at it. Brüks fired every command he could, along every motor nerve in his body. His fingers wiggled.

Moore smiled a sad little smile. "Nobody's in *control*, Daniel. Do you really think you don't have one of these zombie switches in your own head, you don't think *everyone* does? We're *all* just along for the ride, it's the coming of the Lord is what it is. God's on Its way. It's the Angels of the Asteroids, calling the shots . . ."

Angels again. Divine teleoperators, powerful creatures with neither soul nor will. God's sock puppets.

Jim Moore was turning into one before his eyes.

"What if it's not—Siri?" Brüks managed. His tongue seemed to be thawing a bit. "What if, what if it's something *else* . . ."

The Colonel smiled again. "You don't think I'd know my own son."

"*It* knows your son, Jim." *Of course it knows him, it* mutilated *him, can't you remember the goddamn slide show?* "It knows Siri, and Siri knows you, and—and it's *smart* Jim, it's so fucking smart . . ."

"So are you." Moore eyed him curiously. "Smarter than you let on, anyway."

If only.

He wasn't smart enough to get out of this. Not smart enough to outthink some interstellar demon who could hack a man's brain across five trillion kilometers and a six-month time lag, who could trickle its own parasitic subroutines into the host's head and lead him around in real time. Assuming that Moore hadn't just gone batshit crazy on his own, of course. That was probably the most parsimonious explanation.

Not that it mattered. Brüks wasn't smart enough to get out of that, either.

Moore lowered his eyes. "I didn't want to do that, you know. She was a good person, she was just—misguided. I suppose I may have overreacted. I only did it to protect you."

Behind him, up among the crossbeams that ribbed the ceiling, one shadow stirred among others. Brüks blinked and it was gone.

"I wonder if that was such a good idea . . ."

"It was," Brüks croaked. "Really. It—"

Faster than he could finish: a shape detached itself from the ceiling, swayed silently against the light, and folded down over Moore like a praying mantis. Inhuman fingers, blurred in motion; silhouetted lips in motion.

Without any fuss at all, Moore stopped moving.

Valerie dropped soundlessly to the deck, crossed the room, stared down at Daniel Brüks as he slowly, painfully bent one knee. It was the closest thing to fight/flight left in him. She bent close and whispered—

"The tomb at Aramathea."

His body unlocked.

He gulped air. The vampire stood, stepped back, gave him a small cryptic smile.

Brüks swallowed. "Saw you *burn,*" he managed. *Twice.*

She didn't even dignify it with an answer.

We expect a trick, and we find one, and we pat ourselves on the back. We find her pinned to the hull—think we do, anyway—and just stop looking. Of course she's out there: there she is. There goes her hab and all its tripwires. Why look any further?

Why look inside the Crown? Why check the hatches in the shuttle . . . ?

He propped himself up on his elbows; the sodden jumpsuit peeled from the deck as if steeped in half-set epoxy. Valerie watched impassively as he got to his feet.

"So what now? You give me a ten-second head start to make it sporti—"

A blur and a hiss and he was off his feet, strangling and kicking a meter from the deck with her hand around his throat. In the next instant he was back on the floor, collapsed in a heap while Valerie grinned down with far too many teeth.

"All this experience," she remarked while he gasped for breath, "and you're still an idiot."

Catch and release. Cat and mouse. Just having fun, he supposed. In her way.

"Aircraft are all dead," Valerie said. "I find a ride in the moon pool, though. Get us to the mainland at least."

"Us," Brüks said.

"Swim if you'd rather. Or stay." She dropped her chin in the direction of the statue frozen on its chair. "If you stay you should kill him, though. Or he kills you when he unlocks."

"He's my friend. He *protected* me, before—"

"Only part of him. OS conflict. It resolves soon enough, it's resolving *now*." Valerie turned toward the door. "Don't wait too long. He's on a mission from God."

She stepped into the light. Brüks looked back at his friend: Jim Moore sat staring at the floor, face unreadable. He blinked, very slowly, as Brüks watched.

He did not cry out against his abandonment.

Brüks followed the monster along slanting corridors and companionways, down endless flights of emergency-lit stairs into the bowels of the gyland, unto its very anus: an airlock that would have felt too small at five times the size, given present company. The chamber beyond echoed like a cave and looked a little like one, too: pipes and hoses and cylinders of compressed gas jutted like stalactites from the angled ceiling. The room was half-underwater; the ocean had breached the banks of the moon pool as the gyland listed, flooded down to some temporary equilibrium halfway up the far bulkhead. Diffuse gray-green light filtered up from outside and wriggled dimly across every surface.

It was only a small port in the storm. There was probably a bay big enough to dock a Kraken or a Swordfish somewhere else on this floating behemoth, but here the berths were for smaller vehicles. A dozen parking racks hung from an overhead conveyor train, most of them empty. A two-person midwater scout rested snuggly in one clenched set of grappling claws, the end of a service crane still embedded in its shattered crystal snout. Another dangled precariously from the ceiling, nose submerged, tail entangled in its broken perch.

A third, apparently intact, floated just off the flooded deck: broad shark body, whale's flat flukes, the great saucer eyes of some mesopelagic hatchetfish bridging the snout. *Aspidontus*, according to the letters etched just above the countershade line. It bumped gently against the edge of the moon pool—tail to the bulkhead, nose poking out over the hole in the floor—a waist-deep wade down the flooded incline.

A fucking *cold* wade, as it turned out. Valerie leapt the distance from a standing start, sailed over Brüks's head and landed one step from the hatch. The vessel dipped and rolled under the impact; she didn't even wobble. By the time Brüks had dragged his soaking legs and shriveled testicles onto the hull, she was inside and the little sub was humming awake.

Three seats. Brüks dropped into shotgun, pulled the hatch down overhead, dogged it. Valerie tapped the dashboard; *Aspidontus* shook herself, thrashed her flukes, humped forward half-stranded over loose canisters and bits of broken podmates. She hung balanced for a moment, belly scraping the submerged edge of the pool; her flukes slapped the water like a dolphin's and she was free.

Still dark overhead, though, for all the hours that must have passed since sunrise. The derelict gyland loomed above them like the belly of a mountain, all too visible from underneath, ready to drop down and squash them flat without warning. There was nothing beyond the cockpit: no fish, no plankton swarms, no sun-dappled waves sending shafts of light dancing through the water. Not even the indestructible drifts of immortal plastic debris so ubiquitous from pole to pole. Nothing but heavy blackness above and dim green murk everywhere else. And *Aspidontus*: a speck embedded in glass.

And where to now? he wondered. *Why did I even come along, why did she even take me, what* am *I to this thing other than a walking lunch? How the hell did I ever decide that Jim Moore was less dangerous than a goddamn* vampire?

But he knew it was a meaningless question. It was predicated on the assumption that the decision had ever been his to begin with.

Darkness receded above, encroached from below: *Aspidontus* was diving. A hundred meters. A hundred fifty. They were in the middle of the Pacific. The seabed was four kilometers down. There was nothing in between, unless Valerie had arranged a rendezvous with another submarine.

Two hundred meters. *Aspidontus* levelled off.

Right. Beneath the thermocline. Stealthed to sonar.

The vessel angled to port. Valerie hadn't touched the controls since they'd left the surface. She'd probably given the sub its marching orders while Dan Brüks had been pleading with a brain in a tank. The course was laid out right there on the dashboard, a faint golden thread wound along the eastern North Pacific. The viewing angle was bad, though; too small, too many contours. He could not make out the details.

He knew where he'd have chosen to go. This had all started in the desert; the Bicamerals had manipulated him onto their goddamned chessboard for reasons of their own, and if they'd ever planned on letting him in on the joke, *Portia* and Valerie and taken them out of the game before they'd had the chance. But the Bicamerals were legion, and not all of them had been burned on the altar. If there were answers to be had, the hive would have them.

He leaned sideways until the road map angled into clearer view: grunted to himself, completely unsurprised. Valerie stared into the abyss and said nothing.

She'd laid in a course for the Oregon coast.

PROPHET

There are people here who repeatedly drown themselves in the name of enlightenment. They climb into glass coffins called "prisms," seal the lid, and open the spigot until they're completely submerged. Sometimes they leave a bubble of air at the top, barely big enough to stick their noses into; other times, not even that much.

This is not suicide (although occasional deaths have been reported). They would tell you that it is exactly the opposite, that you haven't lived until you've nearly died. But there's more to this than the superficial thrill-seeking of the adrenaline junkie. The Prismatic kink derives from the evolutionary underpinnings of consciousness itself.

Put your hand in an open flame and subconscious reflex will snatch it back long before you're even aware of the pain. It is only when some other agenda is in *conflict*—your hand hurts, but you don't want to spill the contents of a hot serving tray all over your clean rug—that the self awakens and decides which impulse to obey. Long before art and science and philosophy arose, consciousness had but one function: not to merely implement motor commands, but to mediate between commands *in opposition*.

In a submerged body starving for air, it's difficult to

imagine two imperatives more opposed than the need to breathe and the need to hold your breath. As one Prismatic told me, "Put yourself in one of those things, and tell me you aren't more intensely *conscious* than you've ever been in your life."

The fetish—it seems grandiose to call it a "movement"— would itself seem to be the manifestation of an opposing impulse, a reaction *against* something. By all accounts drowning is an intensely unpleasant experience (although I did not take my interviewee up on her offer). It's difficult to imagine what kind of stimulus might provoke such intense pushback, why the need to assert one's *consciousness* of all things would seem so pressing. None of the Prismatics I asked were able to cast any light on this question. They simply didn't think of their actions in those terms. "It's just important to know who you are," one twenty-eight-year-old TATmaster told me after a few moments' thought, but his words seemed as much question as answer.

—Keith Honeyborne, *Travels with My Ant:*
A Baseline Guide to Imminent Obsolescence, 2080

MONSTERS GIVE US *COURAGE TO CHANGE THE THINGS WE CAN*: THEY ARE OUR PRIMAL FEARS GIVEN FORM, TERRIBLE PREDATORS WHO CAN BE VANQUISHED IF ONLY WE RISE TO THE CHALLENGE. GODS GIVE US *SERENITY TO ACCEPT THE THINGS WE CAN'T*: THEY EXIST TO EXPLAIN FLOODS AND EARTHQUAKES AND ALL THAT WHICH LIES BEYOND OUR CONTROL.

IT DID NOT SURPRISE ME IN THE LEAST TO LEARN THAT VAMPIRES DO NOT BELIEVE IN MONSTERS. I'LL ADMIT THEIR BELIEF IN GODS WAS A BIT OF A SURPRISE.

—DAVID NICKLE

DEEP IN THE Oregon desert, crazy as a prophet, Daniel Brüks opened his eyes to the usual accumulation of wreckage.

The monastery lay in ruins. The broad stone steps of the main entrance sloped away before him, cracked and fissured but still intact for the most part. Past them, to the left of some small patch of desert mysteriously slagged to glass, his tent shivered in the morning breeze. He'd salvaged it from across the valley—he must have, along with his supplies and his equipment, although he wasn't quite sure when—but he could barely remember the last time he'd slept there. Too constraining, somehow. The sky made a better ceiling. These days he didn't use the tent for much more than storage.

He stood and stretched, felt his joints crack as the sun peeked through a gap in the fallen stonework behind him. He turned and surveyed his domain. One end of the monastery stood reasonably intact; the other was a tumbledown pile of broken stone. The damage had been inflicted along a gradient, as though entropy were slowly devouring the structure from north to south.

Entropy had left a path, though: a small canyon through the rubble, leading back to the garden. The parts of the lawn that hadn't been buried outright were brown and brittle and long dead, except for a small green patch struggling bravely around one of the Bicamerals' washbasin pedestals. That pedestal, blessed with some kind of magic, was intact and unmarked by the devastation that had rained down everywhere else. The basin even held half an aliquot of stagnant water; blazing noon or frozen midnight, the level never changed. Some kind of capillary action, probably. A core of porous stone that wicked up moisture from some deep aquifer. Together with the rations left over from his sabbatical, it was enough to keep him going for now.

For *what,* though: that was another matter.

He still had doubts, sometimes. Wondered occasionally—after some especially fruitless dig through the ruins—what he was really accomplishing out here, day after day. Whether this whole exercise might be a waste of time. A little voice in the back of his head wondered even now, as he squinted into the rising sun.

Brüks bent over the pedestal, splashed water on his face, and drank. He washed his hands.

That always made him feel better.

He spent that day as he spent every other: as an amateur archaeologist, sifting the wreckage in search of answers. He didn't know what exactly had happened here after he'd left, why such massive physical destruction had proven necessary in the wake of their escape. Those left behind had been in no position to mount much of a defense, as far as he could tell. Maybe someone had just wanted to make an example of them. Back when he'd still been sleeping in his tent Brüks had gone to it for answers, voiced queries and search strings to the fabric and trawled through the closest hits that the clouds had to offer, but relevant insights seemed impossible to find. Perhaps humans had covered up the details.

Perhaps networks, fearful of impending schizophrenia, had simply forgotten them.

It had been a long time since Brüks had used ConSensus. It didn't really matter. Those weren't the answers he was looking for.

He realized now that Luckett had been right; there *had* been a plan, and all had happened in accordance with it. It was the only model that fit the data. The idea that mere baselines had been able to vanquish the Bicamerals made about as much sense as positing that a band of lemurs could outthink Jim Moore at battlefield chess. The hive had only lost because they'd been playing to lose; Dan Brüks had only escaped because they'd wanted him to; he was only back here now, looking for answers, because they had left answers for him to find. Eventually he would find them. It was only a matter of time.

He knew this. He had faith.

A great pit gaped off the northeast corner of the ruin: walls had shattered and spilled toward it during the purge, but that loose scree had only made it halfway. Some other force had flattened the waist-high guardrail that had once ringed the pit at a safe distance. Brüks stepped over it with ease, and across the concrete apron.

He could not see the bottom, not clearly. Sometimes, when the sun was high, he caught the dim glint of great radial teeth, deep in the earth, cutting across the shaft. He would kick pebbles over the edge: water splashed, after a long time, and occasionally he would see the fitful blue spark of short-circuiting electricity. Still life down there, then, of a sort. He idly considered exploring farther—there had to be some kind of access to those depths, an air intake at least—but there was plenty of time for that.

There were other, more ambulatory hazards to contend with. Rattlesnakes seemed to be making a comeback, or at least changing their distribution; an unthinking reach into dark places while clearing debris resulted in a couple of close calls, and a welcome supplement to his freeze-dried rations. Some exotic species of locust had discovered fire while he'd been away, set a patch of dead grass alight one morning while Brüks was digging nearby. He watched it crackle and blacken and only later discovered the charred little carcasses along the edge of the burn, not quite strong enough to leap clear of their own conflagration. The coder couldn't ID them below Family but named *Chortoicetes* as the closest known relative: Australian plague locust, too far from home and freshly equipped with a novel variant of chitin whose frictional coefficient proved positively incendiary during mating calls.

Plagues and firestorms in a single package. How very apocalyptic. Some splicer somewhere had a refreshingly biblical approach to weaponized biologicals.

He had a visitor that afternoon, watched for almost an hour as it grew from speck to heat-shimmer to biped staggering across the eastern flats. Stuck with roach vision he almost didn't identify it in time, almost started out to meet it before that peculiar stagger tipped him off and sent him scuttling for cover. The newcomer wasn't running, but he moved fast and unencumbered: no pack, no canteen, only one sneaker on the end of a leg as dark and leathery as beef jerky. Whoever he was, he was more than dehydrated; he was almost skeletal. His left arm hung as if snapped at the humerus.

He didn't seem to care. He kept up that jerking half-panicked stride, stumbled past the monastery without a glance, zigzagged on to the western horizon under a lethal simmering sun. Brüks hid in the ruins and watched him pass and did not get a good look at his eyes. He didn't think they danced, though. He was not that kind of undead.

He hunkered down in the calm between the stones, and tried to remember which way the wind was blowing.

. . .

Valerie appeared after sundown. She materialized from the darkness, half-visible in the bloody flickering light of his campfire, and dropped a bag of supplies at his feet: tinned food now, mostly. No more of the magic foil pouches that instantly heated your stew or froze your ice cream when you ripped them open. The pickings out there must be getting slim.

He grunted a greeting. "Haven't seen you since—since . . ."

He couldn't exactly remember. She'd brought him here, he remembered that much. Hadn't she? He had flashes sometimes: a rain-soaked shoreline, a man who'd thought a contraption of metal and plastic was worth dying for. A disembodied eye trailing ragged shreds of nerve and tendon, almost too cloudy to unlock the retina-coded driver's door. A pair of polarized sunglasses in Valerie's hand, terrible backlit eyes staring right through him while she clicked bared teeth and asked *Do I?*

He remembered saying *Yes.* He'd said *Please*, and hadn't even tried to keep the whine from his voice. She had been merciful. She had masked herself a little, a lion's concession to the lamb.

Tonight there was a light beyond his own: a dim orange glow on the northwestern horizon, some distant fire reflecting off the underbelly of a low-hanging cloud bank. Brüks put it in the general direction of Bend.

He pointed back over her shoulder. "Did you do that?"

She didn't look. "You do."

He nodded at the lizard mash sizzling on the fire, held out the half-eaten Vitabar he'd been nibbling to take the edge off. Valerie shook her head: "I eat already."

Even now, it was a relief to hear that.

He sat back down on the corner of a shattered and empty mausoleum. "Found my room today." More precisely, he'd uncovered his goggles—one lens gone completely, the other a spiderweb of cracks embedded in the frame—and finally recognized the remains of the cell where he'd spent his last night on Earth before escaping to the sun. He'd spent the rest of the day searching those foundations on his hands and knees. "Thought someone might have left something there, but . . ."

Her pupils glowed like embers in the firelight. "Doesn't matter," she told him, but somehow there was something *under* the words, an unspoken addendum. Brüks wasn't entirely sure how he knew that; some subtle telltale in the way Valerie held herself, perhaps, some twitch of the lip that his subconscious had parsed and served up as an executive summary—

—*wrong scale; look* down—

—and suddenly Brüks saw the truth of it: they'd *known* him, these hive-minded transHumans who'd called him back home. They'd known his background, and what he'd been doing in the desert all those months before. Any answers they'd left for him would be for him alone: too subtle to show up under the ham-fisted forensics of mortal Man, too durable for bombs or bulldozers to destroy. They'd be ubiquitous, indestructible, invisible to all but their intended recipient.

He mentally kicked himself for not having seen that before.

He wasn't exactly sure how he'd seen it now—exactly what cues he'd read in Valerie's body language, or even whether those cues had been deliberate or inadvertent. It had been happening more often, though; as though the desert had cleared his head, washed away the electronics and the interference and the ubiquitous quantum chaos of the twenty-first century to leave his mind as sharp and pristine as an undergrad's. His newfound clarity might have even saved his life on occasion; he'd gotten the strong sense that a wrong answer to some of Valerie's campfire questions might have carried severe penalties.

Is this what augmentation feels like? he wondered, but it couldn't be. He hadn't even taken Cognital for weeks.

He was seeing things more clearly now, though, no doubt about it. Faces in the clouds. Patterns that made his brain itch. Rakshi would have been proud.

Even Valerie seemed to be.

. . .

Her visits, once rare, had become more frequent. The first time she'd been a shadow with a face, there and gone so quickly that Brüks had written her off as a posttraumatic flashback. But she'd returned six nights later, and two nights after that—and then she had *stayed,* lurking just beyond the campfire, twin spots of eye-shine hovering in the darkness.

At first he'd thought she was toying with him again, getting her usual sadistic kicks out of scaring prey. But then he remembered that she wasn't like that after all, and she obviously didn't want him dead; the fact that he was alive was all the proof he needed. One night he'd shouted a challenge into the darkness—"Hey! Don't you ever get bored playing the Monster Card?"—and she'd stepped into the light: hands spreads, lips sealed, watching him watching her. She'd left a few minutes later but by then he'd realized what she was doing. She was an anthropologist, incrementally accli-mating some primitive tribesman to her presence. She was a pri-matologist of days past, easing her way into a doomed colony of bonobos: one last behavioral study before the species checked out for good.

Sometimes now she sat across the fire and asked him riddles, like some demonic inquisitor assessing his fitness to survive another night: questions about traveling salesmen or Hamiltonian circuits. He'd been terrified at first: afraid to answer, afraid not to, convinced somehow that whatever Valerie's interest in keeping him alive, it could end in an instant with the wrong response. He had done his best, and knew that it wasn't good enough—what did he know about bin packing or polynomial time, how could *any* mortal keep up with a vampire?—but she hadn't killed him yet. She had not turned him back to stone with a few words. She no longer drummed out strange tattoos with her fingertips or left mind-altering hiero-glyphics scratched into the sand. They were beyond that now.

Besides. He didn't quite know how, but he was starting to guess some of the right answers.

. . .

He began again with the most obvious signpost: the magic wash-basin, the defiant patch of grass that circled it like a green pupil. He sampled the water, scraped flecks from the stone, pulled leaves from the ground and ran them through his barcoder. He found a thousand common bacteria, a few purebred, most rotten with lateral transfer.

He only found one that glowed in the dark.

It wasn't obvious, of course: it wouldn't have lit up the night to any naked eye, not in the minuscule densities the machines reported. The only way he could tell it fluoresced was from the gene sequence itself: 576 nucleotides that shouldn't have been there, an assembly line for a protein that glowed red in the presence of oxygen. A marker of some kind. A beacon.

He couldn't read it at first. He had seen the light, but the genes to either side seemed unremarkable. It was a road sign in the desert, with no roads in sight.

He let his hands and feet guide him. The answer would come.

He explored corridors and wood-paneled chambers at the south end of the complex, more than merely intact: *pristine,* stripped bare, light rectangles punctuating the faded dumb paint where pictures had once hung. He found a pair of Masashi's mahogany knuckles hiding in the corner behind a smashed door. He found what was left of his bike: a pair of mangled handlebars, an axle fork, a distended bladder of tire bulging from beneath a fallen wall like a hyperinflated football.

But it wasn't until the dead of night that he found the body.

He hadn't found any others. Most likely the authorities had disposed of them—or perhaps, against all the evidence of his own eyes, they had escaped somehow. Stranger things had happened.

But he woke in the night to the echo of rock falling nearby, and his memory was somehow able to pick a path through the ruins when mere starlight failed. His feet found their way through the wreckage without a missed step; his ears tracked the soft rattle of gravel flowing down new slopes in the darkness ahead. Eventually he came to a jagged shadow where none had been before, a fresh cave-in gaping through the shattered tiles. Brüks stood shivering at its edge and waited for the sky to lighten.

The corpse resolved in shades of gray at the bottom of the pit: a dim shapeless blob against darkness, a shadow extruded from jumbled debris, a bundle of dark sticks wrapped in a tunic on the basement floor. It lay on its back, buried to its waist by the cave-in. The body had mummified in the desert air, shriveled down to bones and brown leather. The eyes through which it stared at the sky had long since collapsed into empty sockets. Perhaps, once, the arms had been folded peacefully across the chest; now they were hooked and twisted as if bent by some disfiguring disease, wrists torqued inward, fingers clawing at the sternum.

It's pointing at itself, he realized. *At* itself . . . And with the sparkling clarity of his newfound faith, Daniel Brüks finally saw the body for what it was.

It was a sign.

"It *was* a marker," he told Valerie the next time she appeared (two nights later? Three?). "It was pointing at itself."

So obvious, in the hindsight of revelation: the same sequence that coded for fluorescence contained other information as well, the same tangled thread of amino acids both serving a mundane biological function *and* spelling out a more esoteric message to anyone who knew the right alphabet.

Not just a marker, not just a message. It was a *dialogue:* gene and protein, talking to each other. It was a straight transposition of amino into alphabet: valine-threonine-alanine into *t-h-e*, phenylalanine-glutamine-valine-alanine into *f-a-t-e*, serine press-ganged into hard-space or hard-return depending on the iteration. The fluorescent protein spelled out a message—

the faery is rosy
of glow

in fate
we rely . . .

And the complementary codons directing its construction spelled out another, in a different alphabet:

any style of life
is prim
oh stay
my lyre . . .

A free-verse call-and-response packed down into a measly 140 codons. It was a marvel of cryptographic efficiency, and it was obvious once Brüks had seen the light.

"The sequence spells a message *and* codes for a protein. The protein fluoresces *and* contains a response. It's not contamination or lateral transfer. It's a *poem*."

"Not for you," Valerie said. "You're looking for something else."

No, he thought. *You are.*

"This is not a kink," he said after a while, and ignited the campfire.

"You mean I don't get off on keeping retarded pets." Her eyes flared red orange. "I'm not Rakshi Sengupta."

"And I'm pretty sure you're not here for the sheer enjoyment of my company." She did not cry out in disagreement. "So what is this?"

Valerie's face was unreadable. "What do you think?"

"I figure I'm cheap labor. The odds of finding something useful here are too high to ignore and too low to waste much effort on. You've got a lot of irons in the fire. So now and then you wait until the sun goes down, and drop by to see what I've dug up."

She eyed him for a moment. Brüks looked back at that vaguely lupine face alive with dancing shadows, and wondered when he had stopped finding it so terrifying.

"Daniel," she said at last. "How you underestimate yourself."

The truth was, though, Valerie *did* seem to enjoy his company. The tone of their conversations had changed; no longer an inqui-

sition, their forays into philosophy and viral theology were turning into something almost conversational. She no longer thought
rings around him; occasionally now he even seemed able to
challenge her. He still wasn't sure where this newfound facility
was coming from. His subconscious simply served up the right
responses without bothering to show its work. It frightened
him, at first—the way new thoughts spilled from his mouth before he could check them for veracity, before he could even parse
their meaning. He bit down, to no avail, grew queasy—almost
terrified—by his own insights, while Valerie cocked her head and
watched from some prehistoric remove.

It was those same insights that eventually calmed him. After
all, wasn't this the way the human brain had *always* behaved?
The bolt from the blue, the classic fully formed eureka moment?
Hadn't the structure of benzene come to Kekulé in a dream?

He began to have his own dreams. He heard voices in them,
insistent whispers: *She's behind it all. She set it all up, can't you see
that? Broke out of jail, snuck through the nets and the ether, got past
the best firewalls baselines could build. Flashed false ID to False In-
telligences, snuck a carousel out of the garage with a whole squad of
zombies on board and didn't wake anyone up on her way out. She
bluffed her way onto the* Crown of Thorns. *Conveniently made it
back from Icarus when everyone else burned.*

You think it was a bunch of monks *that locked you up with the
woman who'd sworn to kill you, a diversion-on-demand tripwired to
go off like a flash grenade? It was the vampire. It was the vampire,
and everyone else is dead, and the only reason you're not is because
she wants to know God's plan for Daniel Brüks. She'll get what she
wants and then she'll kill you, too.*

On waking, he only remembered the voices. He couldn't quite
remember what they'd said.

Valerie kissed him two nights later.

He didn't even know she was there until her hand snapped

closed around the back of his neck, spun him around faster than even his brain stem could react. By the time his heart had jumped through the roof of his mouth and his body remembered fight/ flight and his cache had a chance to think *This is it she's done with me I'm dead I'm dead I'm dead* her tongue was already half-way down his throat and her other hand—the one not crushing his cervical vertebrae—had pincered his cheeks, forcing his teeth apart. He could not close his jaws.

He hung paralyzed in her grip while she tasted him from the inside. He felt something through her flesh that might almost have been a heartbeat if it weren't so slow. Finally she released him. He collapsed on the ground, scuttled sideways like a frantic crab caught in the open with nowhere to run.

"What the *fuck*—" he gasped.

"Ketones." She looked down through him, silhouetted by purpling twilight. "Lactate."

"You can taste cancer," he realized after a moment.

"Better than your machines." She leaned in close, grinning. "Maybe not so precise."

Even eye to eye, she didn't seem to be looking at him.

He knew it an instant before she moved—

—She's going to bite me—

—but the sharp stabbing pain bolted up his arm and her face hadn't moved a centimeter. He looked down, startled, at the twin puncture marks—only a centimeter apart—on his forearm. To the dual-punch biopsy gun in Valerie's hand; his own, he saw. From the field kit lying on the ground, flap open, vials and needles and surgical tools glinting in the firelight.

"Sun gives you problems," Valerie said softly. "Too much radiation, not enough shielding."

At Icarus, he remembered. *When we thought we were burning you off the hull like a moth . . .*

"But you're easy to fix."

"Why?" Brüks asked, and didn't even have to say that much to know that she understood:

Why help prey?
Why help someone who tried to kill you?
Why aren't I dead already?
Why aren't we all?
"You bring us back," Valerie said simply.
"To be slaves."
She shrugged. "We eat you otherwise."
We bring you back, then enslave you in self-defense. But maybe
she really did regard it as a good deal; given a choice between
captivity and outright nonexistence, who would choose the latter?
I'm sorry, he didn't say.
"Don't be," she replied, as if he had. "*You* don't enslave us.
Physics does. The chains *you* build—" Her fangs gleamed like
little daggers in the firelight. "We break them soon."
"I thought you already had."
Rising moonlight lit her eyes for a moment as she shook her
head. "The Glitch still works. I see the cross and a part of me
dies."
"A par—a part you *made.*" *Of course. Of course. They're parallel
processors, after all . . .*
The truth dawned on him like daylight: a *custom cache,* a sac-
rificial homunculus brought into existence and *isolated,* to suffer
the agony of the cross while more vital threads of cognition
wound about it like a stream around a stone. Valerie didn't avoid
the seizures at all; she—encysted them, and carried on.
He wondered how long she'd been able to do that.
"Just a workaround," she said. "Need to undo the wiring."
Not to go up against the roaches, of course. *That* war was already as good as over, even though the losing side didn't know it
yet. This creature with a dozen simultaneous entities in her head,
this prehistoric post-Human, could speak so openly—without
animosity, or resentment, or the slightest concern for the impact
one Daniel Brüks might have on her revolution—because baseline Humanity was already beneath her notice. Valerie and her
kind were perfectly capable of shrugging off Human oppression

without breaking their chains; they needed their arms free to pick on things their own size.

"You are not so small as you think," she said, reading him. "You might be bigger than all of us."

Brüks shook his head. "We're not. If I've learned *anything* these—"

Emergent complexity, he realized. *That's what she means.*

A neuron didn't know whether it fired in response to a scent or a symphony. Brain cells weren't intelligent; only brains were. And brain cells weren't even the lower limit. The origins of thought were buried so deep they predated multicellular life itself: neurotransmitters in choanoflagellates, potassium ion gates in *Monosiga*.

I am a colony of microbes talking to itself, Brüks reflected.

Who knew what metaprocesses might emerge when Heaven and ConSensus wired enough brains together, dropped internode latency close enough to zero? Who knew what metaprocesses already had? Something that might make Bicameral hives look as rudimentary as the nervous system of a sea anemone.

Maybe the Singularity already happened and its components just don't know it yet.

"They never will," Valerie told him. "Neurons only speak when spoken to; they don't know why."

He shook his head. "Even if something is—coalescing out there, it's left me behind. I'm not wired in. I'm not even augged."

"ConSensus is one interface. There are others."

Echopraxia, he wondered.

But it didn't matter. He was still Daniel Brüks, the human coelacanth: lurking at the outskirts of evolution, unchanged and unchangeable while the world moved on. Enlightenment was enough for him. He wanted no part of transfiguration.

I will stay here while the tables turn and fires burn out. I will stand still while humanity turns into something unrecognizable, or dies trying. I will see what rises in its place.

Either way, I am witnessing the end of my species.

Valerie watched him from the darkness. *These chains you build—we break them soon.*

"I wish we hadn't needed them," he admitted softly. "I wish we could have brought you back without Crucifix Glitches or Divide and Conquer or any of those damn *chains*. Maybe we could have dialed down your predatory instincts, fixed the protocadherin deficit. Made you more . . ."

"Like you," she finished.

He opened his mouth, found he had nothing to say. It didn't matter whether shackles were built of genes or iron, whether you installed them after birth or before conception. Chains were chains, no matter where you put them. No matter whether they were forged by intent or evolution.

Maybe we should have just left you extinct. Built something friendlier, from scratch.

"You need your monsters," she said simply.

He shook his head. "You're just too—complicated. Everything's linked to everything else. Fix the Crucifix Glitch, you lose your pattern-matching skills. Make you less antisocial, who knows what else goes away? We didn't dare change you too *much*."

Valerie hissed softly, clicked her teeth. "You need monsters so you can defeat them. No great *victory* in slaughtering a lamb."

"We are not that stupid."

Valerie turned and looked to the horizon: the firelight flickering off the clouds was all the rejoinder she needed.

But that's not us, Brüks thought. *Even if it is. It's—urban renewal. Tear-down and development for the new owners.*

Pest control.

The monster's shoulders rose and fell. She spoke without turning—"Wouldn't it be nice if we could all just get along?"—and for the life of him Brüks could not tell whether she was being sincere or sarcastic.

"I thought we were," he said, reaching for the biopsy needle in his half-open field kit. And leapt like a flea onto her back, faster than he had ever moved in his life, to plunge it up through the base of her skull.

THE CLOTHES HAVE NO EMPEROR.
—STEWART ELLIOTT GUTHRIE

NOW HE WAS alone. By day tornadoes marched across the desert like pillars of smoke, under no control but God's. At night the distant glow of burning bushes encircled the horizon: the Post-Anthropocene Explosion in full swing. Brüks thought about what might be going on out there, thought about anything but the act he'd just committed. He imagined battles unseen and ongoing. He wondered who was winning.

The Bicamerals, perhaps, shaping the Singularity, planting that first layer of bearings in the box. Laying a foundation for the future. Perhaps this was their linchpin moment, the first dusting of atoms on the condensor's floor. From these beginnings Humanity could resonate out across time and space, a deterministic cascade designed to undo what the viral God had wrought. Debug the local ordinances. Undo the anthropic principle. It could take billions of years from such humble butterfly beginnings, but in the end life itself might be unraveled from Planck on up.

What else could you call it, other than Nirvana?

There would be other forces, other plans. The vampires, for one: the smartest of the selfish genes. They might prefer their human prey just as they were, slow and thick-witted, minds dulled by the cumbersome bottleneck of the conscious cache. Or maybe some other faction was rising in the east, any of the other monstrous subspecies that humanity had fractured into: the membrains, the multicores, the zombies or the Chinese Rooms. Even

Rhona's supraconscious AIs. They all had their causes, their reasons to fight; or thought they did.

The fact that their actions all seemed to serve the purposes of something *else*, some vast distributed network slouching toward Bethlehem—sheer coincidence, perhaps. Perhaps we really do act for the reasons we believe. Perhaps everything's right on the surface, brightly lit and primary colored. Perhaps Daniel Brüks and Rakshi Sengupta and Jim Moore—each burning for their own kind of redemption—all just *happened* to end up in the white-hot radiance of solar orbit, obsessed enough to rush in where Angels feared to tread.

Perhaps it really was Daniel Brüks, on some level, who had just murdered his last and only friend . . .

He thought of Jim Moore and Jim was in his head, nodding and offering sage advice. Rhona reminded him to *Think like a biologist* and he saw his mistake; he'd heard *Angels of the Asteroids* and he'd seen heavenly bodies, not earthly ones. He'd seen chunks of dead spinning rock, not the extinct echinoderms that had once crept across the world's intertidal zones. *Asteroidea*: the sea stars. Brainless creatures, utterly uncephalized, who nonetheless moved with purpose and a kind of intelligence. Not the worst metaphor for the Icarus invader. Not the worst metaphor for what seemed to be happening out beyond the desert . . .

There were other voices: Valerie, Rakshi, some he didn't recognize. Sometimes they argued among themselves, included him only as an afterthought. They told him he was becoming schizophrenic—that they were nothing but his own thoughts, drifting at loose ends through a mind being taken apart in stages. They whispered fearfully about something skulking in the basement, something brought back from the sun that stomped on the floor and made things move upstairs. Brüks remembered Jim Moore cutting the cancers from his body, felt his friend's head shaking behind his mind's eye: *Sorry, Daniel—I guess I didn't get it all . . .*

Sometimes he lay awake at night and clenched his teeth and

strained, through sheer effort of conscious will, to undo the slow incremental rewiring of his midbrain. The thing in the basement came to him in his dreams. *You think this is* new? it sneered. *Even in this miserable backwater, it's been happening for four billion years. I'm going to swallow you whole.*

"I'll fight you," Brüks said aloud.

Of course you will. That's what you're for, that's all you're for. You gibber on about blind watchmakers *and* the wonder of evolution *but you're too damn stupid to see how much faster it would all happen if you just went away. You're a Darwinian fossil in a Lamarckian age. Do you see how sick to death we are of dragging you behind us, kicking and screaming because you're too stupid to tell the difference between success and suicide?*

"I see the fires. People are fighting back."

That's not me out there. That's just you folks, catching up.

It was such an uphill struggle. Consciousness had never had the upper hand; *I* had never been more than the scratchpad, a momentary snapshot of a remembered present. Maybe Brüks hadn't heard those voices before but they'd always been there, hidden away, doing the heavy lifting and sending status reports upstairs to a silly little man who took all the credit. A deluded homunculus, trying to make sense of minions so much smarter than it was.

It had only ever been a matter of time before they decided they didn't need him.

He no longer sought his answers among the ruins. He looked for them across the whole wide desert. His very senses were coming apart now; each sunrise seemed paler than the last, every breeze against his skin felt more distant than the one before. He cut himself to feel alive; the blood spilled out like water. He deliberately broke his little finger, and felt not pain but faint music. The voices wouldn't leave him alone. They told him what to eat and he put rocks in his mouth. He could no longer tell bread from stone.

One day he came across a body desiccating in the parched desert air, its side torn open by scavengers, its head abuzz in a halo of flies. He was almost sure this wasn't where he'd left it. He thought he saw it move a little, undead nerves still twitching against their own desecration. Guilt rose like acid in his throat.

You killed her, Brüks told the thing inside.

And that's the only reason you're alive. I am your salvation.

You're a parasite.

Am I. I pay the rent. I do renovations. I've only just got started and this system's already clocking fast enough to outsmart a vampire. What did you ever do except suck glucose and contemplate your navel?

What are you, then?

I'm manna from heaven. I'm a Rorschach blot. The monks look at me and see the Hand of God, the Vampires see an end to loneliness. What do you see, Danny Boy?

He saw a duck blind, an ROV. He saw some other Singularity looking back. He saw Valerie's body twitching at his feet. Whatever was left of Daniel Brüks remembered her last words, just after she'd pierced him with a biopsy that wasn't a biopsy: "Wouldn't it be nice if we could all just get along?"

You know she wasn't talking about you.

He knew.

He found himself on the edge of a cliff, high above the desert. The ruined monastery shimmered in the heat but he felt nothing. He seemed a million miles away, as though watching the world unfold through distant cameras. *You have to crank the amplitude,* his tormentor said. *It's the only way you'll feel anything. You have to increase the gain.*

But Brüks was onto it. He wasn't the first to be tempted in the desert, and he knew how that story went. He was supposed to defy the voice. *Do not test the Lord thy God,* he was supposed to say, and step back from the precipice and into history. It was in the script.

But he was so very fucking sick of scripts. He couldn't remember a time when he'd made up his own lines. Herded into the desert by invisible hands, packed into some post-Human field kit with the nanoscopes and petri dishes and barcoders: a so-called biologist barely smart enough to poke at things he didn't understand, too stupid to know when those things were poking back. They'd used him; they'd all used him. He'd never been their colleague, never a friend. Never even the accidental tourist he'd first supposed, the retarded ancestor in need of babysitting. A cargo container: that's all he'd been. A brood sac.

But he was not an automaton, not yet. He was still Daniel Brüks, and for just this moment he was slaved to no one's stage directions. He would make his *own* fucking destiny.

You wouldn't dare, something hissed in his head.

"Watch me," he said, and stepped forward.

POSTSCRIPT

An End to Loneliness

THERE'S NOT MUCH to work with. Barely a melanoma's worth. Enough to rewire the circuitry of the midbrain, certainly; but to deal with shattered bones? Enough to keep osteoblasts and striated muscles alive in the face of such massive damage, to keep the metabolic fires flickering? Enough to keep decomposition at bay?

Barely. Perhaps. One piece at a time.

The body shouts, wordless alarm-barks, when the scavengers come calling. Judicious twitches scare away most of the birds. Even so, something pecks out an eye before the body is whole enough to crawl for shelter; and there will be necrosis at the ex-tremities. The system triages itself, focuses on feet and legs and the architecture of locomotion. Hands can be replaced, if need be. Later.

And something else: a tiny shard of God, reprogrammed and wrapped in a crunchy encephalitis jacket. A *patch*, targeted to a specific part of the vampire brain: *Portia* processors, homesick for the pattern-matching wetware of the fusiform gyrus.

There's no longer any light behind these eyes. The parasitic, self-reflective homunculus has been expunged. The system still has access to stored memories, though, and if there was sufficient cause it could certainly replay the awestruck words of the late Rakshi Sengupta.

Can you imagine what those fuckers could do if they could actually stand to be in the same room together?

An end to loneliness. By now, the system that was Daniel Brüks seethes with it. His is the blood of the covenant; it will be shed for many.

It hauls its broken, stiff-legged chassis to its feet—only an observer for now, but soon, perhaps, an ambassador. The resurrection walks east, toward the new world.

Valerie's legacy goes along for the ride.

ACKNOWLEDGMENTS

It's been a while. Three editors, three family deaths, one near-fatal brush with flesh-eating disease. A felony conviction. A marriage.

Now this.

I'm not quite sure what "this" is, exactly—but for good or ill, I couldn't have pulled it off without help. In fact, I wouldn't even be *alive* now without help. So first and foremost, let me acknowledge the contribution of one Caitlin Sweet. *Echopraxia* would not exist without her, because I would not exist without her; I would have died of necrotizing fasciitis on February 12, 2011. (Darwin Day. Seriously. Look it up.) As a perverse reward for saving my life, Caitlin got to endure endless hours in the shower, or in bed, or at restaurants, listening to me whinge endlessly about how this scene was too talky and that climax too contrived; she would then suggest some elegant solution that might have occurred to me eventually, but probably not before deadline. Her insights are golden. If their implementation sucks it's my fault, not hers.

The first couple of chapters also had the benefit of being work-shopped by two different groups of writers: those at Gibraltar Point (Michael Carr, Laurie Channer, John McDaid, Becky Maines, Elisabeth Mitchell, Dave Nickle, Janis O'Connor, and Rob Stauffer); and those at Cecil Street (Madeline Ashby, Jill Lum, Dave Nickle—again—Helen Rykens, Karl Schroeder, Sara Simmons, Michael Skeet, Doug Smith, Hugh Spencer, Dale Sproule, and Dr. Allan Weiss).

I've kept lists over the years, tried to document the various insights, references, and crazy-ass hallucinatory what-ifs that informed the writing of this book. I've tried to keep track of those who sent me papers and those who actually *wrote* the damn things, those who made offhand remarks in blog posts or jabbed a finger at my chest while making some drunken point during a barroom debate. I wanted to list everyone by the nature of their contribution: beta reader; scientific authority; infopipe; devil's advocate.

For the most part, I couldn't do it. There's just too much overlap. All those superimposed colors turn the Venn diagram into a muddy gray disk. So, for the most part, I'll have to fall back on alphabetical order when I thank Nick Alcock, Beverly Bambury, Hannu Bloomila, Andrew Buhr, Nancy Cerelli, Alexey Cheberda, Dr. Krystyna Chodorowksa, Jacob Cohen, Anna Davour, Alyx Dellamonica, Sibylle Eisbach, Jon Enerson, Val Grimm, Norm Haldeman, Thomas Hardman, Dr. Andrew Hessel, Keith Honeyborne, Seth Keiper, Dr. Ed Keller, Chris Knall, Leonid Korogodski, Do-Ming Lum, Danielle MacDonald, Dr. Matt McCormick, Chinedum Ofoegbu, Jesús Olmo, Chris Pepper, Janna Randina, Kelly Robson, Patrick "Bahumat" Rochefort, Dr. Kaj Sotala, Dr. Brad Templeton, and Rob Tucker. And some mysterious dude who only goes by the name "Random J."

Some folks, however, went above and beyond in singular and specific ways. Dr. Dan Brooks ranted and challenged and acted as occasional traveling companion. Kristin Choffe did her best to teach me the essentials of DNA barcoding, although she couldn't keep me from sucking at it. (She also fronted me a vial containing the refined DNA of a dozen plant and animal species, with which I washed out my mouth before submitting a cheek swab to the Department of Homeland Security.) Leona Lutterodt described God as a Process, which lit an LED in my brain. Dr. Deborah McLennan snuck me through the paywalls. Sheila Miguez pointed me to a plug-in that made it vastly easier to insert citations into Notes and References (I will understand if, after reading that section, you decide to hate her for the same reason). Ray Neilson kept me on my toes and kept my Linux box running. Mark Showell saw me working on a laptop that was literally held together with binder clips, and took pity. Cat Sparks moved me halfway around the world; she was the fulcrum that tipped the worst year of my life into the best.

Some of these people are meatspace friends; others are pixel-pals. They've argued with me online and off, punched holes in whatever bits of *Echopraxia* leaked out during gestation, passed me countless references on everything from hominid genetics to machine consciousness to metal-eating bacteria. They are a small army but a very smart one, and despite my best efforts I'm probably forgetting some of them. I hope those I've neglected here will forgive me.

Howard Morhaim. After dealing with agents whose advice ran the gamut from *Buy my book* to *I'll only represent you if you write a near-future techno-thriller about a marine biologist,* Howard told me to write what I was inspired to: selling it, he insisted, was *his* job. This might not be the most opportunistic attitude to adopt in a Darwinian marketplace, but man it was nice to run into someone who put the writing first for a change.

Ironically, my next novel is most likely going to be a near-future techno-thriller about a marine biologist.

NOTES AND REFERENCES

I am naked as I type this.

I was naked writing the whole damn book.

I aspire to a certain degree of discomfort in my writing, on the principle that if you never risk a face-plant you never go anywhere new. And if there's one surefire way to get me out of my comfort zone, it's the challenge of taking invisible omnipotent sky fairies seriously enough to incorporate into a hard SF novel. The phrase "faith-based hard SF" may, in fact, be the ultimate oxymoron—Clarke's Third notwithstanding—which means that *Echopraxia* could be my biggest face-plant since *βehemoth* (especially in the wake of *Blindsight,* which continues to surprise with all the love it's garnered over the years). And thanks to a lack of empirical evidence (as of this writing, anyway) for the existence of deities, I can't even fall back on my usual strategy of shielding my central claims behind papers from *Nature.*

I can try to shield everything else there, though. Perhaps that will do.

PSY-OPS AND THE CONSCIOUSNESS GLITCH

I'm not dwelling too much on consciousness this time around—I pretty much shot my load on that subject with *Blindsight*—except to note in passing that the then-radical notion of consciousness-as-nonadaptive-side-effect has started appearing in the literature,[1] and that more and more "conscious" activities (including math![2]) are turning out to be nonconscious after all[3,4,5] (though holdouts remain[6]).

One fascinating exception informs Keith Honeyborne's report on "Prismatics," who nearly drown themselves to achieve a heightened state of awareness. The premise of Ezequiel Morsella's PRISM model[7,8] is that consciousness originally evolved for the delightfully mundane purpose of mediating conflicting motor commands to the skeletal muscles. (I have to point out that exactly the same sort of conflict—the impulse to withdraw one's hand from a painful stimulus, versus the knowledge that you'll

---

1. D. M. Rosenthal, "Consciousness and Its Function," *Neuropsychologia* 46, no. 3 (2008): 829–840.

2. Asael Y. Sklar et al., "Reading and Doing Arithmetic Nonconsciously," *Proceedings of the National Academy of Sciences* (November 12, 2012): 201211645, doi:10.1073/pnas.1211645109.

3. Ap Dijksterhuis et al., "On Making the Right Choice: The Deliberation-without-Attention Effect," *Science* 311, no. 5763 (February 17, 2006): 1005–1007, doi:10.1126/science.1121629.

4. Christof Koch and Naotsugu Tsuchiya, "Attention and Consciousness: Two Distinct Brain Processes," *Trends in Cognitive Sciences* 11, no. 1 (January 2007): 16–22, doi:10.1016/j.tics.2006.10.012.

5. Ken A. Paller and Joel L. Voss, "An Electrophysiological Signature of Unconscious Recognition Memory," *Nature Neuroscience* 12, no. 3 (March 2009): 349+.

6. C. Nathan DeWall, Roy F. Baumeister, and E. J. Masicampo, "Evidence That Logical Reasoning Depends on Conscious Processing," *Consciousness and Cognition* 17, no. 3 (September 2008): 628–645, doi:10.1016/j.concog.2007.12.004.

7. Ezequiel Morsella et al., "The Essence of Conscious Conflict: Subjective Effects of Sustaining Incompatible Intentions," *Emotion (Washington, D.C.)* 9, no. 5 (October 2009): 717–728, doi:10.1037/a0017121.

8. E. Morsella, "The Function of Phenomenal States: Supramodular Interaction Theory," *Psychological Review* 112, no. 4 (2005): 1000–1021.

die if you act on that impulse—was exactly how the Bene Gesserit assessed whether Paul Atreides qualified as "Human" during their *gom jabbar* test in Frank Herbert's *Dune*.)

Everything else comes down to tricks and glitches. The subliminal "gang signs" Valerie programmed onto the *Crown*'s bulkheads seem a logical (if elaborate) extension of the newborn field of optogenetics.[9] The "sensed presence" Dan Brüks and Lianna Lutterodt experienced in the attic results from a hack on the temporoparietal junction that screws up the brain's body map[10,11] (basically, the part of your brain that keeps track of your body parts gets kicked in the side and registers a duplicate set of body parts off-center). Sengupta's induced misiphonia is a condition in which relatively innocuous sounds—a slurp, a hiccup—are enough to provoke violent rage.[12] All of this *was* inflicted in the service of education, though: as Brüks points out, fear promotes memory formation.[13,14]

Fear and belief can also kill you,[15] a trick used to good effect in

9. Matthew W. Self and Pieter R. Roelfsema, "Optogenetics: Eye Movements at Light Speed," *Current Biology* 22, no. 18 (September 25, 2012): R804–R806, doi:10.1016/j.cub.2012.07.039.

10. Shahar Arzy et al., "Induction of an Illusory Shadow Person," *Nature* 443, no. 7109 (September 21, 2006): 287, doi:10.1038/443287a.

11. Michael A. Persinger and Sandra G. Tiller, "Case Report: A Prototypical Spontaneous 'Sensed Presence' of a Sentient Being and Concomitant Electroencephalographic Activity in the Clinical Laboratory," *Neurocase* 14, no. 5 (2008): 425–430, doi:10.1080/13554790802406172.

12. Joyce Cohen, "For People with Misophonia, a Chomp or a Slurp May Cause Rage," *New York Times*, June 9, 2011, http://www.nytimes.com/2011/09/06/health/06annoy.html.

13. Rachel Jones, "Stress Brings Memories to the Fore," *PLoS Biol* 8, no. 12 (December 21, 2010): e1001007, doi:10.1371/journal.pbio.1001007.

14. V. S. Ramachandran, *The Tell-Tale Brain: a Neuroscientist's Quest for What Makes Us Human* (New York: W. W. Norton, 2012).

15. Alexis C. Madrigal, "The Dark Side of the Placebo Effect: When Intense Belief Kills," *The Atlantic*, September 14, 2011, http://www.theatlantic

certain religious practices.[16] And in case you were wondering what was up with the fusiform gyrus there at the end (a couple of my beta readers did), it's the structure containing the face-recognition circuitry[17] we tweaked to amp up the mutual-agonism response in vampires. It's part of the same circuitry that evolved to let us see faces in the clouds, involved—once again—in the evolution of our religious impulse (see below).

The brain's habit of literalizing metaphors—the tendency to regard people as having "warmer" personalities when you happen to be holding a mug of coffee, the Bicamerals' use of hand-washing to mitigate feelings of guilt and uncertainty—is also an established neurological fact.[18]

I pulled "induced thanoparorasis" out of my ass. It's a cool idea, though, huh?

UNDEAD UPDATE

Back in *Blindsight* I laid out a fair bit of groundwork on the biology and evolution of vampires. I'm not going to revisit that here (you can check out FizerPharm's stockholder presentation[19] if you need a refresher), except for the citation in *Blindsight* imply-

.com/health/archive/2011/09/the-dark-side-of-the-placebo-effect-when-in-tense-belief-kills/245065/.

16. Vilayanur S. Ramachandran and Sandra Blakeslee, *Phantoms in the Brain* (New York: Quill, 1999).

17. Mark Brown, "How the Brain Spots Faces—Wired Science," *Wired Science*, January 10, 2012, http://www.wired.com/wiredscience/2012/01/brain-face-recognition/.

18. Simon Lacey, Randall Stilla, and K. Sathian, "Metaphorically Feeling: Comprehending Textural Metaphors Activates Somatosensory Cortex," *Brain and Language* 120, no. 3 (March 2012): 416–421, doi:10.1016/j.bandl.2011.12.016.

19. FizerPharm, Inc. "Vampire Domestication: Taming Yesterday's Nightmares for a Better Tomorrow," 2055, http://www.rifters.com/blindsight/vampires.htm.

ing that female vampires were impossible (the gene responsible for their obligate primatovory being located on the Y chromosome[20]). More recent work by Cheberda et al have established a more general protocadherin dysfunction on both X and Y chromosomes,[21] resolving this inadvertent paradox. At any rate, zombies are more relevant to the current tale. Both surgical and viral varieties appear in *Echopraxia*; the surgically induced military model is essentially the "p-zombie" favored by philosophers[22]; it already got a workout back in *Blindsight*. Examples of the viral model would include victims of the Pakistan pandemic: "civilian hordes reduced to walking brain stems by a few kilobytes of weaponized code drawn to the telltale biochemistry of conscious thought."

What telltale signatures might these bugs be targeting? Consciousness appears to be largely a property of distributed activity—the synchronous firing of far-flung provinces of the brain[23,24]—but it is also correlated with specific locations and

20. Patricia Blanco-Arias, Carole A. Sargent, and Nabeel A. Affara, "A Comparative Analysis of the Pig, Mouse, and Human PCDHX Genes," *Mammalian Genome: Official Journal of the International Mammalian Genome Society* 15, no. 4 (April 2004): 296–306, doi:10.1007/s00335-003-3034-9.

21. Alexey Cheberda, Janna Randina, and J. Random, "Coincident Autapomorphies in the γ-PCDHX γ-PCDHY Gene Complexes, and Their Role in Vampire Hominovory," *Vampire Genetics and Epigenetics* 24, no. 1 (2072): 435–460.

22. "Philosophical Zombie," *Wikipedia, the Free Encyclopedia*, October 25, 2013, http://en.wikipedia.org/w/index.php?title=Philosophical_zombie&oldid=576098290.

23. Giulio Tononi and Gerald M. Edelman, "Consciousness and Complexity," *Science* 282, no. 5395 (December 4, 1998): 1846–1851, doi:10.1126/science.282.5395.1846.

24. Jaakko W. Långsjö et al., "Returning from Oblivion: Imaging the Neural Core of Consciousness," *The Journal of Neuroscience* 32, no. 14 (April 4, 2012): 4935–4943, doi:10.1523/JNEUROSCI.4962-11.2012.

structures.[25] In terms of specific cellular targets I'm thinking maybe "von Economo neurons" or VENs: disproportionately large, anomalously spindly, sparsely branched neurons that grow 50 to 200 percent larger than the human norm.[26,27] They aren't numerous—they occupy only 1 percent of the anterior cingulate gyrus and the fronto-insular cortex—but they appear to be crucial to the conscious state.

Zombie brains—freed from the metabolic costs of self-awareness—exhibit reduced glucose metabolism in those areas, as well as in the prefrontal cortex, superior parietal gyrus, and the left angular gyrus; this accounts the fractionally-reduced temperature of the zombie brain. Interestingly, the same metabolic depression can be found in the brains of clinically insane murderers.[28]

PORTIA

I'd like to start this section by emphasising how utterly cool *Portia*'s eight-legged namesake is in real life. That stuff about improvisational hunting strategies, mammalian-level problem-solving, and visual acuity all contained within a time-sharing bundle

25. Navindra Persaud et al., "Awareness-related Activity in Prefrontal and Parietal Cortices in Blindsight Reflects More Than Superior Visual Performance," *NeuroImage* 58, no. 2 (September 15, 2011): 605–611, doi:10.1016/j.neuroimage.2011.06.081.

26. Franco Cauda et al., "Functional Anatomy of Cortical Areas Characterized by Von Economo Neurons," *Brain Structure and Function* 218, no. 1 (January 29, 2012): 1–20, doi:10.1007/s00429-012-0382-9.

27. Caroline Williams, "The Cells That Make You Conscious," *New Scientist* 215, no. 2874 (July 21, 2012): 32–35, doi:10.1016/S0262-4079(12)61884-3.

28. Adrian Raine, Monte Buchsbaum, and Lori Lacasse, "Brain Abnormalities in Murderers Indicated by Positron Emission Tomography," *Biological Psychiatry* 42, no. 6 (September 15, 1997): 495–508, doi:10.1016/S0006-3223(96)00362-9.

of neurons smaller than a pinhead—God's own truth, all of it.[29,30,31,32]

That said, the time-sharing cognitive slime mold at Icarus is even cooler. Given the limitations of Human telematter technology at the end of the twenty-first century—and given that *any* invasive agent hitching a ride on someone else's beam would be well-advised to keep its structural complexity to a minimum— the capacity for some kind of self-assembly is going to be highly desirable once you reach your destination. Miras et al describe a process that might fit the rudiments of such a bill, at least.[33,34] Once it starts assembling itself, I imagine that *Portia* might function something like Cooper's "iCHELLs"[35]: inorganic metal cells, capable of reactions you could call "metabolic" without squinting too hard. Maybe with a sprinkling of magical fairy-

29. Duane P. Harland and Robert R. Jackson, "Eight-legged Cats and How They See—A Review of Recent Research on Jumping Spiders (Araneae: Salticidae)," *Cimbebasia* 16 (2000): 231–240.

30. D. P. Harland and R. R. Jackson, "A Knife in the Back: Use of Prey-Specific Attack Tactics by Araneophagic Jumping Spiders (Araneae: Salticidae)," *Journal of Zoology* 269, no. 3 (2006): 285–290, doi:10.1111/j.1469-7998.2006.00112.x.

31. M. Tarsitano, "Araneophagic Jumping Spiders Discriminate Between Detour Routes That Do and Do Not Lead to Prey," *Animal Behaviour* 53, no. 2 (n.d.): 257–266.

32. John McCrone, "Smarter Than the Average Bug," *New Scientist* 191, no. 2553 (2006): 37+.

33. H. N. Miras et al., "Unveiling the Transient Template in the Self-Assembly of a Molecular Oxide Nanowheel," *Science* 327, no. 5961 (December 31, 2009): 72–74, doi:10.1126/science.1181735.

34. Katharine Sanderson, "Life in 5000 Hours: Recreating Evolution in the Lab," *New Scientist* 209, no. 2797 (January 29, 2011): 32–35, doi:10.1016/S0262-4079(11)60217-0.

35. Geoffrey J. T. Cooper, "Modular Redox-Active Inorganic Chemical Cells: iCHELLs," *Angewandte Chemie International Edition* 50, no. 44 (2011): 10373–10376.

dust plasma[36] (although I'm guessing those two processes might be incompatible).

ADAPTIVE DELUSIONAL SYSTEMS ...

An enormous amount of recent research has been published about the natural history of the religious impulse and the adaptive value of theistic superstition.[37,38,39,40,41,42,43,44] It's no great surprise that religion confers adaptive benefits, given the near-universality

36. V. N. Tsytovich, "From Plasma Crystals and Helical Structures Towards Inorganic Living Matter," *New Journal of Physics* 9, no. 8 (August 1, 2007): 263.

37. Ara Norenzayan and Azim F. Shariff, "The Origin and Evolution of Religious Prosociality," *Science* 322, no. 5898 (October 3, 2008): 58–62, doi:10.1126/science.1158757.

38. Richard Sosis and Candace Alcorta, "Signaling, Solidarity, and the Sacred: The Evolution of Religious Behavior," *Evolutionary Anthropology: Issues, News, and Reviews* 12, no. 6 (2003): 264–274, doi:10.1002/evan.10120.

39. Jesse M. Bering, "The Folk Psychology of Souls," *Behavioral and Brain Sciences* 29, no. 5 (2006): 453–462, doi:10.1017/S0140525X06009101.

40. Azim F. Shariff and Ara Norenzayan, "God Is Watching You: Priming God Concepts Increases Prosocial Behavior in an Anonymous Economic Game," *Psychological Science* 18, no. 9 (September 1, 2007): 803–809, doi:10.1111/j.1467-9280.2007.01983.x.

41. Melissa Bateson, Daniel Nettle, and Gilbert Roberts, "Cues of Being Watched Enhance Cooperation in a Real-World Setting," *Biology Letters* 2, no. 3 (September 22, 2006): 412–414, doi:10.1098/rsbl.2006.0509.

42. Azim F. Shariff and Ara Norenzayan, "Mean Gods Make Good People: Different Views of God Predict Cheating Behavior," *International Journal for the Psychology of Religion* 21, no. 2 (2011): 85–96, doi:10.1080/10508619.2011.556990.

43. Jeffrey P. Schloss and Michael J. Murray, "Evolutionary Accounts of Belief in Supernatural Punishment: A Critical Review," *Religion, Brain & Behavior* 1, no. 1 (2011): 46–99, doi:10.1080/2153599X.2011.558707.

44. ... to name but a few.

of that impulse among our species.[45,46,47,48] If you're interested and you've got ninety minutes to spare, I'd strongly recommend Robert Sapolsky's brilliant lecture on the evolutionary and neurological roots of religious belief.[49]

It's not all food taboos and slashed foreskins, though. Far more relevant to the current discussion is the fact that religious minds exhibit certain characteristic neurological traits.[50] Believers, for example, are better than nonbelievers at finding patterns in visual data.[51] Buddhist meditation increases the thickness of the prefrontal cortex and right anterior insula (structures associated with attention, interoception, and sensory processing).[52] There's even circumstantial evidence that Christians are less ruled by their

45. Eckart Voland and Wulf Schiefenhovel, eds., *The Biological Evolution of Religious Mind and Behavior,* 2009, http://www.springer.com/life+sciences/evolutionary+%26+developmental+biology/book/978-3-642-00127-7.

46. Justin L. Barrett, "The God Issue: We Are All Born Believers," *New Scientist* 213, no. 2856 (March 17, 2012): 38–41, doi:10.1016/S02624079(12)60704-0.

47. Paul Bloom, "Is God an Accident?," *The Atlantic,* December 2005, http://www.theatlantic.com/magazine/archive/2005/12/is-god-an-accident/304425/?single_page=true.

48. Elizabeth Culotta, "On the Origin of Religion," *Science* 326, no. 5954 (November 6, 2009): 784–787, doi:10.1126/science.326_784.

49. *Dr. Robert Sapolsky's Lecture About Biological Underpinnings of Religiosity,* 2011, http://www.youtube.com/watch?v=4WwAQqWUkpI&feature=youtube_gdata_player.

50. Sam Harris et al., "The Neural Correlates of Religious and Nonreligious Belief," *PLoS ONE* 4, no. 10 (October 1, 2009): e7272, doi:10.1371/journal.pone.0007272.

51. Lorenza S. Colzato, Wery P. M. van den Wildenberg, and Bernhard Hommel, "Losing the Big Picture: How Religion May Control Visual Attention," *PLoS ONE* 3, no. 11 (November 12, 2008): e3679, doi:10.1371/journal.pone.0003679.

52. Sara W Lazar et al., "Meditation Experience Is Associated with Increased Cortical Thickness," *Neuroreport* 16, no. 17 (November 28, 2005): 1893–1897.

emotions than are nonbelievers[53] (although whether the rules they follow instead are any more rational is another question). Certain religious rituals are so effective at focusing the mind and relieving stress that some have suggested coopting them into a sort of "religion for atheists."[54]

An obvious significant downside is that most religious beliefs—gods, souls, Space Disneyland—are held at best in the complete absence of empirical evidence (and are more frequently held in the face of *opposing* evidence). While it remains impossible to disprove the negative, for most practical purposes it's reasonable to describe such beliefs as simply *wrong*.

It was only during the writing this book that it occurred to me to wonder if one couldn't say the same about science.

Lutterodt's comparison of religious faith with the physiology of vision came to me while I was reading Inzlicht et al,[55] a paper that describes religion as an internal model of reality that confers benefits even though it's wrong. While that idea is nothing new, the way it was phrased was so reminiscent of the way our brains work—the old survival-engines-not-truth-detectors shtick—that I had to wonder if the whole right/wrong distinction might be off the table the moment any worldview passes through a Human nervous system. And the *next* paper[56] I read suggested that certain cosmic mysteries might not be a function of dark energy so much as inconstancies in the laws of physics—and if that *were* the case, there'd really be no way to tell . . .

53. Laura Saslow, "My Brother's Keeper?: Compassion Predicts Generosity More Among Less Religious Individuals," *Social Psychological and Personality Science* 4, no. 1 (January 1, 2013): 31–38.

54. Graham Lawton, "The God Issue: Religion for Atheists," *New Scientist* 213, no. 2856 (March 17, 2012): 48–49, doi:10.1016/S0262-4079(12)60708-8.

55. Michael Inzlicht, Alexa M. Tullett, and Marie Good, "The Need to Believe: a Neuroscience Account of Religion as a Motivated Process," *Religion, Brain & Behavior* 1, no. 3 (2011): 192–212, doi:10.1080/2153599X.2011.647849.

56. George Ellis, "Cosmology: Patchy Solutions," *Nature* 452, no. 7184 (March 13, 2008): 158–161, doi:10.1038/452158a.

Of course, there's absolutely no denying the functional utility of the scientific method, especially when you compare it to the beads and rattles of those guys with the funny hats. Still, I have to admit: not entirely comfy with where that seemed to be heading for a bit.

...AND THE BICAMERAL CONDITION

The Bicameral Order did not begin as a hive. They began as a fortunate juxtaposition of adaptive malfunctions and sloppy fitness.

The name does not derive from Julian Jaynes.[57] Rather, both Jaynes and the Order recall a time when paired hemispheres were the only option: the right a pragmatic and unimaginative note-taker, the left a pattern-matcher.[58] Think of "gene duplication," that process by which genetic replication occasionally goes off the rails to serve up multiple copies of a gene where only one had existed before; these become "spares" available for evolutionary experimentation. Hemispheric lateralization was a little like that. A pragmatist core; a philosopher core.

The left hemisphere is on a quest for meaning, even when there isn't any. False memories, pareidolia—the stress-induced perception of pattern in noise[59]—these are Lefty's doing. When there are no data, or no meaning, Lefty may find it anyway. Lefty gets religion.

But sometimes patterns are subtle. Sometimes, noise is almost all there is: a *kind* of noise anyway, at least to classically evolved

---

57. Julian Jaynes, *The Origin of Consciousness in the Breakdown of the Bicameral Mind* (Boston: Houghton Mifflin Company, 1976).

58. Michael S. Gazzaniga, "The Split Brain Revisited," *Scientific American Special Edition* 12, no. 1 (August 2, 2002): 27–31.

59. Jennifer A. Whitson and Adam D. Galinsky, "Lacking Control Increases Illusory Pattern Perception," *Science* 322, no. 5898 (October 3, 2008): 115–117, doi:10.1126/science.1159845.

senses. Smeared probabilities, waves that obscure the location or momentum of whatever you're squinting at. Virtual particles that elude detection anywhere past the edges of black holes. Maybe, when you move a few orders of magnitude away from the world our senses evolved to parse, a touch of pareidolia can take up the slack. Like the feather that evolved for thermoregulation and then got press-ganged, fully formed, into flight duty, perhaps the brain's bogus-purpose-seeking wetware might be repurposed to finding patterns it once had to *invent*. Maybe the future is a fusion of the religious and the empirical.

Maybe all Lefty needs is a little help.

Malfunctions and breakdowns showed them the way. Certain kinds of brain damage result in massive increases in certain types of creativity.[16] Strokes provoke bursts of artistic creativity,[60] fronto-temporal dementia supercharges some parts of the brain even as it compromises others.[61] Some autistics possess visual hyperacuity comparable to that of birds of prey, even though they're stuck with the same human eyes as the rest of us.[62] Schizophrenics are immune to certain optical illusions.[63] At least some kinds of synesthesia confer cognitive advantages[64] (people who literally *see*

---

60. Helen Thomson, "Mindscapes: Stroke Turned Ex-Con into Rhyming Painter" *New Scientist*, May 10, 2013, http://www.newscientist.com/article/dn23523-mindscapes-stroke-turned-excon-into-rhyming-painter.html.

61. Sandra Blakeslee, "A Disease That Allowed Torrents of Creativity," *New York Times*, April 8, 2008, sec. Health, http://www.nytimes.com/2008/04/08/health/08brai.html.

62. Emma Ashwin et al., "Eagle-Eyed Visual Acuity: An Experimental Investigation of Enhanced Perception in Autism," *Biological Psychiatry* 65, no. 1 (January 1, 2009): 17–21, doi:10.1016/j.biopsych.2008.06.012.

63. Danai Dima et al., "Understanding Why Patients with Schizophrenia Do Not Perceive the Hollow-Mask Illusion Using Dynamic Causal Modelling," *NeuroImage* 46, no. 4 (July 15, 2009): 1180–1186, doi:10.1016/j.neuroimage.2009.03.033.

64. Heather Mann et al., "Time-Space Synaesthesia–A Cognitive Advantage?,"

time, arrayed about them in multicolored splendor, are twice as good as the rest of us at recalling events from their own personal timelines[65]). And—as Daniel Brüks reflects—brain damage is actually a prerequisite for basic rationality in certain types of decision-making.[66] The Bicamerals set out to damage their brains, in very specific ways. They manipulated the expression of NR2B,[67] tweaked TRNP-1[68] production, used careful cancers to promote growth (their genes tagged for easy identification,[69] should anything go wrong) and increase neurosculptural degrees of freedom. Then they ruthlessly weeded those connections, pruned back the tangle into optimum, isolated islands of functionality.[70] They improved their pattern-matching skills to a degree almost inconceivable to mere baselines.

Consciousness and Cognition 18, no. 3 (September 2009): 619–627, doi:10.1016 /j.concog.2009.06.005.

65. Victoria Gill, "Can You See Time?," *BBC*, September 11, 2009, sec. Science & Environment, http://news.bbc.co.uk/2/hi/science/nature/8248589 .stm.

66. Michael Koenigs et al., "Damage to the Prefrontal Cortex Increases Utilitarian Moral Judgements," *Nature* 446, no. 7138 (April 19, 2007): 908–911, doi:10.1038/nature05631.

67. Deheng Wang et al., "Genetic Enhancement of Memory and Long-Term Potentiation but Not CA1 Long-Term Depression in NR2B Transgenic Rats," *PLoS ONE* 4, no. 10 (October 19, 2009): e7486, doi:10.1371 /journal.pone.0007486.

68. Ronny Stahl et al., "Trnp1 Regulates Expansion and Folding of the Mammalian Cerebral Cortex by Control of Radial Glial Fate," *Cell* 153, no. 3 (April 25, 2013): 535–549, doi:10.1016/j.cell.2013.03.027.

69. Robert M. Hoffman, "The Multiple Uses of Fluorescent Proteins to Visualize Cancer in Vivo," *Nature Reviews Cancer* 5, no. 10 (October 2005): 796–806, doi:10.1038/nrc1717.

70. Anonymous, "Autism: Making the Connection," *The Economist*, August 5, 2004, http://www.economist.com/node/3061282.

Such enhancements come at a cost.[71,72] Bicamerals have lost the ability to communicate effectively across the cognitive-species divide. It's not just that they've rewired their speech centers[73] and are now using different parts of the brain to talk; they *think* now almost entirely in metaphor, in patterns that contain meaning even if they don't, strictly speaking, exist.

Things get even messier when linked into networks, which can literally scatter one's mind even at today's rudimentary levels of connectivity. The "transactive memory system" called Google is already rewiring the parts of our brains that used to remember facts locally; now those circuits store search protocols for remote access of a distributed database.[74] And Google doesn't come anywhere close to the connectivity of a *real* hive mind.

Which is not to say that hive minds aren't already a ubiquitous part of Human society. *You* are a hive mind, always have been: a single coherent consciousness spread across two cerebral hemispheres, each of which—when isolated—can run its own stand-alone, conscious entity with its own thoughts, aesthetics, even religious beliefs.[75] The reverse also happens. A hemisphere forced

---

71. Fabienne Samson et al., "Enhanced Visual Functioning in Autism: An ALE Meta-Analysis," *Human Brain Mapping* 33, no. 7 (2012): 1553–1581, doi:10.1002/hbm.21307.

72. Deborah Halber, "Gene Research May Help Explain Autistic Savants," *MIT's News Office*, 2008, http://web.mit.edu/newsoffice/2008/savants-0212 .html.

73. Fumiko Hoeft et al., "Functional and Morphometric Brain Dissociation Between Dyslexia and Reading Ability," *Proceedings of the National Academy of Sciences* 104, no. 10 (March 6, 2007): 4234–4239, doi:10.1073/ pnas.0609399104.

74. B. Sparrow, J. Liu, and D. M. Wegner, "Google Effects on Memory: Cognitive Consequences of Having Information at Our Fingertips," *Science* 333, no. 6043 (July 14, 2011): 776–778, doi:10.1126/science.1207745.

75. V. S. Ramachandran and Stuart Hameroff, "Beyond Belief: Science, Reason, Religion & Survival. Salk Institute for Biological Studies, Nov 5–7,

to run solo when its partner is anaesthetised (preparatory to surgery, for instance) will manifest a different personality than the brain as a whole—but when those two hemispheres reconnect, that solo identity gets swallowed up by whatever dual-core persona runs on the whole organ.[16] Consciousness expands to fill the space available.

The Bicameral hive takes its lead from Krista and Tatiana Hogan, conjoined craniopagus twins whose brains are fused at the thalamus.[76] Among other things, the thalamus acts as a sensory relay; the twins share a common set of sensory inputs. Each sees through the other's eyes. Tickle one, the other laughs. Anecdotal evidence suggests that they can share thoughts, and although they have distinct personalities each uses the word "I" when talking about the other twin.

All this resulting from fusion at a *sensory* relay. Suppose they were linked farther up? A thought doesn't know to stop and turn back when it reaches the corpus callosum. Why would it behave any differently if it encountered a callosum of a different sort; why should two minds linked by a sufficiently fat pipe be any more distinct than the halves of your own brain?

Sufficiently high bandwidth, therefore, would likely result in a single integrated consciousness across any number of platforms. Technologically, the links themselves might exploit so-called "ephatic coupling"[77] (in which direct synaptic stimulation is bypassed and neurons are induced to fire by diffuse electrical fields generated elsewhere in the brain). Synchrony is vital: unified con-

2006 (Session 4)," *The Science Network*, 2006, http://thesciencenetwork.org/programs/beyond-belief-science-religion-reason-and-survival/session-4-1.

76. Jordan Squair, "Craniopagus: Overview and the Implications of Sharing a Brain," *University of British Columbia's Undergraduate Journal of Psychology (UBCUJP)* 1, no. 0 (May 1, 2012), http://ojs.library.ubc.ca/index.php/ubcujp/article/view/2521.

77. Costas A. Anastassiou et al., "Ephaptic Coupling of Cortical Neurons," *Nature Neuroscience* 14, no. 2 (February 2011): 217–223, doi:10.1038/nn.2727.

scious only exists when all parts fire together with a signal latency of a few hundred milliseconds, tops.[23,24] Throttle that pipe and it should be possible to retain individuality while accessing memories and sensory data from your fellow nodes.[78]

I've kept the extent of Bicameral hive integration flexible, allowing internode connections to throttle up and down as the need arises—but whether those bandwidth-versus-dialup decisions are made by the nodes themselves or by something more *inclusive* remains ambiguous. If you want some hint of the ramifications of total cognitive integration, I point you to the (apparently) catatonic Moksha Mind of the Eastern Dharmic Alliance.[79]

However the hive links up—whatever its degree of conscious coherence—it is a religious experience. Literally.

We know what rapture is: a glorious malfunction, a glitch in the part of the brain that keeps track of where the body ends and everything else begins.[80] When that boundary dissolves the mind feels connected to *everything,* feels literally at one with the universe. It's an illusion, of course. Transcendence is experience, not insight. That's not why Bicamerals feel the rapture.

They feel it because it's an unavoidable side effect of belonging to a hive. Sharing sensory systems, linking minds one to another—such connections really *do* dissolve the boundaries between bodies. Bicameral spiritual rapture isn't so much an illusion as a bandwidth meter. It still feels good, of course, which has its own implications. Bicams rap out when they hook up to

78. Kaj Sotala and Harri Valpola, "Coalescing Minds: Brain Uploading-Related Group Mind Scenarios," *International Journal of Machine Consciousness* 04, no. 1 (June 2012): 293–312, doi:10.1142/S1793843012400173.

79. The Pontifical Academy of Sciences, "An Enemy Within: The Bicameral Threat to Institutional Religion in the Twenty-First Century (An Internal Report to the Holy See)," (Internal Report, 2093).

80. A. B. Newberg and E. G. d' Aquili, "The Neuropsychology of Religious and Spiritual Experience," *Journal of Consciousness Studies* 7, no. 11–12 (November 1, 2000): 251–266.

solve problems. They actually *get off* on discovery; if baselines got those kind of rewards they wouldn't need tenure.

The side effect has side effects, though. The activation of rapture-related neurocircuitry generates glossolalia even in baseline brains[81,82]; given the modifications that Bicamerals use to enhance transcendence,[83,84] the occasional bout of speaking in tongues is pretty much a given. Brüks should be thankful the hive doesn't just scream all the time.

In hindsight, it is apparent that describing the Bicamerals as a religious order is a little misleading: the parts of the brain they've souped up simply overlap with the parts that kick in during religious neurobehavioral events, so the manifestations are similar. Whether that's a distinction that makes a difference is left as an exercise for the reader.

GOD AND THE DIGITAL UNIVERSE

The idea of God as a virus only really works if you buy into the burgeoning field of digital physics.[85] Most of you probably know what that is: a family of models based on the premise that the

---

81. Andrew B. Newberg et al., "The Measurement of Regional Cerebral Blood Flow During Glossolalia: A Preliminary SPECT Study," *Psychiatry Research: Neuroimaging* 148, no. 1 (November 22, 2006): 67–71, doi:10.1016/j.pscychresns.2006.07.001.

82. M. A. Persinger, "Striking EEG Profiles from Single Episodes of Glossolalia and Transcendental Meditation," *Perceptual and Motor Skills* 58, no. 1 (February 1984): 127–133.

83. Cosimo Urgesi et al., "The Spiritual Brain: Selective Cortical Lesions Modulate Human Self-Transcendence," *Neuron* 65, no. 3 (February 11, 2010): 309–319, doi:10.1016/j.neuron.2010.01.026.

84. Dimitrios Kapogiannis et al., "Neuroanatomical Variability of Religiosity," *PLoS ONE* 4, no. 9 (September 28, 2009): e7180, doi:10.1371/journal.pone.0007180.

85. "Digital Physics," *Wikipedia, the Free Encyclopedia*, September 17, 2013, http://en.wikipedia.org/w/index.php?title=Digital_physics&oldid=571364996.

universe is discrete and mathematic at its base, and that every event therein can therefore be thought of as a kind of computation. Digital physics comes in several flavors: the universe is a simulation running in a computer somewhere[86,87,88]; or the universe is a vast computer in its own right, where matter is hardware and physics is software and every flip of an electron is a calculation. In some versions matter itself is illusory, a literal instantiation of numbers.[89,90] In others, reality is a hologram and the universe is empty inside[91,92,93]; the real action takes place way out on its two-dimensional boundary, and we are merely interferences patterns projected from the surface of a soap bubble into its interior. There's no shortage of popular summaries of all this stuff, either online[94] or off.[95]

86. Nick Bostrom, "Are We Living in a Computer Simulation?," *The Philosophical Quarterly* 53, no. 211 (2003): 243–255, doi:10.1111/1467-9213.00309.

87. Nick Bostrom, "The Simulation Argument," n.d., http://www.simulation-argument.com/.

88. Brian Whitworth, *The Physical World as a Virtual Reality*, arXiv e-print, January 2, 2008, http://arxiv.org/abs/0801.0337.

89. Max Tegmark, *The Mathematical Universe*, arXiv e-print, April 5, 2007, http://arxiv.org/abs/0704.0646.

90. Amanda Gefter, "Reality: Is Everything Made of Numbers?," *New Scientist* 215, no. 2884 (September 29, 2012): 38–39, doi:10.1016/S02624079(12)62518-4.

91. Zeeya Merali, "Theoretical Physics: The Origins of Space and Time," *Nature* 500, no. 7464 (August 28, 2013): 516–519, doi:10.1038/500516a.

92. Marcus Chown, "Our World May Be a Giant Hologram," *New Scientist* no. 2691 (2009): 24–27.

93. Dave Mosher, "World's Most Precise Clocks Could Reveal Universe Is a Hologram," *Wired Science*, October 28, 2010, http://www.wired.com/wiredscience/2010/10/holometer-universe-resolution/.

94. "Rebooting the Cosmos: Is the Universe the Ultimate Computer? [Replay]," accessed September 10, 2013, http://www.scientificamerican.com/article.cfm?id=world-science-festival-rebooting-the-cosmos-is-the-universe-ultimate-computer-live-event.

95. B Greene, *The Hidden Reality: Parallel Universes and the Deep Laws of the Cosmos* (New York: Vintage Books, 2011).

Lee Smolin (of Waterloo's Perimeter Institute) goes against the grain: he rejects digital physics outright and serves up a single universe in which time is not an illusion, reality is not deterministic, and universes themselves grow, reproduce, and evolve via natural selection writ *very* large (think of black holes as offspring; think of entropy as a selective force).[96,97,98] Even Smolin's model, however, is vulnerable to inconstancy in the laws of physics; the model actually predicts that physical laws evolve along with the rest of reality. Which kind of leaves us back at the question of how one can legitimately assume constancy in an inconstant universe.

You can't get through these references without realizing that, whacked out as it sounds, digital physics has a lot of scientific heavy-hitters on its side. I, of course, am not one of them; but since so many smarter people are defending the premise, I'm happy to sneak viral deities onto the back of all their hard work and hope it slips through.

MISCELLANEOUS BACKGROUND AMBIANCE

The fieldwork preoccupying Brüks at the start of the story descends from the "DNA barcoding" that's all the rage today: a quick-and-dirty taxonomic technique for distinguishing species based on a chunk of the cytochrome oxidase gene.[99] There's no

96. Lee Smolin, *The Life of the Cosmos* (New York: Oxford University Press, 1997).
97. Lee Smolin, "Time Reborn," 2012, http://perimeterinstitute.ca/videos/time-reborn.
98. Lee Smolin, *Time Reborn: From the Crisis in Physics to the Future of the Universe* (Boston: Houghton Mifflin Harcourt, 2013).
99. "DNA Barcoding," *Wikipedia, the Free Encyclopedia*, September 17, 2013, http://en.wikipedia.org/w/index.php?title=DNA_barcoding&oldid=573251556.

way it'll still be around in its present form eight decades from now—we've already got handheld analyzers[100] that put conventional wet analysis right out to pasture—but the *concept* of a genetic barcode will, I think, persist even as the technology improves.

The vortex engine[101] powering the Bicameral monastery derives from work patented by Louis Michaud,[102] a retired engineer who basically came up with the idea while tinkering in his garage. I have no idea whether two-hundred-megawatt, twenty-kilometer-high wind funnels are in our future, but the patents went through,[103] and the project's got some serious attention from government and academic agencies. Nobody's saying the physics are wrong.

We are already closing in on learning techniques that bypass conscious awareness,[104] à la Lianna Lutterodt's training at the hands of her Bicameral masters. Likewise, the precursors of the gimp hood that Brüks uses in lieu of a brain implant can be seen taking shape in a diversity of mind-reading/writing tech

100. Kevin Davies, "A QuantuMDx Leap for Handheld DNA Sequencing," *Bio-IT World*, 2012, http://www.bio-itworld.com/2012/01/17/quantumdx-leap-handheld-dna-sequencing.html.

101. "Vortex Engine," *Wikipedia, the Free Encyclopedia*, September 18, 2013, http://en.wikipedia.org/w/index.php?title=Vortex_engine&oldid=573492083.

102. Tyler Hamilton, "Taming Tornadoes to Power Cities.," *The Toronto Star*, July 21, 2007, http://www.thestar.com/business/2007/07/21/taming_tornadoes_to_power_cities.html.

103. Kurt Kleiner, "Artificial Tornado Plan to Generate Electricity," *Technology: New Scientist Blogs*, 2008, http://www.newscientist.com/blog/technology/2008/06/artificial-tornado-plan-to-generate.html.

104. Kazuhisa Shibata et al., "Perceptual Learning Incepted by Decoded fMRI Neurofeedback without Stimulus Presentation," *Science* 334, no. 6061 (December 9, 2011): 1413–1415, doi:10.1126/science.1212003.

already extant in the literature.[105,106,107,108,109] Brüks's dependence on Cognital, on the other hand, marks him truly as a relic of a past age (ours, in fact): memory boosters are already in the pipe,[110,111,112] and as far back 2008, one in five working scientists already indulged in brain-doping to help keep up with the competition.[113]

The use of massively multiplayer online games as a tool for epidemiological simulation was first proposed by Lofgren and Fefferman[114]; they, in turn, were inspired by an unexpected pan-

105. Jack L. Gallant et al., "Identifying Natural Images from Human Brain Activity," *Nature* 452, no. 7185 (March 20, 2008): 352+.

106. T. Horikawa et al., "Neural Decoding of Visual Imagery During Sleep," *Science* 340, no. 6132 (May 3, 2013): 639–642, doi:10.1126/science.1234330.

107. Kendrick N. Kay and Jack L. Gallant, "I Can See What You See," *Nature Neuroscience* 12, no. 3 (March 2009): 245–245, doi:10.1038/nn0309-245.

108. Thomas Naselaris et al., "Bayesian Reconstruction of Natural Images from Human Brain Activity," *Neuron* 63, no. 6 (September 24, 2009): 902–915, doi:10.1016/j.neuron.2009.09.006.

109. Jon Stokes, "Sony Patents a Brain Manipulation Technology," *Ars Technica*, April 7, 2005, http://arstechnica.com/uncategorized/2005/04/4785-2/.

110. Johannes Gräff and Li-Huei Tsai, "Cognitive Enhancement: A Molecular Memory Booster," *Nature* 469, no. 7331 (January 27, 2011): 474–475, doi:10.1038/469474a.

111. Dillon Y. Chen et al., "A Critical Role for IGF-II in Memory Consolidation and Enhancement," *Nature* 469, no. 7331 (January 27, 2011): 491–497, doi:10.1038/nature09667.

112. Reut Shema et al., "Enhancement of Consolidated Long-Term Memory by Overexpression of Protein Kinase Mζ in the Neocortex," *Science* 331, no. 6021 (March 4, 2011): 1207–1210, doi:10.1126/science.1200215.

113. Brendan Maher, "Poll Results: Look Who's Doping," *Nature News* 452, no. 7188 (April 9, 2008): 674–675, doi:10.1038/452674a.

114. Eric T. Lofgren and Nina H Fefferman, "The Untapped Potential of Virtual Game Worlds to Shed Light on Real World Epidemics," *The Lancet Infectious Diseases* 7, no. 9 (September 2007): 625–629, doi:10.1016/S1473-3099(07)70212-8.

demic of "corrupted blood" in World of Warcraft,[115] which occurred because people in RPGs—like those in real life—often don't behave the way they're supposed to. I don't know how many have since picked up this ball and run with it—at least one paper speaks of using online gaming for economics research[116]—but if that's all there is I think we're missing a huge opportunity.

Near the end of this novel there's a teaching moment on the subject of natural selection. Most people seem to think that organisms develop adaptive traits in response to environmental change. This is bullshit. The environment changes and those who *already* happen to have newly adaptive traits don't get wiped out. A deteriorating Daniel Brüks muses on an especially neat case in point, the curious fact that the building blocks of advanced neural architecture already exist in single-celled animals lacking even the most rudimentary nervous systems.[117,118,119,120]

115. "Corrupted Blood Incident," *Wikipedia, the Free Encyclopedia*, August 12, 2013, http://en.wikipedia.org/w/index.php?title=Corrupted_Blood_in cident&oldid=566358819.

116. John Gaudiosi, "Gameworld: Virtual Economies in Video Games Used as Case Studies," *Reuters*, October 1, 2009, http://www.reuters.com/article /2009/10/01/videogames-economies-idUSSP15565220091001.

117. Alexandre Alié and Michaël Manuel, "The Backbone of the Post-Synaptic Density Originated in a Unicellular Ancestor of Choanoflagellates and Metazoans," *BMC Evolutionary Biology* 10, no. 1 (2010): 34, doi:10.1186 /1471-2148-10-34.

118. P. Burkhardt et al., "Primordial Neurosecretory Apparatus Identified in the Choanoflagellate Monosiga Brevicollis," *Proceedings of the National Academy of Sciences* 108, no. 37 (August 29, 2011): 15264–15269, doi:10.1073/ pnas.1106189108.

119. X. Cai, "Unicellular Ca2+ Signaling 'Toolkit' at the Origin of Metazoa," *Molecular Biology and Evolution* 25, no. 7 (April 3, 2008): 1357–1361, doi:10.1093/molbev/msn077.

120. B. J. Liebeskind, D. M. Hillis, and H. H. Zakon, "Evolution of Sodium Channels Predates the Origin of Nervous Systems in Animals," *Proceedings of the National Academy of Sciences* 108, no. 22 (May 16, 2011): 9154–9159, doi:10.1073/pnas.1106363108.

A couple of isolated factoids. Fruit flies save energy in impoverished environments by becoming forgetful[121]; the construction and maintenance of memories is, after all, a costly affair. I imagine that Rhona McLennan's "Splinternet" is suffering the same sort of energetic triage after Icarus drops offline. And that bit where Brüks wondered why Moore even bothered exercising to stay in shape? That's because we're within spitting distance of a pill that puts your metabolism into hardbody mode even if you spend the whole day sitting on the couch snarfing pork rinds and watching *American Idol.*[122,123]

The poem Brüks discovers in the desert as his mind is coming apart is not, contrary to what you might think, a hallucination. It is real. It is the warped brainchild of Canadian poet Christian Bök,[124] who has spent the past decade figuring out how to build a gene that not only spells a poem, but that functionally codes for a fluorescing protein whose amino acid sequence decodes into a *response* to that poem.[125] The last time we hung out he'd managed to insert it into *E. coli*, but his ultimate goal is to stick it into *Deinococcus radiodurans*, aka "Conan the Bacterium,"[126] aka the toughest microbial motherfucker that ever laughed at the inside

121. Pierre-Yves Plaçais and Thomas Preat, "To Favor Survival Under Food Shortage, the Brain Disables Costly Memory," *Science* 339, no. 6118 (January 25, 2013): 440–442, doi:10.1126/science.1226018.

122. Margaret Talbot, "Brain Gain," *The New Yorker,* April 27, 2009, http://www.newyorker.com/reporting/2009/04/27/090427fa_fact_talbot.

123. Vihang A. Narkar et al., "AMPK and PPARδ Agonists Are Exercise Mimetics," *Cell* 134, no. 3 (August 8, 2008): 405–415, doi:10.1016/j.cell.2008.06.051.

124. "Christian Bök," *Wikipedia, the Free Encyclopedia*, September 14, 2013.

125. Jamie Condliffe, "Cryptic Poetry Written in a Microbe's DNA," *CultureLab, New Scientist Online,* 2011, http://www.newscientist.com/blogs/culturelab/2011/05/christian-boks-dynamic-dna-poetry.html.

126. *"Deinococcus Radiodurans,"* **Wikipedia, the Free Encyclopedia**, July 29, 2013.

of a nuclear reactor. If Christian's project comes through, his words could be iterating across the face of this planet right up until the day the sun blows up. Who knew poetry could ever get that kind of a print run?

Finally: free will. Although free will (rather, its lack) is one of *Echopraxia*'s central themes (the neurological condition of echopraxia is to autonomy as blindsight is to consciousness), I don't have much to say about it because the arguments seem so clear-cut as to be almost uninteresting. Neurons do not fire spontaneously, only in response to external stimuli; therefore brains cannot *act* spontaneously, only in response to external stimuli.[127] No need to wade through all those studies that show the brain acting before the conscious mind "decides" to.[128,129] Forget the revisionist interpretations that downgrade the definition from *free will* to *will that's merely unpredictable enough to confuse predators*.[130,131] It's simpler than that: the switch cannot flip itself. QED. If you insist on clinging to this *free will* farce I'm not going to waste much time arguing here: plenty of

---

127. Yes, there may be random elements—quantum flickers that introduce unpredictability into one's behavior—but slaving your decisions to a dice roll doesn't make you free.

128. Benjamin Libet et al., "Time of Conscious Intention to Act in Relation to Onset of Cerebral Activity (Readiness-Potential): The Unconscious Initiation of a Freely Voluntary Act," *Brain* 106, no. 3 (September 1, 1983): 623–642, doi:10.1093/brain/106.3.623.

129. Chun Siong Soon et al., "Unconscious Determinants of Free Decisions in the Human Brain," *Nature Neuroscience* 11, no. 5 (May 2008): 543–545, doi:10.1038/nn.2112.

130. Björn Brembs, "Towards a Scientific Concept of Free Will as a Biological Trait: Spontaneous Actions and Decision-Making in Invertebrates," *Proceedings of the Royal Society B: Biological Sciences* (December 15, 2010), doi:10.1098/rspb.2010.2325.

131. Alexander Maye et al., "Order in Spontaneous Behavior," *PLoS ONE* 2, no. 5 (May 16, 2007): e443, doi:10.1371/journal.pone.0000443.

others have made the case far more persuasively than I ever could.[132,133,134,135]

But given this current state of the art, one of the more indigestible nuggets *Echopraxia* asks you to swallow is that eight decades from now, people will still buy into such an incoherent premise—that as we close on the twenty-second century, we will continue to act as though we have free will.

In fact, we might behave that way. It's not that you can't convince people that they're automatons; that's easy enough to pull off, intellectually at least. Folks will even change their attitudes and behavior in the wake of those insights[136]—be more likely to cheat or less likely to hold people responsible for unlawful acts, for example.[137,138] But eventually our attitudes drift back to pre-enlightenment baselines; even most of those who accept deter-

132. Anthony R Cashmore, "The Lucretian Swerve: The Biological Basis of Human Behavior and the Criminal Justice System," *Proceedings of the National Academy of Sciences of the United States of America* 107, no. 10 (March 9, 2010): 4499–4504, doi:10.1073/pnas.0915161107.

133. David Eagleman, *Incognito: The Secret Lives of the Brain* (New York: Vintage Books, 2012).

134. Daniel M. Wegner, *The Illusion of Conscious Will* (Cambridge, MA: MIT Press, 2002).

135. *Sam Harris on "Free Will,"* 2012, http://www.youtube.com/watch?v=pCofmZlC72g&feature=youtube_gdata_player.

136. Davide Rigoni et al., "Inducing Disbelief in Free Will Alters Brain Correlates of Preconscious Motor Preparation: The Brain Minds Whether We Believe in Free Will or Not," *Psychological Science* 22, no. 5 (May 2011): 613–618, doi:10.1177/0956797611405680.

137. Roy F. Baumeister, E. J. Masicampo, and C. Nathan DeWall, "Prosocial Benefits of Feeling Free: Disbelief in Free Will Increases Aggression and Reduces Helpfulness," *Personality and Social Psychology Bulletin* 35, no. 2 (February 1, 2009): 260–268, doi:10.1177/0146167208327217.

138. Kathleen D. Vohs and Jonathan W. Schooler, "The Value of Believing in Free Will: Encouraging a Belief in Determinism Increases Cheating," *Psychological Science* 19, no. 1 (January 1, 2008): 49–54, doi:10.1111/j.1467-9280.2008.02045.x.

minism somehow manage to believe in personal culpability.[139,140] Over tens of thousands of years we just got used to cruising at one-twenty; without constant conscious intervention, we tend to ease back on the pedal to that place we feel most comfortable. *Echopraxia* makes the same token concessions that society is likely to. You may have noticed the occasional reference to the concept of personal culpability having been weeded out of justice systems the world over, that those dark-ages throwbacks still adhering to the notion are subject to human rights sanctions by the rest of the civilized world. Brüks and Moore squabble over "the old *no-free-will* shtick" back at the monastery. Adherents to those Eastern religions who never really took free will all that seriously anyway have buggered off into a hive-minded state of (as far as anyone can tell) deep catatonia. The rest of us continue to act pretty much the way we always have.

Turns out we don't have much choice in the matter.

139. Hagop Sarkissian et al., "Is Belief in Free Will a Cultural Universal?," *Mind & Language* 25, no. 3 (2010): 346–358, doi:10.1111/j.1468-0017.2010.01393.x.
140. Wasn't it Joss Whedon, in one of his X-Men comics, who stated that "Contradiction is the seed of consciousness"?